SAUCER

*Also by Stephen Coonts
in Large Print:*

America
Liberty

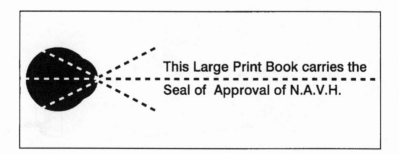

This Large Print Book carries the
Seal of Approval of N.A.V.H.

SAUCER

STEPHEN COONTS

Thorndike Press • Waterville, Maine

Published in 2004 by arrangement with
St. Martin's Press, LLC.

Thorndike Press® Large Print Famous Authors.

The tree indicium is a trademark of Thorndike Press.

The text of this Large Print edition is unabridged.
Other aspects of the book may vary from the original edition.

Set in 16 pt. Plantin.

Printed in the United States on permanent paper.

Library of Congress Cataloging-in-Publication Data

Coonts, Stephen, 1946–
    Saucer / Stephen Coonts.
        p. cm.
    ISBN 0-7862-6602-3 (lg. print : hc : alk. paper)
    1. Unidentified flying objects — Fiction.   2. Americans
— Sahara — Fiction.   3. Space flight — Fiction.
    4. Sahara — Fiction.   5. Large type books.   I. Title.
PS3553.O5796S28 2004
    813′.54—dc22   2004051798

To Rachael and Tyler

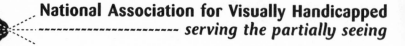
As the Founder/CEO of NAVH, the only national health agency solely devoted to those who, although not totally blind, have an eye disease which could lead to serious visual impairment, I am pleased to recognize Thorndike Press* as one of the leading publishers in the large print field.

Founded in 1954 in San Francisco to prepare large print textbooks for partially seeing children, NAVH became the pioneer and standard setting agency in the preparation of large type.

Today, those publishers who meet our standards carry the prestigious "Seal of Approval" indicating high quality large print. We are delighted that Thorndike Press is one of the publishers whose titles meet these standards. We are also pleased to recognize the significant contribution Thorndike Press is making in this important and growing field.

Lorraine H. Marchi, L.H.D.
Founder/CEO
NAVH

* Thorndike Press encompasses the following imprints: Thorndike, Wheeler, Walker and Large Print Press.

There are at least 100 billion
stars in the Milky Way.

1

Rip Cantrell was holding the stadia rod, trying to blink away the sweat trickling into his eyes, when a bright flash of light caught his eye. The light was to his left, near the base of an escarpment almost a mile away.

Careful not to disturb the stadia rod, he turned his head to get a better view.

"Hold that thing still for a few more seconds, Rip."

The shout echoed off the rock formations and tumbled around in the clear desert air, rupturing the profound silence. Occasionally one could hear the deep rumble of a jet running high, but normally the only sound was the whisper of the wind.

Dutch Haagen was at the transit, reading the rod. He and Bill Taggart were the engineers surveying a line for a seismic shoot. Rip was the gofer, working a summer job before he returned to college in a few weeks.

Rip concentrated on holding the rod still. Fifteen seconds passed, then Dutch waved his arms.

Now Rip looked again for the bright spot of reflected light.

There! Shimmering in the hot desert air, at the base of that low cliff, maybe a mile to the north. The afternoon sun must be reflecting on something shiny.

But what?

Trash? Here in the central Sahara?

The three men were a hundred miles from the nearest waterhole, two hundred from the nearest collection of native mud huts. A twin-turboprop transport with fixed landing gear dropped them here three weeks ago. "Your nearest neighbors are at an archaeological dig about thirty miles west," the South African pilot said, and gestured vaguely. "Americans, I think, or maybe British."

As Rip thought about it now, it occurred to him that he hadn't seen a single piece of man-made trash since he arrived. Not a crushed Coke can, a snuff tin, a cigarette butt, or a candy wrapper. The Sahara was the cleanest place he had ever been.

He put the stadia rod on his shoulder and waited for Dutch to drive up.

"Had enough for today?" Haagen asked as Rip stowed the rod in the holder on the side of the Jeep.

"We could do a couple more shots, if you want."

Dutch wore khaki shorts and a T-shirt, was deeply tanned and pleasantly dirty. Water to wash with was a luxury. In his early thirties, Haagen had been surveying seismic lines for ten years. The job took him all over the world and paid good money, but at times he found it boring. "We've done enough for today," he said with a sigh.

Rip looked again for the flash from the sun's reflection as he got into the passenger's seat.

"Look at that, Dutch."

"Something shiny. Candy wrapper or piece of metal. Old truck, maybe. Maybe even a crashed plane. Found one of those once in this desert."

"Let's go look."

Dutch shrugged and put the Jeep in motion. Rip was still a kid. He hadn't burned out yet. The central Sahara was a big adventure for him, probably the biggest of his life.

"Did you find that plane around here, Dutch?"

"Closer to the coast, in Tunisia. Old German fighter plane. A Messerschmitt, as I recall. Pilot was still in the cockpit. All dried out like a mummy."

"Wow. What did you do?" Rip held on to

the bouncing Jeep with both hands.

"Do?" Haagen frowned. "Took a few photos, I guess. Stuck my finger in some of the bullet holes — I remember that."

"Did you get a souvenir?"

"One of the guys pried something off the plane. I didn't. Didn't seem right, somehow. It was sort of like robbing a grave."

"Did you bury the pilot, anything like that?"

"No," Haagen said softly. "We just left him there. The cockpit was his coffin. The plane had been half uncovered by a windstorm a few weeks before. The cockpit had a lot of sand in it. The wind probably drifted sand back over the plane within days after we found it."

Rip pointed at the sandstone cliff they were approaching. "About there, I think."

"Yeah."

Haagen stopped the Jeep and watched Rip bound away. He was a good-looking, athletic kid and smart as they come. The boss picked his résumé from a pile of two hundred engineering students who applied for this summer job. The kid worked hard, never complained. Still, this was just a summer job to young Cantrell. Rip was too bright to settle for seismic surveying when he graduated next May.

Haagen sighed, turned off the Jeep, and stretched.

The low cliff rising in front of him was sandstone sculpted by the wind, like thousands of similar formations in this section of the desert. It was perhaps twenty feet high, Haagen guessed. The slope of the face was about thirty degrees, gentle enough to scramble up.

"Better come up here and look, Dutch."

"What did you find?"

"Looks like metal. Right in the rock."

"A survey marker rod?"

"Come look."

Haagen slowly climbed to where Rip was perched about ten feet above the desert floor.

"It's metal of some kind, Dutch. Curved, right in the rock."

Haagen reached out, touched it. The metal was exposed for a length of about a foot. Vertically, perhaps four inches of metal were showing. At the maximum, the metal protruded about an inch from the stone.

"Looks a little like the bumper of an old Volkswagen Beetle polished by windblown sand."

"It's no bumper," Rip muttered.

13

Haagen bent down to study the exposed surface. It resembled steel, yet it didn't. A titanium alloy? It seemed too shiny, too mirrorlike to be titanium, he thought, and the color was wrong. The metal was dark, a deep gray, perhaps.

"Funny thing is, it's right in the rock. *Inside* the rock. Now how do you suppose someone got that in there?"

"Looks like it was exposed as the wind and rain weathered this cliff."

"That can't be right," Rip Cantrell countered stubbornly. "That would mean it was older than the rock."

"It's a mystery," Haagen said dismissively and turned to look out over the desert. Dirt, sand, and stone, but it *was* beautiful. He loved being outdoors. Even though he had an engineering degree he had never wanted an "inside" job.

Rip picked up a handy stone and swung it against the exposed metal. It made a deep *thunk*.

Haagen turned around to watch. Cantrell swung the rock three times, hard, then examined the metal closely.

"Didn't even mark it," he announced finally, straightening. "Not even a scratch."

Haagen bent down and again examined the surface, which was smooth, extraordinarily

14

so, without a mark of any kind, like a mirror. Amazing how sand can polish metal. Well, wind-driven sand wears away the hardest rock.

"There're lots of mysteries in this desert. Lots of things we'll never know." Dutch Haagen shook his head, then climbed down the ledge toward the waiting Jeep.

Rip followed him. "Maybe we ought to report this, eh?"

Haagen chuckled. "To Harvey Quick?" Harvey was their boss. "What are we going to tell him? That we found a funny piece of metal out in the desert? Ol' Harve will wonder what we've been drinking."

Haagen grinned at Rip. "Someday you're going to own this oil company, kid, and I'm going to win a big lottery, but right now we both need these jobs."

That evening Rip told Bill Taggart about the find. "It's right in the rock, Bill. The rock is weathering away, and as it does, more and more of the metal is exposed. That's the way it looks to me, anyway."

"What do you think, Dutch?" Bill asked. He was about forty, a heavyset, jowly guy who didn't like the heat. He spent most of his afternoons in the tent plotting the team's work on a computer.

"The kid is leveling with you. I don't

15

know any more than he does. Never saw anything like it."

"Show it to me in the morning, will you?"

"Sure. If we can find it again."

Taggart smiled. "Did I ever tell you fellows about the time we found a still in the Louisiana swamps? Mash was cooking and shine was dripping out the tube. There wasn't a soul around, so we helped ourselves. Didn't get any more work done that day, I can tell you. Ah, that was good stuff."

"There's something inside that rock," Rip Cantrell said, unwilling to see his find so quickly relegated to the tall-tale file.

"Maybe it's Martians," Bill Taggart suggested with a chuckle.

"Or a big black rock," Dutch put in, "like they had in *2001: A Space Odyssey.* You guys ever see that old flick?"

"Before my time," Rip said crossly.

"I hate to bring you wild adventurers back to earth," Taggart said, "but we are going to have to do something about the food supply."

"There's nothing wrong with the food," Rip said.

"You should know. You ate it all. We're darn near out."

"Maybe we should take an inventory, make a list," Haagen suggested.

"I already did that." Taggart passed him a sheet of paper. "Since the food delivery last week, this kid has personally hogged his way through enough grub to keep a caravan of camel drivers eating for a year. Honest to God, I think he has a tapeworm."

"The tapeworm theory again! Thank you, Professor." Rip stalked away. Haagen and Taggart had been kidding him all summer.

"There's something wrong with him," Bill Taggart assured Dutch. "Real people don't eat like that."

Before he went to bed, Rip Cantrell walked a few yards from the fire and sat looking up. Since the desert lacked the haze and light pollution that obscured the night sky in the major cities of the temperate world, the stars were stunning, a million diamonds gleaming amid the black velvet of the universe. Only in this desert had Rip seen the night sky with such awe-inspiring clarity.

The searing memory of this sky, with the Milky Way splashed so carelessly across it — that was what he would take back to college this fall.

Billions of galaxies, each with billions of stars.

As he had done every night this summer, Rip Cantrell lay down on his back in the sand. The warmth of the sand contrasted pleasantly with the rapidly cooling desert air. Lying spread-eagle on his back it almost felt as if he were free of the planet and hurtling through space.

A meteor shower caught his eye, dozens of streaks all shooting across the star-spangled sky at the same angle.

What was buried in that sandstone ledge?

He made a promise to himself to find out.

"See, Bill. I wasn't kidding. It's *in* the rock. And it wasn't pounded in. The rock is real rock, not concrete or some kind of artificial aggregate."

"Hmm." Bill Taggart examined the stone carefully. The sun had been up less than an hour and was shining on the metal at an angle.

When Taggart straightened, Rip set his feet, got a good grip on the sledgehammer, and started swinging.

Each blow took off a few small chunks of sandstone. When he tired, he put the head of the hammer on the ground and wiped his forehead. The humidity was nonexistent, yet the air was just plain hot. Already the thermometer was into the nineties. It seemed as if the heat just sucked the moisture from you.

Dutch brushed away the chips with his fingers. "Well, you didn't dent it. Exposed a few more inches of it, I'd say."

"What the hell is it?" Taggart asked.

"Something man-made from damn good metal before that rock was laid there," Rip told him.

"And what might that be?"

"I don't know," Rip admitted. "Dutch, you been knocking around these deserts for a lot of years. What do you think?"

Haagen took his time before answering. "What's the weather forecast?"

"Clear and sunny," Rip replied, "as usual." He got the weather off the satellite broadcast every morning. "Not a cloud in the forecast."

"We're a day or two ahead of schedule. What say we take today off, drive over to the archaeology dig, introduce ourselves to our neighbors? Maybe they'll let us borrow an air compressor and jackhammer, if they got one."

"Yes!" Rip shouted and tossed the hammer to the sand below, near the Jeep.

"An air compressor," Bill Taggart mused.

"I thought those folks used dental picks and toothbrushes for their excavating."

"We can ask," Dutch said and kicked at the metal sticking out of the rock. He frowned at it. It shouldn't be there, and that fact offended him. Frogs don't fly and dogs don't talk and sandstone ledges don't contain metal.

Bill brightened. "Might get a decent meal over at the dig."

"Might even see some girls," Rip said with a laugh. "You two old farts wouldn't be interested, but I sure am."

There weren't any girls within ten years of Rip's age at the archaeology dig. In fact, the only two females in sight had been on the planet at least half a century and weighed perhaps thirty pounds more than he did. Taggart kidded Rip about it as they walked toward the office tent.

"What are these people digging up?" Rip asked, to divert Taggart from the subject of women.

"Old stuff," Taggart replied. "The older the better."

The head archaeologist was Dr. Hans Soldi, from a famous Ivy League university. He shook hands all around, then listened with a skeptical expression as Dutch explained why they needed a jackhammer.

"We have one, to do the heavy digging," Soldi said when Dutch ran out of steam. "Now tell me the real reason you want it."

"It's diamonds, Prof," Rip said. "We found King Solomon's mine. We're gonna jackhammer the place, steal everything we can carry, and skedaddle."

Soldi ignored the young man. "Metal inside rock is an impossibility," he said to Haagen and Taggart.

"It's there, sure enough," Dutch replied quietly. "Whoever put it there didn't know it was impossible."

"I will let you borrow the compressor and hammer, if you will swear to me that you are not disturbing an archaeological site."

"I swear," Rip said. "Cross my heart."

"You others?"

Dutch Haagen got out his pipe and slowly tamped the bowl full of tobacco. "I don't know what we have, Professor. Tell you what — you loan us the equipment and come along. Take a look. We'll bring you back this evening before dark."

Soldi didn't mull it long. He was in his fifties, a healthy, vigorous man wearing a cowboy hat. "Okay, I'll come. I need to think about something besides stone tools."

"Stone tools? That's what you're digging

up?" Rip asked incredulously. "People used to live around here? In this desert?"

"This wasn't always a desert," the professor said as he led them to where the compressor was parked. "The climate didn't become extremely arid until about five thousand years ago. Then the wind carried in most of this sand, which covered up the valleys and low places. What we see protruding from the sand today are the tops of hills and mountains."

"So the site you are exploring is at least five thousand years old?"

"More like fifteen thousand years old, I suspect. Man lived here during the Ice Age. We are trying to find evidence that these people cultivated grain."

"By the way," Rip put in, "do you folks have any food left over from lunch? Maybe I can get a snack to take along. I'm sorta hungry."

"Sure, son." The professor pointed toward a tent and gave him the name of the cook.

Hans Soldi made his examination of the sandstone ledge while the surveyors started the compressor and manhandled the jackhammer into position. Rip waited until Soldi was out of the way, then began hammering.

The heat wasn't unbearable if one were accustomed to it. Wearing jeans, long-sleeve cotton shirts, and hats with wide brims, the men instinctively spent as much time as possible in the shade and swigged on water.

"I never saw anything like it," Soldi admitted to Dutch as he watched Rip work the hammer. The scientist had been scrambling around with his video camera, shooting footage from every angle.

"We'll see what Rip can do."

Haagen picked up one of the shards of stone kicked out by the hammer and handed it to the archaeologist. "How old is this, anyway?"

"Offhand, I could only guess. I'll get it analyzed."

"More than five thousand years old?"

"Oh, yes. The desert and the ocean came and went through the ages, many times. Time is so . . ." He flung his arms wide. "We talk blithely of time — as we do death and infinity — but humans have difficulty grasping the enormity of it. Perhaps if we could comprehend the vastness of time we would be able to understand God."

Soldi put the piece of sandstone into a pocket. He gestured at the cliff. "This is a windblown deposit, I think. You can see

23

how the wind sculpted the sand as it was laid down."

"I thought those designs were made by wind cutting the rock."

"I don't think so," the professor replied. "The wind made the designs before the sand hardened to stone. After the sand was deposited, it was covered by dirt, probably this red dirt that you see everywhere else. Water and the weight of the dirt transformed the sand into stone. Through the millennia there were repeated periods when the desert encroached. Sooner or later the rains always came again and pushed it back. The desert is winning now, but someday the rains will come again. Everything changes, even climates."

"Whatever is in that ledge now was there when the sand covered it."

"So it would seem."

"Playing it safe?"

"It looks as if the thing is embedded in the stone, but . . ." Soldi picked up another rock shard and examined it closely. He hefted it thoughtfully as he gazed at the face of the cliff.

"Give me your guess. How old is this rock?"

Soldi took his time before he replied. "Anywhere from a hundred thousand to a million years old," he said finally and tossed away the rock. He grinned. "Doesn't make sense, does it?"

"Don't guess it does."

Three hours of vigorous, sweaty work with the jackhammer under the desert sun uncovered a curved expanse of metal fifteen feet long. It protruded from the raw stone at least three feet. The structure seemed to be a part of a perfectly round circle, one with a diameter of about seventy feet.

The four men squatted, touching the metal with their hands, examining it with their eyes.

Amazingly, the surface seemed unmarred. Oh, here and there were a few tiny scratches, but only a few, and very small. The dark metal was reflective yet lacked a patina. The water that had percolated through the stone for ages apparently had affected the metal very little. "Assuming the metal was in the stone," Dr. Soldi muttered.

"Excalibur," Rip said as he wiped his face.

Bill Taggart didn't understand the reference.

"The sword Arthur pulled from the rock . . . Excalibur was its name."

"Whatever this is," Dutch remarked, "it isn't going to make us kings."

"It's going to take us a couple days to hack this thing completely out of the rock," Bill Taggart said gloomily. "The ledge is thicker back there, so the going will be slower. Maybe we ought to just leave it here. Forget about it."

"So what the hell is it?" Dutch Haagen wondered.

"That's obvious, isn't it?" Rip said. "I thought you three were sitting here like store dummies because you were afraid to say it. The damned thing is a saucer."

"A saucer?"

"A flying saucer. What else could it be?"

Dr. Soldi closed his eyes and ran his hands across the metal, rubbing it with his fingertips. "Two days. Whatever it is, we'll have it out of the rock in a couple of days."

"Are you trying to tell us that this thing we're sitting in front of is a spaceship?" Bill Taggart demanded.

"Yeah," Rip Cantrell said with conviction. "Modern man didn't make this and put it here. Ancient man couldn't work metal like this. This is a highly engineered product of an advanced civilization. That's a fact beyond dispute."

"I don't believe in flying saucers,"

Taggart scoffed. "I've seen the shows on TV, watched those freaky people from the trailer parks say they saw UFOs in the night sky while the dogs howled and cats climbed the walls." He made a rude noise. "I don't believe a word of it."

Rip was beside himself. "It's a saucer, Bill," he insisted.

"Bet it ain't. Bet it's something else."

"What?" Professor Soldi asked sharply.

The next day they got to the cockpit. It was in the middle of the thing, at the thickest point. The canopy was made of a dark, transparent material. When they wiped away the sand and chips, they could stare down into the ship. There was a seat and an instrument panel. The seat was raised somewhat, on a pedestal that elevated the pilot so he — or she or it — could see out through the canopy.

"It *is* a saucer!" Rip Cantrell shouted. He pounded Bill on the back. "See! Now do you believe?"

"It's something the commies made, I'll bet," Taggart insisted. "Some kind of airplane."

"Sure."

When he finished with his video camera, Professor Soldi eased himself off the ship, climbed down the ledge, and found a shady spot beside the Jeep where he could sit and look at the thing.

He sat contemplating the curved metal embedded in stone. After a bit the other three men joined him in the shade and helped themselves to water from the cooler.

"There hasn't been a discovery like this since the Rosetta Stone," Soldi said softly. "This will revolutionize archaeology. Everything we know about man's origins is wrong."

"You're going to be famous, Professor," Bill Taggart said as he helped himself to the water. Soldi gave him a hard look, but it was apparent that Bill meant the words kindly.

"Shouldn't we be taking more pictures or something?" Rip asked Soldi. "Something that will prove we found it buried in the rock?"

"We have the videotape," Bill reminded them.

"If it is a spaceship, then it must have been manufactured on another planet," Soldi mused. "Once we examine it, there should be no doubt of that. Where and how it was found will be of little importance." He held his hands to his head. "I can't believe I said that, me — a professor of archaeology. Yet it's true. For fifty years we've been inundated with UFO photos, most of them faked. The thing must speak for itself or all the photos in the world won't matter."

"So what should we do?" Dutch asked.

"Do?" Soldi looked puzzled.

Rip gestured toward the saucer. "Should we keep hammering? Uncover it?"

"Oh, my, yes. Before we tell the world about this, let's see what we have. Is it intact? Is it damaged?"

"What I want to know," Rip said, "is there a way in?"

"I'm not a nut," Bill Taggart announced, "and I still don't believe in flying saucers."

"A spaceship," Soldi muttered. "No one is going to believe this. Not a soul." He couldn't have been more wrong about that, but he didn't know it then. He sighed. "When this hits the papers, the faculty is going to laugh me out of the university."

"Perhaps we should keep this under our hats," Rip Cantrell suggested. "When we do go public we don't want anyone laughing."

"I hear you," Dutch murmured.

Rip looked toward the sun, gauging its height above the horizon. "We have three or four hours of daylight left, but it's almighty hot and we have only a gallon or two of gasoline for the compressor. I think we have ten gallons at camp."

"I want to go back to my dig," the professor said. "Get some clothing and a toothbrush. We have four five-gallon cans of gasoline, I think. At the rate we're going, my guess is that it will take us another two days to completely uncover this thing."

"I'll drive the professor over to his camp and bring him back," Rip said eagerly, "if it's all right with you, Dutch?"

"Sure, kid. Sure."

"Bring back some food, kid," Bill called mournfully. "And don't eat all of it on the way."

"What's he talking about?" Soldi asked.

"He's a big kidder," Rip replied curtly.

Rip took Dutch and Bill back to their camp, then drove away with the professor.

"Twenty-two years old, and Rip's a take-charge kind of guy," Dutch said as he watched the Jeep's dust plume tail away on the hot wind.

"Got a lot of his mother in him, I suspect," Bill said. "The kid told me his father was a farmer in Minnesota and died when Rip was twelve. His mother has run the farm ever since. She must be quite a woman."

"He gets on your nerves, doesn't he?" Dutch remarked.

"A little, I guess." Taggart shrugged.

Dutch slapped Bill on the shoulder. "We're going to be famous too, you know. Finding a flying saucer sounds like a new career to me. Maybe they'll stick us on the cover of *Time* magazine."

"We'll have to shave, then, I reckon."

"We'll put the saucer in a parking lot in Jersey City and charge five bucks a head to go through it. We'll make millions. Our ship has come in, Bill."

2

"So whaddaya think, Professor?" Rip asked as they bounced along in the Jeep at thirty miles per hour, at least ten miles per hour too fast for the ancient caravan trail that he was generally following.

"The thing in the rock?"

"The saucer. Yeah."

"It's too soon to say. I don't recognize the metal, if it is metal. I don't yet have explanations for anything."

Hans Soldi weighed his words. "I feel over-whelmed. This discovery is unexpected. If it is what it seems to be, the scientific benefits are going to be extraordinary. Think of the spillover from the American space program of the sixties and seventies — this could be many times that big. Ultimately the life of everyone on this planet could be affected." He released his death grip on the side of the Jeep momentarily to wipe his forehead with his sleeve. "I just don't know what to think, where to start."

"We need some other scientists in on this, wouldn't you agree?"

"Of course. Experts in a variety of fields. First, however, I think we should uncover the ship, see what is there, satisfy ourselves that it is what it appears to be. If we even hint to the outside world that we've found an alien spaceship and it isn't, I'll be laughed out of the profession. I won't be able to get a job digging basements."

"Uh-huh."

"When we are absolutely convinced that it could be nothing else, then we tell the world."

"I was thinking about the local government," Rip said with a glance at the professor. "The Libyan border is just a few miles north, isn't it?"

Soldi frowned. "Our dig is in Chad. They issued the archaeological permit."

"The saucer may be in Libya, Chad, or the Sudan for all I know," Rip remarked. "Borders are political — you can't see or touch them. Qaddafi might run us off and confiscate the saucer if he gets wind of this. We've got to get it out of this desert before we say anything to anybody."

"Let me do the talking at the dig," Professor Soldi told him.

By evening the following day, the four men had the sandstone completely removed from the top of the spaceship, which was indeed circular in form, with a diameter of a few inches over seventy feet. The top of it seemed to be in perfect condition, although the bottom was still embedded in stone.

"The thing looks like it's sitting on a pedestal in front of a museum," Dutch remarked.

"That's probably its ultimate fate," Rip replied, then went back to work clearing the last of the stone from the four exhaust pipes that stuck out the rear. Each of these nozzles was about a foot in diameter.

Arranged around the circumference of the ship, but pointing up and down, were more exhaust nozzles, small ones. These, everyone agreed, must be maneuvering jets, to control the attitude of the ship in yaw, roll, and pitch. The upper ones were packed with sandstone.

Although it was late in another long day, Rip still had plenty of energy. He had ceased asking Professor Soldi questions only when the scientist quit supplying answers. Soldi was lost in his own private world. He and Bill measured the ship with a tape as carefully as they could. Soldi took notes on a small computer and shot more videotape. He also shot up several rolls of 35mm film.

The archaeologist studied the surface of the ship with a pocket magnifying glass, dripped a bit of acid from the Jeep's battery on one tiny spot, and muttered over the result.

"It's a giant solar cell," Rip remarked.

"What is?"

"The skin. Put your fingers on it. You can feel it absorbing energy from the sun. And notice how the reflectivity has changed — it seems to change with the temperature, and probably the state of the battery charge."

The professor gave Rip a surprised look. As soon as the younger man turned away, he caressed the skin with his fingers. A solar power cell, absorbing the sun's energy and converting it to electricity! Of course!

He drew back suddenly, as if he had been shocked. Rip implied that the solar cells were absorbing energy *now!* Could that be true?

He lay for an hour on top of the ship with a mirror to direct the sun's rays down inside the cockpit like a spotlight. Each of the men joined him there, looking at the seat and controls, the blank white panels. The cockpit looked like nothing they had ever seen, and yet it was familiar in a way that was hard to describe.

"It's human-size," Rip remarked.

"Isn't that extraordinary?" Soldi muttered.

Most of the afternoon Soldi spent sitting in the shade tapping on his computer, with long pauses to stare at the ship.

They had found no blemish on the upper skin of the ship and no way in. The skin was seamless.

"The hatch must be underneath," Rip told Dutch and kept working with the jackhammer. He seemed almost immune to the heat and dust.

Twice the jackhammer slipped when Rip was working close to the ship's skin. The hard steel bit whacked the ship several smart raps. Soldi examined the spots with his magnifying glass and said nothing.

Finally, with the evening sun fully illuminating the ship, Soldi shot two more rolls of 35mm film.

The rock under the ship was difficult to remove. After it was broken up, the shards and remnants had to be shoveled away.

Just before dusk, they managed to clear the first landing gear. It was a simple skid protruding from the bottom of the saucer, held down by what appeared to be a hydraulic ram.

"No wheels," Soldi muttered and resumed chewing on his lower lip.

"It must land vertically," Rip Cantrell said.

"So it would seem."

"That means it must have some other mode of thrust besides the rocket engines to hold it up."

"One would think so, yes."

"What kind of thrust?"

"I dig up ancient villages," Soldi said irritably. "How would I know?"

"Well, Professor, I never saw an airplane like this. No, sirree. Did you?"

Soldi pointed at the stone. "Hammer some more rock out. There's another fifteen minutes of daylight left."

Just before he quit for the evening, Rip uncovered the first landing light. The material that covered it seemed as hard and impervious as the canopy. Still, through the covering he could see the bulb of a powerful spotlight.

That night they ate dinner sitting on folding camp stools in the circle of light cast by a propane lantern mounted on a pole. "We have a supply plane from Cairo scheduled in tomorrow afternoon," the professor told his hosts. The transport landed on unprepared flat, sandy places as if they were a huge paved airfield.

"It would be best if the crew of the plane didn't see the saucer," Dutch Haagen remarked.

"I think that's wise," the professor said. "We have several large tents at my dig. I suggest that after dinner we drive over and get one. We can erect it over the saucer tomorrow morning."

"Okay," Dutch agreed. "And I was thinking that perhaps we should move our camp closer to the saucer."

They talked about the day's events, about what the ship looked like. They were winding down, watching Rip eat the last of the cooked vegetables as they sipped their coffee, when Rip asked, "What have we really got here, Doc? Give us your off-the-record opinion."

Soldi puffed on his pipe as he scrutinized each face. "It's very, very old. Ancient man didn't make it. That much I am reasonably sure of."

"Is it a spaceship?" Dutch asked.

"You see, that's the danger of loose language. The thing may fly, probably does — the shape is a symmetrical, saucer-shaped lifting body — but whether it is capable of flying above the atmosphere . . ." He shrugged. "Later, if we can get inside, we'll get a better idea."

"So who brought it here?"

Soldi puffed slowly on his pipe and said nothing.

"Why did they leave it?"

"I have seen no exterior damage."

"Where are the people who flew it?"

"People?"

"Whatever."

Soldi waggled a finger. "The answers to those questions, if we can find answers, are going to rock civilization." He nodded in the direction of the saucer, several miles away in the night. "That thing is going to revolutionize the way we think about the universe, about ourselves. We must be very careful about the words we use because they have enormous implications." He smoked some more, then repeated the phrase, "Enormous implications."

Bill Taggart ran his fingers through his hair. "Maybe we should have left it in the rock."

Rip Cantrell looked up at the sea of stars almost within arm's reach. "We couldn't, Bill," he said softly. "We had to dig it out because it's our nature to wonder, to explore."

"Maybe that's why *they* came," Dutch Haagen remarked.

Soldi, Rip, and Dutch were deep in a

discussion of the physics of atmospheric entry when Bill Taggart wandered off into the darkness. When he was well away from the light of the camp lanterns, he walked quickly to the supply tent. By the light of a pencil-thin flash, he found the satellite telephone. He opened the dish antenna and turned the thing on.

Bill removed a small book from his hip pocket and consulted it by the light of the pencil flash. He dialed in the frequency he wanted, picked up the telephonelike handset, and waited for the phone to lock onto the satellite.

He punched a long series of numbers into the keyboard, waited some more. He looked again at the numbers. That country code, that was Australia, wasn't it?

He heard the number ringing. A sleepy voice answered.

"This is Bill Taggart. Is Neville there?"

"Neville who?"

"Just Neville."

"I'll see. Say your name again, mate."

"Bill Taggart."

"Wait."

Time passed. A minute, then two. Taggart glanced through the tent flap at the three figures sitting in the light near the camp stove. They hadn't moved.

Finally the voice came back on. "Neville isn't here. Why don't you tell me what you want, mate?"

"I met Neville about eighteen months ago. In Singapore. He mentioned that he would be interested in buying certain kinds of information."

"That Neville . . ." the male voice said noncommittally.

"I have some information to sell. It's very valuable."

"All information has value. The question is, is it valuable to us? We will discuss price with you after we have evaluated what you have. Sorry about that, but it's the only way we can do business. You have to trust us."

"How do I know you will play fair?"

"As I said, you have to trust us. Do you?"

"No."

"Well, you have our number. If you —"

"Wait a minute! Okay? I have to think about this for a minute."

"We're on your dime, mate."

Soldi was standing, looking into the darkness toward the ship. Rip lay in the sand, looking skyward at the stars. Dutch was sipping coffee.

"I work for an oil company," Bill Taggart

said to the man on the other end of the satellite phone. "I'm on a seismic survey crew working in the Sahara Desert. I'll give you the coordinates in a minute. We've found something, something extraordinary that I think would be of interest to Neville and his associates."

"I'm listening, Bill. Talk away."

"I want two million dollars."

"I'd like ten my own self."

"I'm serious."

"I am listening, my friend. You're paying for this call."

Captain Kathleen Sullivan was the duty officer in the operations center at Space Command, in Colorado Springs, Colorado, when one of the enlisted technicians called her over to his computer console.

"We were processing data from the equatorial satellite when the computer found an anomaly, Captain. I think you should take a look at this."

"Okay," Captain Sullivan said.

"The area we are looking at is the Sahara, on the border between Libya and Chad. The computer says the area of interest is a few meters inside Libya, but as I recall, the exact border has never been formally agreed upon."

"What do you have?" Sullivan asked brusquely. She was in no mood for a long wind-up.

"This." The sergeant punched a key on the computer keyboard and a picture appeared. He used a track ball to make the picture larger, and larger, and larger. In the center was a perfect circle. The sergeant stood back from the console with his hands behind his back.

"That circular shape is made of metal, is highly reflective, is about twenty meters in diameter, and wasn't there four days ago on the satellite's last look at that area."

Sullivan leaned close to the computer screen. "This is a new one on me," she muttered.

"Yes, ma'am," the sergeant agreed. "Me too. If I didn't know better, I'd say the damn thing is a flying saucer."

"Or the top of a water tank."

"There? In the middle of the Sahara?" The sergeant reached for the computer keyboard. "There is one vehicle near it and one small piece of wheeled equipment."

"People?"

"At least one, perhaps two. If we had a little better angle on the sun we might have gotten a shadow . . ."

Sullivan straightened up and frowned.

"You don't believe in flying saucers, do you?"

"I have an open mind, Captain. An open mind. I'm just saying that circular shape looks like a saucer. It could be a water tank. It could be the top of a nuclear reactor. It could be a twenty-meter metal sunshade for the queen of England's garden party."

Sullivan picked up a notepad, jotted a series of numbers off the computer screen, then tore off the sheet of paper.

"Thank you, Sergeant," she said and walked back to her office.

"Since I'm not an officer," the sergeant muttered under his breath, "I can believe any damned thing I want. Sir."

Captain Sullivan consulted the telephone number list taped to her desk, then dialed a secure telephone. After two rings, a male voice answered.

She explained about the anomaly and dictated the latitude and longitude coordinates. She was very careful not to label the anomaly a flying saucer. "It appears to be the top of a water tank, but it's in an empty, barren godforsaken place. I suggest, sir, that we request a more thorough examination of this site."

"Libya?"

"Near the place where the borders of Libya, Chad, and Sudan come together."

"I'll be down for a look in five minutes."

Exactly six and a half minutes later, the general was leaning over the sergeant's shoulder while Captain Sullivan watched from several paces away.

"We're doing an initial analysis before we send this data to NIMA," she explained. NIMA was the National Imagery and Mapping Agency, which collected, analyzed, and distributed imagery for the various agencies of the U.S. government.

"Hmm," said the general.

"Yes, sir," the sergeant agreed flippantly.

"What do you think it is, Sergeant?"

"Looks like a flying saucer to me, General, but I just work here."

"Darned if it don't," the general said. He straightened, checked the lat/long coordinates on the screen, nodded at Captain Sullivan, then walked away.

In less than an hour a computer printer spit out a sheet of paper in a windowless office on the ground floor of a hangar in Nevada, at an airfield that wasn't on any map, in a place known only as Area 51.

Two hours later a pilot wearing a helmet and full pressure suit manned an airplane that had just been pushed from the hangar.

The airplane was all black and shaped like a wedge, with seventy-five degrees of wing sweep. An enlisted crew helped the pilot get into the cockpit, then strapped and plugged him in.

The airplane was receiving electrical power from a piece of yellow gear. The pilot set up his cockpit switches, then spent fifteen minutes waiting.

Only when the minute hand of his wristwatch was exactly on the hour did he signal the ground crew for an engine start.

Precisely ten minutes later he advanced the throttles of his four rocket-based, combined-cycle engines and released the brakes. The noise from the engines almost ripped the sky apart. Even snuggled in the cockpit under a well-padded helmet, the pilot found the noise painfully loud.

As he rolled down the runway, the engines were burning a mixture of compressed air and methane, augmented with liquid oxygen. As the plane accelerated, the mixture would be automatically juggled to maintain power.

The spy plane rolled on the fourteen-thousand-foot runway for a long time before it lifted off. With a flick of a switch the pilot retracted the gear. Then he pulled the nose up steeply and climbed away at a forty-five-degree angle. Passing Mach 2, the pilot toggled a lever that hydraulically lifted an opaque metal screen to cover the windshield and protect it. He had been using computer displays as his primary flight reference since liftoff, so being deprived of an outside view was of no practical consequence.

He watched his airspeed carefully, and at Mach 2.5 monitored the computer-controlled transition to pure ramjet flight. The air compressor inlet doors were closed and the flow of LOX secured. When the transition was complete, methane burning in the free airflow through the four ramjets provided the aircraft's propulsion. Fifteen minutes after lifting off, the plane leveled at one hundred twenty-five thousand feet above the earth and accelerated to fifty-four hundred miles per hour.

The pilot kept a careful eye on the computer screen that displayed the temperature of various portions of his aircraft. He was especially vigilant about the temperatures of the leading edges of the wings, which he knew were glowing a cherry red even though he couldn't see them.

Despite the deafening roar of the engines and the shock wave that trailed for miles behind the hypersonic plane, a placid calm had descended upon the cockpit. Engine noise reached the pilot only through the airframe. Amazingly, almost none of this noise reached the ground. The sonic wave of aircraft flying above one hundred thousand feet dissipated before reaching the ground, as did ninety-nine percent of the engine noise. And at this altitude the stealthy plane was invisible to radar and human eyes. Only infrared sensors trained skyward could detect it, and there were few of those.

The pilot ensured that his two Global Positioning System (GPS) devices agreed with each other, then coupled the primary autopilot to one of them. The autopilot would take him to the first tanker rendezvous, over the Atlantic. He would drop down to thirty thousand feet and slow to subsonic speed on the turbine engines to refuel from a KC-135 tanker, then climb back to altitude while accelerating to hypersonic cruise for the flight across Africa.

The night would not yet have passed when he arrived over the central Sahara, but no matter. His synthetic-aperture radar could see through darkness, clouds, or smoke. The digital signals would be encrypted and transmitted via satellite to NIMA for processing into extraordinarily detailed images.

With its mission in the Sahara complete, the hypersonic spy plane would make another pass over the Mideast — this pilot made the Mideast run at least once a week — then turn and head for a second tanker rendezvous west of the Azores on the way back to Nevada.

Just another day at the office, the pilot told himself, and tried to make himself comfortable in his padded seat.

When Bill Taggart got back to the circle of light from the propane lamp, the professor was explaining: ". . . Modern man appears in the archaeological record about one hundred thousand years ago, but the story is mixed, hard to decipher. At least two other species of hominids lived at the same time. All we know for a fact is that modern man survived and the other hominids became extinct."

Professor Soldi gestured into the larger darkness. "A hundred millennia ago this area was probably a lot like parts of Arizona are today, with wooded hills and mountains rising above the arid desert floor. People lived wherever there was a dependable source of water — didn't have to be much, just a little, but steady. The desert encroached and retreated with variations in rainfall."

"How do you see what's under the sand?"

"We use radar. We look through the sand with radar, map the terrain, locate places that we think it likely that water might have been more plentiful than elsewhere. If these sites aren't buried too deep, we dig."

"Any luck so far?"

"Oh, yes," Soldi said, and from a trouser pocket he removed a large flint blade. "This knife," he said, cradling it in his hand, "may be fifty thousand years old."

"The saucer might be that old," Rip said. "Or older."

"Extraordinary, isn't it?" Soldi exclaimed, his voice vibrant and full of energy. "The technology in that saucer and the technology represented by this knife blade. They were found just thirty miles apart and are apparently so dissimilar. And yet . . ."

The sky was just beginning to lighten in the east when Rip Cantrell awoke. He was too excited to sleep. He could think of nothing except the saucer.

He rolled off the cot, pounded his boots to make sure that they were empty, then put them on. He pulled on his shorts and a T-shirt he had worn only a couple of days, then slipped out of the tent.

The air was invigorating, cool, and crisp. Actually, it was cold. He went back into the tent and rooted through his clothes for a sweatshirt. And a sweater.

After a long, delicious drink of cool water and a couple of leftover rolls from last night's dinner, Rip set off on foot for the saucer. Dutch and Bill and the professor could bring the Jeep later.

As he walked he watched the first light of dawn chase away the shadows. This summer job was his first real experience with the desert, and he loved it.

He was at least a mile away when he saw the saucer reflecting the dawn's pink light. God, it looked . . . so . . . sublime! Mysterious and sublime.

Today would be the day they got some answers. Yes. He could feel it.

He climbed around on the rock, looking at the saucer from every angle. He put his hands on it, felt the cool, smooth, sensuous surface. When he lifted his hands, their outline remained in the surface dust.

From the top of the stone ledge that had imprisoned the saucer, he watched the sun rise over the rim of the earth.

Why here? Why had they landed here, in this place? Was it a desert then?

51

When the sun was completely above the horizon, Rip got the shovel and began removing sandstone debris from under the saucer. He brushed loose sand and rubble away from the exposed landing gear skid with his fingers.

He almost missed it in the darkness of the early morning light. There, in the stone!

A handprint!

Just like the ones he had left in the dust on the skin of the ship . . . a handprint in the rock.

He blew all the sand from the print. Placed his own right hand in it.

The print in the stone was just a tiny bit smaller.

He sat down and stared at the print, trying to understand.

Finally he covered the print with loose sand, then packed the sand in hard.

He had the compressor going and was jackhammering rock under the saucer when the others arrived in the Jeep. He heard them drive up when he paused to move the hammer and rearrange the handkerchief he had tied over his mouth and nose.

Rip Cantrell grinned to himself. Yes. Today was going to be the day!

About nine that morning the men took a break from moving rock and rigged the tent, which was really a large tarpulin without sides. An hour after they resumed work they uncovered a corner of the hatch in the bottom of the saucer. It was just aft of dead center, the thickest part of the ship.

The hatch cover joined the rest of the fuselage in a joint that was so fine it was easy to miss. As usual, Rip noticed it first.

They worked feverishly to break the rock loose from under the rest of the ship.

Panting from exertion and excitement, Professor Soldi crawled in and lay on his back, looking up at the hatch, which was about two feet above his head. Rip and Dutch lay on each side. In the center of the hatch was a drumstick-shaped cutout. At first blush, the cutout channel looked like an engraving. It was no more than a hundredth of an inch wide, if that.

Soldi wiped his hands on his shirt, then used his fingers to wipe the dust from his glasses. "Look at the workmanship," he whispered.

"Should we open it?" Dutch asked.

"You're assuming that we can," Soldi remarked.

"Of course we can," Rip said, his voice reflecting his optimism. "I'll bet this whole ship is just the way they left it. There isn't a speck of rust on it."

Soldi reached up and caressed the hatch with his fingertips. "We are on the threshold of a new age."

"Let's do it," Rip said. He was out of patience.

"Relax, Rip," Taggart rumbled.

"Perhaps we should wait for experts," Soldi muttered, probably just to rag the young man beside him, who was almost quivering.

Dutch Haagen was kneeling beside a landing gear skid. "I really don't want to meet anyone who claims to be an expert in flying saucers," he said. "Let's just get on with it before Qaddafi's boys arrive and run us off. Besides, the suspense is killing me."

Soldi reached over his head. He pushed gently on the small cutout. Nothing. Pressed on one end, then the other. "This is like pushing on a bank safe," he said with his teeth clenched.

He pushed, tugged, pried with his fingers. Nothing.

"There's gotta be a trick to it," Dutch remarked.

"I'm sure there is," Dr. Soldi agreed.

"Let me try." Rip bumped his hip against the professor, who glanced at the youngster's eager face, then moved over.

Rip put his hand against the cutout and held it there for a moment. Then he pressed on the large end. It gave. The small end moved down away from the fuselage.

"How about that!"

"It's sensitive to the heat of your hand."

"How did you know that?"

"It just makes sense. Doesn't it?"

Carefully Rip grasped the handle. He applied pressure downward, then sideways. Finally he tried to rotate it. Now the handle turned, then the rear edge of the hatch moved inward.

The hatch opened slowly, making a tiny hissing sound.

When the sound stopped, the four men lay frozen looking at the gaping hole in the ship's hull.

"Oh, man!" Dutch exclaimed.

3

Professor Soldi crawled toward the open hatch and sniffed the escaping air. "It *is* air, all right," he said, "but the aroma is a little strange . . ."

"That hatch has been closed for a very long time," Dutch Haagen remarked, more to himself than the others.

The professor stuck his head into the open hatchway and inhaled a lungful through his nose. Then he sagged back onto the sandy rock. "Stale. Very stale."

Rip Cantrell snorted. "I like your scientific method," he said and laughed.

Soldi didn't even bother to glare at him. The open hatch beckoned.

"Rip, you found this ship," Dutch said. "Would you like to go first?"

Rip didn't have to be asked twice. He scooted over to the hatch and positioned himself immediately under it as Bill Taggart told Dutch, "Thanks for not asking me."

Rip got his knees under him and eased his head higher in the hole. His eyes ad-

56

justed to the dim light.

His stomach felt like it was full of butter-flies.

He inched his head up.

His eyes cleared the rim of the hatchway, and he could see into the ship.

The only light came into the ship through the canopy over the pilot's seat, which was on a pedestal of some kind. No doubt the pedestal kept the pilot high, so he could see out.

Maybe seven feet of headroom in the center of the ship around the pedestal, less as the distance from the pedestal increased. The compartment was only about ten or twelve feet in diameter. There were six seats with seat belts lying beside them, but no bunks. All the seats faced forward. One seat on each side of the pedestal faced a blank white panel. On each panel were some switches and knobs, but no instruments were in sight — none.

After he had surveyed the entire compartment and his eyes were completely adjusted, Rip stood up in the hatch. His head just cleared the hatchway. The air in the ship was cool. That was unexpected. A metal ship, sitting in the sun. It must be well insulated.

He climbed in. Now he realized that

there was a handhold and cutout for his foot, so that he could climb in easier. He hadn't seen that before.

Standing inside the ship, he breathed deeply. Was there a faint odor of salt? Of perspiration? Or was it just his imagination?

Rip Cantrell took a careful look around, then climbed up into the pilot's seat and seated himself. The canopy was deeply tinted and offered the pilot a good view in all directions.

He was examining the knobs and levers and switches on the control panel in front of him when he realized that Professor Soldi was standing on one side and Dutch on the other.

"Can you believe this?" Rip asked. "*Look* at this! I've never seen anything like it."

"It's a shuttle ship," Dutch decided, "for taking people and supplies from a spaceship in orbit down to the surface."

"There's not much room for supplies in here. Maybe they used it for exploration. Or emergencies. Maybe it was a lifeboat."

"There's a thought."

"What are all these controls?"

There was a small stick on the right arm of the pilot's seat, which Rip suspected was the control stick. Another lever was mounted on the left side of the seat, but it ran forward at a forty-five-degree angle from a pivot point at the rear of the seat. Rip tugged on it experimentally. This lever moved only up and down. Both of the controls had several knobs and switches near the handgrips.

Where the pilot's feet would rest were pedals. Rudder pedals, Rip thought, then remembered that the saucer had no rudder. Some of its maneuvering jets were mounted beside the rocket exhaust nozzles, he recalled, pointed away from the axis of the saucer at a forty-five-degree angle. No doubt these pedals activated those jets, simulating a rudder.

"The insulation sure keeps the heat down in here," Rip remarked when he had finished examining the major controls. "I guess if this thing goes in and out of the atmosphere, it has to be well insulated."

"These panels have to be computer screens," Dutch said and pointed to the black panel areas directly in front of each control station. "Wouldn't Bill Gates like to see these? Then he could get *all* the money."

"Wonder why they left this ship here," Bill Taggart muttered. He was standing behind Haagen, looking over his shoulder.

Rip picked a switch and flipped it. Nothing happened, of course.

"No electrical power," Dutch murmured.

"But there is," Rip said. "I'll bet the skin is absorbing energy from the sun. We just don't know how to turn on the power."

"Man, don't go touching stuff, flipping those switches," Bill pleaded from behind him. "Makes me nervous as a naked cat."

"This joystick must control the ship somehow," Rip said, wrapping his right hand around the handgrip projecting from the right arm of the pilot's seat.

"Man, we don't even know what makes this thing work," Bill explained. "Let's not take foolish chances."

Dutch Haagen chimed in. "I think that —"

He stopped there, because Rip had reached for a reddish knob protruding from the instrument panel at a sixty-degree angle, near one of the computer screens. He tried to turn it, and when that didn't work, pulled it out. The knob came. As it did, the computer screens burst into life, red and yellow lights appeared all over the panels, and a low rumbling noise came from behind the passenger compartment.

Startled, Rip pushed the knob back in.

The lights died, the computer screens went blank, the noise stopped.

"Oh, sweet Jesus!" Bill exclaimed, then turned and clambered quickly out the hatch.

"It's got to be nuclear-powered," Dutch said, looking over the blank, dark panels. "That noise must have been the reactor."

"Must be."

"Professor, if this thing has sat here for eons, how could a reactor have any juice left? Wouldn't it go dead, like a battery?"

"Over a terrific span of time, yes. The half-life of plutonium is a quarter million years. After five hundred thousand years, a reactor would still have twenty-five percent of its energy remaining."

Rip reached for the knob again. Dutch's hand shot out.

"Not just now, son. Bill had a valid point. I know you're a tiger, but let's think this over very carefully."

"This ship may have been abandoned because it was no longer in operational condition," Dr. Soldi suggested.

"Yeah," Bill said from the hatch. Only his head was visible. "You go turning stuff on willy-nilly and we all may wind up knocking on the pearly gates sooner than we figured, Rip."

"We've got to figure out what makes this thing go," Rip argued.

"Let's study up a bit more," Dutch insisted and put his hand on Rip's shoulder.

Rip got out of the seat and Taggart climbed back into the ship. The four men began poking and prodding. The low panels between the seats were on hinges. The latches were pushbuttons.

Behind the panels was the machinery. Pipes, pumps — well . . . they looked like pumps — lines for carrying fluid, insulated wires.

"This insulation must be rotten," Dutch muttered and laid a rough hand on the nearest wire. He flexed it, twisted it, and still it remained intact.

"What *is* this stuff?"

"Somebody built this thing to last."

"Over here is the reactor."

It was small, not much bigger than a forty-gallon can. It was almost invisible, nestled amid a tangle of wires, pressure hoses, and other machinery.

"Yeah, that's it."

"Isn't it awful small?" Bill asked.

"How big should it be?"

"I dunno. I guess I thought it would be about the size of a car or something."

"If that thing's cracked, we're probably

absorbing a fatal dose of radiation," Dutch pointed out.

"It isn't cracked," Rip replied, suddenly sure of himself. "There's nothing wrong with this ship. Nothing."

"And on what do you base that scientific conclusion?"

"I just know." The youngster shrugged. "Call it instinct."

"I call it wishful thinking," Bill said from the equipment room hatch. He had not crawled in, which was a good thing. The other three filled up all the space not occupied by machinery.

"Maybe you should stay as the mine canary, Rip," Dutch suggested, "while the rest of us wait outside."

"Exploring this ship is dangerous," Soldi told them. "We are surrounded by unknown technology, in a ship with unknown problems. Radiation, bacteria, viruses from space . . . this ship should be explored by engineers wearing full-body clean suits."

Bill Taggart's head disappeared. Despite Soldi's comment, neither Haagen, Rip Cantrell, nor the professor moved toward the hatch.

They found the batteries, the wires that seemed to lead to them from the skin of the ship, bundles of wires that led away from them to buses, and from there to a bewildering conglomeration of strange boxes and devices. They studied the devices one by one, trying to decide what each might be.

"Whoever built this was well ahead of where our civilization is today," Dutch Haagen said finally. "This is like looking into the equipment bay of the space shuttle, only more so."

Although he was still an engineering student, Rip had the most recent experience with high-tech applications. "This ship is less cluttered," he decided, thinking about last summer's trip to Cape Kennedy. "In a way, things are simpler, more . . ." He ran out of words. After a bit, he said, ". . . refined. Advanced. Better."

They continued their explorations, until finally the compartment was so hot and stuffy they wanted out.

Rip held them back. "Come look at this, Professor."

The young man was on his hands and knees, looking at something wedged between the machinery. He was holding his flashlight in his left hand.

Soldi crawled over for a look.

"It's a pile of something that has deteriorated over the years."

"Looks like it, doesn't it?"

The professor adjusted his glasses, stuck his nose down almost in the pile, which looked somewhat like the pages of a very old book that had lost its binding.

"Paper? Pages?"

"Pages of something, I'll bet. Let me get my camera and a bag."

"What do you think it is?"

"My God, Rip! I have no idea."

When Rip crawled out of the engineering spaces, Dutch was sitting with his back to the pilot's seat pedestal, his arms curled around his legs.

"What do you think?"

"I feel as if I'm in a museum. This thing is ancient."

"They've been dead a long time."

"A long, long time. Too long for us even to comprehend the enormity of it."

"I still don't understand how everything works," Rip mused. "It's got electrical power, a reactor, but what powers the ship?"

Dutch ran his fingertips slowly across the deck. He touched everything in reach, taking his time, looking, feeling.

"We aren't alone in the universe," he said after a bit.

"Gives me the willies." Rip shivered.

"This shouldn't be real. Can't be real. Yet it is."

"What would it be like to take that saucer into space?" Rip asked. Everyone else had finished lunch, but he was still eating. They were sitting under a tarp rigged as a sunshade.

Dutch just shook his head. He watched Rip stuff food into his mouth. Maybe the kid *does* have a tapeworm, he thought.

"The limiting factor would be the heat on reentry," Rip said thoughtfully as he chewed. "I'll bet the material that ship is made of is almost impervious to heat."

"One wonders," Dr. Soldi murmured.

"There is no food storage or prep area," Dutch pointed out. "The ship must be a shuttle, used to ferry people and supplies between a ship in orbit and the surface."

"Why is the saucer here?" Rip asked, with his mouth full. "I mean, why in this place and not in another?"

"Questions, questions, questions . . . all we have are questions, but no answers." Soldi said this, but he didn't seem upset. Difficult problems had always fascinated him.

"Dutch, this afternoon you must examine the ship more closely. I want to take this pile of whatever that Rip found to the archaeology dig and examine it in the lab."

They cleaned up perfunctorily, then Soldi left in the Jeep.

Standing outside the saucer, looking it over, Dutch told Rip, "We should start at the reactor. That is the heart of this thing."

"Okay."

"You want to help, Bill?"

"No thanks." Bill Taggart was sitting in shade smoking a cigar. "You guys are nuts to poke around inside this thing. You have no idea what could be in there."

"So we're nuts."

"Soldi wasn't whistling Dixie."

"You don't have to help."

"I know that. And I don't intend to."

"Ease up, Bill."

"Dutch, you're acting the fool. That damn thing has been sealed up tight since Christ was a corporal. You're breathing viruses that haven't had a host for a zillion years. Maybe the germs are from another planet, another solar system. God only knows what you'll catch."

Rip grabbed his throat, staggered, made a rasping noise. His eyes bugged out.

"Stop that, Cantrell," Bill barked. "You half-wit!"

Rip made a dismissive gesture at Taggart.

"Come on, Dutch," he said. "Let's look at the reactor." The youngster climbed into the ship without another glance at Bill, who hadn't moved from his seat.

"Hey, Dutch. Look at this. This pipe is marked."

Rip held his flashlight beam on a pipe. Dutch studied the markings.

"Looks like scratches."

"Maybe a little. But they're markings. They've marked the pipe."

"Doesn't look like anything I ever saw."

"Course it doesn't. But this proves this thing was made by people, doesn't it?"

Dutch Haagen held his flashlight so the beam illuminated the inscription from an angle. "Looks like it's painted on or something. Maybe etched in." The symbol on the left was small and elegant. Above it and to the right was a small marking, like an upside-down cone but with no bottom. Following that was another symbol, different from the first, but even with it.

"Never saw anything like this."

"It's probably a label, telling us what the line carries," Rip explained.

"Yeah, kid. That's a good guess. But I can't read it. Can you?"

"Ahh, yes . . . 'Bill Taggart is a jerk.'

That's the translation, anyway." Rip shrugged. "I think they covered this stuff in the sixth grade, but I had the flu that week."

"This couldn't be the only marking. Look around."

It took Rip only fifteen seconds to find another marking, this time on a pressure line. This was different from the first set of symbols.

Over the next half hour they found that almost every line was marked, and many of the symbols seemed to be the same.

"If we could read these damn marks, we could figure this thing out," Rip exclaimed.

Dutch didn't reply. He continued to look for marks, examine fittings, study everything he saw. After a bit he said, "This piece of gear in front of me looks like a generator. See all these electrical wires coming off it? They go down there, hook into those cable ends."

The two men continued to explore. Finally Dutch said, "Well, it looks to me like the generator makes power, which is sent to these circular cables that go around the bottom of the ship." There were six of these cables, making six concentric rings that circled the bottom of the saucer. "More juice goes into those big buses over there. I'll bet a nickel those things are circuit breakers or fuses of some kind. From the buses, the juice goes all over the ship."

"Antigravity rings?" Rip suggested. "Maybe the big circular cables cut the gravity force lines of the planet?"

"Maybe, kid. Maybe." Dutch crawled on.

In the hour before dark, Rip worked on clearing sandstone from the saucer's maneuvering ports. He used a small screwdriver as a chisel, pounding on the handle with a hammer. Blowing into the hole cleaned out the shards. The job went pretty fast.

Rip enjoyed touching the ship, running his fingers over it. The saucer fascinated him. As the sun got lower and lower on the horizon, he found himself sitting, staring at the ship, mesmerized. Who flew this ship here? Who were these people?

"I had to get our geologist involved," Professor Soldi reported that evening when he returned from his dig. He poured himself a cup of coffee from the pot on the propane stove. "He examined the sandstone sample under an electron microscope."

"What did he think?" Rip asked as Soldi paused to sip coffee.

"It took him a while to sort out the pollens."

"Uh-huh."

"One hundred and forty thousand years, plus or minus ten."

Dutch Haagen whistled. Soldi sipped coffee. Rip Cantrell wrapped his arms around his legs and stared into the fire.

Tonight the seismic crew was camped in front of the ledge, less than a hundred yards from the saucer. Moving the camp was no big deal, a chore the crew normally accomplished every other day. The camp consisted of two tents, one for sleeping, one for cooking, and a sunscreen rigged to keep the sun off the two water wagons, each of which was a two-hundred-gallon tank welded to a wheeled chassis. Most evenings Rip slept outside in a sleeping bag.

"We're going to have to tell somebody about the saucer," Dutch said after a bit.

"Like our boss in Houston," Bill Taggart rumbled. "That poor fool thinks we're doing honest work."

"What do you think, Professor?"

"The geologist is a gossip. My assistant wanted to know where I've been. Maybe I should have taken more time to listen to him tell me what they have accomplished."

He shrugged, drained the coffee cup. "I asked them to keep quiet for two more days. Maybe they will, maybe they won't."

"You mean you told them about the saucer?"

"I had to."

"I'll bet they're on the horn this very second," Rip said glumly.

"Well . . ."

"What about that pile of stuff we found in the machinery spaces?" Rip asked.

"Our lab man was working on that when I left. The stuff isn't paper." Soldi poured a second cup of coffee. "He's running some chemical tests, but I think we'll have to send it to a lab in the States to get a reliable analysis."

It was one a.m. when Rip awakened with a start. He had been dozing, examining the saucer inch by inch in his mind when the answer came to him. He sat up in his sleeping bag.

No one else was awake. The camp lanterns were out, a million stars looked down from a deep black sky.

In the starlight he could just see the outline of the tarp that covered the saucer.

Shivering in the chill air, he felt for his boots, knocked them out, slipped them on.

Pulled on a sweater, fumbled for his flash-light.

Inside the saucer the temperature had not changed. It was insulated equally well from heat and cold.

Warmer, Rip crawled straight into the machinery compartment and put his light on the inscription he had first noticed.

Well, it could be. Maybe. If that raised figure between the two symbols stood for the number two, then the inscription might mean H_2O. Water.

If so, then there should be a cracker, some device that separates the hydrogen and oxygen. Mix gaseous hydrogen and oxygen together, burn the mixture in the rocket engines, use some of the oxygen for the cabin atmosphere.

Rip traced the line. Okay, this thing could be a tank. This could hold water. The line went . . . This thing with the reinforcing bands must be the cracker, or separator.

Lines leading out, yes, they are labeled with one of the two symbols from the water line. This one must be hydrogen, this one oxygen.

Full of his discovery, Rip sat on the floor staring at the machinery. Everything was packed so tightly it was difficult to see how the system functioned, but he had it figured out now. He hoped. Well, it made sense . . . sort of.

The water intake valve must be on the outside of the ship. How had he missed it?

He had been busy with the jackhammer breaking rocks. He hadn't had time to examine the surface of the ship inch by inch or the nooks and crannies of the exhaust nozzle area. There must be a water intake there somewhere and he hadn't seen it.

He went outside, began exploring with the flashlight.

Water!

Oh, man. Water is everywhere. Except here in the desert, of course. Maybe they ran out of fuel over the desert . . .

But it might not have been desert then. Maybe the crew was out exploring and something happened to them. Something ate them, or they got sick . . . Or humans attacked them.

He found it. He found a tiny hairline crack and used his pocket knife to pry on it. Finally it opened. A cover. Yes.

Inside the cover was a cap, a bit like a fuel cap on a car. This must be where the water goes in.

He had just closed the cover when a flashlight beam hit him. He turned toward it and heard a male voice say, "Well, hello friend. Didn't expect you." The words were English, the voice definitely American.

The flashlight played over the skin of the ship. Did he have the cover closed before the flashlight beam hit him? He decided he did.

The voice reflected its owner's amazement. "By all that's holy! It *is* a flying saucer!"

"Or a good mock-up." That was an American voice too, a woman's.

4

"Who are you people?" Rip asked and pointed his own flashlight toward the voices. He saw a khaki uniform and a gray-green flight suit.

"U.S. Air Force. And just who are you?" A male voice with a flat Texas twang to it.

"Name's Rip Cantrell."

"Did you fly this thing here?"

"Yeah, sure. I just park it under this tarp when we need to work on it. Don't want it to get rained on."

"Who you work for, smart-ass?"

"Wellstar Petroleum. We're seismic surveyors."

"Uh-huh." They were standing just above him, near the edge of the rock ledge, looking under the flap of the tarp at the saucer. The man was in his thirties, maybe, and the woman was . . . well, with just the flashlight, it was hard to tell. Mid-twenties. Late twenties, perhaps. Pretty, with her hair pulled back in a ponytail, wearing a flight suit and a flight jacket.

"You people got names?" Rip asked.

"I'm Major Stiborek and this is Captain Pine." He gestured toward the woman.

"Not anymore," the woman said. "Now it's just plain ol' Charley Pine. I got out of the Air Force two weeks ago."

"What are you doing hanging around with these flyboys?"

"Now I'm a civil servant. Same job."

"Get acquainted later," the major snarled at her.

"Easy, buddy," Rip said. "Don't be so touchy."

"We didn't expect to find Americans here," Charley remarked.

"Who *did* you expect to find?"

She didn't answer. The major merely played his flashlight back and forth across the saucer.

"Unbelievable," he muttered to the woman, so softly that Rip almost missed it.

Rip cleared his throat. "So," he said as matter-of-factly as he could, "did your camel break down near here, or are you just scoping out desert real estate?"

"Something like that."

"Or are you out snooping around?"

The major was still running his flashlight back and forth over the saucer. After a moment or two he asked, "Did your survey crew uncover this thing?"

Rip flipped off his flashlight and stuck it in his hip pocket. "Tell you what, Tex," he said. "This isn't Uncle Sam's business. Why don't you folks just buzz off into the wild black yonder?"

"Sorry," the woman said. She actually did sound sorry. "This *is* government business."

"Bullshit," Rip shot back, feeling his face flush. He hated being talked down to. "We're smack in the middle of the Sahara Desert. You people get back on your camels and fork 'em out of here."

"There's six of our people down at the camp, kid," the major said brusquely. "You have two options. You can walk down like a gentleman to join your friends, or I can take you down there by the scruff of the neck."

Rip took two steps toward the ledge. The major's ankles were within range, so he grabbed them and pulled. The major smacked down hard on his butt, and groaned.

"You've made your brag, buddy. You think you're man enough, you take me there."

"*Rip!*" Dutch Haagen's shout split the night. "Get down here. We got company."

"Holy Jesus, Charley!" the major exclaimed. "I think my left hip is broken."

"Mr. Cantrell," the woman said, exasperated. "Would you please be so kind as to help me carry Major Big Mouth to the camp?"

"Just a minute," Rip said and slipped under the saucer. He closed the hatch.

When he got back to the groaning major and the woman, he said, "So your name is Charley?"

"Charlotte. Charley."

"Who are you people?" Rip asked her as they hoisted the major. Rip had the major's left arm over his shoulders, Pine his right.

"I'm a test pilot," she said. "Major Macho is an aerospace engineer. Our boss, Colonel West, whom you will meet shortly, is head of the Air Force's UFO project."

"UFOs! Oh, wow. Did someone around here call you about one?"

"Very funny. Our primary mission is to keep the public from panicking over unexplained phenomena."

"Let's not talk out of school, Charley," Major Stiborek muttered.

"How about I drop you again, Tex?"

"Please be nice, Mr. Cantrell," Charley Pine said. "We've had a very long day. We started out thirty-six hours ago in Nevada."

"Charley!"

"Shut up, Mike."

"Are you two married or something?" Rip asked.

"Or something. A mistake I made in one of my weaker moments."

"Do you really like him or just need sex?"

Major Stiborek cussed; Charley laughed. Rip thought she had a good laugh.

"So you guys flew in from Cairo?"

"From Aswan. And then rode twenty miles across the desert at night in a hummer."

Colonel West was talking when Rip and Charley Pine deposited the major by one of the lanterns that was brilliantly illuminating the camp area. The colonel and five enlisted men stood facing Bill, Dutch, and Professor Soldi. The Air Force people wore sweat-stained fatigues. The enlisted men carried rifles on straps over their shoulders. For the first time, Rip noticed that Major Stiborek and Charley Pine were wearing pistols in holsters, as was Colonel West. The vehicles the Air Force people had used were not in sight.

West was saying: ". . . are here by the direct order of the National Command Authority. By that I mean the president of the United States. I certainly hope you

80

gentlemen are going to give the United States government your full and complete cooperation."

"Well, of course, Colonel," Dutch Haagen said, then looked curiously at the major, who was rubbing his hip and chewing savagely on his lower lip.

"He had an accident," Rip explained. "Fell."

West had other things on his mind. "I want to see this saucer shape. Will you please lead the way, Mr. Haagen?"

"Before we go anywhere, Colonel," Professor Soldi put in, "perhaps we should have an understanding. This is an archaeological site, as defined by the United States Code. The Air Force has no jurisdiction whatever over an archaeological site. As a professional archaeologist, as defined by the United States Code, I do. I am in charge here."

"Don't go quoting law to me, Professor. We aren't in the United States, and I have my orders."

"I don't care about your orders, Colonel. I know American and international law. As an archaeologist, I have a moral and legal obligation to protect that artifact. I promise you that if it's harmed in any way you're going to wind up in front of a federal judge."

The colonel gave the professor a hard look.

The professor glared right back. Rip had thought the archaeologist something of an old fossil, but now he revised his opinion.

"Sergeant," said Colonel West in a flinty voice, "search these men and their gear for satellite telephones. Confiscate all the com gear you find."

"Yes, sir."

"This is my party, Professor," West snarled. "I intend to examine that thing. What happens after that depends on what I find."

"Is that a threat?"

"Take it any way you like."

Soldi busied himself with his pipe before he spoke. "No one is above the law, Colonel. The brass will swear they never told you to do anything illegal; they will fry you without a qualm to protect themselves. If I were you I'd keep that fact firmly in mind."

The colonel apparently decided to let Soldi have the last word.

The sergeant frisked each of the civilians while several of the other men went through the gear in the tents. After he had been searched, Professor Soldi took a seat on one of the camp stools. Dutch sat down beside him.

Rip found a seat in the sand beside Bill Taggart.

"You are welcome to accompany me, Professor," the colonel said gruffly.

"I warn you," Soldi replied. He raised his voice. "I warn all of you people. That artifact is protected by American and international law."

"We'll be careful," the colonel rumbled. He picked up one of the camp lanterns and marched away. Captain Pine followed.

Major Stiborek got slowly to his feet, massaging his rump. "I owe you one, kid," he told Rip and limped after the others.

The sergeant detailed three men to watch the civilians. He went into the darkness and came back in a few minutes driving a hummer. He parked it with the headlights pointed at the saucer.

"I guess we should have called your university yesterday," Dutch said to Soldi.

"I suppose." Soldi fussed over his pipe. When he had it going well, he muttered, "Damnation," so softly that Rip almost missed it.

The Air Force rigged lights. Soon the saucer was lit up like a museum exhibit.

"How did they find out about the saucer?" Soldi wondered aloud. "What do you think, Rip?"

83

"Satellites, I suspect," Haagen said. "Or someone at your camp called someone. Does it matter?"

"I guess not."

"Why does that guy owe you one?" Bill asked Rip.

"He got mouthy. I dumped him on his ass."

One of the Air Force NCOs took a seat fifteen feet away facing them.

"What the hell is going on here?" Rip demanded of the NCO. "Are we prisoners or what?"

"Can it, kid."

Rip went into the tent and shook out his sleeping bag. Haagen came in after him. "The officers will be right back," Rip told him. "Unless they can figure out how to open the hatch."

"You closed it?"

"Yeah."

"If we don't open the hatch for them, they might damage the saucer."

"You're kidding!"

"They're going in one way or the other, I suspect. A detachment of U.S. Air Force people *here,* in the Sahara? By order of the president?"

"Okay, okay. But I found that saucer. It's mine."

"Don't get cute with me, Rip. I'm no lawyer, but I don't think you have a claim. You don't even have a prayer. I don't think anybody knows exactly what country we're in."

"I know this," Rip Cantrell whispered heatedly. "My father left me a quarter of a million dollars and a third interest in a farm in Minnesota. I've got an uncle in Des Moines who's a junkyard dog lawyer; his speciality is biting people on the ass. You'll need a rabies shot if Uncle Olie gets anywhere close. With dad's money and my uncle's mouth, I can cause the Air Force a hell of a lot of grief."

"Hey, you!" they heard the major call.

"Yeah." That was Bill Taggart outside.

"You know how to open the hatch on the saucer?"

"This is your show, flyboy. I don't know shit."

Inside the tent, Haagen gestured with his thumb. "Go open it for them, Rip. Stay with them, see if you can learn anything."

Rip went. The major was standing outside near the camp stove.

"I can open that hatch, Big Mouth."

"Come on, kid."

He could feel Charley's eyes on his back as he crawled under the saucer and placed his hand on the hatch latch. He held it there for fifteen seconds or so, then pushed gently on one end. It moved out, and he grasped it and turned.

The hatch came open, just as it had that first time, several days ago.

The military officers sat stunned, amazed. Without a word Rip climbed into the ship and seated himself in the pilot's chair. He was sitting there when Colonel West stuck his head through the hatch. The glare of the floodlights outside through the pilot's canopy was the only light in the interior. It took several seconds for one's eyes to adjust to the dim lighting.

West stood in the open hatch blinking and gawking. He looked all around, then slowly climbed in. Behind him came Major Stiborek, then Charley Pine.

"Oh," she murmured when she got her first good look at the interior. She climbed all the way in, then stood near the open hatch. "Oh, my!"

"It's really cool, huh?" Rip said softly, watching the expression on her face.

"A real . . . flying . . . saucer!"

"They don't make 'em like this any-more," Rip said expansively, once again running his eyes around the instrument panel. With his hands he caressed the controls, fingered them gently, molded his hands around them.

"Unbelievable!" Charley said again and stepped over beside him.

"It's mine, you know," he said.

She didn't reply, just stood looking.

Behind her the colonel and major were touching and feeling. They peered into the equipment bay with flashlights, then stuck their heads in. They weren't paying any attention to Rip or Pine.

"And I'm going to keep it," Rip said softly.

He sat in the pilot's seat listening to the exclamations and startled comments. All three of them crowded into the equipment bay, which had just enough excess room to accommodate them. They quickly figured out what the nuclear reactor was. They were musing about what fuel the ship might use when Colonel West stuck his head out of the equipment bay, glared at Rip, then told him in no uncertain terms to leave.

Reluctantly, Rip climbed out of the pilot's seat and exited the hatch. The colonel was right behind him, calling for one of the enlisted men to bring a video camera and radiation detector.

Rip wandered slowly back toward camp.

He paused halfway and seated himself in the dirt.

The saucer looked stark under the lights. Had he done the right thing by uncovering it?

After a bit, exhaustion overtook him. It had been a long day.

He struggled to his feet, then went directly to the tent he shared with Dutch and Bill. They were still seated with the professor outside by the lanterns.

As Rip was getting into his sleeping bag, he overheard the professor ask, "Just who is that kid, anyway?"

"He was one of two hundred applicants for this job," Dutch replied. "My boss picked his application out of the pile. He could finish his engineering degree in one semester, but I think he's going to stretch it into two."

"Most of the time I think he is just what he appears," Soldi said thoughtfully, "a kid in blue jeans with a dirty T-shirt. Then there are moments when I think he is brilliant."

"Rip works real hard to appear normal," Dutch said. "But he's a straight-A engineering student with a genius IQ. And he may be the smartest man I ever met."

Inside the tent Rip Cantrell snorted in

derision. He pulled a pillow over his head and promptly went to sleep.

The *whop-whop* of helicopters awakened him. The sun was well up in a brassy sky when Rip stuck his head through the tent flap. He squinted, looked around until he saw them. Two large machines.

They circled the area, then went into a hover downwind of the saucer.

Rip pulled on his jeans, put on his boots.

Dutch and Bill were fixing breakfast on the propane stove while Soldi smoked his pipe and sipped coffee.

"Looks like more company, huh?" Rip said.

"Unexpected, looks to me like," Bill said, nodding at the Air Force enlisted men, who were watching the choppers with their rifles in their hands.

Rip hurriedly filled a plate and started forking in fried potatoes and reconstituted eggs. He watched the choppers and ate as quickly as he could.

"Damn, kid, it makes me sick to see you wolf your food like that." Bill Taggart made a face.

"I got a bad feeling about this, Bill. This may be all the food we get for a while."

"You've been making every meal your

last for twenty years," Taggart replied and turned his back so he wouldn't have to watch.

Rip finished eating as the choppers settled onto the ground a hundred yards from the camp. About a dozen armed men got out of each one. Even from this distance, the weapons were unmistakable.

"What have we got ourselves into, Dutch?" Bill Taggart whispered.

The men from the helicopters spread out into a ragged line and started this way with their rifles in the ready position. About fifty yards out they halted and plopped on their bellies.

The Air Force sergeant tersely ordered his men to lie on the ground.

When the first bullets whizzed over their heads, Dutch, Bill, and Rip also dove for cover.

"You chaps in the camp! Drop your weapons and come out with your hands in the air. No one will be hurt if you do as I say."

Rip asked Dutch, "What the hell is that? A British accent?"

"Aussie, I think."

Another burst of automatic fire went over their heads.

The airmen were having a whispered

conference with the sergeant when the major crawled over. He and the sergeant talked while the other enlisted men listened. The major must have slipped over from the saucer while the choppers were circling.

Now the major stood and called, "We are a detachment from the United States Air Force. Who are you?"

Back came the answer: "I don't care if you are the pope's eldest son, mate. Drop your bloody weapons, stand up with your hands in the air, or we are going to start shooting for real. It's going to be a hot day in this sandbox and I don't feel like screwing around. You've got exactly five seconds."

"Do as he says," the major ordered the airmen. Reluctantly, they tossed down their assault rifles and stood with their hands raised.

"I'm beginning to think we should have left that damn saucer in the rock," Dutch announced to whoever might be listening.

Professor Soldi sat up and brushed the sand from his shirt. He sucked experimentally on his pipe, found it had gone out, and fired it off again.

The leader of the group that surrounded the camp was a tall, rangy redhead. He plucked the pistol from the holster on Major Stiborek's belt and pocketed it as several of his men picked up assault rifles and frisked the Americans.

He put his hands on his hips and stood staring at the saucer. "As I live and breathe. Wouldn't have believed it if I hadn't seen it with me own eyes. If that don't beat all! A bloody flying saucer!"

"This saucer is the property of the United States government," Major Stiborek said with a straight face.

"Damn, Major. I don't know exactly where in the hell we are, but I'm pretty sure it ain't the U. S. of A."

"That thing is U.S. government property," Stiborek insisted.

Rip Cantrell shook his head in amazement. If he didn't know the truth, he would have been tempted to believe the major.

"Well, tell you how it is," the redhead replied, obviously amused. "I'm not going to waste air arguing about legal title. Details like that are way above my pay grade. We came to look that thing over and that's what we're going to do. Now you sit down, shut up, behave yourself, and we'll get along fine." He glanced around at the other Americans. "That goes for all of you."

Red turned to the two men behind him, men in short-sleeve white shirts wearing glasses and nerd buckets — pocket protectors. In their arms were cameras and portable computers. They hadn't taken their eyes off the saucer since Rip first saw them. "There it is," Red said. "Have at it."

The two scurried forward. They passed Charley Pine and Colonel West, who were being marched back to camp by two of Red's men. Both of the Americans had apparently been relieved of their sidearms. Their holster flaps were open.

"Professor Soldi?" the redheaded man asked, looking at the archaeologist, who was still sitting in the sand with his pipe.

"That's right."

"Pleased to meet you, sir. My name is Sharkey." Red reached down and helped the professor to his feet. "Perhaps you could come with me, sir, and tell me what you have found out about this flying saucer."

"How did you know my name?"

"We did a bit of research before we choppered over, Professor. Never hurts to know the lay of the land, who's in the neighborhood."

"The saucer is a valuable archaeological artifact. It belongs to all mankind."

"Yes, sir. You are absolutely right. My employer is merely interested in examining it, learning as much as possible about the technology. Obviously time is of the essence. The more you tell us, the sooner we will leave. Then you can go on with your research."

"Don't believe him," Colonel West interjected.

Soldi looked at West with undisguised antagonism. "Just what would you like to know, Mr. Sharkey?"

"Everything you can tell me, sir. Believe me, we have no desire to harm the artifact, steal it, or deprive you of your opportunity to study it for the benefit of science. We couldn't transport it out of here even if we wanted to. We merely wish to learn if there is technology here that we can put to immediate commercial use."

"Who is your employer?"

"I would be indiscreet to name him here and now. Suffice it to say he is a curious industrialist. If his use of technology that we learn about here is illegal, of course the courts will haul him up short."

Soldi knocked out his pipe and refilled it. He lit it and took a few puffs as he looked at the civilians with rifles guarding the Air Force officers and enlisted. He glanced at Rip and Dutch, looked again at the saucer.

"Why not?" Soldi said. "Everything will come out in a few days anyway."

"Professor, I apologize for my confrontational manner when I first arrived," Colonel West said earnestly. "Still, this is not a time for bruised egos or hurt feelings. This matter affects the national security of our country."

"Hardly, Colonel," Soldi shot back. "As I explained to you when you first arrived, that saucer is an archaeological treasure belonging to all mankind. It is quite ancient, at least a hundred and thirty thousand years old. Everything we learn about it will be made public as soon as possible. Every human alive is entitled to the benefits of the technology embodied in that saucer."

"You don't know what you are saying," the colonel protested. "Civilization is not ready for that kind of knowledge."

"That's what the pope told Galileo three and a half centuries ago," Soldi snarled. "Poppycock!"

"Colonel, you are on the losing end of this philosophical disagreement," Sharkey said lightly. "Come, Professor."

The Aussie put his arm around Soldi's

shoulders and gently steered the archaeologist toward the saucer.

The day grew hot. It was funny, but
when he was working, surveying, or running the jackhammer or moving the camp,
Rip didn't notice the heat. Now, sitting in
the shade with nothing to do, he found the
desert heat oppressive. It enveloped him,
made it difficult to breathe, and he per-
spired freely.

So did everyone else sitting there under
the watchful eyes of the Aussie's friends.
Those worthies didn't look like they had
seen a bath or clean clothes in quite a
while, but their weapons looked well cared
for. Russian-made assault rifles, British
army web gear, automatic pistols . . . they
were ready to fight a minor war. Fortunately they didn't point the weapons at
anyone. The rifles stayed on their shoulders or across their laps, the pistols stayed
in their holsters.

Still, they stayed alert. A bit of moving
around by the Americans seemed to be tol-
erated, but two or more people moving
brought a curt admonishment.

"Think the prof is telling Sharkey all the
secrets?" Rip asked Haagen.

"He doesn't know any to tell."

"He shouldn't have gone off as pals with that guy."

"That Aussie was going to look at the saucer with or without the prof. Maybe with Soldi there he won't tear up anything."

"You are an incurable optimist," Bill Taggart told Haagen.

"Don't you start grousing again," Haagen shot back. "I'm not in the mood. And another thing . . ."

Leaving those two to squabble, Rip moved over to where Charley Pine was sitting.

"Hot day, huh?"

Pine looked him over, didn't say anything.

After a bit, Rip asked, "What did you think of the saucer?"

"I don't know what to think. I've been sitting here trying to decide."

"It's really old," Rip offered.

"Yes," she murmured.

"Did you see anything wrong with it?" Rip asked softly.

"What do you mean?"

"Well, we were wondering why it came to end up in that sandstone ledge. Maybe there was a malfunction of some kind. What do you think?"

"It's possible. We didn't have time to do more than give it a superficial look last night."

"I'm sort of curious about what you experts found," Rip said. "How does that thing work, anyway?"

"All I could give you are guesses."

"The thing doesn't have wheels on the landing gear. It must take off vertically."

Charley Pine looked thoughtful. "I'd love to fly it someday," she said.

"You could figure out what all those levers and things actually do?"

"That would be the easy part," Charley Pine replied. "It's funny, when you think about it, how vastly different cultures arrive at very nearly the same answers to engineering problems. The controls have to give the pilot control. How the systems work, how it's powered, what the controls operate — it will take weeks or months of investigation to answer those questions."

"Ever flown a saucer before?" Rip asked matter-of-factly.

Charley smiled. "No."

"Have you flown many different kinds of planes?"

"Most of the tactical machines in the Air Force inventory and a half dozen helicopters."

"Bet being a test pilot takes a lot of education, huh?"

"It's a specialized field. I have a masters

in aero engineering too. That's why Mike is so testy at times." A faint smile crossed her lips.

"I've had a few aero courses myself," Rip said.

Charley merely nodded and brushed a loose hair from her forehead.

Rip gestured toward the saucer. "Flying that thing couldn't be too hard," he suggested.

Charley cocked her head, looked at the saucer as if weighing his comments. "Shouldn't be all that difficult," she agreed, "if all the systems were in working order and we had the manual to study. Everything isn't working, of course. Not a chance in a million."

"You're serious? You could fly that thing?"

"No. I couldn't. Not unless we have a crew of Martians check it out, repair it, service it, and sign it off as ready to fly. And I would need to read the manual; I don't fly anything without reading the book."

"Bummer."

"That's one of the really big rules."

"That's cool," Rip said. "Only two small caveats. I like that."

Rip tried to envision what it would be like going Warp 7 in the saucer with the controls in your hand.

"The major there," he said after a bit, "I'll bet he's a pretty good pilot."

"He designs planes, he doesn't fly them," Charley Pine said, a bit vinegary Rip thought.

He grinned at her. She managed a small grin in return.

"So why did you get out of the Air Force, anyway?"

"My being in uniform was driving Mike crazy."

"Umm . . ."

"It was time . . . time to move on. I've landed a job with Lockheed Martin that starts in six months. The Air Force asked me to stay with the UFO team until they can order in someone else."

"I see."

"Sorry to bore you. My life is a mess."

"So exactly what does a UFO investigation team do?"

"Learn all we can. Write reports. Debunk the myths."

"Are there UFOs?"

"That's classified," Charley Pine said curtly.

"Government's been doing UFO stuff for fifty years or so, hasn't it?"

"About that, I guess."

"Seems like they could tell us something, after all that time."

"If the authorities chose, perhaps they could."

"Must be a lot of flying saucers to justify spending all that money."

"There certainly are a lot of people who think they've seen one," the test pilot admitted.

"Have you guys got any other flying saucers lying around? Out there in Nevada or somewhere else?"

Another tiny smile crossed Pine's face. "Not to my knowledge. Of course, if we did and I told you, I'd have to kill you."

Rip smiled easily. "Maybe we oughta call you Charley Manson."

"Just kidding, of course."

"You're sorta cute," Rip told her. "For an older woman."

Charley Pine rubbed at the dirt and sweat mixture on her forehead. Sitting in the desert in front of a flying saucer with an amorous kid! She looked at the Aussie's troops with their big flop hats and their rifles and gritted her teeth.

5

At lunchtime Bill passed around some freeze-dried fruit sealed in see-through bags. "This is it?" Rip asked incredulously.

"I'll eat yours if you don't want it."

As they munched, Rip tried to make conversation with Haagen, who was in a dark mood. He got like that sometimes, and Rip usually tried to avoid him until the mood passed. Today he decided to take his chances.

"What do you think these Air Force types really want, Dutch?"

"They want the saucer, kid. Believe it. So does the Aussie."

"If the Air Force gets it, this will be big back in the States, huh?"

Haagen ate another piece of dried prune before he answered. "If the Air Force gets that saucer, you'll never see or hear of it again. The government's position is that saucers don't exist."

"That's crazy."

"Why do you think the Air Force has UFO teams? I'll tell you — to rush to the

102

site of any 'unexplained phenomenon' and explain it away, get everybody calmed down. The people who saw strange things are dismissed as kooks."

"But saucers *do* exist. There one is!" Rip pointed with his head.

"You know that and I know that, but the powers that be don't want Joe Six-Pack and the Bible thumpers to get all sweaty. My God, kid, where have you been? There are still people in America who think evolution should not be taught in schools. Darwin will rot impressionable little minds, destroy their faith in religion, bring civilization crashing down around our ears, et cetera and so on."

"Do you believe that?"

"Doesn't matter what I believe. What matters is that the bigwigs in the government believe it."

Major Stiborek dozed some during the heat of the day. He did it sitting up, with his head back against one of the poles that held up the shade tarp. It didn't look comfortable, but he snored a bit.

Stiborek awoke when the Aussie, Sharkey, brought Professor Soldi back to the camp and helped himself to some water. After he had a long drink, Soldi grunted at Dutch and Bill, then went into the sleeping tent and lay down on one of the cots.

Sharkey tried to make conversation with the Air Force officers. He gave that up after a few minutes as a waste of time.

When Sharkey wandered back toward the saucer, Rip went over to where Stiborek was sitting on one of the camp stools.

"Captain Pine says you're a pretty good engineer."

Stiborek merely grunted. He didn't even look at Rip.

"Bet a good aeronautical engineer like you has that saucer all figured out, huh?"

"What do you want, kid?"

"Just trying to be nice, Major, get acquainted. Let bygones go by the by."

"What do you want to know?"

"How does it work?"

"Amazingly enough, it burns hydrogen. Cracks water into hydrogen and oxygen in some sort of electrolysis process."

"Ever see anything like that?" Rip asked casually.

"It's an extraordinary engineering triumph."

"What holds it up when the hydrogen engines aren't going?"

"That's the mind-boggling part. It uses a force field of some type to modulate the earth's gravitational field."

"Does Charley know that?" Rip asked with a glance at the female pilot, who was sitting at least fifty feet away, well out of earshot.

"She was there when we discussed all this."

"I see."

Mike Stiborek frowned, glanced at Charley Pine, then studiously ignored her.

"Think the reactor is intact?" Rip asked.

Stiborek laughed. "You do the dumb kid act very well. Have I told you anything you don't know?"

"What about the reactor?"

"We brought a small radiation detector with us, and as near as we can tell, the reactor is still a sealed unit." Stiborek shrugged. "Can you believe it? A flying saucer?"

"Whoever flew it here, why did they leave it?"

Stiborek took his time before he answered. "I don't know, kid. I really don't. I don't think the answer is in the saucer. It looks like it was parked there yesterday."

"But it wasn't," Rip replied. "I dug away most of that rock myself. That's real sandstone." He took a small piece from a pocket and passed it to Stiborek, who gave it a cursory glance and rubbed it between his fingers.

When Stiborek passed it back, Rip pocketed the stone, then asked, "Could Charley fly it?"

Stiborek laughed. "Now, I never even thought about that. That woman can fly anything. But, no. There isn't a chance that saucer is airworthy. Or spaceworthy. Whatever. Not a chance in a zillion."

"Why?"

"My God, man. Everything deteriorates over time. Metal crystallizes, dissimilar metals react to each other, corrosion eats on everything . . . Entropy in a closed system increases over time — that's the second law of thermodynamics. Time has taken a toll on that ship, even if the toll isn't readily apparent to our eyes."

"If it could fly, I mean. Could Charley fly it?"

"Kid — what's your name? Cantrell? Well, Cantrell, if elephants had wings, car windshields would be made of bulletproof glass and it would be dangerous to walk around outside. 'If' is the biggest word in the English language."

"Okay."

"All those systems in working order, after a hundred and thirty thousand years?

Whoever made that thing was good, I'll grant you, but not that good."

"One hundred forty thousand."

"Give or take. What's ten thousand years among friends?" Stiborek picked up a small rock and tossed it a few feet. After a bit he added, "The reactor is the critical unit."

Rip looked puzzled. "You said you guys checked the reactor. Isn't that a radiation counter there?" Rip pointed to a small battery-operated device lying on the sand near Stiborek's feet.

"I made a cursory check," Stiborek acknowledged, "with a battery-operated unit that is used only to ensure personnel safety. We found only background radiation. Which proves nothing."

"At least —" Rip began.

"Insulation — that ship probably has several hundred thousand miles of wire in it. If the insulation has come off a wire in just one place, you got a short, maybe a fire."

"The insulation looked okay to me," Rip murmured. "In the places I could see."

"Kid, you don't know what you're talking about. Let's look at one more example, just one. If you try to fire off that reactor and something critical breaks, that ship will melt down. If there is no explosion — and there might be — the whole ship will dissolve into a puddle of molten-hot radioactive goo. You won't care because you'll have already been fried."

Stiborek tossed another pebble. "Anybody who tries to fly that thing has found a flashy way to commit suicide."

"Just thought I'd ask. A theoretical question."

"Go away, kid. Leave me alone."

"How come you and Charley are on the outs?"

Stiborek frowned. "Did she say we are?"

"Oh, come on! Give me a break. I've got a mother and a sister and have even had a couple girlfriends through the years."

Stiborek looked glum. "She's going to move to Georgia, be a test pilot for Lockheed Martin. I tried to talk her out of it, but she's made up her mind, she says."

"Does she have a reason?"

"Says this UFO team is a career dead end."

"Maybe it used to be, but it isn't anymore. You two are about to become famous."

Stiborek made a rude noise, then picked up another rock and threw it out into the desert.

In late afternoon Sharkey left his experts in the saucer and settled in to interrogate the Air Force officers in the sleeping tent. Colonel West was his first victim.

West was still in there when the sun set. Dutch passed around cold food to his people and the Air Force crowd. The Aussie's men ate food from a cooler they carried from one of the helicopters, which hadn't moved all day.

When Red Sharkey finished with Colonel West, he sent for Major Stiborek.

Darkness came quickly in the desert. Rip went around lighting the lanterns, checking that they had enough propane.

A small breeze came up, easing the heat of the day.

Most of Sharkey's troops were gathered around their choppers, eating and talking loudly and laughing, when Rip rooted in his bags for his passport and wallet. Then he made his usual pilgrimage to the portable outhouse. He kept the door cracked while he did his business, watched the two Aussies with guns across their laps sitting outside the tent. They weren't looking in his direction.

When he got his pants up, Rip eased the door open and slipped away into the darkness.

He made his way to the Jeep. The glove compartment contained a roll of duct tape, which Rip pocketed.

Two five-gallon plastic cans full of water were attached to the rear of the Jeep. Out here in this desert, water was life. Rip checked these cans every day, and both Dutch and Bill did too.

He unfastened them both, lifted them down into the sand. They weighed about forty pounds apiece.

After a last check around, he hefted both cans, one in each hand, and set off in the direction of the saucer, which was still illuminated by two spotlights. The other spotlights, at least six, had been turned off.

Rip could hear Sharkey's two experts talking inside the saucer. He made sure the water cans were out of sight, then stuck his head up into the thing. The two Aussie technicians had a battery-operated lantern going and were disassembling one of the computer displays. Maybe the whole computer.

"Hey," Rip said.

"Yeah," one of the men said, not looking around.

"Sharkey said to tell you guys to go get some dinner."

"He did?" Now the man looked around. "Yep."

One of the men straightened up. "I could use something to eat. Come on, Harry."

"I'm not hungry," Harry said. "You go. Bring me back a bite."

"Okay, mate."

As the first man climbed down off the ledge, Rip crawled up into the ship. Harry didn't turn around.

"What are you working on?"

"A computer. Really extraordinary. Never saw anything like it."

"Did you guys take anything else apart?"

"Not yet." Harry sat back on his heels. "We really should disassemble that electrolysis unit." He pointed with a thumb. "I think that thing separates water into hydrogen and oxygen. Ol' man Hedrick could make a mint with a thing like that, believe me, mate. Put every oil company on earth out of business. The possibilities are mind-blowing. Still, he said to examine the computers first."

Hedrick could only be Australian billionaire Roger Hedrick, the second richest man on earth. "Hedrick's rich enough, don't you think?" Rip asked lightly. "He's worth what? Fifty billion?"

"More like eighty," Harry replied. "He owns half of Australia now. But a man can never be too rich. At least Hedrick doesn't think so."

Rip tapped Harry on the shoulder. As he

111

turned his head, Rip delivered a haymaker on the point of his chin. Harry went down hard.

Rip got busy with the duct tape. By the time he had Harry's mouth, hands, and ankles taped, the man was moaning. At least he wasn't dead.

"Sorry, buddy," Rip told the half-conscious man and grabbed his ankles. He pulled the man over to the hatch and dropped him through it. There was a satellite phone on the floor near where Harry had been working, and Rip pitched that through the hatch too, along with Harry's tool kit.

He didn't have much time. He pulled the man as far from the ship as he could, hoisted him, and set him up on the ledge. That would have to do.

Working fast, he opened the fueling hatch between the exhaust nozzles and got the lid off the first water can. He lifted it into position and poured.

He was halfway through the first can when a voice behind him said, "You didn't kill that man, did you?"

It was Charley Pine.

"What are you doing here?"

"I wondered where you went when you didn't come back."

"Anyone see you leave?"

"I don't think so. Now tell me, how bad did you hurt that man?"

"Just slugged him with my fist, taped his mouth shut. He'll be okay."

"What is that you're putting in there?"

"Water."

"After one hundred and forty thousand years? Rip, don't be silly."

"We'll find out in about three minutes."

"Are you kidding me?"

The words were just out of her mouth when two helicopters sporting floodlights flew over. Low.

"Now what?" Rip demanded.

He could see two more choppers settling onto the sand near Sharkey's two machines.

"Pine, are these more Air Force?"

"I don't think so."

Someone in the door of the chopper just landing started shooting. Muzzle flashes.

One of the choppers overhead came into a hover and someone spoke over a loud-hailer. In Arabic.

"Uh-oh," Rip said through clenched teeth. He finished the first can of water and reached for the second.

The floodlight hit the tarp over the saucer.

"Get down quick," he shouted at

Charley. "Get in the saucer."

She leaped off the ledge, crawled under the saucer toward the hatch.

"Raise your hands. Drop your weapons. Surrender and you will not be harmed." The voice over the loud-hailer was using English now.

"In the name of the Islamic Republic of Libya, surrender or be shot down."

"Boy, it's in the fan now," Rip muttered to himself as the water gurgled out of the second can. The can was still draining. It seemed to take forever.

"Come on, come on . . ."

Then the can went dry. He made sure the saucer's refueling cap was firmly in place. Ingenious how they did that.

He tossed both cans into the ship, then crawled in himself and pulled the hatch shut behind him.

Charley Pine was standing beside the pilot's seat on a step that jutted out from the pedestal, trying to see out the canopy.

"One of us is going to have to fly this thing," Rip said. "I flew my Uncle's Aeronca Champ three or four times. I'll give it a go if you want to wait to read the manual."

She got into the pilot's seat, reached for the seat belt and fastened it.

"That was the easy part," she said. "Got any bright ideas on how to get this thing started?"

"As a matter of fact . . ." Rip muttered and reached across for the power knob. He pulled it all the way out. The instrument lights illuminated, the dials and gauges came alive, the computer screens came on, and from the equipment bay behind them they heard a welcome hum.

"My God!" The exclamation just popped out of Charley Pine. "I thought you were kidding."

"This is the third time I've fired it off. The other night I had it running for over an hour while the other guys were asleep."

She merely stared, her mouth agape.

"The neat thing is the computers," Rip told her with a grin. "Everything's done symbolically. I'm not sure I understand all the symbols yet, but I think I can figure them out in flight."

She turned to examine his face. "Who *are* you, anyway?"

"Name's Rip Cantrell, lady. Now, can you fly this thing or can't you?"

She looked at the panel and controls, trying to take it all in.

"This lever here," Rip reached and touched, "has got to be the control stick. I think this will fly like a helicopter. You see the pedals? They function like a rudder, I think, activating the maneuvering jets."

"You've flown a helicopter?"

"I rode in one. Watched the pilots fly it." He grinned at her to allay her fears. He was feeling none too confident himself, but he didn't want her to know that.

"That thing in your left hand is the collective, which controls the antigravity field, I think. If you'll lift it the tiniest bit . . ."

As she did, the saucer lifted itself from the earth. It rocked slightly from side to side, touching on the skids that were still down. Charley overcontrolled with the stick in her right hand, then had the sense to let go of it. The pedals at her feet she barely touched . . . and felt the ship slew.

"Awesome!" breathed Rip Cantrell, holding on tight to the pilot's seat.

The tarp was still covering the saucer, so Charley couldn't go up very far or that thing would drape itself over the canopy. She eased the right-hand stick forward just a touch.

The saucer moved ever so gently out from under the tarp. Some sand flew around, about as much as a helo would raise.

Dutch Haagen was standing with his

hands raised when he heard Bill Taggart cry out. He looked back at the saucer.

The spaceship was a silent silver shape, coming out of the glare of the floodlights toward them.

It was moving slowly, like a helicopter. Only there was no sound. Without even a whisper of sound, the thing was uncanny, like something from a silent movie.

"Sweet Jesus!" Bill said.

"If that kid crashes that thing . . ." Professor Soldi swore. He knew to a certainty that Rip Cantrell was in the pilot seat.

The Libyan officer in charge couldn't believe his eyes.

He screamed something in Arabic, pointed his pistol at the saucer, and pulled the trigger.

His troops let fly with bursts of automatic fire. Sparks appeared along the body of the ship where the bullets were bouncing off.

Charley raised the collective and pulled back on the stick. The saucer tilted up. She and Rip could hear the whump of bullets striking the ship.

"I can't see," she shouted as the illuminated camp disappeared under the nose.

"Fly the instruments!" Rip cried.

Sure enough, there was an artificial horizon on the computer screen in front of her. Charley lowered the nose to get the ship level.

"We're not going very fast," Rip pointed out.

"I haven't lit the burners yet. I need to feel this thing out, fly it around a while."

"Lady, I don't think this is the time or place. We gotta boogie."

Charley Pine felt completely out of her depth. Panic swept over her as she scanned the instrument panel. She pushed a button. Nothing happened. Flipped a lever. Symbols appeared above the lever. Three arrows pointing up. Then little green lights.

"Gear up."

Maybe the rockets were controlled by the buttons on the grip of the collective.

She took her eyes off the artificial horizon to examine the grip. When she pushed a button on the very end of the stick, she heard a rumble.

"Watch where you're going," Rip urged, his voice an octave higher than normal.

Charley got her eyes back on the artificial horizon and leveled the ship with the stick in her right hand. Then she twisted the grip on the left-hand control. She heard the rocket engines ignite, a throaty rumble, and acceleration pressed her back hard into the seat. Rip Cantrell lost his fight against the acceleration G and fell toward the rear of the compartment.

Somehow Charley managed to pull the stick back; the nose of the ship came up. Straight ahead, through the canopy, was a sky full of stars.

The fire from the rocket engines lit the desert for miles in every direction. The light was blinding, like a small sun.

And the noise was deafening, the loudest noise Dutch Haagen had ever heard. It vibrated his skull and teeth, massaged the flesh of his face. Dutch clapped his hands over his ears and fell to his knees. He kept his eyes shut against the searing light, which was so bright he could see it through his eyelids.

When the sound and light had faded somewhat, he opened his eyes to slits. The saucer was fifteen degrees above the horizon, accelerating away, the exhaust a sheet of white fire.

6

The severe acceleration forces held Charley Pine imprisoned against her seat. Rip was on the floor, trapped against the bottom of a forward-facing seat.

Rip pushed off with his legs until he could reach the pedestal that supported the pilot's seat. He pulled himself to it, then clawed his way erect. That he was able to accomplish this task under at least four G's of acceleration was a tribute to his physical condition.

"Get off the juice, Charley, for God's sake!"

She twisted the grip on the left-hand stick back somewhat and the G eased considerably.

"How much water did you put in this thing?"

"Ten gallons," he replied.

"That isn't going to get us far."

"Maybe we can make the Nile. Lake Nasser. We're heading east, I think."

"How can you tell?"

"Look at this computer display. You tell

me." In front of them was a globe with a small arrow in the middle, which now pointed to the right.

In the crystal-clear desert air the earth below was an empty, dark wasteland under an infinite sea of stars. The sliver of moon that had been just above the horizon when they took off was now well up in the night sky and rapidly climbing higher as the saucer gained altitude.

"Oh, God!" Pine exclaimed. "What in the world have we done? How are we going to get down?"

Rip tried to swallow and couldn't. "We'll make it," he said, his voice an octave too high.

"We can't even see to land!"

Rip searched the control panel. "There has to be a light switch on here someplace," he said. "There are two big landing lights on the bottom of this thing."

Charley let the saucer tilt slightly. "Watch your attitude," Rip said sharply, causing her to pick up the left wing, if there had been a left wing.

"How high are we?" she asked plaintively. She tried to keep the fear out of her voice, but she knew it showed a little.

"God knows," Rip Cantrell answered, his voice tight.

He played with buttons and switches on the instrument panel until he found the lighting panel. Confident that he was turning on lights, Rip turned on every switch on that panel. Landing lights made the leading edge of the saucer glow, although the air was too clear to see the beams.

"Look at the displays," Charley demanded. "Figure it out!"

"I'm trying! I'm trying!"

She still had a little nose-up attitude on the artificial horizon, so she assumed she was climbing. She had no idea what her speed might be.

Almost as if he could read her thoughts, Rip Cantrell remarked, "We must be supersonic. This saucer shape is optimal for hypersonic flight."

Charley twisted the grip to add a little more power.

Off to her left, at about her ten o'clock position, she glimpsed the twinkling of city lights embedded in the vast blackness. Aswan? Luxor? It couldn't be Cairo, could it?

Her heartbeat and respiration rate were almost back to normal when she said to Rip, "This is pretty cool, huh?"

The saucer responded to every twitch of her hands and feet. Never had she felt this wonderful, felt such a feeling of command.

"Too cool for school. But how are you going to land this thing?"

"Uh . . ."

Before she could say another word, the sound of the rocket engines died; they felt a decelerating force push them forward.

"We're outta water," Rip said bitterly. "Keep flying, keep flying!" he quickly added. "This thing is going like a bullet. Lower your nose just a tad to level flight and hold it there while we decelerate."

"I *know* how to fly, Junior."

"Just trying to do my bit."

"The saucer is glowing," she reported. By craning her neck, Charley could just see a bit of the fuselage.

"I think that glow is from the landing lights."

Charley Pine's mind was racing. She studied the displays on the computer screen. The graphics were alive. One of them must display angle of attack or relative airspeed, margin above stalling speed, something like that. Which one?

Perhaps . . . She reached up and touched the buttonlike protrusions that surrounded the main screen. Yes. Each button produced a different graphic on a small segment of the screen.

She quickly found what appeared to be an analog display of angle of attack. Suddenly sure, she told Rip, "I'll fly this," and explained how the needle on the screen would give her the best gliding angle. "When that needle gets to about this position," she pointed with her fingertip, "I'll hold it there by adjusting the nose attitude. Or try to, anyway."

"And if you can't?"

Charley swallowed hard. The magnitude of the task before her hit her like a hammer. She had been a damned fool to try to fly this thing. Now she was going to kill herself and this idiot kid. She had trouble swallowing.

"Relax," Rip said, squeezing her hand. "You got us this far."

"You're crazy!"

Rip laughed. At a time like this, he laughed!

"This thing will glide like a brick," he told her. "It's a lifting body, but the sink rate is going to be spectacular." He checked the position of the lever to the left of the pilot's seat. "Better lower that." He pointed. "It works the antigravity rings, and we're going to need all the help they can give us to cushion our descent at the bottom."

Tears trickled down Charley's cheeks. She swabbed at them with her left hand while she kept her eyes moving between the artificial horizon and the angle of attack presentation.

"We're way high up," she said when she finally trusted herself to talk. "It's going to take us a long time to coast down."

"Not as long as you think. Believe me."

"I'll bet this thing has radar," she suggested.

Rip began playing with the other computer displays. One computer hung half out of the panel, partially disassembled. There were three others. Luck being what it is, Rip was sure the radar display was probably presented on the computer that Harry and his mate had operated on.

He felt the nose dip. Heard the hiss of gas being ejected from the maneuvering jets as Charley moved the control stick. Now he understood the system: gaseous oxygen and hydrogen had been automatically stored so the pilot could control the machine with the rocket engines off, as she would have to do to rendezvous with a mother ship in orbit.

There, a radar presentation! Amid the sea of return was a black ribbon angling left and up. That would be the Nile.

"I've got it, but I don't know the scale."

"We're coming down pretty fast," Charley said in a worried voice.

He checked. Almost ten degrees nose down on the artificial horizon.

"Look for lights along the river. The river's out there, all right. We're aiming straight for the southern end of Lake Nasser."

"Lights . . ."

"Little towns along the river. Villages."

"There," Charley Pine said, relief evident in her voice, "I'll steer for that." She consulted the radar presentation.

That bright spot along the riverbank . . . that could be the town. She looked again through the canopy, examined the radar presentation one more time.

"Are we high enough?" he asked Charley. She knew what he meant, which was, Can we glide that far?

"Jesus, I hope so," she told him and inadvertently waggled the control stick.

"I wouldn't do that," Rip told her nervously as he braced himself against the twitching of the saucer. "The gas in the reservoirs for the maneuvering jets must be oxygen or hydrogen from the water. When it runs out, we'll have no way to control this thing."

Charley had an almost overpowering urge to urinate. She fought it back.

The lights of the town were coming rapidly closer. The gliding saucer rapidly closed the distance at a velocity of four hundred knots true.

They crossed over the town several miles above it. It was on the Nile, the southern end of Lake Nasser, so Rip had Charley turn to the northeast to fly along the lake. "We'll have to land beside it regardless of obstacles."

Charley's head bobbed.

"When you near the ground, level off. As our speed bleeds off, lift up on the collective, that left-hand lever. Those antigravity rings will keep us airborne, I hope. Keep flying the saucer with the control stick and the rudder. Pick a flat place near the water and bring us down gently."

Charley nodded again. Her head just kept bobbing up and down.

"Can you do this, Charley?"

More head bobbing.

"I'd feel better if you said something to me, Charley. Anything."

She glanced at him. Her face was white. She was too scared to say anything. It was written all over her face.

Rip kissed her on the lips. "Thanks for the ride, babe."

"Better" — she cleared her throat explosively — "better sit down and strap in."

Charley Pine stared into the darkness ahead. She could see . . . absolutely nothing.

No, wait! There was a light, reflecting on water. A boat.

Too low!

She pulled back sharply on the control stick and up on the collective. The G's mashed her into the seat as the nose rose.

Oh, too much, *too much!*

She felt the ship shudder . . . the edge of a stall . . . rammed the stick forward . . . pulled the collective toward her armpit, as high as it would go. She knew she was grossly overcontrolling, but what choice did she have?

The earth appeared suddenly in the landing lights; quick as thought she lifted the nose sharply, although not as precipitously as the first time.

The saucer leveled, then the nose dipped and the landing lights revealed the ground racing to meet her. She pulled the stick as far back as it would go.

The saucer hit something a glancing blow that threw it back into the air.

Still slowing, the ship would have crashed were it not for the antigravity rings, which prevented contact with the earth. Once again the saucer seemed to carom off an invisible rail.

A cliff appeared dead ahead in the landing lights.

She had no time to think. She dropped the collective, slammed the stick and rudder to the left. The saucer hit the earth, bounced once, then stayed on the ground.

Rip lost his grip on the pilot's seat. The deceleration slammed him forward onto the instrument panel. He went out like a light.

When Rip Cantrell awoke, the sun was in his eyes. He was lying in sand, he discovered, and the sun was reflecting off the saucer. He squinted, tried to rise and couldn't, rolled over to see where he was. He could hear an airplane, a buzzing.

He held up an arm to shield his eyes from the sun. The plane was a high-wing Cessna, only a couple hundred feet up, circling. The pilot must be looking the saucer over.

"About time you woke up," Charley Pine said. She was pouring water into the fuel tank using one of the plastic cans Rip had thrown into the saucer last night.

He had a hell of a headache. He rolled

over, levered himself up to a sitting position. He fingered his forehead. A large scab. Dried blood on his skin, in his eyebrows. He picked at it.

Finally he checked his watch. Ten o'clock.

The saucer was sitting on its landing gear, as neat and pretty as a pigeon on her nest. Fifty or sixty yards away, mostly downhill, was the riverbank. The river was perhaps two miles wide at this point; this must be Lake Nasser. The view was worth looking at, but his eyes ached from the sun's glare. He shut them to let them rest.

The drone of the airplane's engine brought him fully awake. "How long has that plane been circling?" he asked.

"Oh, fifteen minutes or so."

"I thought we crashed, last night."

"We did. Nothing damaged, though. I lifted the saucer and put the gear down. Got you out here in the sand so you would sleep better."

"Is the thing okay?"

"Sure."

"Didn't hurt it?"

"Honest."

She finished pouring and set out for the river. Rip started to get up, then thought better of it.

The Cessna made one last circle, then flew away to the northeast.

Rip watched it go. He was still sitting beside the saucer when she returned carrying the heavy can with both hands. Unassisted, she hoisted it to the refill receptacle and began pouring.

"You're pretty strong."

"You'd better be, this day and age."

"How many gallons is that?"

"Fifty. Ten trips. I'm going to sit a while and watch you add the next fifty."

"Isn't that just like a woman! You do your work in the cool of the day and leave the hot work for a man."

"Isn't that just like a man!" she shot back. "Sleeps late, watches the woman work, then gripes."

Rip struggled to his feet and took the empty can from her. He picked up the second one in the other hand, then set off down the hill.

The river was a flat sheet of brown, opaque water. In every direction, all he could see was sand, mud, rock, and water. There wasn't much breeze. Sweat dripped off his chin as he forced the can first into the water and let the water run in the opening.

Liquid mud. This brown water wouldn't

131

do the saucer's machinery any good, that's for sure. Still, there was nothing else.

After he filled the second can, he paused, staring morosely at the brown water, which didn't seem to be flowing. He was thirsty and hot, but if he drank that stuff he would get the runs for sure. He squatted and splashed water on his face, in his hair, then swabbed it with a rolled-up sleeve. His sleeve picked up most of the dirt.

Maybe this afternoon they would get to a place with cool, clean water.

A bath wouldn't hurt either. And food.

If he could work up the courage to fly in the saucer again. He had never been so scared in his life as he was last night, in the darkness, with the earth rushing toward them . . . He shivered once, remembering.

Climbing the hill with the cans, he told himself he could do it. "It was dark last night," he told Charley. "Couldn't see a darn thing."

"Uh-huh."

"Flying in the daytime will be different."

"Yeah."

"You can see things."

She nodded her head and brushed the hair back out of her eyes.

"You'll do better today," he said.

"Maybe."

"No, really. I'd be dead right now if you hadn't crawled into that saucer with me."

"You would really have flown this thing by yourself?"

"I was going to."

"Seriously?"

"I intended to."

"Uh-huh."

"I didn't know what was involved."

"Life's like that, isn't it?" she said and brushed a wisp of hair off her forehead.

He trudged down the hill for another ten gallons.

When he had poured his fifty gallons into the saucer, he flopped down on the sand beside Charley. "Wonder how much that thing holds."

"Let me see your head." She put her hands on the side of his head and examined his forehead. "You may have a scar. That's a pretty good whack. Blood's still oozing from it."

Her hands were strong. He liked that.

"Are you married to that major?" he asked.

"What made you ask that?"

"You're not wearing a ring, but some women don't these days."

"I'm single."

"Live with him?"

She made a dismissive gesture.

A gentle breeze stirred her hair. She looked like a fine hunk of woman, Rip Cantrell thought. Pretty old, though. Heck, she must be pushing thirty.

"So how come you got into that saucer with me?"

"I didn't want to see you kill yourself."

"Oh, come on. Give me a straight answer. I'm not a kid."

She shrugged. "I figured you might try to fly it, and I thought, why not? A girl can only die once."

Charley Pine started to laugh, then thought better of it and bit her lip. She got up, picked up one of the cans, set off for the river.

Rip picked up the other can and trailed after her.

"So are you in trouble with the Air Force?"

"I will be, sooner or later. When they find out this thing will fly, they'll want me to fly it to Nevada."

"Where in Nevada?"

"Area Fifty-one."

"That's the top-secret base?"

"Yes."

"So are you going to?"

"Can't take you there, can I? You don't have a clearance."

"They'll fire you, maybe. Talk Lockheed Martin out of hiring you."

Charley grunted.

On the next trip back up the hill with full cans, Rip relieved Charley of her can. "What do you think we ought to do?" he asked as he poured water into the saucer.

"We should fly this thing to the States, give it to the Air Force."

Rip tilted the can, listened to the gurgling water. When the can was empty, he tossed it in the sand and picked up the other one.

"No," he told her.

"Well, where do you want to go?"

"I don't know," he confessed.

"This ship is designed to shuttle back and forth between an orbiting mother ship and the surface of a planet. I doubt if it carries enough fuel to operate continuously in the atmosphere."

"What are you saying?"

"This craft is designed to shuttle up and down from the surface, not fly cross-country like an airplane."

"Can we safely go into space without knowing how to run the computers?"

"Don't kid yourself. There's nothing we can safely do with this ship except let it sit right where it is."

"I don't want to leave it here and I don't

want to give it to the Air Force."

She didn't say anything to that.

"I don't want to let those Aussies have it," Rip added. "Qaddafi either."

"Uh-huh."

"I just don't know," Rip Cantrell said.

"Well, we're going to have to do something. Sitting here on this riverbank is going to attract a crowd before long. And I could use something to eat and something tall and frosty to drink."

Finally they got the saucer's tank full. They could tell by the sound that the tank was filling up. Rip poured water in until it overflowed, then tossed both cans inside the ship. The tank had taken about one hundred and sixty gallons.

They were sitting in the shade of the saucer, neither of them saying anything, when a small steamer drifted to a stop about fifty yards from the riverbank. It must have been in sight for at least fifteen minutes but they hadn't noticed it. The small ship was perhaps seventy feet long, with two decks above the waterline, and crammed with people and animals. All the people were looking this way. So many had crowded to this side of the boat that it was listing.

"Uh-oh!"

Everyone on the boat seemed to be talking at once and pointing this way. The gabble of voices carried across the water.

"Do you speak Arabic?" Charley asked Rip.

"Nowhere near enough to talk to those guys." Rip stood and dusted off his trousers.

"Maybe we better get aboard and bop on out of here."

"Boy, look at 'em," Rip said. "You'd think they'd never seen a flying saucer."

"Ha, ha, and ha."

Rip waved at the mob on the boat. Several waved back, but most just stared. They seemed to be silent now.

With his hands on his hips, Rip looked around as if he were trying to memorize the setting. "This place is gonna be famous," he said with a grin. "The Roswell, New Mexico, of the Nile Valley. People will come from miles around just to see the place where the saucer sat." He waved at the boat crowd again. "Who knows, there are probably some folks aboard that boat who will eat out for the next twenty years on their story of what they saw today. 'And then, just before he went aboard his spaceship and blasted off, one of the aliens waved. Damnedest thing I ever did see.'"

"That's enough, E.T. Into the ship."

After one last wave to the people on the boat, the imaginary fans on the landward side, and an unseen television audience all over the globe, Rip Cantrell ducked down and waddled his way under the saucer to the open hatch.

"We must do something about the method of ingress. It's just plain undignified."

He fired off the reactor, waited a bit for some water to percolate through the system, then helped Charley Pine into the pilot's seat. She wiggled the stick and rudder. Little puffs of dirt and dust rose from each of the maneuvering jets. She kept wiggling the stick until the puffs stopped.

Rip stood beside her on the step where he had stood last night.

"You want to get strapped in or something?"

"Just take it easy, lady. Don't do anything exciting."

She slowly lifted the collective, concentrated on making only tiny movements with the stick. The saucer became light on the skids, then rose off the ground in a little cloud of dust. She lifted it into a hover about six feet above the ground, then used her left hand to reach for the gear switch. A humming noise was audible from the machinery spaces until the gear legs were in.

Charley took a deep breath and let it out slowly. *Please, Lord, don't let me screw this up.*

She turned the ship with the rudder, pointed it ahead of the boat, which was still dead in the water fifty yards or so from the shore.

She let the saucer move that way. The ship was at least a hundred feet in the air and climbing when it crossed the river-bank. The test pilot kept lifting the collective, lifting the saucer higher and higher. She ran out of collective when the ship was about two hundred feet high; it would go no higher without rocket power.

Taking her time, Charley slowly circled the drifting boat. As she crossed behind the stern, the boat listed the other way as everyone on board shifted sides for a better view.

"If that boat capsizes, a lot of those people will drown," Rip pointed out.

"Okay."

Charley turned west and leveled out, nudged the control stick forward to coax more speed out of the saucer. They crossed the lake leisurely, accelerating slowly. On the far shore they passed over a railroad track and a highway. Only then did Charley Pine light the rocket engines.

The acceleration pushed her deeper into the seat. Rip Cantrell held on tightly.

Yes!

A smile lit up her face.

The saucer was accelerating nicely, but it was only a couple thousand feet above the sand and rock wilderness when Rip spotted the first jet fighter and pointed it out to her. The plane was a silver speck in the deep blue sky, glinting in the sun. There was another behind the first, offset to one side.

The fighters were coming in from the right, pointed almost directly at the saucer.

"We stayed too long at the party," Charley told him.

Even as she spoke, a series of flashes lit up the nose of the first fighter.

"He's *shooting!* Let's *go!*"

She cranked the rocket engines wide open. The G struck her like a fist.

Rip Cantrell shouted something, lost his grip on the pilot's seat and instrument panel, and tumbled toward the back of the compartment.

Despite the push of the rockets at full cry, the fighter was closing. Instinctively she banked the saucer toward the fighter, forcing the other pilot into an overshoot. The saucer ripped by the silver delta-winged fighter at a scant hundred yards, accelerating through Mach 2.

At Mach 3, Charley pulled back on the control stick and pointed the saucer almost straight up. She stayed on the juice.

The saucer roared skyward on a cone of fire.

Aboard the boat, the passengers stared with open mouths as the rising fireball began slowly tilting toward the northeast. They could still hear the distant thunder of the engines echoing back and forth between the steep shores of the lake when the bright fire from the rockets merged with the great golden orb of the sun.

7

The computer displays consisted of graphics and short rows of symbols that both Rip and Charley thought were probably words and numbers. Since they couldn't read any of it, Rip held on tightly to the pilot's seat with his left hand and flipped through the displays with his right, looking for . . .

"I've never seen graphics like these," he shouted. "They're so real, like you should be able to touch them. They almost look like holographs."

"They are holographs," Charley said. "That's it, right there! That display is the one we want."

Rip held tight with both hands and stared. A curving pathway led upward and eastward. A series of analog needles arranged vertically along the left side of the display might indicate altitude, airspeed, direction . . . but which was which?

Ah, yes. The second one down from the top must be altitude, and the one under it airspeed. He said as much to Charley, who told him, "I think you're right."

She had the juice full on now. At least four G's were pushing them toward the rocket engines in the rear of the ship. Rip was holding on as best he could, but he was tiring.

Finally he could hold on no longer and let himself go. He crashed into the aft bulkhead.

Charley Pine was shouting, a primordial yell of pure triumph as she concentrated on the computer graphics before her. She felt so good. All those years of flight training, all those years of school, the sweat, the tears, the sacrifices, and now she was flying this thing into space! Her fellow Air Force test pilots would turn green with envy when they found out. And they *would* find out, of that she had no doubt.

She inhaled deeply and let out another rebel yell. "Yee-haaaa! Oh, yes. Go, baby, go!"

Charley kept the steering centered on that pathway into space. No doubt there was an autopilot in this thing somewhere and a simple push of a button would couple the ship to it, but she had no idea where it was or how to work it. Even if she had known, she probably would not have used it.

Outside the sky was almost black, a deep

obsidian black arcing over the blue planet. They were high, twenty or thirty miles, she guessed, and going higher. The ship was still accelerating at four G's with the canopy pointed toward earth, climbing at about a forty-degree angle. With the earth above them, the concept of up and down seemed to no longer apply.

The glowing of the saucer's nose faded as the ship raced through the last remnants of the atmosphere. Although slightly muffled now, the dull roar of the rocket engines still filled the saucer's cabin with sound.

Orbital velocity was eighteen thousand miles per hour. Charley Pine had to accelerate to at least that speed or she would merely go over the top and begin reentry. Excess speed would cause her to orbit higher and higher. If she accelerated past twenty-five thousand miles per hour, escape velocity, the saucer would fly off into space on a voyage into eternity.

Charley knew the physics cold; what she didn't know was the computer program that she was using as a flight director. If only she could read the words and numbers!

This had to be the right program! It had the right look; the physics seemed right; everything about it seemed right.

But how was she going to know when

she reached orbital velocity? And how high would this orbit be?

Why was she asking herself these questions? The saucer flew, whoever designed it obviously knew their stuff, whoever made it sure as hell built it right. Whoever they were . . .

She was well out over the Indian Ocean now, which appeared above her since the saucer was inverted. The curvature of the earth was quite prominent, the atmosphere a hazy blue line on the curved horizon. Clouds, small gauzy cotton things, stuck to the sea's surface. A squall line, a front, obviously, appeared as a row of clouds, tiny things with minuscule shadows.

The earth hanging over her head, the deep black of space, the roar of the rocket engines hurling her into that blackness, the G pushing her into her seat like the hand of God . . . the experience was sublime, a sensory feast, and Charley Pine shouted again from pure joy.

Beside her Rip Cantrell was fighting to get erect so he could see out of the canopy. She glanced at him. Sweat coated his face, the veins in his arms stood out like cords. He lifted himself even with her, fighting the G.

"Oh, wow!" he breathed, then filled his

lungs and joined her in a shout.

Just then the pathway disappeared from the computer screen. One second it was there, then it was gone.

Charley Pine shut down the rocket engines, and Rip shot forward as the G instantly stopped. His contracted muscles propelled him right into the instrument panel.

He bounced off the panel and floated toward the back of the cabin, weightless. "Hot damn! We made it!"

Charley laughed. She felt so terrific.

Rip kicked off a bulkhead and caught himself on the arm of the pilot's seat. He anchored himself there and studied the earth hanging above them, the riot of subtle colors, the blackness of space framing it all.

"There's the Persian Gulf and the Himalayas."

"Earth," said Charley Pine and laughed again.

"Are we in orbit?"

"Maybe. Maybe not. If the ship starts heating up, we didn't make it." All of the red had now disappeared from the saucer's skin.

The earth seemed to be rotating slowly above them. Cloud systems and smears of land moved steadily along. They watched mesmerized as they crossed the zone from day into darkness.

"It's really weird with the earth above us," Rip commented. "Can you turn the ship?"

Charley Pine nudged the stick sideways a trifle, then recentered it. The nudge was enough. Slowly the saucer rolled until the earth was below them. Then Charley stopped the roll with another small displacement of the stick.

"Oh, man!" Rip exclaimed. "What a show!"

Charley felt the same way. It came to her then that she had lived her whole life to get to this moment. Everything led to this.

Without thinking she rubbed her hand absently through Rip's hair. He didn't seem to notice.

Rip was the first to come back to reality. He began punching up displays on the computer, studying the graphics, looking for something, anything, that might tell him the dynamics of their orbit.

He found a display, finally, that depicted an elongated oval. "This is us, I think," he muttered, studying the symbols.

"Anything on how to get down?" Charley Pine asked.

"Not that I've seen yet. If you have any ideas, this might be a good time to trot them out."

She too began playing with the computers. In the weightless environment, being strapped to the pilot's seat was a distinct advantage. Floating in the air, Rip held himself in position with the fingertips of one hand.

Charley was scrolling through displays one by one when she hit it — a presentation of the descent path over a planet. The two of them studied the presentation, a complex three-dimensional graphic.

On impulse Charley reached for the screen with a fingertip. The planet rotated under her touch.

"It's earth," she said. "There's North and South America, the Azores . . ."

"Well, look at that!" Rip exclaimed, and pointed. The Mediterranean Sea was dry, without water. "And there, the English Channel." On the presentation the British Isles weren't islands at all, but part of the mainland.

"That's Earth as it looked long ago," Charley said, thinking aloud. "I wonder how long?"

"Use your finger to spin the planet to Missouri, then touch it."

"Is that where you want to land?"

"Yeah. If we can get down, we'll put this thing on my uncle's farm."

"He's a farmer?"

"Uncle Egg lives on a farm, but he's no farmer. He's a bit of everything — inventor, wizard, mechanic extraordinaire . . . He has about twenty patents in a variety of fields, lives off his royalties."

She did as he suggested. A tap of the fingertip on Missouri caused the graphic to change. Now the point of a long cone rested there. The body of the cone rose and bent westward a third of the way around the globe, with the wide mouth just west of the Hawaiian Islands.

"We'll have to try it on our next orbit," Rip said. He pointed. "See the small dot of red light? That's us, I think, and we're in the wrong orbit. We need a trajectory change to get us to the reentry point."

Charley kept scrolling through the displays. "Here it is, I hope." She studied the three-dimensional graphic, then pointed. "The minimum burn will be right here."

"How much fuel will it take?"

She played with the displays for almost a minute before she said, "I don't know. If we burn up all our fuel maneuvering, we won't have enough to get out of orbit. If we

149

lose orbital velocity but don't burn long enough to hit the cone, we'll skip off the atmosphere like a rock, over and over, until finally we go in steeply."

"Steeply? I don't like the sound of that."

"We'll probably burn up in the atmosphere like a meteor."

"How much fuel do we have remaining?"

"See this display?" Charley pointed at another computer presentation. "This might be fuel remaining. We're under five percent, I think."

Rip looked slowly around. "These saucer people must have taken on another load of water from the mother ship while they were in orbit."

"No more than a few gallons. Water in space is precious. One suspects they used the mother ship to make cross-track trajectory changes."

"So what do we do? Missouri or where?"

"Let me work with the computers," she said and bent to study the screens.

Finally she took a deep breath. "I think we can make North America. Missouri. We'll make the orbit change, then fire the rockets to drop us into that cone on the computer."

Rip nodded vigorously. "We'll coast down over the Pacific and plop into the good ol' U. S. of A. If we overshoot, we'll hit the Atlantic." Rip smiled confidently. "But not to worry, Charley baby. North America is a big target. We'll be okay."

"Uh-huh."

"Trust me."

"Don't call me baby."

"Nothing personal, Captain Pine, you being an older woman and all."

The ship had rotated on its axis about ninety degrees, or so it seemed. The dark planet was off to their left, filling half the sky. They fell silent then, stared at the massive orb.

"We're coming up on the U.S. now," Charley whispered.

Sure enough, the lights of Los Angeles soon came into view, twinkling merrily, covering the hills and valleys. The huge city was a vast smear of light. The orbiting saucer soon left it behind. The Mojave Desert was black and empty, the inter-states tiny twinkling ribbons, the little towns mere splotches in the darkness.

When Rip finally looked into space he saw only unwinking stars against an obsidian sky. A shiver ran through him.

The peril of their position washed over him like a cold shower. They were several hundred miles above the surface of the earth in an ancient spaceship that he had jackhammered from a rock ledge. If anything went wrong, both he and Charley were going to die. In this saucer. Very soon.

He felt slightly nauseated. It's the weightlessness, he told himself, wanting to believe that. The reality of his recklessness he tried to ignore. Pine wanted to come, he thought; she was here of her own free will.

He wondered about the water, how much remained in the tank.

Would the rocket motors start? An anxious dread came over him, brought a layer of sweat to his brow.

The motors have to start. They must! It can't end like this, the two of them marooned in orbit, condemned to die when the air went bad.

Here came the sun!

With a dazzling rush the sun rose over the earth's rim and filled the inside of the saucer with its light.

Charley Pine watched the sun climb toward the zenith, then went back to playing with the computers. She went back and forth between the three displays before her. She looked calm, as placid as if she were receiving e-mail on the Internet.

"If the engines don't start, we're toast," Rip told her. "You know that?"

She glanced at him, her expression unchanged. "I tried to focus your attention on the risk before we started."

"I'm focused as hell now."

"The risk hasn't changed. We are no more or less in jeopardy than we were when we were fifteen feet above the ground."

"It sure feels more dangerous," he replied, his eyes inadvertently drawn to the planet looming over the ship. Towering cumulus clouds low in the atmosphere cast distinct shadows with military precision. There were thousands of clouds.

She went back to the computers.

"I got a bad feeling about this," he told her, but she was concentrating on the machines and didn't hear him.

He pushed gently away from the pilot's seat and floated effortlessly across the small compartment. When he came within reach of a bulkhead, he pushed off, continued slowly back and forth across the compartment while the earth sped by beneath the saucer and Charley Pine played with the computers.

Okay, she's a tough broad. Tough.

He was floating along thinking about things when the rocket motors fired. He went crashing into the rear bulkhead. After about three seconds, the motors stopped.

"Hey!"

"Sorry. Forgot to warn you."

"Well, at least the engines work," he acknowledged grudgingly. "What was that all about, anyway?"

"That was the cross-trajectory burn. Now we are in the proper orbit, lined up with the descent cone."

He floated over to look at the display.

As he hung on, Charley turned the saucer and pointed it backward, lining it up with a set of crosshairs that showed in the holographic display on the computer. "About five more minutes, more or less."

"Okay."

He wasn't frightened anymore. Maybe he should have been, but he wasn't. A great peace came over him. Whoever made this saucer was long dead, yet he felt a kinship to those creatures . . . people . . . whoever they were. He was flying their ship as they must have done, and somehow that seemed all right. They had the courage to face the unknown, and now, with no boasting or bravado, Rip Cantrell knew that he had it too.

"We're going to be okay," he said to Charley, who was busy fooling with the computer again.

"Yeah," she replied, intent on examining another display.

Then she brought the reentry holograph back on-screen and rearranged herself in the chair.

"Perhaps you should strap into a seat," she said.

"Just for the burn."

"Okay."

He settled himself into the nearest seat and put on the belt.

He got a glimpse of the display blossoming as they entered the cone and the flame on the display that commanded engine power. Charley came on with the juice and didn't stint. She went smoothly up to full power while keeping the ship properly oriented.

Just as she reached full power, the motors cut out for a second or so. When they came back on, they weren't at full power. Maybe half, a little less. Despite his resolve, Rip's heart threatened to leap up his throat.

The engines burped again, two, three, four times . . .

"Come on!" That was Charley, talking to her steed. "Don't do that to me."

Rip was out of the seat, clawing his way up toward the pilot's seat so he could see the displays. "What's wrong?"

More burping from the rocket motors.

Then they quit. On the main display, the holograph was commanding full power.

"Uh-oh."

"This isn't good . . ."

"Oh, man!"

Charley fiddled with the controls, jiggled the throttle grip, pushed on it fiercely.

The motors came up to power for a second, two . . . three . . .

"We're out of the cone," Charley said, her voice taut.

"Keep flying it. There's nothing we can do." Rip's voice was calm and controlled.

She got a steady burn of about four seconds, then the computer commanded a shutoff. The cone was well below the flight path recommended by the computer, which presented its recommendation as a crosshair of attitude and heading.

Charley used rudder and side stick to turn the ship, point it down the cone facing forward.

"Are you going to dive into the cone?"

"Too dangerous," she replied and gestured toward the scene out the canopy. The earth filled most of the windscreen. The nose was definitely down, maybe fourteen or fifteen degrees.

She held the precise attitude recommended by the computer and let the saucer race downward toward the waiting air.

Minutes passed. The earth seemed no closer. Rip asked nervously, "Are you sure we got slowed down enough?"

"No, I'm not sure. Maybe you better strap in and hold on."

Reluctantly Rip propelled himself into the nearest seat. He had just got the straps fastened when he felt the forward tug of deceleration as the ship bit into the upper edge of the atmosphere.

Telltale flecks of fire raced over the canopy, too fast to really see. They were just streaks.

By moving her head as high as she could, Charley Pine could just see a pinkish glow radiating back from the nose and growing redder by the second as the ship dove deeper and deeper into the atmosphere.

Due to some freak combination of light and moisture, a visible shock wave developed on the canopy aft of the apex about ten minutes into the descent. It played across the transparent material as Rip watched, then was swept aft as the air thickened.

Charley Pine concentrated on keeping the attitude and heading crosshairs centered on the computer display as the saucer plunged into the earth's atmosphere like a meteor coming in from deep space.

8

The saucer appeared on a computerized display console at the North American Air Defense Command (NORAD) inside the Cheyenne Mountain bunker near Colorado Springs. It appeared as a blip on the radar screen displaying the Pacific sector west of California. The computer was programmed to remove orbiting satellites and space junk from the display and present only objects traveling faster than or below orbital velocity.

Halfway through a long four-hour watch, the operator was drinking coffee and listening to background music piped in over the loudspeakers as she flipped listlessly through the two dozen possible presentations available at her watch station. She was also thinking about her new boyfriend, who had made it crystal clear last night that he had serious designs on her body.

She stared at the fast-moving blip for several seconds before it cut through the fog of boyfriend, music, and ennui. She slid an icon over the blip and clicked once. Above the blip this information appeared:

C082 S143 52NM. Course in degrees true; speed in hundreds of knots; height in thousands of feet until one hundred thousand was reached, then in nautical miles.

The operator rang the alarm bell to attract her supervisor, then pushed buttons to put the blip on the main display of the United States that occupied most of the wall in the front of the room.

The supervisor arrived at her console within seconds. The operator pointed.

"Fourteen thousand miles an hour?"

"It almost looks like a space shuttle coming in, but there isn't one up there. Maybe space junk reentering, or . . ."

The unspoken possibility was that the blip was an inbound ICBM warhead. In fact, the primary mission of this facility was to detect and track ICBMs launched from anywhere on the planet.

"Any launch indications?"

"No, sir."

"Anybody," the supervisor thundered over the PA system, "do we have any indications of missile launch anywhere on the planet in the last two hours?"

Silence.

"Anywhere?" he repeated, his amplified voice sounding in the operator's headset as well as over the public address system.

"The target appeared a few seconds ago, sir. As if it dropped out of orbit."

The supervisor was an old hand. He had seen space junk come in dozens of times. It always decelerated very quickly and burned up long before it could reach the ground. He was watching the numbers on this blip now, waiting for the quick deceleration. Its speed was slowly dissipating, but nowhere near quick enough.

"Coming in pretty shallow for a meteor," the operator added, quite superfluously.

Warhead, meteor, or space junk — whatever it was, it was going to hit the earth before it burned up.

The supervisor said a cuss word and picked up the red telephone.

From San Diego to San Francisco, people out and about three hours before dawn saw a fiery red streak cross the sky heading slightly north of east. Slower than a shooting star yet faster by far than any airplane, the fireball had a short tail and glowed reddish yellow. Despite the hour, a few thousand people saw it. Several managed to get underexposed photographs. One man near Bakersfield engaging in his hobby of amateur astronomy caught the saucer's passage on a time-lapse exposure.

Most of the viewers just watched in awe, unaware of what they were seeing or its significance.

The saucer was far too high for the sonic boom to reach the ground, which was perhaps just as well.

As quickly as it came, the fireball disappeared into the eastern sky. A few dozen people called in the sightings to local radio stations, and within seconds reports were on the Internet.

As the saucer dropped below Mach 10, the on-board computer commanded a steeper descent. Charley Pine was reluctant to obey — the surface of the saucer was a cherry red — but after a second of hesitation, she lowered the nose a few degrees. Not as many as the computer commanded, but a few. The airspeed was dropping a bit, she thought, scanning the displays for something that might indicate airspeed, but her primary concern was the saucer's skin temperature. Of course it was designed to take these astronomical temps, but still, the skin was very, very old.

The glow of the saucer's skin seemed to lessen.

She lifted the nose still higher, and the redness faded rapidly. Now she lowered the nose, let the saucer hunt for a descent angle that felt right.

The saucer was still traveling in excess of Mach 4 when Charley descended through a hundred thousand feet just west of St. Louis. Behind her the shock wave touched the ground, a stupendous clap of thunder that shook houses, rattled windows, and frightened livestock and wildlife. It was, perhaps, the loudest noise ever heard in St. Louis. Every human not comatose or stone deaf heard it as a deep, bass boom of overwhelming power, painfully loud, but not loud enough to shatter eardrums. Many thought they had just heard a large explosion a few blocks away. Lights came on all over the metropolitan area and the telephone system was overloaded as everyone within reach of a telephone tried to dial 911.

Charley Pine felt for the earth. The saucer descended through a layer of low broken clouds, then came out in a dark area with few lights. She had carefully milked the glide, never using engines, all the way down. When she was about a thousand feet above the ground — it was hard to tell from looking outside, and she had no idea about the increments on the cockpit indicators — she used the antigravity control. Pulled it as high as it would go, then let the saucer fly down until the descent slowed.

The descent stopped at about two hundred feet. Low. Too low.

She almost flew into a radio tower that loomed in front of her, lit by only a few red beacon lights.

Safely around that, she followed a road toward a town she had seen when she came out of the bottom of the clouds.

Thank heavens the land hereabouts was relatively flat. Coming down in this thing into a mountainous region at night would be a good way to commit suicide.

Rip was standing beside her now. "Where are we?" he asked, looking out the canopy for lights.

"I don't know."

"Missouri, you think?"

"Not very likely."

"The United States?"

"Maybe."

"Pinpoint accuracy. I like that."

The sky was getting light in the east when she brought the saucer to a stop on the edge of a small town.

It wasn't much of a town, just a conglomeration of houses on a small paved road in farming country.

They looked the town over from a hundred feet up. Not a car was stirring. "It must be about four-thirty or five in the morning here," Charley muttered.

"Yeah." Rip pointed. "Try that filling station. Maybe they got a water hose."

"I'm getting pretty desperate for a bathroom, now that we're back in civilization."

"Bet everything's locked."

She maneuvered the saucer through some trees and set it down in a vacant lot beside the filling station, as close to the building as possible. Rip opened the hatch and dropped through.

The smells of earth and summer and motor oil were like perfume. He inhaled deeply. The sky and clouds were pink in the east, which bathed the landscape in soft light. After two and a half months in the desert, Rip thought he had never seen a prettier place than this little town.

There was a water tap on the corner of the building but no hose. He turned on the tap, just to make sure. Water came out. He turned it off and stood up, looking around. Across the street from the filling station was a diner, still closed, of course. Four little houses were in sight, with pieces of others visible through the trees. Might as well try the house next door, Rip thought.

He walked through the trees. The house was a white one-story with a single-car garage. The garage door was open, revealing a Chevy pickup and lawn mower parked inside. A coil of garden hose hung from a hook on the wall. Rip helped himself.

Two minutes later he had water flowing into the saucer. He tried the door of the filling station's men's room. Unlocked.

He was standing beside the saucer looking around at the trees, the buildings, the flat fields stretching away toward comfortable horizons when Charley came out of the women's rest room.

"Ah," she said, adjusting her gray flight suit.

"Maybe you should take off your name tag and captain's bars," Rip suggested.

"You're right. The saucer *is* going to attract a lot of attention."

Rip thought Charley's remark a masterpiece of understatement. Still, he was desperately hungry. "Let's get something to eat when the diner opens, okay? And please let me do the talking."

"Okay," she said without much enthusiasm as she removed the rank devices and name tag from her flight suit. "I should have taken off the captain's bars two weeks ago," she said and tossed them away.

"Why did the rockets hiccup when we did that reentry burn?"

"Your guess is as good as mine."

"If we can get this thing to Uncle Egg's, he can figure it out."

Rip Cantrell laughed. He felt wonderful. "This is so *cool!*" He opened his arms to take in the filling station, the diner, the houses stretching down the street, then pirouetted and gestured grandly at the saucer as he bowed from the waist.

Charley Pine applauded.

"Thank you, thank you. For you, ma'am, we have a seat front row center."

She checked the water tank. The hose was delivering water under a good head of pressure, yet from the sound the tank was a long way from full.

When she turned around an old dog was sniffing at the ship, then at Rip. He waited until the dog had had its sniffs, then he bent carefully and offered an ear scratch.

Rip is just an overgrown boy, she thought.

She turned back to the saucer, laid both hands upon it.

She had flown it.

Yes! She closed her eyes and remembered how it felt, how it was with the rocket engines going and the ship quivering in her hand.

When she turned back toward him, Rip was looking at her strangely.

"What's wrong?"

"In this light . . . well, you look awful pretty," and he reddened nicely.

She grinned at him then, at the boy still in him and the man he had become.

He shuffled over to listen to the water rushing into the tank to hide his embarrassment. "Half full, maybe."

The sound of a car coming down the street made them turn and look. The car turned into the station and parked on the other side of the building, well away from the pump. The driver came walking over. He was a kid, maybe sixteen, wearing dirty jeans, with a face splotched with acne. The dog lying beside the saucer's nearest landing gear thumped its tail in the dirt.

"Hey," the kid said. "What the hell *is* this?"

"An oversize hauler off-loaded it about a half hour ago," Rip said matter-of-factly, without inflection. "He said it was gonna be a sign for an amusement park in St. Louis. Said there was an overpass down the interstate that it wouldn't go under."

"Well, I'll be . . ." the kid said. "Why'd he leave it here?"

"Didn't have anywhere else to leave it. Said another trucker would be along to get it in a couple hours."

The kid tore his eyes from the saucer and directed his attention to Charley and Rip. "Why you putting water in it?"

"Darn thing is so light it needs some water to hold it down if the wind kicks up. Fellow next door brought his hose over." Rip nodded with his head. "Hope you guys can spare a few gallons of water."

"I reckon we can."

The kid put his hands on the saucer. Then he rapped on it with a knuckle. Before he could speak, Rip said, "I'd be careful. Just Styrofoam under there and you're liable to dent it."

"Oh." The kid put his hands in his pockets and tried to look nonchalant.

"By the way," Rip continued. "My sister and I broke down a few miles east of here. After we get some breakfast, could we get someone to tow the car in? I think the water hose broke."

"Lots of steam, huh?"

"I should say."

"Well, the owner drives the tow truck. He'll be in after a while. You got Triple A?"

"I think so. Somewhere in my wallet." Rip touched his hip.

"How much more water you gonna put in there?"

"Oh, this is enough, I reckon. It's just to give it some weight." Rip turned off the water tap and disconnected the hose. Charley closed the cap on the water tank.

As Rip coiled the hose, he said to Charley, "Meet you at the diner."

"Nice of you to let the trucker have a little water," Rip told the kid as Charley strolled away.

"Ain't my water," the kid said, still looking over the saucer. "Sure looks real, huh? Looks like it's full of little E.T. guys."

"Uh-huh."

"Make these things in Hollywood, I guess."

"Somewhere in New Jersey, actually." Rip got the last of the hose coiled up on his arm and took it back to the garage where he had borrowed it.

After another long look at the saucer, the kid went over to the door of the filling station and unlocked it.

Rip and Charley were sitting on the front stoop of the diner when the sun peeped over the horizon and under the cloud deck, illuminating everything in town, including the saucer.

"The kid bought it, I think," he said.

"You're quite the liar."

"I'm practicing to be a politician."

"What do you think happened to our friends?"

"Guess the Arabs will let 'em loose before long. Oil workers are the rainmakers; they come and go all the time. Doesn't pay for the Arabs to hassle 'em. Can't say the same about the Air Force types, though. And God only knows what they'll do with the Aussies."

The fate of the Aussies didn't interest Charley Pine very much. Of course the United States government would eventually bestir itself on behalf of her Air Force colleagues, who would probably all get medals and a trip to Washington to shake hands with the elected ones.

She sat staring at the saucer. "That antigravity device is something else," she said after a bit.

Rip agreed. "I think those coils on the saucer's belly reverse the polarity of the saucer's gravitational field, so the saucer and earth repel each other."

They sat watching the sun rise behind the saucer, each lost in his or her own thoughts.

General Hoyt Alexander, commanding general of Space Command, was awakened from a sound sleep by the Cheyenne Mountain duty officer and informed that an unidentified object had entered the atmosphere, one that appeared to remain intact all the way to the ground. The Pentagon watch team had already been notified, the duty officer said.

Ten minutes later, the watch officer called back with the news from California.

By the time the watch officer learned of the sonic booms in St. Louis, the Air Force chief of staff, General "Bombing" Joe De Laurio, had already called General Alexander.

"Morning, Hoyt. What the hell is going on? Space invaders?"

"I don't think so, sir," General Alexander said. His sense of humor was invisible, if he had one at all.

"Is your television on, Hoyt?"

"No, sir," Alexander said, as if that were a routine question to be asked by a superior officer at — he looked at the luminescent hands of his watch — 4:14 a.m. Mountain Daylight Time.

Bombing Joe sighed. "The media is in a feeding frenzy this morning," he continued. "The public affairs people are already besieged, and I haven't even had a cup of coffee. Objects entering the atmosphere over California, possible sonic booms over St. Louis . . . What in hell is going on?"

171

"Sir, we don't have any answers . . . yet."

"Humpf," grunted Bombing Joe. After a few seconds of silence, he added, "How about making sure none of our hot-rock fighter jocks buzzed St. Louis this morning. Call me back as soon as you can."

"Yes, sir."

"Too many UFO stories around, if you ask me," Alexander's boss grumped. "The world is getting weirder and weirder."

Alexander hadn't a clue what that remark was in reference to since he had not been briefed about the discovery of a saucer-shaped object in the Sahara, confirmation by the hypersonic spy plane, or the fact that a UFO team had been dispatched to investigate. He kept his mystification to himself, however, because he well knew the Air Force was a compartmentalized outfit. His was not to wonder why . . .

After a few more grumbles for the record, Bombing Joe hung up. He immediately called his aide at home on the secure telephone and asked him what he had heard about the UFO team that had been sent to the Sahara two days ago.

"Nothing, sir," the aide said.

"I want a complete report when I get to the office," rumbled Bombing Joe. The political people were going to be all over him before he got very much older. He sat in bed frowning as CNN's reporters got wound up about explosive noises in St. Louis.

Just another Rolaids morning, he thought as he climbed out of bed.

Rip and Charley heard the car coming down the street when it was still two blocks away. After parking it beside the diner, a hefty woman got out, took a good look at the saucer across the street, then came walking toward the front door. She glanced at Charley and Rip, then stuck her key in the door.

"You know anything about that?" she asked, nodding at the saucer.

"Truckers off-loaded it there a little while ago," Rip volunteered. "Said there was an overpass down the four-lane that it wouldn't go under."

"Well, I guess. What is it, anyway?"

"Gonna be part of a sign for an amusement park over in St. Louis. That's what the trucker told us. We broke down on the four-lane and walked into town."

"Come on in and I'll put the coffee on."

Rip and Charley followed her into the diner.

"You folks been driving all night?"

"Yeah. Then the car gave out."

"That's the way the world works, I guess. Some days you just can't have no luck. Find a seat and I'll get you some coffee as quick as I can."

"Thanks."

They sat in the first booth, with the sun's rays streaming through the window. The clouds were patchy now, breaking up.

"It's going to be a pretty day," Charley Pine said.

"Feels good to be home," Rip replied and helped himself to a package of coffee sugar. Then he yawned.

"I'm sleepy too," Charley said. "And I could use a bath."

"Uncle Egg's got hot water and beds. I'm going to sleep all day."

When the woman brought the coffee, Rip said, "We didn't see the sign on the way into town. What's the name of this place, anyway?"

"Lordy, how did you miss that sign? This is Upshur, Indiana, boy, 'where the prairie begins.'"

"It was sorta dark when we walked in."

"Honey, Upshur, Indiana, is a good place to be from. Been here all my life, though. Just can't seem to wind myself up to get up and go."

"Sounds like a country song."

"Don't it, though? What do you all want to eat this fine summer morning?"

"Half dozen eggs scrambled," Rip said. "Lots of fried potatoes, a couple slabs of ham, maybe four biscuits, two big glasses of whole milk. What about you, Charley?"

"That's all for you?" Charley and the diner lady both stared at him.

"I'm hungry."

"Two eggs and dry toast for me, thank you," Charley said.

As she went into the kitchen, the woman turned on the television in the corner. The thing took a few seconds to warm up. Rip helped himself to another packet of sugar.

". . . Authorities have no explanation for a loud noise that rocked St. Louis approximately one hour ago, shattering windows throughout the metro area and causing thousands of people to telephone police and fire departments."

Charley and Rip looked at each other. Rip shrugged.

The reporters went on to another story. "A suspected meteor raced across the California sky in the early hours this morning. Hundreds of people saw the large object, apparently burning up in the atmosphere, streak across the sky from west to east. Was it a meteor or a satellite falling out of orbit? The Air Force has yet to say. There have been no reports of a meteor striking the earth this morning, but if one hit in a remote area, it may be days before the report comes out. Here is Air Force spokesman Major Don Williams."

The station cut to a man in uniform. "The object was tracked by Space Command, of course. We will have a statement later when we know more about the object's trajectory."

A reporter asked the officer, "A very loud explosion was reported just minutes ago in St. Louis. Could the meteor have struck the earth near St. Louis?"

"We don't know," the major said. "We're trying to determine that now."

Charley sipped her coffee and looked out the window at the saucer, which was casting a long shadow in the early morning sun.

"When I was hunting for a hose," Rip said, "for a second there I thought you might fly off and leave me."

"Did you really?"

"Just for a second."

"If I hadn't needed to go to the rest room so badly, maybe I would have."

"Why didn't you?"

"I want to know everything there is to know about that ship before I walk away from it."

She turned over the paper place mat in front of her, took a pen from the left sleeve pocket of her flight suit, and began making notes. She wanted to get down her impressions of flying the saucer while they were still fresh. The handling was excellent at low speeds but at large Mach numbers the saucer was almost impossible to maneuver. She wrote fast and quickly, scribbling thoughts as they came to her.

They were working on their second cups of coffee when a man parked outside, took a long look at the saucer, then walked over to it. He walked around it slowly, touching it, rapping on it, then he came over to the diner.

"Flo," he called, "what in hell is that thing across the street?"

"That you, Oscar?"

"Yeah. What's that thing across the street?"

Flo walked out of the kitchen carrying three plates. As she set them on the table before Charley and Rip, she said, "That thing is a flying saucer, Oscar, you ignorant boob. These folks here flew it in from Mars." She put two plates in front of Rip, one in front of Charley, then winked at her.

Charley tried to grin. She folded up the paper place mat and stowed it in a flight suit pocket.

"Don't you know a flying saucer when you see one, Oscar?"

"That's my first one this week, woman. How about some coffee?"

Rip picked up his knife and fork and went to work as Flo and Oscar bantered back and forth and the TV played in the background.

He was working on the second glass of milk when a deputy sheriff parked his patrol car out front and came inside. Soon a man parked a medium-sized farm tractor alongside the deputy's car and joined him on a stool at the counter. Oscar told them about the sign for the St. Louis amusement park and everyone tried to think up something witty to say about saucers. Meanwhile a small crowd of half dozen people had gathered by the saucer. Some of the people were from vehicles sitting at the pumps, but the rest were from pickups that had parked on the side of the road.

The television went back to the California meteor story as Rip gobbled the last of his potatoes. Charley had finished five minutes earlier and was watching him with an amused expression on her face.

She started to get out of the booth. "I'll pay the bill while you finish," she said, to his obvious discomfiture.

"Please! I'll do it. I've got some money."

Charley was amused.

"Just doesn't look right, a woman paying," he muttered.

He stood up, strolled casually to the register. Flo came over after a bit. She was figuring the bill when a picture of the saucer in flight came on the television behind her. "Here's a curiosity," the announcer began. "This morning in Aswan, Egypt —"

Rip reached over and changed the channel on the television. A commercial came on. He smiled at Flo and handed her a fifty. "Sorry, this is the smallest I have."

"We're seeing more and more pictures of U.S. Grant these days, honey. I got change."

Down the counter the deputy was telling an off-color joke.

Rip took his change, then lingered until Flo went down the counter to pour coffee.

"That was close," Charley muttered. "Somebody on that lake boat must have had a camera."

"Let's mount up and start kicking, amigo."

They sauntered out the door and across the street, two people with no place to go and all day to get there.

Ten people were standing around the saucer now and three more were looking at it as they pumped gas into their vehicles. The kid who worked in the filling station was telling them all about it, apparently. "Here they come now," he said. He addressed Rip as he walked up. "Hey, buddy. Didn't you say this thing is going into an amusement park in St. Louis?"

"Yeah."

"Is that Six Flags?" a woman asked. She had a baby in her arms.

"Well, I don't know, ma'am. Fella didn't say."

"Sure looks real, don't it?"

"My dad saw a real saucer, one night, few years back," said another.

"Where was that, Butch?"

"Out at the farm. Darn thing was hovering over the cows. Got 'em all upset, so it did." The speaker continued, telling his rapt audience of the close encounter.

Charley walked once around the saucer, looking it over, then she went underneath and opened the hatch. As she climbed in, Rip said to the crowd: "You folks might want to move back a bit, give us a little room here." Then he ducked down, went through the hatch, and pulled it shut behind him.

Charley already had the reactor on.

Apparently the crowd heard the hum. They were stumbling backward now. Many were agape, too stunned to say anything. Rip waved at them through the canopy as Charley gently lifted the ship. The usual cloud of dirt and pebbles flew into the air.

She took the saucer up about ten feet and stabilized there as the landing gear retracted. The crowd below was scattering; several of the men were in full flight. The mother with the baby went onto her knees by the gas pumps, clutching the child fiercely. People poured out of the diner across the street. The deputy sheriff ran this way.

Rip waved at him as Charley eased the stick forward and pulled up on the collective. She soared over the cornfield by the diner and put the sun behind the saucer.

"Missouri?"

"Missouri."

"Wish we had some charts."

"I can recognize the rivers and stuff. I'll get us there."

"Hold on," Charley said and twisted on the throttle grip. The rocket motors hiccuped once, then lit with a pleasant roar.

"Yeah!" Rip shouted. The G's felt terrific.

Charley pulled the nose up and the saucer accelerated into the Indiana morning sky.

9

Like the million other Americans who happened to be watching television that August morning as they dressed or ate breakfast, General Bombing Joe De Laurio, U.S. Air Force chief of staff, stared in unbelieving amazement at the flying saucer zipping around on his television screen.

"Holy smokes," he muttered through his toothbrush, which was still in his mouth.

When the camera zoomed in on the fighter chasing the saucer, he dropped the toothbrush. The quality of the picture was poor as the amateur Egyptian cameraman tried to zoom in and focus on fast-moving machines, but one glimpse of the telltale puffs of white smoke zipping back over the fighter's wing was more than enough for Bombing Joe — the fighter was shooting at the saucer. The general grabbed for the telephone.

"White House!" he roared at the operator when she came on. "Get me the White House!"

The cameraman centered the saucer's

exhaust flame in his viewfinder and managed to keep it there as the saucer went almost straight up, accelerating. The saucer got smaller and smaller until all that was visible against the heavens was the spot of light that was the flame from the rocket nozzles. Then the flame merged with the sun.

"Oh, my God!" roared Bombing Joe De Laurio and rushed for the uniform hanging in his closet.

The general was charging through his outer office on the Pentagon's E-ring when a junior staffer arrested his progress.

"General, you must take a moment to look at the television! A little town in Indiana — people there claim that a flying saucer was there this morning!"

Bombing Joe rocked with the punch. When he saw that video from Egypt, he was convinced. Now they're in Indiana? Was this an invasion?

"How many saucers?" he demanded.

"One saucer, sir. Two crewmen. Aliens. They wore gray, one-piece flight suits, ate a prodigious quantity of food . . ."

Bombing Joe stood speechless, rooted to the floor. Nothing in his thirty-six years in the Air Force had prepared him for this moment. He was trapped in a fevered nightmare, some weird, drug-addled Hollywood epic.

He pinched the back of his left hand. Yep, he was awake.

"The aliens paid for their meal with U.S. dollars," the staffer said, pointing at a man talking to a reporter on the television screen.

"They *what?*"

"Yes, sir. U.S. dollars. A fifty-dollar bill that the owner of the diner says is counterfeit. Then they got in the saucer and flew it the hell out of there."

The light began to glow for Bombing Joe.

"Where is that UFO team that we sent to the Sahara?" he roared. "I want answers *right now* or I'm going to eat somebody's head for breakfast!"

Egg Cantrell came by his name honestly, Charley Pine concluded. His body, neck, and head formed a perfect ovoid shape, marred only by his short, stubby legs. He waddled when he walked and his fat jiggled. A permanent layer of perspiration was beaded on his upper lip and brow. Buried in his fleshy face were quick, intelligent eyes.

"How do, ma'am," he said and gave a short, nervous bow.

"Well, Unc, what do you think?" Rip stepped back and gestured expansively at the saucer.

Egg Cantrell quivered with joy as he regarded the saucer. He touched it, caressed it, fondled it, stroked it.

"Amazing," was all he could find to say.

Charley Pine grinned broadly and looked around the old army hangar with interest. She had slipped the saucer into the ramshackle wooden structure after Rip pushed the doors open. There was barely room for the saucer amid the junk that looked as if it were wearing the accumulated dust of centuries; old farm tractors, antique farming equipment, a Model A Ford, an Indian Chief motorcycle, and an Aeronca Champ were just some of the items in sight in this former Army Air Corps hangar, the only one still standing at what had once been a thriving World War II training base. Egg jackhammered the crumbling concrete on the runways years ago — now the runways were grass, perfect for little airplanes like Egg's Champ. Charley ran a hand along the Champ's prop as Rip told his uncle about the saucer.

When Rip had covered the high points, Egg remarked, "You two have been on television, I think."

"You mean Egypt? Yeah, that was us, getting water from the Nile to power this thing."

"I mean LA, St. Louis, Aswan, Egypt, and just now on CNN, some little burg in Indiana. They're going nuts in Indiana."

"Are they now?" Rip's face looked almost angelic.

"I hope to shout," said Egg Cantrell, his belly quivering. "They had a genuine flying saucer right there in Upshur, Indiana; dozens of folks saw it, three or four even got religion. One woman claims she served breakfast to two Martians in gray, one-piece flying suits. After they ate they paid with counterfeit money, left a three-dollar tip, strolled across the street like they were going to Wal-Mart, then blasted out of there like a bat outta hell."

"Did they now?"

"The diner woman said they ate more food than any human could. Six eggs apiece, giant slabs of ham, a quart of milk each. When she said that ten minutes ago on the TV, I do declare, Rip, I thought of you."

"I was mighty hungry, Uncle Egg."

"I know, boy. You come by it honest. I spent my life in that condition."

"Well, what do you think of the saucer?"

"Hell of a nice piece of machinery. God Almighty, it's nice. I just hope you and the lady here came by it legal."

"Unc, I told you how we got it. Cross my heart. It was a stroke of pure luck that I saw the gleam where the rock had weathered. Honest sweat dug it out of that rock."

"You think somebody'll be coming after it?"

"It's mighty valuable, all right."

"Somebody or something, I should have said. It's like something from a dream . . . or a nightmare."

"I don't figure whoever lost it originally will come back for it, but these days, who knows?"

"Never can tell," Egg agreed.

"No one around here knows it's here," Rip declared. "We kept low the last forty or fifty miles, below radar coverage, right above the treetops, kept the rockets off. It was sorta tough finding this place in the rain, what with the clouds and all. If anyone saw us I doubt if they could figure out where we were going."

"What do you say, young lady?" Egg asked.

"The Air Force will come looking before long. In a day or two, I think. Three at the most."

"Uh-huh. Are you going to call 'em, tell 'em where to look?"

"Not just now. To the best of my knowledge, Rip is the lawful owner of the saucer."

"Is he really, you think?" Egg asked shrewdly.

"I doubt it."

"So do I, ma'am," Egg said.

"Now see here, Uncle," Rip said hotly, "you're supposed to be on my side."

"I am, I am," Egg said. "I know you didn't do anything immoral — I just think you have a legal problem."

Rip set his feet and squared his shoulders. "Possession is nine-tenths of the law, I always heard. I've got it and I intend to hang on to it. Whoever hopes to take it away is going to have to prove better title than mine."

"Finders keepers, losers weepers," Egg said thoughtfully. After another sideways appraisal of Charley Pine, he added, "That'll have to do for now, I guess."

Egg pointed toward the hatch hanging open under the saucer. "Any way I can get up through that hole?"

"If you kinda suck yourself up, I reckon you can," Rip replied, grinning. "We got a little problem with the engines. They

188

hiccup from time to time. Was hoping you could look at that." With that Rip led the way under the saucer. Egg got down on his hands and knees to crawl after him.

"Uh, Mr. Cantrell. Mr. Egg. Before you go. Do you have someplace I could freshen up?"

"Why, I guess I'm forgetting my manners, Miss Pine. Go up to the house and help yourself. I'm a bachelor and the place is messy, but avail yourself of all the conveniences. Towels are in the closet."

"Thank you, sir."

The small house wasn't messy, of course. As Charley suspected, Egg Cantrell was a fastidious housekeeper. Everything had a place and everything was in it.

Charley Pine went straight to the bathroom and took a long, hot shower. With her flight suit in the washing machine, she retired to Egg's guest bedroom, a cozy nook with a television. On the walls were frames containing flint arrowheads, dozens of them, perhaps a hundred. Each arrowhead was neatly labeled.

Rain from a turbulent gray sky spattered on the windowpane. She got under the covers and surfed television channels.

On CNN she found what she was

looking for. Yes, the network was showing the video from Egypt one more time. Then there were more interviews with the citizens of Upshur, Indiana. Charley looked at her watch. Lord, she and Rip had blasted out of there just two and a half hours ago and already the place was famous.

She sat in bed watching the citizens express their wonder and awe at the abilities of the saucer. Ordinary people who had seen an extraordinary thing. The adventure seemed to affect each of them in a slightly different way; some were thoughtful, others exuberant, some frightened, some angry or resentful.

One, the lady at the diner, Flo, was thankful:

"Of all the places on God's green earth they could have lit, they picked this one. I always thought Upshur was special, and now I know. I am so happy this happened."

"Why?" the interviewer asked.

"That flying saucer gave us something besides ourselves to think about, reminded us that there's more to life than our little bean row."

Charley flipped channels, found some government type explaining that flying saucers were figments of people's imaginations. "There is no scientific proof whatsoever that flying saucers exist," the scientist on television argued. "The Air Force has been investigating sightings for fifty years and has come up with exactly nothing."

"They found what they were ordered to find, buster," Charley Pine growled and flipped the channel again.

More talking heads, offering opinions about what this "rash" of saucer sightings might mean. One woman was plainly nervous. "Aliens" might already be here, she explained.

Another scoffed, insisted that what was being reported were top-secret Air Force test vehicles. "The government never tells us the truth," she said. "*They* know and won't tell."

Charley flipped off the television finally and laid her head back on the pillow. She was tired but not yet sleepy.

What had she gotten herself into? Would the Air Force demand that Lockheed Martin fire her? For flying the saucer? For not calling to tell them where she was? Would the publicity ultimately make it impossible for her to get a test-flying job anywhere?

She thought about Rip, who was down at the hangar with his Uncle Egg, two boys playing with a new and exotic toy. Rip hadn't a clue about the extent of the stir the saucer had caused . . . would cause.

Perhaps Rip was taking all this the right way. He didn't really care what other people thought. He didn't care about the talking heads on television or their carefully crafted opinions. Nor did he care a fig about the Air Force.

How did Australians get involved?

Maybe she should take a tip from Rip, ignore all of this.

She unfolded the diner place mat and read her notes. The saucer flew very, very well across an amazing variety of flight regimes. That had been no accident, she well knew. The designers of that ship knew precisely what they were doing.

Staring at the notes, Charley Pine could once again feel the ship in her hands, feel the rudder pedals under her feet, feel the power of the rocket engines. She looked out the window with blind eyes, thinking about how it had been. With a blanket wrapped around her, she went looking for paper. In Egg's little office she found a notebook.

Back in bed she wrote quickly, with a sense of deep purpose, trying to capture all of it. Never in her life would she get another chance to fly such a unique machine.

No two ways about that!

Finally her eyelids became heavy. She lay back on the pillow and slept.

"Oh, wow, Rip! This thing is something else!" Egg Cantrell marveled at the extraordinary engineering manifest in the saucer, the way things fit together, the tidy, neat solutions to problems.

Egg was wedged into the engineering spaces. When they had first come aboard, Rip had pulled the power knob out to the first notch, firing off the reactor. Amid the computer displays and cabin lights, Egg stood in awe. Rip secured the reactor before the men entered the engineering compartment.

Now, wedged between machines, Egg tapped on the walls, looked at each component, examining everything with his flashlight. He did so with a sense of curiosity and wonder.

"You say you put some muddy water in this thing?" Egg asked after a bit.

"Yeah. It was all we had."

"Gotta be mud in this separator. Gotta be. Go get my little toolbox on my workbench, please."

Rip did as requested.

Egg soon found that the wrenches didn't

quite fit. Neither metric nor American wrenches worked. Worried that he might ruin a nut or two, he had to use adjustable wrenches and pliers.

"It's good to see you again, Rip. Missed you this summer."

"Yeah," said Rip. "This old farm . . ." Rip had been spending his summers with his Uncle Egg since he was twelve. Ever since his father died. "The desert was a new adventure," he told his uncle now as a partial apology.

"A man needs new adventures," Egg admitted as he worked on the separator. "Yes he does. Expands his horizons, lets him learn new things. I still missed you."

Rip didn't reply, and Egg didn't expect him to. He knew Rip pretty well.

"What's the story on the woman?"

"No story. She was the test pilot the Air Force UFO team brought to the desert to look at this thing. She's a civilian, got off active duty two weeks ago. She crawled into the saucer when I was getting ready to fly outta there. People were shooting; I couldn't leave her."

"Lucky for you she happened by."

"I could fly this thing, Uncle Egg. Honest."

"Be sorta messy if you happened to be wrong."

"Flying's an instinct thing."

"We have birds in our family tree?"

"I flew your Aeronca. Remember? You taught me how to fly. This saucer is sorta like the Aeronca, I think. Course it's a little faster and has some other complications, but I could figure it out. It'd come to me."

Egg changed the subject. "When I got out of bed this morning I never expected anything like this. A flying saucer! What a day this is! And the gal is something else. Everyone needs a nephew like you, Rip, who just might drop by. Every morning for a lot of years I'll wonder if you're coming by today."

"Well, owning this saucer, I just might."

A warm glow suffused Rip as he contemplated the prospect of flying around the country in his own saucer, able to go when and where he chose, anywhere he chose . . . He rubbed the metal of the bulkhead beside him.

When he realized Egg was looking at him, Rip grinned.

"Come any time," Egg said. "And bring the woman. I like her."

Rip flipped a hand. "Charley will be gone soon. She isn't a girlfriend or anything like that, Egg."

Egg got back to the separator. "She sure

looks healthy," he said. "Brainy, cute . . ."

"She's pushing thirty. She's too old for me."

"She's not too old; you're too young."

"Yeah. I really missed you this summer, Egg. All the romantic advice and opinions and trips to town for pizza."

"How's your mom?"

"Oh, so-so, I guess. Haven't had a letter in a while. Maybe I ought to call her while I'm here."

"Maybe you should."

Egg finished taking the separator apart. He had a knack for things mechanical.

There was mud in the separator all right. "There should be a plastic bag and some paper towels on the workbench."

When they had the separator as clean as they could get it, Egg muttered, "Didn't anybody on this planet make this thing."

"You sure about that?"

"Yeah. I've never seen anything like it, and I keep up with all the latest. This thing is built with technology that's so damn up-to-date it hasn't been invented yet."

"Who built the saucer, Egg?"

"People! Obviously. Take a look. This thing is sized for people our size, maybe a few inches smaller. Look at this twist grip I'm holding." Rip eased into position to see. "See this? It's designed to be twisted with a human hand. I'd bet money on it."

"Tell you what, Egg. You get that separator back together and let me turn on the garden hose, fill this thing with water. We may have to get out of here in a hurry, if Charley is right."

"I sorta think she is, Rip-boy. This is some piece of machinery — the Air Force is gonna be looking hard for it."

"It's mine, Egg. Not theirs."

"You told me that before. Go hook up the hose and turn on the water."

When Rip got back, Egg was examining the computer that the Australian mechanic had partially disassembled. "You didn't do this, did you?" Egg grunted.

"Heck no."

Egg looked it over. After a few seconds, he whipped out a magnifying glass. "I think I can get it back together," he said after a bit. "The fool was trying to get to the chip, but he didn't know what it looked like. This whole case is the chip." He picked up the three pieces that formed the case. They were dangling, held only by some wires.

"That's the chip?"

"Yeah. Probably has billions and billions of transistors. If they are transistors, which

I doubt." Egg scrutinized the inside surface of the case with the glass.

"Are they even talking about stuff like this at your school?" Egg wanted to know.

"Uh-huh."

Egg cradled the three pieces with both hands. "What's the rule? The number of transistors industry can cram on a chip doubles every eighteen months?"

"That's it," Rip affirmed.

"If we knew how many transistorlike things are in this case, we could calculate how far ahead of us technically these creatures are."

"Of course," Rip said, "the function may cease to be straightline after a while."

"See this screen. It's a quarter inch thick and flexible." The screen was also hanging by a wire. Egg twisted it in his hands, pulled it and kneaded it. "Unbelievable."

He laid the screen aside and began examining parts. Soon he laughed. "Look at this headband. This must be the keyboard."

"Naw," Rip said, hunting through the parts for something he might recognize.

"Yes. My glory, this has gotta be *it!* This *must* be the way you talk to the computer."

The headband was a collection of very fine wires, thousands of them, fashioned into a complete loop. The wires seemed to be held together with some flexible material, plastic perhaps.

It took Egg only about five minutes to reassemble the computer. "Turn on the power."

Rip pulled out the master power knob to the first detent, which fired off the reactor. Then he passed Egg the headband. Egg carefully placed it over his head.

"This isn't the smartest thing you ever did, Unc."

"We're engaged in a scientific inquiry. If I freak out, get this thing off me."

"What if — ?"

But Egg had already closed his eyes. He sat impassively.

Rip waited.

He could hear the water running into the fuel tank. The water was from a well, and the hose delivered only three or four gallons a minute, so it was going to take a while.

Now Egg was grinning. Widely. His eyes were open, his hands moving, reaching . . . Now they were still.

A variety of emotions registered on Egg's face: amazement, happiness, joy.

What was in that computer?

Rip moved his hand back and forth in front of Egg's face. His open eyes didn't track or blink.

199

Egg's breathing seemed okay. Rip sat watching Egg and listening to the running water and the silence. The silence was exquisite. Rain was pounding on the hangar's tin roof, but the interior of the saucer was quiet as a tomb.

If Professor Soldi was correct, the interior of the saucer had known no sound for a hundred and forty thousand years. God, that was a long, long time! Man became man, the African diaspora spread man all over the planet, the ice sheets came and went, people walked across the land bridge to America, the pyramids rose, Moses led his people from Egypt, Greece flourished, then Rome . . . The entire human story happened while this machine sat, just like this, silent under the sand.

Rip shivered.

Egg's eyes came open. He took off the headband. His grin got wider and wider. "Yes, yes, yes! This is the cat's nuts, man. Oh, Rip, it's *fantastic!*"

"What is?"

Egg offered the headband. "Put it on. Follow the picture of the saucer. It's the maintenance manual for this ship . . . some sort of three-dimensional holograph. You can see everything: how the ship works, how each component functions, how to take it apart, how to repair it. It's so real you'll want to reach out and touch. I never in my life saw anything like it."

He leaped from the seat and tossed the headband onto it. In seconds he was on his knees working on the compartment's forward bulkhead. A panel opened. Egg reached in and withdrew a package encased in a soft material. He held it out toward Rip.

"Look at this! It's a tool kit. Take a look! It's the tools to fix the machinery on this ship. And here are some more headbands — you wear one to access the computers."

Rip placed the headband on his head. It was a tad small, but there was some give to it, so it was not uncomfortable.

The saucer was one of three objects before him. He approached them, looking . . . They were *real!*

He jerked the headband off.

Egg broke into laughter. "I told you! I told you!" He bent down, his face inches from his nephew. "Try it again, Rip."

Rip went toward the saucer, merely desired to go closer, and it moved toward him or he toward it — it was hard to say which. The saucer was whole, yet it wasn't. From several feet away the ship was transparent, allowing him to see every piece, every fastener, wire, valve, pipe, etc. And it was *real*, a three dimensional object with perspective and shadows and a tangible reality. Like Egg, he tried to touch.

The reactor, the water cracker, the antigravity system . . . Rip leaned closer to examine a computer. The closer he looked, the more he could see. He dove deeper and deeper into the chip in the main computer in front of the pilot, deeper and deeper until he could see the microscopic circuits.

When Rip Cantrell finally took off the headset, he was drained. It took him several seconds to reestablish where he was, whom he was with.

His Uncle Egg was sitting across from him, a smile playing over his lips. "Amazing, eh?"

"Oh, Egg, I never dreamed . . ."

"Now you know how the Indians felt when they went aboard Columbus's ship."

Rip sat stunned, replaying the experience in his mind.

"One thing," Egg mused. "One thing we know: Humans built this saucer."

"But . . . We — I and the two men I work with — dug it out of sandstone, Egg. I breathed the dirt and dust and dug it out with these two hands. There's no way that was fake rock. That stone had been there for one hundred and forty thousand years, the archaeologist said."

"This computer, the headband . . ." Egg pointed. "That machine reads *our* thoughts, tells us what *we* want to know. The machine is designed to communicate with *our* brains. With *human* brains. I can't explain it, but there it is."

The president and his advisers were serious men (and one serious woman), engaged every day in the serious business of politics, i.e., dividing the pie in such a way as to create maximum advantage for themselves. They didn't smile much; on those rare occasions when they did it was at an enemy's discomfiture. They had a goodly number of enemies. Friends were blindly and intensely loyal to the president and his administration, enemies were everyone else. The great saucer scare left these serious people at a loss over what to do. Nothing in their experience quite fit this situation.

The saucer hullabaloo was perfect for television, a made-to-order media event that glued an extraordinary percentage of the populace to the tube, where they could be sold everything from automobiles to Zantac, brokerage services to suppositories. One of the things television wanted were ten-second sound bites from the serious people. Television reporters and camera crews lay in wait anywhere that an ambush of a serious person was even a remote possibility.

Yet even if the serious people were uncooperative, the insatiable appetite of the medium had to be filled somehow. Enterprising producers sent their minions after the God squad.

"How dare the networks air this trash," one prominent divine raved on camera. "This talk of flying saucers and aliens is all right for the movies, but it has no place in serious conversation."

The president's advisers nodded in sympathy. What could they say on camera? In television everything is on the record. The camera captures every moment, good or bad. If, as seemed probable, the saucer scare turned out to be some kind of hoax, the serious ones would be covered in ignominy if they treated it seriously now. On the other hand, if buried under all this sensationalism was a real flying saucer filled with real aliens, the serious ones had to be out there in the arena ready to fight or shake hands. At least, they had to appear to be ready.

"How did we get into this fix?" the president's chief of staff, P. J. O'Reilly, demanded of Bombing Joe De Laurio. The serious people were very unhappy with the Air Force and Bombing Joe, whom they suspected was somehow responsible for this unholy mess.

Bombing Joe glowered at O'Reilly, who would blame the weatherman for a thunderstorm.

"This whole thing is very troubling," the president said. "I don't know what our options are."

"Mr. President," Bombing Joe began, "the CIA tells me that Qaddafi may have our UFO team in custody, and —"

"Don't try to blame this on Qaddafi," O'Reilly snarled, interrupting.

"I was trying to say that —"

"I know high-tech when I see it. That thing" — O'Reilly pointed at the video from Egypt — "sure as hell looks high-tech to me."

"Who knows what it is?" Bombing Joe sneered. "You ought to go to the movies more often. It's absolutely amazing what the special effects crowd can do with computers these days."

The national security adviser picked up a wad of computer printouts of wire service stories on the St. Louis boom and the

Indiana appearance and fluttered them. "Twenty-seven sane people in Indiana swore they saw a flying saucer in broad daylight from a range of less than a hundred yards. Four of those twenty-seven swore they touched it! Special effects?"

Bombing Joe tried earnestly to explain: "I'm telling you that nothing in anybody's inventory looks like that thing on television or flies like that. Sure, we have some black projects, but they are airplanes, for God's sake. You know that! I resent the implication that the Air Force has developed some magic machine without the knowledge of the government."

"What if it's really a flying saucer?" the president asked. The president was a politician because he enjoyed being in front of a crowd. He wanted to be liked, yet he hated making decisions. "From somewhere *out there?* Do you realize the implications? Technically advanced beings from another world? Would I have to meet them in the Rose Garden, surrender the nation?"

Just then Dr. Jim Bob Cantwell, the famous evangelist, appeared on CNN. "The events we are witnessing today herald the coming of the Antichrist," he intoned.

Furious, P. J. O'Reilly grabbed the television remote control and shut off Cantwell. "Cantwell is a fool," he growled.

Another serious person pointed out, "A sizable percentage of the voters are church-goers. They are worried about the implications of this saucer mania on their faith."

"I don't do religion," the president said firmly. "Other than a few platitudes on holidays —"

Bombing Joe excused himself and walked from the room, looking for a telephone. He should have retired years ago and got seriously into golf; he knew that now.

10

It was early evening when Rip and Egg Cantrell climbed the gentle grade to the small house nestled in the trees. Charley Pine was wearing her gray flight suit, now clean, and pacing back and forth in front of the television.

Both the men looked tired, she thought. "The water cracker was full of mud," Rip told her. "Egg cleaned it out. We're ready to go."

"Go where?"

"I don't know," Rip said crossly. "Somewhere that the Air Force and Qaddafi and those Aussie nuts can't find us." The injustice of the pursuit bothered him. The saucer was *his*.

Charley gestured toward the television. "Sit down, you two. Watch some of this. It's a media meltdown. Every channel has flying saucers continuously or is offering instant updates for breaking news."

They sat. CNN was running the video of the saucer lifting off from the shore of Lake Nasser one more time. "This has been on every channel on earth ten dozen times today," Charley explained. "The only saving grace is that the tape starts with the saucer lifting off, not with Rip and me pouring water into it or climbing aboard."

"Humpf."

"The West Coast . . . St Louis . . . Upshur, Indiana . . . the press has done it up brown. They've interviewed everyone who might have a pebble to contribute. Just for balance, they've also interviewed every UFO nutcase in the country who is willing to say something outrageous."

She flipped through the channels to give them a taste of it.

Five minutes was enough. "Turn it off," Rip said. "Let's go get something to eat. I'm starved."

As Charley reached for the clicker, the talking head mentioned Clarksville, Missouri. Egg held up his hand. "Wait," he said. "Clarksville is just east of here."

A farmer appeared. "I saw a saucer this morning, so I did," he announced solemnly. "Right over the treetops, flying along quiet as a prayer. Round it was, sorta dark, black-like in the mist and rain, sinister as all get-out. I was on the tractor, going down to plow the winter-wheat field, when it caught my eye . . .

"Wouldn't be talking about it now, you understand, but I called my minister. He said it was my Christian duty to tell what I know so the government can take steps, do what has to be done to protect us from *them*."

"Them?" Egg asked.

"Them," Charley said firmly and turned off the television. "The hunters are close, Rip. Just a few miles from here. They'll be here soon."

Egg swiveled to examine her face. "The government is looking for the saucer?"

"Absolutely. Satellites photographed the saucer in the Sahara. My UFO team was sent to investigate." She wasn't about to mention the hypersonic reconnaissance plane, the very existence of which was a top secret. "The other members of the team were there when Rip and I flew it out. As soon as the U.S. government knows who we are, they'll find out where our parents live, where we grew up. They'll look for us by talking to all those people, checking every place we might be."

"You're speculating," Rip said, his face ominous.

"Bet on it, Rip," Egg replied, not in the mood for argument. "Go on, Ms. Pine. Tell us all of it."

"The only reason the FBI isn't knocking on your door right now is that the Libyans probably are holding Rip's colleagues and mine — and the Aussies — incommunicado. As soon as the Air Force learns our identities from the UFO team, the FBI will be called in to find us."

"The FBI will try to hold on to the information," Egg mused. "They won't want to get trampled by reporters."

"It'll get out anyway," Rip said, rubbing his chin.

"Of course it will," Charley said. "Someone will leak it or one of our relatives will talk to a friend, who will talk to a reporter or talk to someone who will. This is too hot. The press will find out. The FBI will be trying to stay a jump ahead."

"How long do we have?" Rip asked.

"However long the Libyans give us. As soon as they release our crowd, all of them will dive for a phone. I think we'll know when it happens because Professor Soldi has to get on television as fast as he can. If he doesn't get the story out, the Air Force will scarf the saucer when they find it, and neither he nor you nor anyone else will ever see it again. It'll go straight to Area Fifty-one; no one in government will ever admit that it exists. Soldi's no fool. He knows what is at stake."

"It sounds as if you have a little time," Egg said to Rip.

"Uncle Egg," said Charley Pine, "people are out there looking this very minute. Space Command tracked the saucer as it came into the atmosphere. The Air Force will assume the object they saw on radar was the saucer or a meteor. They will use every law enforcement resource available to find where the thing came down: state police, county mounties, National Guard, everybody. Those people are out there right now beating the bushes, looking for little green men. Some of that has been on television. There's an element of public hysteria in all this that television and government are both pandering to. The politicians get on camera and ask that everyone remain calm. It's ludicrous."

"So just what is at stake, Ms. Pine?" Egg asked.

"You've seen the saucer," Charley Pine shot back. "You tell me."

"I can cook here or we can go to town," Egg told his guests. "Town is twenty miles down the road."

"I vote for town," Rip said. "I've been three months in the desert. I want a decent meal, and Charley and I need to buy some clothes."

"Are you insulting my cooking?" Egg asked hotly, which made Rip laugh.

"Can Air Traffic Control see the saucer on their radar?" Rip asked Charley as they rode down the two-lane asphalt in Egg's pickup.

"Only if they are looking for it. Their radars are set up to receive coded signals from aircraft transponders, not pick up skin paints."

"Wouldn't the saucer's shape be hard to see?"

"The shape of the top and bottom would give it some stealth characteristics," she said after a moment's thought, "but the curved leading edge will glint, make a return on a screen, if there is a radar close enough and properly tuned to pick it up."

"So what are our chances of, say, flying to Denver tonight, making an appearance with the saucer, then sneaking back here?"

"Are you serious?" she asked.

"If we can make these people look in Colorado, we've got another day or two we can stay with Egg."

"Why do you want to stay here?"

"Speaking just for myself," Rip replied, "I'd like a decent night's sleep and a couple of good meals. And we need to do some figuring about what happens next."

"What does happen next?"

"Every day you hang out with me is another day deeper in trouble for you. Have you thought about it?"

"Yes," Charley Pine admitted.

"And?"

"My troubles are mine. I'll handle them."

Rip Cantrell shrugged. "Okay, lady. You being an older woman and all, I guess I have to live with that. But back to my question, can we sneak the saucer out of here without blowing the eardrums out of every hick within fifty miles?"

"Let's talk a bit more about Denver. The television people are talking about an invasion of *saucers*. Plural. They've got the American public looking for a swarm of saucers, an aerial armada."

"The more saucers they think there are, the less chance they have of finding just one."

"Denver?"

"Denver."

"If we left after dark," Charley mused, "rode the antigravity rings for a while before we lit the rockets . . ."

"If we used the rockets sparingly to get to

altitude, maybe the ship would sound like a low-flying jet," Rip suggested hopefully.

"It might work," Charley mused. "Or it might not."

"Maybe the best thing to do is leave it right where it is," Egg said.

A state police car passed the pickup going the other way. All three of them watched the car go by.

"So what *are* you going to do with the saucer, Rip?" Egg asked when the police car was out of sight.

"I don't know, Unc." Rip's voice reflected his misery. "Honest, I don't know what the right thing is. Giving it to the Air Force doesn't have much appeal."

"Ms. Pine, what do you think?" Egg asked, his eyes on the road.

"Rip has to make a decision he can live with," Charley replied.

"That's a cop-out," Rip said and sighed. "Maybe you ought to steal the damned thing and fly it to Area Fifty-one."

"Maybe I should," Charley said lightly.

"What is this?" Rip asked the waitress at the cafe.

The woman looked at him as if he were stupid. "It's what you ordered: banana cream pie."

"I didn't want a piece. I wanted the whole pie."

She stared at him for a moment. Then her eyes narrowed. "I remember you. You were here last summer."

"That's right. Would you bring the rest of the pie, please?"

The waitress looked at Charley and Egg with suspicion, then marched for the kitchen. In a moment she returned. The heads of the rest of the kitchen staff were visible behind her, peeking through the door. She put the pie in front of Rip with a flourish. "Enjoy," she ordered and marched away.

As Rip ate, Egg asked, "Why do you want to go to Denver tonight, Rip?"

"You want a ride, don't you?"

"Well, yeah. Who wouldn't? But I don't want to get you guys in trouble giving me one."

"No trouble," Rip said between bites.

"What do you think, Ms. Pine?" Egg asked.

"Someone is liable to see us coming or going from your place."

Rip nodded. "Life's a risk."

"Being around you, it certainly is."

"Hey! I don't know how this saucer adventure is going to turn out. While we have it, let's enjoy it. Let's take Egg for a ride. Twenty years from now he and I can sit in front of his hangar talking about how great it was."

"Makes sense to me," Egg said.

"Try this tonight," Rip said, handing Charley a headband. He had already plugged it into the computer, which presented the main display in front of the pilot. The reactor was on, so the ship had power. "Egg figured out the computers this afternoon. Put it on, try it out before we light out of here."

"You've done this yourself?" Charley asked, checking the expression on his face. She was sitting in the pilot's seat of the saucer with the reactor on, waiting for things to warm up. Egg was standing on her left and Rip on her right.

"Oh, yeah," Rip assured her. "Nothin' to it."

She looked at Egg. "Why the headband?"

"Near as we can determine," Egg explained, "the computer uses the headband to determine what you want to know, then gives you that information. You will have a few choices to make — just move toward the icon or selection you want."

"Will I still be able to fly?"

"We think so," Egg replied, nodding thoughtfully.

"Are you suicidal?"

"Only on Mondays. That's the short answer. The long answer is, the computer that the Aussie's disassembled allows you to see things — you step into the computer's world. When I tried the primary flight computer this afternoon, it seemed to give the pilot displays on the screen and project graphics on the canopy glass. In other words, the pilot stays — how do I say it? — here. The pilot stays here."

She looked at Rip. "You and your uncle spent the afternoon on a psychedelic computer trip?"

"Not the whole afternoon," Rip protested. "And it was pretty cool."

Charley pulled on the headband and arranged her hair around it. She jerked rigidly as the computer screen came alive.

"Takes a little getting used to," Rip added, but Charley Pine gave no indication that she had heard. Her gaze went around the cockpit, taking in everything. Once she reached out and touched the gear lever, which was of course in the down position.

"Can you hear me?" Rip asked loudly.

"Yes," she said finally, after several seconds, then held up her hand for silence so that she could concentrate.

Graphics flashed on the computer screen in the middle of the instrument panel, so quickly they were difficult to follow. It comes and goes as quickly as she thinks, Rip thought. He was watching the screen displays with only a passing interest when the realization struck him that he was looking into Charley's mind. He was watching her think.

A map appeared on the pilot's main display and, instantly, at the speed of thought, resolved itself into the farm, trees, woodlots, the nearby rivers, with a pathway leading away. He could see everything in three dimensions, so clearly that he was tempted to try to reach out and touch. The pathway was long and narrow, ribbonlike, resting almost on the treetops. It ran for several hundred miles southwest, almost into Kansas, before it curled up away from the earth, high into the atmosphere.

Now Charley lifted the collective with her left hand, fed in gentle forward stick with her right. The saucer rose a few feet above the ground and drifted forward out of the hangar.

"You want me to close the door or —" Rip began, but the saucer didn't stop. She was following that thin pathway up to the treetops and then with the contours of the land southwestward. The rocket engines remained silent. That, Rip reflected, had been the plan. Get well away from the farm before using the rockets, which could be heard for miles. The rain and clouds of this warm front should prevent most people from actually seeing the saucer.

Rip looked at Egg. "Maybe we oughta sit down and strap in," Rip said as the saucer accelerated to perhaps a hundred knots using only the antigravity rings.

When he was strapped in, Rip looked up at Charley. She had her hands in her lap and was intently watching the computer screen. The saucer dipped and danced as it followed the contours of the land.

She must have figured out the autopilot, Rip thought, then realized that the computer *was* the autopilot.

A light spot remained on the bulkhead where he and Egg had removed the maintenance computer. The faint outline of it was just visible if you knew what you were looking for. He hadn't told Charley about that machine, and he felt vaguely guilty now. The truth of the matter was that he didn't trust her completely. She was Air Force, she might leave him stranded God knows where, she might steal the saucer . . .

Man, she could fly this thing; you had to admit that.

She could fly like a bird. Or an angel.

Rip was half asleep an hour later when he felt the rocket engines ignite. The G pressed gently at him, perhaps a quarter G of acceleration. Charley must be following that pathway into the sky. Egg was standing up there beside her, taking it all in.

Rip smiled and fell asleep listening to the moan of the rockets.

"Rip, wake up!"

Charley was calling his name, over and over. He unfastened his seat belt and pulled himself up by her chair.

She had the engines running at a low-power setting. The saucer seemed to be in level flight.

"We're about twenty-five miles high, I think," she said and pointed behind them.

Rip looked. He could see something. Red and white lights very close together, coming closer. At this altitude? It couldn't be a plane. Or could it?

"What is it?"

"A hypersonic aircraft. Air Force."

"A what?"

221

"A hypersonic spy plane. It's the replacement for the SR-71. Cruises at Mach five at these altitudes."

The spy plane was closing quickly.

"Does he see us on radar?" Egg asked. He too was hanging onto the pilot's seat, looking aft.

"He must," Charley said. "Hang on." She heeled the ship over in a turn, began pulling back stick, added a bit of juice to the rocket motors. The G shoved all of them toward the floor. Egg grabbed onto the pilot's seat and held on with all his strength.

The hypersonic aircraft tried to turn with the saucer but couldn't.

"How fast are we going?" Egg asked plaintively.

"About Mach five."

"I never even heard of a hypersonic airplane," Rip told her.

"It's highly classified."

"So now you've got to kill us?"

"Don't tempt me, Rip." Charley tightened the turn and twisted the throttle to the stop. The saucer leaped forward, the G increasing ferociously. Egg lost his grip and tumbled aft.

In seconds the lights of the spy plane faded behind them. After a minute or two

Charley killed the rocket motors and let the nose drop toward thicker air.

The lower atmosphere was clear and the bright moon seemed to wash out the stars. All of Denver and the front range of the Rockies were spread beneath them as the saucer came thundering down from altitude. The visibility was unlimited, in excess of a hundred miles, so the lights of Colorado Springs, Denver, Boulder, Loveland, even Fort Collins, glittered in the darkness like jewels. The peaks of the Rockies formed a jagged backdrop to the scene. Some of the peaks still sported a bit of snow, which appeared luminescent in the moon's dim light.

"We're about fifty miles out," Charley murmured. "I'll have to make some turns to bleed off some of this airspeed."

Uncle Egg muttered something that Rip didn't catch. He had managed to get his bulk erect and now was holding on tightly.

"What was that spy plane doing up there, anyway?" Rip asked Charley.

"Looking for us."

"Well, now he's got something to tell the folks at Area Fifty-one, huh."

"Yep."

"Anything else you want to tell me about?" Rip demanded.

"What are you talking about?"

"I'm talking about spy planes looking for us, spy planes that you seem to know all about."

"Oh, shut up," Charley said.

"So what are we? Criminals?"

"They think so. Of course they are looking. They want this saucer."

Rip wanted to enjoy this moment, not think about the future. Charley kept pushing the outside world at him, and he resented it.

"So what do you want to do, Rip?" Charley asked, nodding toward the city dead ahead. It was then that Rip realized that the saucer was on autopilot: Charley had her hands near the controls, not on them.

"I dunno exactly. Get down low, get ourselves seen, then boogie. What do you think?"

"As long as we stay away from the airport, I don't care."

"Let's not cause any heart attacks," Egg admonished.

"Oh, we won't," Rip assured him. "No one will feel threatened. This is just good clean fun."

"Is that all the saucer is to you, Rip?" Charley Pine asked. "Good clean fun?"

"It's not like we're married or something, Charley. I'm not even sure I like you that much."

"Just asked," Charley said, never taking her eyes off the scene before her. The pathway on the computer screen was a ribbon stretching forward and downward, leading her in.

The Los Angeles Dodgers and the Colorado Rockies were tied, 2–2, in the bottom of the eleventh inning at Coors Field on that pleasant August evening. Roughly thirty thousand people remained in the stands watching a Coors Field rarity, a pitching duel.

Wally Greenberg was in the upper deck behind third base with his wife and two teenage sons. The boys were tired and bored and whispering dirty comments to each other about a voluptuous girl three rows down and ten seats left. His wife had been ready to leave for three innings, but Wally wanted to see the "whole game." He didn't get to come see the Rockies very often — the family couldn't afford it — and he wanted his money's worth. He cuffed the boys, growled at them, and tried to ignore his wife's resigned torpor.

For some reason he looked away from

the batter toward the scoreboard behind center field. That was when he saw the saucer, a lenticular shape just a bit lighter than the dark beyond the bank of field lights. It was above the lights, moving slowly into view.

At first he thought it was a balloon, some kind of promotion. Probably the Elway dealerships, which were advertising heavily.

Then Wally realized the moving shape wasn't a balloon.

"Look!" He pointed.

His wife gasped.

"Oh, wow!" The comment escaped his eldest son, who normally was too cool to show pleasure or enthusiasm for anything.

The people sitting behind Wally inhaled so sharply he could hear it.

"It's a saucer!"

"A flying saucer!"

People were standing now, pointing. All over the stadium, people were rising to their feet.

A vast, awed silence fell upon the frozen crowd as the saucer dropped lower and lower toward the center of the field.

A worried Elmer Disquette was on the mound for the Dodgers. He was in his fourth inning of work and was starting through the Rockies' lineup the second time. The catcher had just asked for a curve to this right-handed batter, Disquette's bread-and-butter pitch, in fact, the pitch he had to throw to get people out. His fastball he used merely to set up the curve. He didn't have a decent change-up or slider, a fact he had brooded over for years. Staying too long on the mound was Russian roulette for short-relief men with limited repertoires, as Elmer Disquette well knew.

He glanced at his dugout — all the guys were on their feet — as he went into his windup.

The batter was coiled.

Elmer knew the pitch wouldn't break when he released it, just a millisecond too early.

Ramon Martinez was the batter, and he swung with everything he had. Just up from the AAA farm club, Colorado Springs, Martinez was playing in his third major league game. He had yet to get a hit. If he didn't start getting some hits, he was going to be riding a bus back to the Springs in the very near future. That bus ride was in his mind when he felt the shock of the bat connecting with the ball.

The ball went off the bat climbing. Ramon's heart sank. Another pop fly to center.

He got started toward first as he followed the flight of the ball. It went up, up, up, right under that big black saucer shape . . .

Saucer?

And the ball kept going, going, going . . .

Unbeknownst to Ramon, or anyone else in Coors Field, the ball entered the antigravity field under the saucer and got a free ride for about a hundred feet, just enough. The Dodger center fielder wasn't even trying to catch the ball. He was standing dead in his tracks staring at the saucer. The baseball went over his head and cleared the fence in straightaway dead center by ten feet.

Ramon Martinez leaped straight up at least three feet, his heart filled with joy. He jabbed both fists aloft, then jumped with both feet on first base. After he spiked the bag good and proper, Ramon set off for second, so overwhelmed by the moment that the absence of crowd reaction didn't even register.

While Ramon was bounding around the bases, the crowd was watching the saucer, which was dropping lower and lower toward second base.

As the ship neared the earth, dirt began flying around. The dirt was lifted from the area around second by the saucer's antigravity field and swirled by the gentle breeze blowing in from left.

The cloud of dirt got Ramon's attention. Like everyone else in the stadium, he too looked up. When he got to second he was feeling light on his feet, as if his contact with the earth were being severed. He dropped to his knees and clutched the bag with both hands.

"We better get going before anyone panics," Rip said to Charley. He was eyeing the people near the exits. They were still frozen in place, their mouths hanging open, but that wouldn't last. The urge to flee would strike soon.

"Okay," Charley said softly and eased back the collective while she turned the saucer with stick and rudder.

When the ship was pointing toward the scoreboard in center, she eased the stick forward. As the ship began accelerating, she twisted the throttle grip. The rockets rumbled into life as the saucer shot over the scoreboard.

With Coors Field safely behind her, Charley Pine came on hard with the rockets and pulled the nose up sharply. The G pushed her back hard into her seat.

The thunder washed over Wally Greenberg like an ocean wave. It engulfed him and overwhelmed his senses as the fireball of the saucer's rocket engines rose and rose and rose into the heavens.

When he finally looked around, the boys' faces were shining. "Did you see *that?*" one roared.

"Awesome! Totally cool!"

Wally Greenberg stretched both arms above his head and shouted to the heavens. "Yesssss!"

Ramon Martinez walked to third base, then home. He kept his head down, concentrated on the placement of each foot. As he walked he crossed himself again and again, endlessly.

A thing like that — a man has to think on it, get it into proper perspective.

Elmer Disquette stood on the mound rubbing his face. He took off his glove and rubbed his face some more and spit in the dirt.

The catcher wandered out.

"Tough break, man."

Elmer snorted. "What in hell was that, anyway?"

"Hey, I don't know, man. It didn't land and that's something."

"I didn't even think of that."

"A bunch of aliens running around the diamond . . ." the catcher mused as he watched the crowd stampede for the exits. "I don't think I'm ready for that much diversity."

The television cameras at Coors Field caught it all. Although the game was not being televised live, the saucer was barely out of sight before the networks had the feed on the air nationwide.

In the White House the president and his advisers watched in horror as the saucer slipped into the lights and dropped toward second base.

"My God!" the president whispered. "It's *real!*"

"Sweet holy Jesus," said Bombing Joe De Laurio.

They sat mesmerized until the saucer disappeared from the camera's view.

"They are more advanced than we are," muttered the secretary of state. "We may have to become their slaves."

Bombing Joe looked at her in horror. The old biddy's screws were coming loose.

"People will think that religion is bunk," said O'Reilly. "Morals, ethics, the philosophical underpinnings of civilization are all in question. The government may collapse."

"Where in blazes is my UFO team?" Bombing Joe wondered aloud and trotted away to call the Pentagon again.

The president pounded his fist on the arm of his chair. "An off-year election less than three months away," he said bitterly, "and now *this!*"

11

The night was well along when the saucer settled onto its struts in Egg's hangar. The last hour and a half of the flight back from Denver were spent at two hundred feet using only the antigravity rings for propulsion, well below the coverage of most air traffic control radars. When the main flight computer indicated they were home, Charley Pine flipped on the landing lights. They were right over Egg's hangar.

With the saucer inside the hangar and the doors closed, Egg yawned. "Thanks, kids. That was a ride of a lifetime."

Rip just grinned.

"The sun will be up in a couple hours," Egg added. "This old man is going to bed."

"Me too," echoed Charley and followed him toward the house.

Rip stayed with the saucer. Suffering from jet lag, he was so tired he ached, but he wasn't sleepy.

As they walked up the hill toward the house, Egg thanked Charley again for the ride. "That was an experience of a lifetime."

"Tell me, Mr. Cantrell, who owns the arrowhead collection upstairs? I hope you don't think I was snooping, but this afternoon I was looking for clothes and found that collection."

"Those arrowheads are Rip's. He's spent every summer here with me since his father died. He hunted arrowheads after people plowed their fields, dug likely places himself."

"That's quite a collection."

"Rip's got a good mind," Egg said. "Going to be a good engineer too."

Rip Cantrell sat on the couch in the corner of the hangar contemplating the saucer's ominous curved shape. The dark metallic material that formed the skin seemed to absorb the light from the overhead bulbs. For some reason the reflectivity seemed low just now, in the cool of the dark, humid night.

Finally he had to touch it again. He went over to it, ran his fingertips across the surface.

The saucer was a monument to the immensity of time. A hundred and forty thousand years! More than six thousand generations of humans. *Six thousand!*

Was Egg right? Did humans build it? Surely not.

And yet, it *had* to be. The headbands were for *human* heads, the computer read human thoughts.

So how did the saucer get into that rock?

The secrets this machine could tell, if a man had time to hunt patiently for answers. Professor Soldi intended to look for answers, didn't he?

Strange that he should think of Soldi just then.

Soldi was right about the saucer, of course. It belonged to all mankind. The technology embodied in it should benefit everyone on earth.

So just what *was* he going to do with it?

The hatch was hanging open under the machine, so he climbed back inside and made his way to the pilot's seat. The cockpit was gloomy, dark: the only light came from the bulbs mounted on the roof trusses of the hangar, shining through the canopy.

He pulled the reactor knob out to the first detent. The instrument panel came alive, the computers lit up, the indirect illumination that lit the saucer's main cabin came on. Like magic!

Magic! Those people who were living on the earth one hundred and forty thousand years ago, when they saw this saucer they must have thought it was magic. Dark, black magic, beyond the ken of mere men. And when the spacemen came out of the hatch . . .

What?

Rip Cantrell sat transfixed by his own imagination, wondering how it had been.

They were men, Egg said. This ship was crafted by the hand of man, to fit the hand of man, to fit the *head* of man . . .

He picked up the headband for the computer and settled it around the thickest part of his head.

He had to grab for the arms of the pilot's seat. His vision expanded, he was hunting through possible flight options, thinking rapidly about possibilities.

Possibilities.

The thoughts were in graphic form, almost symbolic. If something appealed to him, he pursued the thought to see where it would lead. Faster and faster, through options and possibilities . . .

Back to possibilities.

Tonight Charley flew the saucer without touching the controls. She just thought about it. How did she do that?

His mind raced along corridors of possibilities. In seconds he came to one that looked like it might be an answer.

Even as he examined it, the saucer lifted ever so gently from the earth. The hangar doors were closed, and the saucer was inside, but it slowly rose until it was suspended about twenty inches above the dark earth floor.

Rip tore off the headband and rushed to the open hatch. The dark packed earth that formed the floor of the old hangar was now at least six feet below him.

He turned and looked back at the instrument panel, all lit up.

Magic!

Oh, yes yes yes.

He would tell the computer to set the saucer onto the ground. Even as that thought formed in his mind and he stepped toward the panel to reach for the headband, he felt a slight jolt as the saucer again came to rest on its retractable legs.

Startled, he turned back to the open hatchway, to verify the thing with his own eyes. He stuck his head down. Yes, the saucer was back on the ground.

Hanging out of the thing, looking at the most forward landing stilt, he asked the saucer for a climb of a few inches. It rocked ever so gently, then lifted. Dust swirled from the hangar floor.

Down. Sit down, boy!

And the saucer again came to rest.

Rip slithered out of the hatch head first, catching himself on the ground with his hands. He crawled from under the machine and sat again on the couch under the old Coca-Cola sign.

Up. And it lifted.

Down.

He opened one of the hangar doors and walked fifty feet or so across the grass. He turned to look through the open door at the saucer under the lights.

Up.

Down.

The thing stunned him. He fell to his knees, rocked back on his heels, stared unbelievingly at the ancient machine.

He picked up a handful of dirt, felt the moistness, the cool, tangible, puttylike consistency.

Finally he lay down, rolled over on his back.

The clouds were completely gone. He could see stars, thousands of stars, a sky full of stars.

After a while Rip went back inside. He asked the saucer to turn off the reactor, and it did so.

He lay down on the couch. He was so filled with marvels, yet so tired . . .

★ ★ ★

The president and his minions got no sleep this night. Huddled in the White House, they raged against the hurricane that was racing down upon them while the television stations played the footage from Coors Field over and over, endlessly. The lights of Washington were visible through the windows, but they knew that beyond the lights was chaos.

"It's as if we are being assaulted by a whole squadron of saucers," someone said after spending another mesmerizing minute staring at the idiot box.

The chief of staff, P. J. O'Reilly, held one finger aloft as he faced Bombing Joe De Laurio. "Our first priority," he said, "is to find out how many saucers there are. Can the Air Force figure that out?"

Bombing Joe seethed like a volcano about to erupt, a towering, molten pillar of fury barely under control. He hadn't been patronized like this since he was a doolie at the Air Force Academy, way back when. Still, now didn't seem to be the right time to squash O'Reilly, the president's geek. So Bombing Joe tried to straighten his twisted lips in his beet-red face and marched away to make more telephone calls.

Despite the lateness of the hour, the telephones were already ringing. Some of the callers were too important for the president to ignore. He took a call from Willard Critenden, a political consultant who had been with him all the way until he was recently disgraced in a sex scandal and banished. Now the president did his consulting with Willard via long distance.

After the pleasantries, which were dispensed with in the first three seconds of the conversation, Willard got down to it:

"You have to do something about these saucers. The Bible-thumpers were freaking out yesterday. They are gonna go nuts when the sun comes up and they turn on their televisions. Already some of the evangelicals say we have arrived at the end of the world. In Revelation —"

"All right, all right," the president said hastily, cutting Willard off. He hated it when people quoted the Bible. It reminded him of those horrible mornings in Sunday school, back when the world was young. "We're doing everything we can."

"Right. Which is nothing."

"Willard, for God's sake! What in hell can I do? Get out on the south lawn with a flashlight and wait for the saucer leader to drop in?"

"All I do is advise. My advice is to go to

DEFCON ONE. People will feel better if the army, navy, and air force are ready to kill somebody. You gotta appear strong, resolute, capable. If you look like a frightened rabbit, the country will panic. And believe me, if the country panics, you and your party can kiss November good-bye."

"No one's going to panic. I can handle that end of it," the president said, reasonably confident. He had discovered long ago that ninety percent of what elected people do is posture before cameras. He was reasonably photogenic, knew how to discreetly use makeup, and for years had practiced setting his jaw just so in front of his bedroom mirror.

Of course that kind of savoir faire went only so far. "Unless they land. What if they land?" the president asked Willard now.

"What do you mean?"

"I mean, what if a goddamn saucer lands on the south lawn and some slimy thing crawls out and says, 'Take me to your leader.' What then?"

"Act presidential. That is critical. Don't pee your pants, don't freeze, don't give away the country."

"Uh-huh," the president said. He never, ever forgot that Willard was a political genius.

"Remind the press that you've always

been a champion of multiculturalism."

"Willard, I really appreciate your taking the time to call."

"I'm pulling for you, pal," Willard said and broke the connection.

The sun was peeping over the horizon in Washington when Bombing Joe De Laurio was summoned to a secure telephone. His repeated calls to the Pentagon demanding to know the whereabouts of the UFO team that had been dispatched to the Sahara had borne fruit.

"Sir, the CIA has confirmed that the members of the UFO team are prisoners of the Libyans."

"They're sure?"

"Positive. CIA says they are being held incommunicado in Tripoli while Qaddafi decides what to do with them. CIA also says there are some other people with them, some Australians and two employees of an oil exploration company."

"What is State doing to get them out of there?"

"Uh, nothing right now, I imagine. The agency has their troubles in Libya. They've moved heaven and earth for us on this one. They just haven't yet passed it on to State."

"The secretary is over here now. I'll tell her, see if I can light a fire under her."

"Sir, if I may make a recommendation. Perhaps we can get someone from the embassy to go see these people. They went to look for a flying saucer and we seem to have a bunch of them flying around . . ."

"Yeah. Thanks."

Bombing Joe hung up and went to find the secretary of state.

The sun was streaming through the open hangar door when Rip awakened. Something was prodding him. He opened one eye.

"Well, hallo, mate. Welcome to the worl'."

"Who are you?"

"Name's Rigby. Like Eleanor in the song."

The man grinned crookedly and used his pistol to tilt the back bill of his cap. Then he pointed the pistol in Rip's general direction and wiggled it. "C'mon, mate. Up. Time's a-wastin'. Let's go."

"You're Australian."

"God, you're quick," Rigby said. "I don't want to get physically violent with you, kid, but if you don't roll your sorry ass off that couch and get yourself erect, I'll have to do something we'll both regret."

Rip got up. That's when he saw that

there were three more men. They were over near the saucer, touching it, looking up into the open hatch, apparently paying no attention to Rigby.

"Let's go," Rigby said, waggling the gun and nodding at the door with his head.

"Where?"

"Up to the house, mate. Let's wake them up."

Rip went. Behind him Rigby said to his friends, "Come with me, people. You can gawk later."

"How did you find us?"

"Took a little doing. Your mother thought you might be here, and lo, here you were."

Rip whirled. "If you hurt my —"

Rigby slapped him. Hard. A casual backhand across the face.

"I've tried this nice, laddie buck. Now I'm telling you. Up to the house and no more running your mouth."

The slap stung fiercely. Tears came to Rip's eyes. He turned away so Rigby wouldn't see them.

They went inside. Rigby made him sit in the living room while the other men searched the house and rousted out Egg and Charley, who were forced to join Rip on the couch. One of the men sat in a chair opposite them. He took a gun from a holster under his armpit and placed it in his lap. Another man made coffee in the kitchen. Rigby removed a cellular telephone from a jacket pocket and made a call.

"It's here," he said exultantly. "In a little wooden hangar by a grass runway, about fifty meters below the house . . . We're in the living room."

He checked on the man making coffee, then looked at Charley. "Your name Pine?"

Charley was staring at her feet. She ignored him. Rigby stepped toward her.

"Yeah," Rip quickly said. "She's Pine."

"She's here," Rigby said into the telephone. He listened a bit more, grunted once, then turned it off and put it back in his pocket.

"Who are you people?" Egg demanded. "Threatening people with a gun is a felony in this state."

"Darn," said Rigby. "I just hope and pray we don't have to shoot you. That's an infraction of the law too, or so I've been told. I try not to do more than six or eight felonies before breakfast. Jack, is that coffee ready yet?"

"Contain yourself," Jack replied in a flat Australian accent.

The four thugs were sipping coffee when Rip heard a car drive up outside. Rigby went to the window and looked out. In less than a minute he opened the door.

The man who entered was a bit above medium height, superbly fit, with a tan that could come only from a tanning bed. He wore a dark blue suit and hand-painted silk tie. He came into the room, looked around at everyone and everything, then stopped in front of Charley.

It was then that Rip realized the man was at least seventy years old. From ten feet away he could have passed for fifty.

"Captain Charlotte Pine, United States Air Force," he said, with just the faintest trace of an Australian accent.

"I used to be in the Air Force," Charley said coolly. "Now it's just Ms. Pine to you."

"I see."

"When people come into my house, mister," Egg said, "I like to know their names."

"You must be Egg Cantrell."

"I am."

"My name is Roger Hedrick."

"I've heard of you," Egg said. "And what I heard wasn't good."

"We're being held here at gunpoint by

246

these thugs, Mr. Hedrick," Rip told the man. "That's a crime in the United States. Would you please help us escape from these people?"

Hedrick looked amused.

"Because if you don't," Rip said, "I'm going to report you to the police and swear out a warrant. Australia is a big place, but it ain't big enough to escape extradition."

Hedrick smiled. "Rip Cantrell. Engineering student, survey worker, young Quixote. A pleasure to meet you, Mr. Cantrell. Rigby, hand him your cell phone."

Rigby tossed the telephone in Rip's lap.

"Call the police, Mr. Cantrell. Tell them who you are, where you are, and that you are being held at gunpoint."

Rip looked from Hedrick to the telephone. Hedrick found a chair and pulled it around. He sat down and crossed his legs.

"Ah," Hedrick said. "I can see the wheels turning. If you make that call, the Air Force will confiscate the saucer and you'll never see it again. The technology will be classified. Perhaps someday one of your children will zip across China in a spy ship based on that saucer, if he or she joins the U.S. Air Force and becomes a pilot. Makes you want to wave the flag, doesn't it?"

Rip picked up the telephone and opened

it, but he didn't dial.

"Before you call the police, Mr. Cantrell, perhaps we should discuss how it was Mr. Rigby and I found you. Would you care to guess?"

Rip shook his head no.

"After you slugged my employee in the saucer in Chad, you made a serious tactical error. He had in his possession a satellite telephone that he had been using to converse with me as he examined the saucer. You discarded that telephone. Before he was captured by the Libyans, another of my employees, a Mr. Hampton, called me on that telephone, Mr. Cantrell. He told me what had just happened. He also gave me your name and that of Ms. Pine."

Hedrick smiled. "Needless to say, I was startled to hear that the saucer had been flown away. Startled? I was *astounded*. That call was the shock of my life."

He leaned forward and put his elbows on his knees. "You can surely appreciate the position in which I found myself. The most valuable repository of high technology on the planet had just been flown away to an unknown destination by an ex–United States Air Force test pilot and a twenty-two-year-old survey party laborer. An artifact worth billions, tens of billions,

of American dollars had just gone . . .
poof!" Hedrick snapped his fingers.

He grinned, displaying perfect white teeth.
"Of course I resolved to get it back. I —"

"It was never yours," Rip put in. "It's
mine."

"Oh, Mr. Cantrell. Surely you don't believe
that any court on this planet would honor
your claim. You discovered it, that is true,
but while you dug it out you were hard at
work for Wellstar Petroleum Corporation.
Mr. Cantrell, I *own* Wellstar Petroleum
Corporation. *You* were *my* employee."

Rip listened to this in bitter silence.
When Hedrick stopped speaking and
leaned back in his chair, Rip said, "So sue
me."

"I have no doubt about my legal position,
Mr. Cantrell. It is impeccable. Unfortunately,
I don't have the time to litigate. The lawyers
can litigate to their hearts' content later."
He made a gesture. "In the meantime, I
am taking possession of the property that
belongs to me."

Rip looked at the phone in his hand and
punched in numbers.

Hedrick held up a finger. "Before you do
that, ask yourself how I knew that you were
here."

Rip's finger froze inches above the phone.

"Perhaps you should call your mother. Talk to her. Then, if you wish, you may call the police."

Rip turned off the telephone, turned it back on, and redialed.

In a few seconds he heard his mother's phone ring. A man answered. "Mrs. Cantrell's residence." A flat nasal voice.

"Mrs. Cantrell, please."

"Who may I say is calling?"

"Her son, Rip."

"Just a moment."

Seconds passed. Then his mother's breathless voice. "Rip, are you okay? Have they —" And the connection broke.

Rip snapped the telephone shut. He eyed Hedrick.

"They're holding Mom hostage," he said to Charley and Egg.

Hedrick stood. "Do you still want to call the police?"

Rip threw the telephone at the kitchen wall. It bounced off the wall and caromed halfway back toward the couch. Rigby picked the thing up and examined it.

"So," Hedrick said, smiling again. "That is the situation. Captain Pine, I have need of your services. We will leave these gentlemen here unharmed if you will fly us and the saucer to Australia. The men with young Cantrell's mother will leave. Everyone will be safe and the world will once again be as it was."

Charley stood up. She looked at Egg, then at Rip. "Okay," she said.

"Hey, Charley," Rip said, "don't let these guys bluff you. They aren't going to hurt anybody. Hedrick doesn't want to spend the rest of his life in a pen somewhere."

"Rigby," Hedrick barked.

Rigby moved toward Egg, who was still seated. He came in light on his feet, moving with deceptive quickness. He was going to kick Egg right in the face.

Rip pushed himself off the couch and dove for Rigby's legs. The two of them went sprawling. Before Rip could recover, Rigby had him by the throat and was shaking him like a terrier shakes a rat. He heard Hedrick say something, then the lights went out.

He came to when someone poured water in his face. Hedrick was kneeling beside him. "See," he said. "He's good as new. He'll have a sore throat for a few days, but he's young."

Hedrick put his face down inches from Rip's.

"She's going with us, Mr. Cantrell. If you

involve the police, create any unpleasant-ness, she will suffer. Do you understand?"

"Why — ?" His voice box wouldn't work. The words came out a hoarse whisper. "Why are you . . . ?"

"Money, Mr. Cantrell. Money. That saucer is very valuable. It's going to make me the richest man on earth."

"Gates is the richest . . ."

For the first time, Hedrick snarled. "I'm going to bankrupt that bastard." He straightened.

"Come, Ms. Pine."

Apparently while he was unconscious, Charley had gone upstairs and changed into her flight suit. Her new clothes, pajamas, and jacket she put into a pillowcase that she was carrying in her left hand.

Now she turned and shook hands with Egg. Rip managed to get himself into a sitting position. He was about to try to get to his feet when Charley bent over and kissed him on the lips. "Thanks for trying," she whispered.

Then she walked from the room. Hedrick followed her.

Rigby and his thugs waited for a minute or so, then followed along.

"It's magnificent, isn't it?" Hedrick said

as his men opened the hangar doors. Charley Pine thought that the morning sunlight seemed to be absorbed by the saucer's dark skin.

"Sublime," Hedrick said and walked over to the saucer, touched it, ran his fingers along the smooth leading edge. He cocked his head and looked at Charley Pine, who also had a hand on the machine.

"When I heard about this saucer," he said, "I didn't believe the report. Fantastic! A great hoax. I see more grandiose schemes than one might imagine, all designed to separate me and my money." He snorted. "As if that were easy to accomplish."

He caressed the saucer's skin, stared at his reflection in the dark material.

"You will fly this saucer for me, Ms. Pine."

"Let's have the rest of it. If I don't . . ."

"Ah, but you will not refuse. You have a mother teaching school in Virginia, a father building houses in Georgia, a sister in New York who wants to paint . . . How long should I make the list? Whom should I add? Egg Cantrell, young Rip . . . ?"

"Extortion is a crime in America, Mr. Hedrick. So is kidnapping and murder."

"Ms. Pine. You are young, beautiful, foolish. You will do what I ask, when I ask it. This saucer is very valuable. I want it. I will do *whatever it takes* to get it. Do you understand?" He was closer now, looking straight into her eyes, without blinking, without a twitch anywhere on his face. *"Whatever it takes!"*

Charley hoped she was doing as good a job controlling her own expression.

"You will do as I ask, Ms. Pine, or no one will ever find the bodies."

"And afterward. You'll let me go?"

"I'll do better than that. I shall pay you for your time and services. Three thousand American dollars per day or any fraction thereof, including today." Hedrick grinned, a disarming, charming grin. "Think of this as a well-paying short-term job, Ms. Pine, and of me as your employer."

"I'll fly it."

"I thought you would see it my way. But first, tell me a little about this machine. What powers it?"

Charley gave him a five-minute brief covering the main points. When she finished, he smiled. "Shall we?" he said, indicating the saucer.

Charley led the way through the open hatch. Hedrick got into the ship with her, as did his chief lieutenant, Rigby. Charley closed the hatch behind them, then climbed into the pilot's seat and fastened the seat belt and shoulder harness.

Pulling out the main power control to the first detent lit off the reactor. As the computers and cockpit panel lights came alive, Hedrick stood frozen, watching.

Rigby looked around curiously.

Gently, gently, Charley lifted the saucer off the ground, snapped up the gear, and eased it out of the hangar, which stood at the western end of the grass runway. She halted the saucer, still about five feet above the grass, then turned it with the foot pedals, the "rudder." A few grass clippings lifted by the antigravity field were picked up by the breeze and swirled away. The windsock near the trees was indicating four or five knots from the northeast.

Hedrick's thugs stood by the open hangar door, their mouths hanging open.

She reached for the computer headband, adjusted it over her head.

Computer, do we have enough hydrogen for full power?

A linear graph appeared on the screen before her. About ninety percent, climbing nicely. Another few seconds.

Hedrick was standing beside her looking at the instrument panel. Rigby was opening the equipment bay, looking inside.

It was doubtful he realized that the saucer was off the ground, so gently had Charley handled it.

"Where to, Mr. Hedrick?"

"A hundred miles due west of Sydney. I have a cattle station — a ranch, if you will — located there."

Charley Pine looked straight ahead, down the runway, put her head back in the headrest, braced her feet on the rudder pedals, and twisted the rocket throttle control to the stop.

The rocket engines lit with a roar and the G came almost instantaneously. Hedrick and Rigby were swept off their feet and smashed against the rear panel of the compartment.

Egg and Rip were sitting on the back porch when the saucer floated from the hangar into sight. It turned there in front of the hangar and stopped with the nose pointed east, down the runway.

Rip massaged his neck.

"I wonder if she told everyone to take a seat and strap in," he whispered to Egg.

The first glimmer of fire from the rocket exhausts made both men clap their hands over their ears. They missed the worst of the noise, a howl rising in pitch and volume to soul-numbing intensity. Behind the saucer the fire from the nozzles scorched the runway grass, lit it on fire.

When the saucer was doing about a hundred knots, Charley pulled the nose up into the vertical. The thunder of the engines massaged Rip and Egg's flesh and vibrated the windowpanes.

The two men sat motionless on the porch until the sound of the rockets had completely faded.

The grass fire burned for a minute or so, then went out, leaving a black, smoking strip on the runway sod.

Hedrick's flunkies came walking up from the hangar. Their suits looked as if they had been rolling in the grass. They were rubbing their ears, opening and closing their mouths repeatedly.

"That close to the rocket exhaust, their eardrums may have burst," Egg muttered.

"Have a nice day," Egg said to the first one as he walked by, going around the house toward the cars parked in the drive.

"Hope the damage is permanent," Rip told the last one, who didn't even look at him.

12

First Lieutenant Raymond Stockert never forgot that morning. For the remainder of his life he would marvel at the combination of luck and fate that put him over central Missouri in an F-16 at the precise moment that a flying saucer came rocketing up from beneath him, missing his plane by a scant hundred yards.

It had been one of those mornings. The military had gone to Defense Condition One, DEFCON ONE — war alert — during the wee hours. Raymond had been awakened at home and ordered to report to his National Guard squadron ready to fly.

The evening before he had been watching the great saucer scare on television, along with every other sentient creature on the North American continent, but he didn't connect this alert to the scare until he got to the squadron.

The skipper was in a rare mood. "Okay, guys. Here is how it is: Washington has ordered all the planes armed. Each of you will be assigned a sector to patrol. You will take off, patrol your sector until fuel requires you to return or you are relieved on station."

"And?" someone asked incredulously. None of the pilots believed this spiel. This was a gag, of course, but what a gag! For this they had forfeited a night's sleep?

"And," said the skipper, "if you see a flying saucer, shoot it down."

His pilots gaped at the colonel as if he had lost his mind.

"Honestly, those are the orders. Shoot flying saucers on sight. That said, I don't want any of you clowns shooting at anything but flying saucers. Anyone who shoots at an airliner had better not come back."

So instead of counting pills behind the pharmacy counter of the supermarket where he labored five days a week, fifty weeks a year, this morning Raymond Stockert was in the cockpit of an F-16 over central Missouri, ready to fire the first shot in the war of the worlds. This was his second patrol this morning. And, by all that's holy, *here* directly in front of him going straight up like a giant bottle rocket was a real, genuine, honest-to-God flying saucer.

Raymond flipped on the master armament switch as he pulled the nose of his fighter into the vertical and slammed the throttle forward into afterburner. Amazingly — the luck of some people! — the saucer was only ten degrees or so off the axis of the airplane. He used both hands on the stick to wrestle the nose toward it.

Sure enough, the first wingtip Sidewinder locked on the saucer's exhaust plume and Raymond heard a tone in his ears.

He squeezed off the heat seeker. The missile shot forward in a gout of fire and smoke. The second Sidewinder locked on too, and Raymond thought, *In for a nickel, in for a dollar,* and fired it.

With both missiles chasing the saucer into the morning sky, Raymond Stockert sat watching until his fighter ran out of airspeed. He was going through forty-two thousand feet at that time, so he rolled onto his left wing and let the nose come down.

When he last saw the saucer, it was merely a brilliant spot of light in the heavens, going off toward the east.

Raymond had no idea what happened to the missiles he had fired.

Charley Pine didn't see the F-16, but she saw the first Sidewinder, which for some reason failed to guide on the exhaust plume. As it flashed by the canopy she recognized it for what it was.

She didn't see the second missile, which fortunately ran out of fuel just seconds before it would have intercepted the saucer. It passed harmlessly through the saucer's exhaust several hundred yards below it.

Charley Pine had been toying with the thought of hovering the saucer over a ship at sea and jumping through the hatch, leaving Hedrick and Rigby to their own devices, but the missile instantly clarified her thinking. Australia suddenly seemed like a solid idea.

She kept the juice full on, accelerating at about four G's. The computer profile led her upward with a gradual tilt of the nose eastward. She flew the saucer manually: She didn't want Hedrick to discover that the computer would fly the saucer on whatever profile the pilot wished.

Hedrick and Rigby stayed glued to the aft bulkhead, pinned there by the G. The blue of the sky gradually grew darker as the saucer roared out of the earth's atmosphere.

Checking the health of the systems, flipping back and forth between computer presentations — merely by thinking about it — Charley flew into space.

The ride into orbit took a bit more than fifteen minutes. When orbital velocity was obtained, Charley shut down the rocket engines.

Hedrick and Rigby floated up from the bulkhead.

Hedrick laughed, a loud, happy laugh. Rigby pushed himself toward Charley, snarling, "You slut! I'm going to make you pay —"

"That's enough, Rigby," Hedrick declared.

"Yeah," said Charley Pine. "Cork it, asshole."

"Please, Ms. Pine, let's not beard the lion." And Hedrick laughed again. He pushed off with his feet and shot across the cabin, all the while roaring his delight.

Through the canopy she could see the eastern seaboard of the United States pass below, although a cloud cover obscured much of the Atlantic. Through occasional rifts one caught glimpses of ocean, a deep blue hue, almost black.

She turned the saucer so that the sun shown full upon her. She was excited, as she always was when she flew the saucer. She took a deep breath, let it out slowly.

Hedrick was beside her now, looking through the canopy. Rigby had retreated to a seat, where he strapped himself in.

"An experience of a lifetime," Hedrick said. "I'm so glad I lived to see this."

What the heck. Charley rotated the saucer so he could see the earth passing below, then got busy with the computer plotting reentry.

"About twenty minutes," she told him. "Then we start the reentry burn. Better find a seat before then."

"Couldn't we do a complete orbit?"

"The scenery is fantastic but the company leaves a lot to be desired. We're going to Australia when we hit the reentry window. I am guessing on the time. The computer isn't programmed with our minutes and seconds."

"Okay, Ms. Pine," Hedrick said reluctantly and pushed off for a seat. "You're the pilot."

After Hedrick's thugs drove away, Rip and Egg sat on the porch without speaking, each occupied with his own thoughts.

Finally, Rip took out his wallet and counted the cash it contained. "Uncle Egg, could you lend me three thousand dollars?"

"Going somewhere?"

"Australia."

"We'll have to go into town. I'll write a check at the bank."

Rip stood and dusted off the seat of his jeans. Then he wiped his eyes. "I'm ready now," he muttered.

"Saw an article about Hedrick in one of those investment magazines down at my dentist's, maybe two or three weeks ago. He has a place west of Sydney, if I remember correctly. Lots of stone and glass and shapely young women. I specifically remember the women."

"Maybe we can stop by the dentist's. I'd like to have that article."

"Sure. And I better lock up the house. No telling who heard that thing climbing out of here."

After he retrieved his passport and new clothes from his bedroom, Rip strolled out to the pickup while Egg went through the house locking doors and turning off lights. He was standing there when a pickup roared in and slid to a halt with a spray of gravel.

"Did you see that thing?" the man at the wheel shouted. He pointed at the sky in the general direction in which the saucer had disappeared. "One of them flyin' saucers?"

"Yeah." Rip turned to point. "Went right down that runway there and then . . ." He made a gesture skyward with his right hand. "Went swooping up, clean out of sight. Darndest thing I ever saw."

"Say, I haven't seen you around here before, have I?"

The man at the wheel was wearing bib overalls and a T-shirt. On his head was a cap bearing a John Deere logo.

"I'm Egg's nephew. Name's Rip."

The man eyed him suspiciously. "The TV says maybe those saucers are dumping aliens around, like in the movies. Maybe they're gonna try to take over. How do I know you're who you say?"

Egg heard that remark. As he strode up carrying a suitcase, he called, "Lemuel, haven't I told you a dozen times to stay the hell off my property? I don't want you over here sniffing around."

"I seen that saucer, Cantrell, and —"

"*Aliens!* You ol' fool. If I had a couple I'd sic 'em on you. Turn that thing around and get out of here before I call the law."

As Lemuel was turning his truck, Egg called, "And fix that hole in the fence that your bull comes through, you skinflint. I think you're running that animal over here on purpose to eat my grass."

Lemuel got his pickup underway in another shower of gravel.

"Let's go," Egg told Rip, jerking his head toward his own pickup. "We'll lock the gate on the way out."

"General De Laurio, Space Command reports that a vehicle just went into orbit from a location in central Missouri. Liftoff was about twenty minutes ago. It is in orbit now, engines secured. Preliminary reports on the wire services seem to indicate the vehicle was extremely loud and saucer-shaped."

De Laurio was back in the West Wing of the White House. He had sent home for a clean uniform and a toothbrush. Two hours ago he went over to the Pentagon for a short nap. P. J. O'Reilly gave him a cold stare as he left. He felt as if he were abandoning the women and children aboard the *Titanic* while he rowed away in the only lifeboat, but he had to get a little sleep.

"It's in orbit now?" Bombing Joe asked the Pentagon duty officer.

"Yes, sir. Achieved a sustainable orbit about five minutes ago. And General, apparently a National Guard F-16 on patrol over Missouri fired two Sidewinder missiles at it."

"*What? Say that again.*"

The duty officer did so.

"Who ordered armed patrols?"

"I believe that order came from the White House, sir."

"Who gave permission to open fire?"

"Sir, that came from the White House."

"Cancel it," De Laurio shouted. "Keep all those trigger-happy morons on the ground. What if they shoot down a United jet?"

"Well, sir, I think the White House understood that risk when —"

"You don't know these people. No one over there would take an iota of responsibility for an accident like that. Get all those airplanes on the ground and keep them there. That's a direct order. *I'll* take the responsibility."

"Yes, sir."

"I'll pass the Missouri launch stuff on to the president. How are we doing on springing that UFO team in Libya?"

"State has people talking to them now. We'll know more in about a half hour."

"Call me back."

"Yes, sir."

Bombing Joe found O'Reilly in his office. "A National Guard F-16 over Missouri just fired two Sidewinders at something," he told the president's man. "Apparently some damned fool gave orders for squadrons of fighters all over the country to fly armed patrols."

"Watch your mouth, General. That 'damned fool' was the president. He felt he had to do something dramatic."

"Why didn't he consult me? I don't even charge for professional opinions."

"You were asleep at the Pentagon. We couldn't wait."

"If some used-car salesman in a jet fighter shoots down an airliner full of voters, that will really be something dramatic, all right. Are you out of your little mind? Get a grip, O'Reilly."

"Shut up, De Laurio!" O'Reilly was on his feet, his face red. "You uniformed popinjays don't seem to realize that the fate of Western civilization is on the line."

Before Bombing Joe could deck O'Reilly, the president darted into the room. He had just completed a press conference in which he had tried to look presidential. Never in his life had he had a day like this, not even when his mistress held a press conference in New York City to tell all. His face was ashen and his hands were shaking.

"Damned flying saucers," he exclaimed as he plopped into a stuffed chair. "Why in hell didn't these things plague the last administration? Why me?" He tugged at the knot in his tie.

"Because you deserve it," Bombing Joe De Laurio muttered under his breath. If anyone heard that remark he gave no indication.

The general took a deep breath, silently counted to ten, then said loudly, "Mr. President." When he had the elected one's attention he told him about the report from Space Command.

"A saucer went into orbit from central Missouri?" O'Reilly asked incredulously.

"Apparently so, sir," Bombing Joe said. "And an F-16 fired two Sidewinders at it. Results unknown."

"I don't believe a word of it," the president said firmly and leaned back in the padded chair. "I don't believe any of this horseshit." He dabbed at his brow with a handkerchief, careful that he didn't swab off any makeup. "The *Washington Post* wanted to know what this administration's position will be when aliens come to negotiate."

"They really asked that?" O'Reilly seemed stunned.

"The college professors say it's time to acknowledge the presence of other life-forms in the universe. The religious types are going nuts. There's a mob of a thousand or so across the street in Lafayette Park waving signs and making speeches, talking about the imminent arrival of the Antichrist."

"It's that bad?"

"It's that bad." The president's face contorted in a grimace. "I sacrificed everything for a career in politics. Now *I'm* the one who has to stand out there and welcome the aliens."

"This is another right-wing conspiracy," P. J. O'Reilly declared.

The telephone rang. General De Laurio grabbed it. He grunted a time or two, listened for about a minute, then carefully placed the receiver back on the hook.

He shook his head, rubbed his eyes. "Okay. Finally we get the real story." Both the president and chief of staff stared at him with their mouths hanging open.

"There is only one flying saucer," Bombing Joe explained. "A seismic survey crew dug it out of a sandstone ledge in the Sahara Desert. The thing was in the stone since Noah was mucking stables on the Ark. It is now being flown by a former Air Force test pilot and one of the survey workers."

The president was horrified. "Oh, my God!" he groaned.

"There is no invasion from Planet X," Bombing Joe said, weighing each word, searching the president's face to see if he was getting through. "There is no fleet of saucers, no aliens out to conquer the universe, no androids who eat human flesh, no battle of Armageddon. This crisis has been caused by two idiots zipping around in a round artifact scaring the bejesus out of people."

"Who says all this? What's your source?" O'Reilly demanded.

"State got somebody in to see the UFO team that's being held in the central prison in Tripoli. The team was there with the saucer in the desert. They were actually inside it. The test pilot was on that team. When the Libyans showed up, she and a survey worker sneaked into the saucer amid all the excitement and flew it away."

"Of all the rotten luck . . ." said the president, staring at his hands. He sagged back into the chair. "Why me, Lord? I just told the *Post* the aliens would be received like any other foreign dignitaries! I'm going to be laughed out of the White House."

"I'm going to get something to eat," said Bombing Joe. He stood and marched out of the room before anyone could order him to remain.

Egg and Rip found the magazine in the dentist's waiting room. The receptionist, who was on the telephone, just nodded when Egg asked with gestures if they could have it. The three people sitting in the waiting area were watching television reruns of the saucer over Coors Field as experts off camera explained everything.

The Cantrells took the magazine and left.

Rip got a new toothbrush and razor at the drugstore across the street, which he put into Egg's suitcase. After a stop at the bank, Egg pulled up at a pay phone at a filling station on the edge of town.

Fifteen minutes later, Rip was confirmed on a flight from St. Louis to Los Angeles, and from there to Sydney. One way.

"Can you get me to St. Louis by noon, Egg?"

"Get in. Let's roll."

"General, the saucer is coming out of orbit." The voice on the telephone sounded smug. "Space Command is tracking it. They're landing in Australia."

De Laurio picked up a fork and whacked it on the table a couple of times. "Okay," he said after a moment's thought. "Call State and the White House and let the duty officers there know. Maybe the Aussies can arrest these people before they scare everybody from Sydney to Perth."

"Sir, our armed forces throughout the world are still at DEFCON ONE. What should we do about that?"

"Let the politicians decide. A little training won't hurt anybody. But under no circumstances is anyone to shoot at anybody or anything without direct authorization from the Joint Chiefs of Staff. Got that?"

"Yes, sir."

Bombing Joe hung up the phone and attacked his breakfast.

Egg and Rip were an hour down the highway when Rip said, "You check on Mom, will ya? See that she's all right. If those jerks are still at the farm, call the police. Send the cops over."

"Sure, Rip. Don't worry about your mom. Hedrick got what he wanted. He's called off the dogs."

"The saucer isn't going to do him any good."

"Kid, you may not be able to get the saucer away from Hedrick. He's filthy rich, got his own private army, owns that part of the world and all the politicians in it."

"I know that, Uncle. I'm going to give it a try, though. But what I'm really after is the girl — I'm not leaving Australia without Charley."

Egg smiled then.

Charley Pine had no trouble finding Hedrick's station even though it was night in Australia. She flew west from the lights of Sydney until she spotted the approach lights of Hedrick's private runway. Hedrick had landed there many times in his Boeing jet, so he stood beside her looking out the canopy and gave her rudimentary directions.

The ranch headquarters was a huge, sprawling complex a short distance from the runway.

"Land in front of the hangar," Hedrick directed. "We'll put it inside."

She did as she was told.

Once the saucer was on the ground, a crowd quickly gathered. Charley opened the hatch for Hedrick. "You fly this thing into the hangar," he told her before he got out. "Rigby," he said, with a glance at his man. He jerked his head at Charley, then let himself down through the hatch.

Rigby grinned broadly. "Back into the seat. I'll be standing behind you. One false move and I'll snap your neck like a dry twig."

"I've waited all my life for a real man like you."

He did stand right behind her. She could smell his breath. As she reached for the controls to lift the saucer to move it, his hands went around her neck.

"Let go of me, you bastard."

He did release his grip, but his hands hovered there by her shoulders. "Goose it," he whispered, his voice urgent. "Go ahead. I want to see you fly with a broken neck."

She moved the saucer through the open door into the dark interior, and set it down again.

She killed the reactor and climbed out of the seat. The hatch was still open, so she dropped through it.

Hedrick was on a cell phone. He gestured to a man, who asked her to accompany him. They got in a golf cart and rode a hundred yards or so to the main house, a monstrous structure as big as a hotel. After walking through endless corridors past enough art to fill a medium-sized museum, she was locked in a bedroom without a telephone.

Only then did Charley Pine begin to shake. That passed after a minute or so, leaving her exhausted. She stood at the window, which was two stories above the ground, staring at the lights of the hangar. Finally she lay down on the bed.

Bombing Joe went back to the White House after he finished breakfast. He was glad he did. He got to watch the president have a conversation with the Australian prime minister that tickled the bottom of his heart, though not a trace of his delight showed on his face.

"Mr. Prime Minister, you don't understand," the president said into the telephone. "We are not asking you to arrest these people. Oh, no, sir. Merely to detain them for questioning . . ."

The president listened a bit, looking very sour. "Yes, sir, we are sure the saucer is there . . . Our satellite tracking network watched it come out of orbit and enter the Sydney area, where we lost it."

He frowned.

"Certainly it is the same saucer . . . I assert to you that it is the same machine. It was tracked from liftoff here to touchdown there . . . Okay, into the Sydney area . . . Not touchdown . . . Indeed, I misspoke. Will you assist us?"

The president listened for almost a minute before he spoke again. "The United States has extensive military, cultural, and economic relations with Australia. Your country and mine are allies.

Why are you being so obtuse?"

The good-byes were short and curt. The president slammed down the phone and glowered at his listeners, the secretary of state, O'Reilly, Bombing Joe, and several aides.

"They won't do anything unless the crew of the saucer violates Australian law. Nothing."

"What?" O'Reilly was furious. "He can't *do* that."

"He just did. He said that other issues, Australian sovereignty issues, were involved. He would not take orders from the American president. He suggested that the American ambassador deliver a note during working hours that sets forth our request and the grounds for it. It will be considered, he said."

"He brushed you off," O'Reilly declared, obviously shocked.

"Someone got to him," the secretary of state said ominously.

"What a day! I don't know about the rest of you people, but I want a drink," said the president and pushed a button to summon the valet even though the clock on the wall said it was still an hour before noon.

Late that afternoon a large helicopter bearing U.S. Air Force markings circled lazily over Egg Cantrell's farm, then dropped very low over the burned grass on the runway. It hovered over the burned area for a bit before it gently touched down. Three men disembarked.

They examined the burned area on the runway, then separated. One man went up to the house to knock on the door, a second went to the hangar to peer in the windows, and the third examined Egg's other outbuildings.

The helicopter pilot remained in his machine with the blades engaged.

Twelve minutes after landing, the three men climbed back into the helicopter and it lifted off. One of the three got on the radio. "It was probably here. The hangar is large enough. It contains a lot of junk and antiques, but there is enough room. No one on the premises."

The man listened to the reply, then motioned for the pilot to fly on.

Rip Cantrell was sitting in a cafeteria in the international terminal of the Los Angeles airport, killing time and sipping a Coke, when Professor Soldi came on the television set mounted high in the corner of the room. The tube had been giving saucer coverage since Rip entered the room an hour ago. Only a few people were paying attention.

Then Professor Soldi appeared on screen, talking about the saucer. "It is very old, one hundred and forty thousand years, give or take ten thousand. We dug it out of the sandstone." Some of his photos appeared on the screen. He explained what each of them were.

"So what happened?" the person interviewing him asked.

"To make a long story short, the saucer was flown away by a former United States Air Force test pilot, a Ms. Charlotte Pine, and a seismic exploration worker, a Mr. Rip Cantrell." He spent several minutes explaining how that came about and what the saucer looked like as it took off.

By now everyone in the room was paying rapt attention to the television, including Rip.

"As you know," the professor continued, "I've been a prisoner of the Libyan government for three days, since the incident happened. We were released just hours ago and taken to the airport in Tripoli, where we boarded a plane for Rome. The other people who were prisoners with me are now en route to the United States, but I wanted to get the story out quickly. That is why I stayed behind to be interviewed."

They talked some more about the saucer, how it worked, how it was discovered.

"Tell me, Professor," the interviewer said, "where did this saucer come from?"

"Obviously it was not made on earth," Soldi said. "It appears to be a shuttle craft, designed to take people and materials from orbit to the surface of a planet, then back into orbit. Apparently it was abandoned where we found it, abandoned all those years ago."

"Who left it there?"

"Ah," the professor said, "if only we knew. I think a careful study of the machine, and I mean a careful, thorough, analysis of every nut and bolt, every aspect of the device, would suggest some answers."

"Do you have a theory?"

"Several. But explanations of each of them would take more time than we have."

"Please share with us the theory that you believe most likely."

"The saucer is man-made."

"You mean people like us?"

"I mean our ancestors."

A murmur ran through the airport crowd that was watching this with Rip. He looked around at the people there, white, black, Hispanic, Asian, some of indeterminate race. All of them were listening intently to Professor Soldi.

"Civilizations don't just happen," the professor explained. "Hunter-gathering Stone Age societies are at one end of the continuum, we are somewhere closer to the other end. Each technological level, if you will, above Stone Age hunter gatherers requires a different level of social organization to support it. Increased specialization is the rule. The industrial age required millions of workers and consumers. The postindustrial age required even more specialization, a larger base of workers and consumers. We are now moving into the era of the global economy, in which the brains, talents, and skills of workers all over the planet will be melded together in gigantic enterprises to create further technical progress. Our destination is the technological future that created the saucer."

"I think I understand," the interviewer prompted.

"The properties of the technological continuum that we have just talked about are rigid; in effect, they are laws. Since each level of technological achievement requires more and more people, more and more social organization, it follows that

281

without the specialized people, the technological level cannot be sustained."

"Keep going," the interviewer said.

"A society that can build a device like the saucer, put it in an interplanetary spaceship, and cross the vastness of interstellar space will not be able to replicate that society anywhere else *unless they bring their whole population, or most of it.* Upon arrival at the planet they intended to colonize, the small number of people who could make that voyage would drop to a technological level that they could sustain."

"You are saying that if the saucer brought colonists, they became hunter-gatherers to survive."

"Precisely," said Professor Soldi. "Spaceships, computers, tools, weapons, lasers, advanced medical devices, books, learning — they lost everything. There weren't enough people to maintain or manufacture any of that. The abandoned saucer was finally covered with sand by the wind. The people lived in caves and learned to make tools with stone and ate their meat raw. The past was passed on as legends and myths. Eventually over the generations the legends and myths became unrecognizable, completely divorced from historical fact. The past was lost, just as the saucer had been."

"So . . . the people who flew the saucer are . . . us?"

"I think the evidence of the saucer will ultimately prove that is the case."

Nine FBI agents, seven men and two women, were waiting for Egg Cantrell when he drove into his driveway. They had driven there in three cars. Egg got out of his pickup and demanded of the closest agent, "Did you pick the lock on my gate?"

"Uh, the gate was open, sir, when we arrived. I never saw a lock. We just drove on in."

"Right! Well, what do you want?"

"We need to have a talk, Mr. Cantrell. We want to know what went on here today."

Egg looked them over and came to a fast decision. If he told them what he knew, they would eventually leave. If he didn't, he was probably going to find himself held in protective custody until he did talk.

"Why don't you people come on inside. I'll make a pot of coffee."

It was after midnight when the agents left. Egg went out on the porch and watched all nine agents get into the cars and drive away. The insects were chirping and fog drifted through the trees. A sliver

283

of gauzy moon was just visible through the luminous fog.

When he could no longer hear the car engines, Egg went down the hill to the hangar and used his key on the padlock. Inside, he turned on the lights. An hour ago he had brought the agents here and they had casually inspected the place. The senior man asked for permission to search, which Egg had refused.

Now he went to a large, dusty cabinet sitting far back in one corner. The cabinet had wooden doors on the lower portion, glass doors on the upper. It had once graced a hardware store in a small town fifty miles from here. Egg bought it at auction when the hardware store went out of business after the Wal-Mart opened. Progress.

Egg opened the lower right door and removed several antique metal signs. Behind the signs was a padded laptop computer case. He took it out of the cabinet, replaced the signs, then carried the computer case out into the light. He laid it carefully on the floor and unzipped it.

The computer from the saucer was unharmed, exactly as he left it. Egg Cantrell zipped up the computer case, turned off the hangar lights, and locked the door behind him.

13

Charley Pine didn't get much sleep her first night in Australia. She didn't really expect to: she had been changing time zones so often that she felt tense and tired all the time. She took a long, hot shower, used the toilet articles the room contained, and tried to rest.

When sleep refused to come, she took a book from the bookshelf in her room while she waited for the world to turn. She sat with the book open on her lap, to no avail; her mind refused to release its grip on the present.

She had flown the saucer for Hedrick because she believed his threats. Standing in Egg's house, watching Hedrick as Rigby worked on Rip, she believed him capable of murder to get what he wanted.

However, if an opportunity presented itself, she intended to get in the saucer and fly away, leaving Hedrick and his thugs as a problem to be solved at another time and place. Of course, Hedrick would not knowingly give her an opportunity. Perhaps she could create one . . .

Slowly, slowly the night ebbed and the sky grew light in the east. Finally the sun crept over the earth's rim.

She was standing at the window, fully dressed, when a knock came at the door. She opened it to find Rigby there. He was a few inches over six feet, with wide shoulders and narrow hips and weight lifter's veins in his forearms.

"He wants to see you."

She closed the door behind her on the way out and walked ahead of Rigby. Instinctively she knew he wasn't the type ever to let anyone get behind him.

He followed her to an elevator, which lifted them to the top floor of the house, the fourth.

Hedrick's office was a large room, with huge windows on every wall. The windows were French doors, which opened onto a deck built above the roof of the rest of the house. The design reminded Charley of a New England widow's walk, only the room and deck were huge.

Roger Hedrick was seated behind his desk. He didn't rise. She sat in one of the chairs facing the desk.

"I'll see you at breakfast, Rigby," Hedrick said, and Rigby left via the stairs, which were beside the elevator.

Hedrick had a presence. He seemed to electrify the air. Charley thought she could feel the tiny hairs on her arms prickle.

"As I told you yesterday," Hedrick said conversationally, "I will pay you for every day of your time, whether you fly or not."

"If you pay me it won't be kidnapping, is that it?"

He seemed to be measuring her, sizing her up. Charley Pine wondered what he was thinking.

Now he said simply, "I don't care how you label your situation, Ms. Pine. I am simply trying to make these few days as pleasant for you as possible. I want your cooperation, and I intend to have it."

He seemed to be looking through her eyes into her soul.

"You will fly the saucer when I ask, where I ask, to demonstrate it for some people I have invited to see it. If you refuse, if you act like anything other than a loyal employee, I will apply pressure to your family in America. We can arrange for telephone calls from your mother or father while someone breaks their fingers, their arms, their legs, their backs . . . whatever you like, Ms. Pine. Whatever you want."

"You're *sick!*"

"Perhaps you would like to listen while

your sister is raped."

"Sick scum," she hissed and involuntarily lowered her gaze from his eyes.

When she raised her eyes, Roger Hedrick grinned. He had a wicked, malevolent grin. Then the grin faded.

"Nothing personal, Ms. Pine," he said crisply. "This is business. It's trite but true. A great deal of money is at stake. A young woman reluctant to listen to reason is not going to be allowed to impede progress. *The wheels are going to turn.* Do you understand?"

She forced herself to meet his gaze.

"I do hope you understand, Ms. Pine. For *your* sake."

Hedrick rose from his chair, came around the desk. She rose from her chair to stay away from him.

"Let's go have breakfast."

He reached for her arm. She fought back the instinctive urge to jerk away.

"After breakfast, perhaps you would care to go for a ride around the station. On the ground, of course."

He smoothly guided her to the elevator. They rode it down in silence, his face perfectly calm, as if the conversation of a moment ago didn't happen.

"I'll find someone to accompany you," Hedrick said easily. "I think you will like

Australia. Most people do."

The dining room was on the ground floor, a rather large room with ten tables, each capable of seating four people. Three of the tables were occupied. Hedrick steered Charley to a table where a stunningly beautiful young woman with blond hair was sitting with Rigby. Charley had to force herself not to stare at the girl.

"Ah, Bernice," Hedrick said, "I wish to introduce you to Charley Pine, our American pilot. She flies the saucer."

Bernice gave Charley a dazzling grin. Then she pecked Hedrick's cheek and he patted her. Charley seated herself beside Bernice.

"You know Rigby, of course."

"I've met the bastard," Charley said.

Bernice didn't turn a hair. She's that kind of broad, Charley thought, dismissing her. Rigby sipped his coffee as if Charley wasn't there.

Hedrick didn't raise or lower his voice, but continued in a conversational tone: "Life is much easier for everyone if the amenities are observed, Ms. Pine. That includes you." Obviously her status here was no secret.

A waiter came to take their order. After he left, Hedrick said to Bernice, "I thought you and Rigby might give Ms. Pine a tour of the station this morning. She said she would enjoy that."

Bernice put her hand on Hedrick's arm. "I'd be delighted," she said and smiled, displaying perfect teeth.

"Interesting weather we're having, isn't it?" Hedrick said and led the conversation to benign topics.

When breakfast was finished, Bernice said to Charley, "Let's walk down to the garage for a vehicle."

Before Charley could reply, Hedrick froze her with his eyes. "You have a choice. You can give me your word you won't try to escape, or we can lock you back in your room. Which will it be?"

Charley Pine stared into his eyes. The man would send hired thugs to murder her family to make her fly the saucer, but not to salve his injured ego. There was no profit in it, and profit was what Roger Hedrick was all about.

The station was certainly guarded. Even if she stole a vehicle and managed to get to a town, what good would it do her? Hedrick's billions undoubtedly bought a lot of cooperation from the local police and politicians.

Finally, there was the saucer. If she left

without it, he would find a way to make a profit from it. The cold certainty that she didn't want Hedrick to have the saucer congealed in her heart.

"I'm not going anywhere," she said as evenly as she could.

"If she tries to escape, Rigby, she's all yours. Just don't kill her."

Rigby grinned.

Roger Hedrick threw his napkin on his plate and rose abruptly. As he walked away he pulled a cell phone from a pocket and punched buttons.

Bernice drove the Land Rover and Charley Pine sat beside her, on the left, in the passenger's seat. Rigby was still at the breakfast table when the women left the room, and if he followed, Charley didn't see him. She didn't even look for him.

She forced herself to look at her surroundings, to see, to observe. When the time for action came, she wanted to be ready. She wanted to know where the enemy was and how he would have to be fought.

Bernice said little until they were bumping along in a Land Rover, then she began explaining about the station, the thousands of cattle, the jackeroos — which were cowboys — airplanes, buildings, etc. Charley soaked it up without asking questions. When a response seemed to be required, she grunted.

Finally Bernice began talking about herself. She was British, she said. A model. She ran into "Roger" several years ago in London at a fashion show. She talked about jetting around with Roger — Paris, Monte Carlo, Rome, Copenhagen, Los Angeles, Chicago, New York, wherever business or pleasure took them. Skiing at St. Moritz one weekend, lying on the beach at Ipanema the next, it was all so magical.

After fifteen minutes of this Charley had had enough. "Sounds like you're bought and paid for," she remarked.

Bernice didn't take offense, didn't argue, didn't pretend the remark hadn't happened. Roger had told her to drive this American pilot around, so she would, regardless. She took a deep breath, then said, "Must be quite the adventure sporting about in a flying saucer, I imagine."

This sally brought forth another Charley Pine grunt.

Bernice clucked her tongue. "We *must* try to get along," she said.

"Why?"

"Because *Roger* said so," Bernice said,

slightly appalled that Charley couldn't see something so plain. "Roger is Roger. He's extraordinarily smart, has made mountains of money. He puts himself under extreme pressure. Deep down he's a generous, warm person. Everyone just loves him."

"You're really not a bad person yourself, are you?" Charley said and patted Bernice on the arm.

Aboard a packed Boeing 747 crossing a great ocean, Rip Cantrell was ready to conclude that Wilbur and Orville should have concentrated on the bicycle business. Nearly five hundred wriggling, sleeping, farting, snoring humans were jammed into the small seats.

Rip managed to cross three sets of knees to get to an aisle, then went back to a tiny open area around an emergency exit. He stood there stretching and looking out the small porthole at the darkness and listening to the hum of the engines. The plane was six hours west of Los Angeles. The sun had set, finally, after a long sunset. A meal had been served to everyone on board, a movie had played, now people slept.

He bent down to see out the window beside the emergency door. Dark out there, nothing to see. An overcast, apparently, obscured the sky.

He couldn't stop thinking about the saucer or Charley Pine.

Somehow the two were bound so tightly together that to think of one was to think about the other.

He pulled the magazine from his hip pocket and read the story on Roger Hedrick one more time, looked carefully at the photos.

Finally he folded the magazine and returned it to the hip pocket of his jeans.

He looked in the window glass at his own reflection. That was the face Charley had seen when she kissed him.

When he straightened up, he was wearing a smile.

The news that a Missouri National Guard F-16 had fired two Sidewinders at a flying saucer the previous day made headlines around the world. Although the Pentagon classified the report, someone in Missouri called a local newspaper. The rest, as they say, was history.

Pharmacist Raymond Stockert was hounded by a mob of reporters at his home and in the supermarket where he worked. The supermarket manager sent

Stockert home for the day to clear the aisles for real shoppers.

Inevitably the White House was forced to admit that the president had ordered the military to patrol the nation's skies and shoot down any saucers encountered. This revelation sparked a debate on Capitol Hill. Once again the White House was under siege.

The president was unapologetic. Safely away from the press, he roared at his aides, "Of course I gave the shoot-down order! I would give it again! The American people elected me to protect the American way of life, and by God I am going to."

"But, Mr. President, there's only one saucer, flown by two American citizens. Surely they —"

"I don't believe a word of that crap. One saucer? Seen in dozens of places? The damn aliens are conducting a disinformation campaign, but they can't fool me!"

"Sir, as a hypothetical, perhaps we should at least consider the possibility that there are . . . no aliens."

"If there are no damned aliens, then this saucer thing is a right-wing conspiracy. Either way, the nation must be protected. Now get the reporters in here. I want the public to know that this administration stands ready to defend the American way of life."

Somehow the fact that the military was no longer flying armed patrols got lost in the hullabaloo. For this, Bombing Joe De Laurio was thankful. He sat in his Pentagon office with the television on wondering why everyone else in Washington had gone off their nut.

That evening he attended a special intelligence briefing for the Joint Chiefs before he went home to dinner. The CIA man was adamant: There was only one saucer, and it was in Australia.

"Roger Hedrick has it," the Joint Chiefs were told. "He forced the test pilot to fly it from Missouri to Australia. He was actually in the thing when that National Guard F-16 pilot fired missiles at it."

"Has the president received this briefing?" Bombing Joe asked.

"He will get it as soon as he finds the time, sir. Right now he is meeting with leaders of Congress."

"Umm," said Bombing Joe.

"To continue, gentlemen, Roger Hedrick has the saucer at his cattle ranch — or station — in Australia. He is currently inviting the governments of China, Russia, and Japan to send representatives to his station to inspect the saucer and bid on it. He intends to sell it to the highest bidder."

"Why would anyone want one saucer?" someone asked.

"Technology, sir. Our scientists say that the technology contained in the saucer will drive worldwide technological development in the twenty-first century."

"Why wasn't the United States invited?"

"We are not privy to Mr. Hedrick's thinking," the briefer replied as respectfully as he could, "but we suspect he is inviting only governments that would not enmesh him in litigation over the ownership of the saucer."

"How much does Hedrick think the saucer will bring?" the chairman asked.

"Our source tells us he mentioned a figure to one of his aides: Fifty billion dollars."

When Charley got back to the main house from her ride, Hedrick was waiting. He had with him two academics, graying, distracted men in cheap clothes. Charley and the professors followed Hedrick the hundred yards to the aircraft hangar where the saucer was parked. Rigby appeared from nowhere and joined the little party.

The machine was right where Charley had left it. She explained the basic functioning of the propulsion system to the professors and Hedrick, then opened the hatch and let them go inside.

They inspected the flight deck, then entered the machinery bay. One of the scientists had a radiation detector with him, a device about the size of a laptop computer, which he used to check the reactor and water separator.

"Extraordinary," one of them muttered, but mostly they kept their comments to themselves.

Rigby ensconced himself in the pilot seat. For a moment or two Charley thought he might be a pilot himself, then she decided he wasn't.

Hedrick stayed with the scientists.

"We could learn a lot more," one of them said, "if you let us take things apart."

"Can you guarantee that you could properly reassemble everything?"

"No, sir. There may be seals and whatnot that would have to be replaced."

Charley got tired of watching Rigby preen, so she let herself down through the hatch and sat beside one of the landing gear pads.

The guards — there were eight of them, all armed — paid little attention to her.

After about an hour, Hedrick lowered himself to the hangar floor. "Ms. Pine, we would appreciate a short demo flight."

"Have you fueled the saucer?"

"Uh . . . no. We haven't touched it."

"We will need some water, the purer the better."

"The well water is quite free of minerals and impurities. I have it checked monthly."

"Get your thugs to rig a hose."

When the tank was topped off, Charley ordered the hangar doors opened.

Only then did she climb back into the saucer and close the hatch behind her.

"Seats, please, and strap yourselves in."

Hedrick stepped up beside the pilot seat as she strapped in. "Ah, Ms. Pine. I know you're the world's hottest jet jock and you could win the world aerobatic competition with this thing, but I want you to take it *easy*." He looked at her with eyebrows raised. "Stay near the farm when you are below a hundred thousand feet. Don't cross over any cities or towns at low altitude. Got it?"

"We're on your nickel, Mr. Hedrick."

Charley Pine lifted the ship gently off the concrete, snapped up the gear, and drifted it out of the hangar. The professors were staring. Whatever they expected, this wasn't it. The only sound was a subdued hum from the machinery spaces. Flight was smooth, effortless, even when Charley lit the rocket engines and added power in a seamless rush.

This, she thought as she put the saucer through a gentle three-hundred-sixty-degree, two-G barrel roll, *is the essence of freedom.*

Out of the corner of her eye she saw Hedrick whispering with the scientists, which shattered her reverie. She leveled the saucer, flew it in a straight line for several minutes, then made a wide, sweeping turn to head back to Hedrick's station.

When the saucer was back in the hangar, the scientists wanted to see the computers in operation. Charley fired off the main flight computer, but she didn't don the headband, preferring to punch the buttons beside the screen to bring up various displays. Hedrick didn't object; he merely watched.

When she had the reactor secured, Hedrick asked Rigby to escort Charley to her room.

She went willingly, leaving the scientists to confer with Hedrick. Rigby trailed along three paces behind her like a well-trained dog.

After his session with the leaders of Congress, the American president was a subdued, thoughtful man. His orders to shoot at saucers had panicked the electorate, the senior legislators said. They demanded that he call off the military and that he publicly reassure the country that under no circumstances would he order or allow rash military action against possible alien ships with unknown military capabilities.

The president caved in to congressional demands. Outraged voters he understood. He had made a mistake, he acknowledged.

Huddled now with his national security team, the president seemed distracted as the CIA briefer went through his presentation. The president's face was gray and sweaty, his shirt a sodden rag. The saucer was for sale, the briefer said, to the highest bidder. If the president thought that fact significant, he gave no sign.

At one point he muttered, "We must be bold," but he didn't explain the relevancy of that observation.

Finally O'Reilly said, "Roger Hedrick seems bent on setting the world economy on its ear, as long as he makes a profit."

That remark seemed to get through to the president. He jerked, then looked around wide-eyed.

"Is the saucer valuable?" he wanted to know.

"Oh, yes, sir. Hedrick seems to think it will bring at least fifty billion in cash. If he sells it to Russia and allows them to pay for it over time, it is possible he might get two or three times that amount."

"Perhaps more," Bombing Joe said. This afternoon he had a long talk with the colonel who headed the UFO team, now just back from Libya. Colonel West thought the saucer worth whatever it took to get it.

"The saucer is everything from computers to metallurgy," Bombing Joe explained to the serious people, "from computers to propulsion. It's a ship that flies into space and returns, a ship that can do it again and again and again. We are still many years away from that capability."

The secretary of state said slowly, "Imagine the competitive advantage we would gain in every technical field if we had that capability *now*."

"So what is your recommendation?" the president asked State.

"Mr. President, we cannot sit idly by and watch Hedrick sell that technology to a rival nation," the secretary said. "He stole the saucer from us. He kidnapped the pilot and forced her to fly it to Australia."

The national security adviser chimed in. "That technology should benefit American industry. If the Chinese or Japanese get it, our economy in the years ahead will be at a serious competitive disadvantage."

"American industry?" Bombing Joe was appalled. "That saucer is a national security treasure. It should be classified, taken to Area Fifty-one. We can use it as the basis for a generation of fighter planes that will be so technologically superior that war will be impossible. Imagine fighter planes that could fly into orbit, then descend and fight anywhere on earth they were needed. Mr. President, war is the oldest scourge of all; we can inoculate ourselves. Surely the American people deserve the greatest gift of all — freedom from war."

"What about Russia?" someone asked. "What if they get the saucer?"

"They don't have a chance if Hedrick wants cash, but if he is willing to take something the Russians are willing to trade, then . . ."

"Don't underestimate the Russians," Bombing Joe remarked. "When you factor in the technology they had to work with, they built the best planes on earth. Russian engineers can work miracles, especially in metallurgy."

"All of you people have overlooked one basic fact," said the chief of staff, O'Reilly.

"The human race is not ready to face up to the reality of other life in the universe. Western civilization is built on the premise that mankind is unique, that we are made in God's image, that somewhere up there is a kindly old man with a white beard who cares about each and every one of us, cares about our little triumphs and disasters, about our cuts and bee stings, and listens to every child's prayers every night. Our uniqueness is the bedrock for religion, philosophy, ethics, morals, for our sense of self-worth."

O'Reilly looked around the room at each of his listeners. "Don't you see? We humans were doing fine without the saucer. We are trapped on this little rock orbiting this modest star on the fringe of a vast galaxy. You" — he pointed at the secretary of state — "want to rip the curtains off the windows, show everyone how insignificant human life is in the grand scheme of things. After you destroy the very foundation of human relationships, with what will you replace it?"

The secretary of state picked up the remote and turned on the television in the corner. In seconds a talking head appeared. The subject was the saucer. She changed channels and got the footage of the saucer over Coors

Field. Professor Soldi was on the third channel she tried, showing still photos of the interior of the saucer that he had taken in the desert.

The secretary of state pointed at the television. "You can't unspill the beans," she told O'Reilly.

"We can do the next best thing," Bombing Joe said. "We can clean up the mess. We could mine the saucer for its technology yet deny it even exists. Soldi will go away after a while. Without new revelations, the media will move on to something else. In a year the saucer will be forgotten."

They argued some more, until everyone had their say. The long silence that followed was broken when the president asked, "So what is the consensus?" He was mopping his face with his handkerchief, wiping off swatches of wet makeup.

No one spoke.

"Can we at least agree that we should try to get possession of the saucer . . . before the new owner can fly it out of Australia?"

Everyone tried to talk at once. When the president finally motioned for order, the secretary of state managed to make herself heard: "The Australians will regard a military adventure as an act of war."

"Everything has a price," the national security adviser said. "The saucer will go to whoever wants it the most. We have to decide if that is us."

Bombing Joe shook his leonine head. "You are all wrong. We have only one option. If we can't get the saucer into a hangar in Area Fifty-one, we should destroy it."

14

After Rip went through immigration and customs at the Sydney airport, he took a taxi downtown and found a hotel. The sun was well up on a brisk morning, but he was whacked with jet lag.

Later he emerged from the hotel and blinked in the late afternoon sun. He had slept for six hours and was famished.

After he had eaten, he went to the car rental booth in his hotel lobby. "I'd like to rent a car," he told the desk clerk, a man in his early thirties, and tossed a credit card and his driver's license on the counter.

The clerk picked up Rip's Minnesota driver's license and scrutinized it carefully. Finally he handed it back. "Sorry, mate. You're too young."

"How old does a fellow have to be?"

"Twenty-five, mate. Those are the rules."

Rip pursed his lips. He pulled a wad of American money from his pocket, peeled off three hundreds, and laid them on the counter.

"Do you own a car?" he asked the clerk.

"Well, mate, this *is* interesting. Indeed, I *do* own an automobile. It's a few years old, but it runs. And you look like a responsible lad. You're not in the drug business by any chance, are you?"

"Lord, no," Rip managed to look a bit sheepish. "There's this woman. She's out on a cattle station and I need wheels to get there."

"How far?"

"Oh, a hundred miles or so."

"How much is that in kilometers?"

"Hundred and sixty, thereabouts."

The clerk reached for the money. "I hate to see true love thwarted," he said with a smile.

Rip's heart sank when he saw the car. The steering wheel was on the *right* side. Oh, yeah, they drove on the left coming in from the airport.

He got into the little car, fumbled with the key in his left hand but finally got it into the ignition. Found first gear, eased the car out of the parking space, and almost collided with a truck. He managed to jerk the car out of the truck's way.

God, it looked weird with the traffic coming at him on the right. He almost had a wreck at the first intersection he came to. He had to concentrate fiercely to keep the car on the proper side of the road. If he let his attention wander the least bit he was going to hit someone head on.

Several times Rip had to pull over to check the map he had purchased in the hotel lobby. After three more near collisions, he managed to get out of the city on a highway heading west.

An hour and a half later he came to the town of Bathurst. There was a hotel in the center of town, so he parked the car and registered for a room. Tomorrow was the time to check out Hedrick's station, not tonight after dark.

Walking the streets after another dinner, he found a clothing store and bought a sweater and a jacket because the air was chilly.

As he walked along the sidewalks he wondered where Charley was and what she was doing.

On the afternoon of the second day of her employment as Hedrick's "saucer pilot," Charley Pine gave a group of Japanese businessmen a ride in the thing. Then she was escorted back to the main house while Hedrick played used-car salesman.

Just before she slipped through the hatch, Charley said to Hedrick, "You don't have the right to sell the saucer, you know."

"I *do* have the right, Ms. Pine." Hedrick smiled genially at one of the Japanese who turned around to listen. "I'll talk to you tonight after dinner. Run along now, please."

Charley went.

A group of five Chinese landed in an airliner a few minutes before the dinner hour. From her room, Charley watched them walk up the gentle incline toward the main house.

At dinner she heard someone mention that a Russian delegation was arriving around midnight.

She had no appetite. She smeared her food around her plate, listened to Bernice expound on the joys of shopping in Paris, and excused herself before dessert was served.

Up in her room she turned on the television. Hedrick had a satellite dish system, she deduced, because several American networks were on the idiot box. She made sure her door was locked, then settled in to watch a rerun of an interview with Professor Soldi broadcast by a Melbourne station.

"The Cantrells are here for their appointment, Mrs. Higginbotham."

"Show them in."

Mrs. Higginbotham didn't rise from her desk. Her office was on the thirty-fifth floor of the Higginbotham Building in downtown Dallas.

She was a white-haired woman in her late seventies with a firm chin and clear blue eyes. The two men came in and reached across the desk to shake hands. One was overweight, shaped like a pear, and the other was completely bald. Both were in their fifties.

The bald man spoke first. "I'm Olie Cantrell, Mrs. Higginbotham, and this is my brother Arthur. We're here on behalf of our deceased brother's boy, Rip. I believe he was employed by your company on a seismic survey crew in the Sahara."

Mrs. Higginbotham nodded. "What can I do for you gentlemen?"

"Well, let me explain the situation, then we'll discuss possible solutions. You've probably been following the saucer crisis . . . ?"

"Indeed. Quite extraordinary." Mrs. Higginbotham's eyes twinkled. "I have followed the story in the newspapers and on television. It's so exciting. That saucer is a hundred and forty thousand years old. Isn't that amazing?"

The Cantrells agreed that it was.

"This is the most fun I've had since Bill Clinton and Zippergate. When I get up in the morning I can't wait to turn on the television and look at the newspaper."

"You probably know that Rip found the saucer while working for your company," Olie Cantrell said.

"Oh, yes. That makes the story sort of personal, don't you think?"

"It's personal, all right. That's why we're here. Several days ago Roger Hedrick showed up at my brother Egg's place in Missouri — Oh, I'm sorry. Egg's real name is Arthur."

Mrs. Higginbotham didn't know quite what to say.

"In any event," Olie continued, "Hedrick told Egg and Rip that he owned Wellstar Petroleum and advanced the theory that the saucer belonged to the company and therefore to him. He then proceeded to kidnap the civilian test pilot who was there and force her to fly the saucer to Australia."

"That sounds like the Roger I know," Mrs. Higginbotham said acidly. "He hates to be thwarted."

"Arthur consulted me because I am an attorney and charge him only modestly for my time, if at all. In the course of my research, I discovered that Hedrick does not own all the stock of this company, although he is indeed a major shareholder and controls one of the seats on the board."

"Hedrick owns about ten percent of the stock," Mrs. Higginbotham said. "I own or control twenty-eight percent, and my sons and daughters have a smidgen over nine."

Olie Cantrell nodded. "I also understand that your late husband founded this company, Mrs. Higginbotham, and both your sons have built their careers here in oil exploration."

"Your research is impeccable."

"With all that said, here is the problem. The saucer is very valuable. Hedrick wants it desperately. He has physical possession right now by virtue of several felonies, none of which are provable in court. He has the saucer in Australia and probably intends to exploit it commercially. Sooner or later he may decide to ask an attorney about Wellstar's claim to title of the saucer by virtue of its discovery by an employee. What he will be told is this: Wellstar does indeed have a claim to the saucer, but it is a poor one because young Cantrell did not discover the artifact in the course of his employment. He was not hired to search

313

for flying saucers. He is in the position of a mailman on his appointed rounds who saw a dollar lying on the sidewalk and picked it up. The dollar belongs to the mailman, not the postal service.

"Still, as an attorney, I can assure you that even a poor claim to a valuable item is better than no claim at all. The rub, for you, is that Hedrick owns ten percent of the company. He may well elect to try to buy control of Wellstar just to be in a position to assert the company's claim."

"I could assert the claim for Wellstar," Mrs. Higginbotham said.

"Indeed you could, ma'am. Unfortunately for you, Hedrick doesn't seem the type who likes to share. And he has the saucer in Australia. Even if you got a court order directing him to return it to the United States, enforcing it will be problematical, at best."

Mrs. Higginbotham looked from one face to another. She scratched an eyebrow. "What do you propose, sir?"

"We came here today, ma'am, hoping that we could persuade you to sell Wellstar's claim to the saucer, whatever it is, to our nephew, Rip Cantrell. This course would avoid any threat to your control of Wellstar by Mr. Hedrick."

Mrs. Higginbotham tapped the desk with one finger. "And the threat of a lawsuit by your nephew?"

Olie Cantrell raised his hands in acknowledgment of her point. "It may never come to that, but it might. Yes, ma'am."

"What haven't you told me that my lawyer will want me to know?"

Olie grinned. "He may want to take a look at the law of Chad, where the saucer was found. I have discussed Chadian law with a firm in New York that practices in Africa. My contact tells me that he can find no Chadian statutes, decrees, or court decisions that deal with found property.

"As you are probably aware, Chad is a miserable, parched little country ruled by a dictator. I'm sure someone could zip off to Chad with a pile of money and the law could become whatever he or she was willing to pay for. I don't think that would play very well in an American court, but it would be another claim, another lever."

Mrs. Higginbotham used her hands to push herself erect. "Gentlemen, I want to talk this matter over with my attorneys. Why don't you come back to see me tomorrow morning at ten o'clock?"

The Cantrell brothers stood, shook hands, then took their leave. When the door closed behind them, Mrs. Higginbotham called her lawyer.

It was three in the morning in New South Wales when Charley Pine finally turned off the television. Roger Hedrick had not called her or come to her room; in fact, no one had. She saw the airplane bringing the Russian delegation arrive just after midnight, a four-engine Tupolev. Lights remained on in the hangar area for another two hours. Finally most of the lights were extinguished.

Charley waited another twenty minutes, then opened her window. Just as she thought. Four feet away was a large downspout. The roof of the porch on the main floor of the house was fifteen or so feet below.

She climbed up onto the windowsill, took one last look around, then leaped for the downspout.

She almost missed it, striking her head on the pipe and slipping several feet before she managed to jam her foot between the pipe and the wall, stopping her descent.

Down she went, straining every muscle, holding on for dear life. Safely on the roof, she felt her lip, spit out something black. Blood. She had bitten her lip. Her right foot was hurting too, so she rubbed it.

Charley Pine tiptoed across the roof and lay full-length so she could look over the edge and see if anyone was on the porch.

One man, smoking a cigarette.

He was forty feet away, facing the other way, listening to music coming through a French door that was open a few inches. Someone was playing a piano. Bach.

From time to time the smoker turned and looked across the lawn. From his position he could see the hangar and the main horse barn, both of which were lit only by security lights.

Moving ever so slowly, Charley crawled across the roof to the corner farthest away from the guard. Here a column held up the roof. As she looked the area over, she decided she would hang by her hands from the gutter and put her feet on the porch rail. The column would help. It would be behind her, breaking up her silhouette if the guard should look this way.

Just as she was about to swing a leg over, the guard left the French door where he had been listening and walked in her direction.

She held her breath. Now she could see that the guard carried some kind of weapon on a strap over his shoulder.

The guard stopped after he had traversed

half the distance between them and stood looking at the hangar and barn. Beyond were low mountains under a clear night sky full of stars.

Charley Pine could just hear the piano, ever so faintly.

The guard took a last drag on his cigarette and flipped it away. Then he turned and walked slowly back toward the open French door.

Charley swung a leg over, then forced her body over the edge. Her hands and arms absorbed her weight. She lowered herself until her feet touched.

She released the gutter and bent over. With her hands on the railing, she pushed off with her feet and dropped between the bushes below and the porch foundation.

She crouched there, scarcely daring to breathe.

The guard must have had his back turned during the descent, which had taken no more than five or six seconds.

Staying bent at the waist, she slipped along the porch to the corner of the house, then peered through the bushes.

Perhaps it was a sixth sense; she felt someone was near. She knelt there, watching and listening. A minute passed, then another.

Now she heard steps, voices. She lay on the ground behind the bushes, looked out underneath.

Two guards with rifles over their shoulders, chatting, pointing flashlights this way and that, walked slowly toward her.

She closed her eyes and lowered her head, just in case.

When the sound had completely faded, she looked again. The yard was clear. Inching her head up, she looked under the porch railing. The porch guard was not in sight.

She slipped out of the bushes and ran toward the dark area to the right of the horse barn. When she got there, she flattened herself against the wall and listened.

Moving slowly, carefully, from one dark shadow to another, she worked her way around the barn and toward the hangar. Another pair of guards passed her near the hangar. She was lying in a slight depression then, in plain sight if the guards had just lowered their flashlights and looked. They didn't.

Heart pounding, Charley Pine ran the last few feet to the personnel door on the side of the hangar and tried the knob. It turned. She let go of the doorknob and looked around one more time. There was a small naked bulb above the door, perhaps forty watts. She reached up and unscrewed it until it went out.

Twelve minutes had passed since she left her room.

She twisted the doorknob and pulled gently. With the door open about an inch, she put her eye to the crack.

The hangar was big, at least a hundred and fifty feet square. There was only one light, a spot that shone down from the roof trusses directly above the saucer.

Charley Pine pulled the door open and stepped into the hangar. She pulled the door completely closed behind her.

In the far corner of the cavernous space was a desk with a small illuminated lamp on it. Someone was seated at the desk, someone reading.

She surveyed the equipment parked and stacked along the walls. Like most hangars, this one was also used to store wheeled equipment that didn't have another home.

She got behind an aircraft tow tractor and lay down so she could see under it, between the wheels.

The hatch under the saucer was open.

Oooh, that tantalized her. If she could just get in the saucer, she could fly it right through the closed main door. With just a

320

squirt from the rockets, the saucer would take that giant overhead door right off its hinges.

She turned her attention to the man at the desk. He seemed to be slumped over, reading a magazine that lay flat on the desk in front of him.

She had watched him for several minutes when she realized the man was asleep.

Lord, yes. The idiot has fallen asleep!

Charley rose noiselessly. She was wearing tennis shoes, which might squeak on that painted concrete floor, so she took them off, tied the strings together, draped them around her neck.

The man at the desk was still slumped over, motionless.

She took a couple of deep breaths, squared her shoulders, then stepped out of the shadows. She walked directly to the saucer, bent down, and went under it toward the open hatch.

Charley stood in the hatchway, climbed up . . .

Rigby was sitting in the chair by the pilot's seat. He had a shotgun in his lap, pointed right at her.

"I thought you'd never get here," he said. He looked at his watch. "Seventeen minutes."

Charley Pine climbed into the saucer,

tossed down her shoes. The shotgun was pointed right at her gut.

"That's close enough, baby," Rigby said. "I'd hate to have to shoot —"

She knocked the barrel aside with her left hand and kicked Rigby square in the face.

Rigby's head bounced off the pilot seat pedestal and he lost his grip on the shotgun, but he didn't go down or out. Charley planted her left foot and kicked again with her right, aiming for his larynx.

She missed. Got him on the shoulder.

Rigby grabbed at her foot. She kicked a third time, but without shoes she wasn't doing enough damage.

Rigby got her ankle that time, held on to it, dragged her to the floor.

He was pounding on her kidneys when Hedrick said, "That's enough, Rigby. We have more rides to give tomorrow." Hedrick's head was sticking up through the hatch.

"I think the bleedin' bitch broke my nose," Rigby said through gritted teeth and thumped Charley in the kidney one more time.

"Tsk, tsk." Hedrick clucked his tongue. "And you gave me your word, Ms. Pine."

15

After a large Australian breakfast, Rip Cantrell set forth from Bathurst in his borrowed car to see what he could of Hedrick's empire. As he drove west the coastal mountains soon petered out, giving way to low, rolling grasslands. Water appeared to be rather scarce, the flora looked semi-arid. Still, plenty of cattle and sheep could be seen from the paved, two-lane road grazing peacefully amid scattered trees, which seemed to grow best near creeks and low places.

The problem was going to be getting in. He suspected that tradesmen from Bathurst, the nearest town to Hedrick's station, must come and go regularly. That was worth looking into. As he drove he kept an eye out for tradesmen's vans. He saw a bakery truck go by on the way back to town, but traffic was sparse. Every now and then a truck, occasionally a car.

He was driving along a particularly long, dull, empty straight stretch when he saw a turnout ahead and a gate. The gate was a steel pole across the road, tended by at least three men. As he drove by he saw the Hedrick name on a sign.

Rip continued on, watched for other roads, other entrances, guards, anything. Ten miles later he was still going by Hedrick's land, he thought, having seen no boundary fences joining the fence alongside the road.

When the road topped a low ridge between watersheds, Rip pulled over and got out to stretch his legs.

The highway in both directions was empty. Fences along both sides of the road, but no livestock in sight. A few trees along a distant creek, and far to the east, the low Blue Mountains. High up, a cloud layer was moving in from the east; soon it would block the sun.

He was about to get back in the car when he heard a distant, low-pitched rumbling sound, like a jet climbing at full throttle. Rip shaded his eyes, searched the sky to the south.

He despaired of seeing it when all of a sudden, there it was — a small black dot low in the sky, moving at a high subsonic speed.

The object turned north, climbing, and headed in his general direction. It was about four miles from him when he realized he was looking at the saucer.

That evening at the Bathurst Hotel, four Japanese in suits and ties sat at a table near Rip. They had apparently just arrived that afternoon.

Rip was quick to notice that these four wore their hair shorter than was stylish, carried no extra weight, and looked remarkably fit. Not a gray hair in the bunch. The oldest was perhaps thirty. Four soldiers, he concluded, and wondered what had brought them to this corner of the earth.

As Rip worked his way through his second large steak, he noticed that these four also had good appetites. Must be the invigorating air down under, he thought, and went back to musing about how he was going to get past Hedrick's security guards.

After dinner Rip Cantrell went for a walk around town. There was a large market just two blocks from the hotel, but then Bathurst was a small town. Delivery trucks were parked out back.

Rip went inside, walked through the aisles looking over the produce and packaged food. The meat counter was well stocked too. Finally he selected a couple of pastries and went to the checkout counter to pay.

The man there rang up his purchases without comment. Rip went back to the sidewalk and took a pastry from the bag to munch on. He walked along the side of the building to a spot where he could look over the market's delivery trucks.

One way or the other, he thought, *I've got to get inside.*

The last delegation to arrive and receive a saucer ride was the one from the European Union. A German, a Frenchman, and an Italian seemed to be the committee in charge. They had engineers along, but the three politicians whispered among themselves all the time.

Charley Pine gave them a gentle ride, no G's, no maneuvering, then sat in the pilot's seat for two hours and watched as the Europeans played with the computers, looked at this, prodded that.

The Frenchman introduced himself as Nicholas Pieraut. "Enchanté, mademoiselle," he said with a grin.

"Same here," Charley Pine replied.

"You are the aviatrix?"

"That's right. Wherever the saucer goes,

I go." She changed positions slightly to ease the pain in her back.

"Ahh," said Pieraut.

After a formal dinner in the huge main dining room of the station mansion, Roger Hedrick led the four delegations back to the hangar. Valets serving cognac and cigars worked the crowd. Tastefully and modestly spotlighted in the center of the hangar was the saucer.

Charley Pine stood nearby with a glass of white wine in her hand, ready to answer questions about the saucer if asked. When she dressed for dinner in a gown loaned to her by Bernice, her lower back was black, blue, purple, and yellow. No blood in her urine, thank God, and apparently no ribs broken. She carried herself gingerly. She was on her third glass of wine, so now her back hurt only when she took a deep breath.

Rigby was just aft of her left elbow, as she was keenly aware. He looked awful: Someone had straightened his nose and taped it to hold it in position. Still, the swelling would take a few days to subside.

She glanced at Rigby again and decided his face was worth the pain in her back.

"Tomorrow, gentlemen, we begin the

auction." Hedrick boomed his words while the translators buzzed to those who didn't speak English. "You delegates representing your respective nations have a chance to change history, to affect the lives of everyone on the planet. The nation that takes the saucer home will become the superpower of the twenty-first century."

In the silence that followed, the delegates looked about them at the other delegations. It seemed to Charley Pine that they thought Hedrick was right. And he *was*.

"Each of you has had a demonstration ride in the saucer, each of you has witnessed its amazing capabilities with your own eyes. You have examined it at great length and have spent hours on the satellite telephones talking to your governments. Our test pilot, the beautiful Ms. Pine, has answered your questions. You are, I hope, fully informed about this remarkable machine, in touch with your governments, and ready to make serious bids."

You have to hand it to the bastard, Charley Pine thought. *He really does it up brown.* The valet with the cigar box strayed within reach, so Charley snagged herself a stogie. *Why the hell not?*

She finished off the wine while the valet used a little guillotine on the butt end of the thing and struck a big long kitchen match. When the cigar was going, she held out her empty wineglass for cognac.

Hedrick nodded at Bernice, who handed a sheet of paper to the senior member of each delegation.

"If you will please refer to your copy of the bidding rules that my assistant is passing out," Hedrick was saying. "As you will see, the bidding will take place in rounds. The minimum bid in the first round will be ten billion American dollars. Each bid in the second and subsequent rounds must be at least one billion dollars more than the highest bid of the last round or the bidder will be disqualified from the auction. The auction shall continue until only one bidder remains, and that bidder shall be the winner. The purchase price of the saucer shall be payable in American dollars or negotiable securities denominated in American dollars unless prior to the auction the bidding party and I agree on the value of the goods being offered in trade. Finally, the purchase price must be paid in full before the winning bidder takes possession."

Hedrick waited until the translators caught up, then said, "Gentlemen, good luck tomorrow."

The members of the delegations puffed

on Cuban cigars and sipped cognac while circling the saucer and surreptitiously eyeing the members of other delegations. In a far corner of the hangar, Hedrick had an ensemble playing chamber music.

One of the Russians approached Charley. He was in his mid-thirties, with shoulders an ax handle wide, narrow hips, high cheekbones. "You fly terrific," the Russian told Charley.

Hedrick approached the senior Japanese delegate, a distinguished corporate type with graying hair and an aide at each elbow. Charley Pine edged closer so that she could hear what was said. The Russian stayed with her. Rigby brought up the rear.

"The saucer is what Japan needs," Hedrick said smoothly, "to power Japan out of the economic malaise that has paralyzed her these last few years."

"Yes, Mr. Hedrick," the senior man replied, in perfectly understandable English. "The advantages inherent in the technology could be very significant."

"I also am a test pilot," the Russian told Charley. "I fly for Mikoyan. Test experimental fighters, fly air shows . . . Have you seen the Paris Air Show?"

"Alas, no," Charley said and concentrated on Hedrick.

"Reactors, antigravity, computers, metallurgy, hydrogen from water . . ." Roger Hedrick shook his head slowly, as if the very thought of all these technological achievements made his head throb. "The money Japan spends each year on foreign oil would purchase a dozen saucers."

"You have a dozen?" the Japanese gentleman asked with a straight face.

"Sorry," Hedrick replied seriously, "just the one."

"We were wondering about the legal title to the saucer, Mr. Hedrick. The reach of American courts is legendary, and we understand the saucer was in the United States recently."

"Very briefly," Hedrick agreed, nodding his head.

"What assurance can you give us that your title is . . . clear?"

"What I am selling, sir, is hardware, not paper. The winning bidder tomorrow will fly the saucer wherever he chooses."

"I see."

"Only the strong survive," Hedrick continued. "The saucer will make some nation very strong."

". . . A beautiful woman," the Russian was saying, "should never sleep alone."

Charley Pine turned to him with a start. "What makes you think I sleep alone?"

The senior Chinese official did not speak English, so Hedrick's translator adroitly appeared at his elbow as Hedrick approached, with Charley Pine and her entourage a few paces behind.

"Mr. Wu, it is a great honor having the vice premier of the People's Republic here as my guest."

Wu nodded and puffed furiously on his cigar.

Hedrick steamed on. "I hope you are as impressed with the saucer as I have been these last few days."

"Yes, yes," said Wu between puffs, according to the translator.

"Perhaps the hour has finally come for China to surpass Japan as the superpower in Asia."

Wu looked at his watch.

A bit nonplussed, Hedrick continued, "With a billion and a half people, China needs the nuclear technology contained in this machine." He laid a manicured hand on the saucer. "Freedom from oil, a clean, safe fuel, computer technology fifty years ahead of its time — the saucer will give some nation a huge technological lift. In the right hands, it might allow a national economy to leapfrog decades of development."

"Perhaps it confers too large an advantage," Wu muttered and appeared to lose himself in thought and tobacco smoke.

"I have had much experience with matters romantic," the Russian test pilot said softly to Charley Pine, who had missed the last sixty seconds of his pickup spiel.

Ten feet away, Roger Hedrick gazed at the saucer as if it were a holy relic for a few more seconds, then moved off toward the small knot of people surrounding the senior European.

Charley looked up into her Russian's warm blue eyes, smiled distractedly, then launched off after Hedrick.

Hedrick made an oblique approach to Pieraut, who was in conference with the German and Italian, as usual. "Here, gentlemen," he said, sweeping his hand at the saucer, "is the catalyst to allow the European economy to catch and surpass the United States. Think what the technology you have seen today could do for the European aerospace industry! Gentlemen, the time has come to expand our horizons, to realize that there are *no limits*. None at all."

"Unfortunately," the German said, "there are always limits, Mr. Hedrick. The saucer has to be paid for, one way or another. But we were wondering, Why are the Americans not here? The British?"

"I did not invite the Americans or the British," Hedrick said. "I suspect they might be tempted to try to take the saucer from me by force or legal process."

"Have they a legal claim?"

"Of course not. The saucer was discovered by an employee of a company of mine. I own the saucer and have the right to do with it what I will. My intention is to sell it to the highest bidder."

The Italian looked skeptical, Charley Pine thought. After handshakes with every member of the delegation, Hedrick moved on.

The senior Russian was a fiery young man named Krasnoyarsk. The Russian translator hovered at Hedrick's elbow. "An extraordinary device, is it not, Mr. Krasnoyarsk?"

"Quite extraordinary."

"The nation that mines the technology embodied in the saucer will gain a large competitive advantage," Hedrick murmured. "Here is the catalyst that will enable Russia once again to become a superpower."

"Russia is a poor nation, Mr. Hedrick,"

said Krasnoyarsk with sadness in his voice. "I am wondering why a man who wants so much money would invite my government to participate in this auction. Surely you don't think we have the foreign exchange to pay twenty, thirty, forty billion dollars or more for this?" He gestured with his left hand.

"Can Russia afford not to own this technology?"

Charley missed Krasnoyarsk's reply because the Russian test pilot moved in front of her. She blew smoke in his face and stepped around him.

Krasnoyarsk was saying, "Mr. Hedrick, if you were selling tickets to heaven for a hundred dollars each, very few Russians could afford to purchase one. Instead, we would jump up and down outside on the sidewalk, shouting, 'Isn't that cheap? Isn't that cheap?' "

"I understand Russia lacks the foreign exchange to make an outright purchase."

"At least this trip offered us a nice airplane ride and some fine cognac and cigars," said Krasnoyarsk after he listened to the translation. "After the collapse of communism, we could no longer afford Mr. Castro's fine cigars."

Hedrick pursed his lips while he considered what to say. "Perhaps your government should consider selling something of great value, something more capital intensive than the saucer."

"More capital intensive? The saucer's technology will soak up capital like a sponge. It will require new raw materials, new manufacturing techniques, new insights in chemistry, physics, mathematics, new factories, new everything. Believe me, Mr. Hedrick, we Russians know all about investing for tomorrow. We did that for seventy years."

Hedrick nodded. He half turned so that he and Krasnoyarsk were both facing the saucer. "Still," the Australian said, "I can think of something that would require more capital than the development of the technology in the saucer."

With a cigar between his teeth, Krasnoyarsk placed both hands on the smooth, dark, curved surface of the saucer and caressed it sensuously. "What?" he asked.

"Siberia," said Hedrick and took another tiny sip of cognac.

Charley Pine took a drag on her cigar and scrutinized Hedrick with new respect. The bastard thinks *big!*

The Russian test pilot whispered in her

ear, "So, we sleep together, yes?"

Charley Pine almost gagged on cigar smoke. She exhaled explosively and coughed. When that subsided, she whispered to Ivan the Russian Romeo, "If only we could, but I have a social disease. It's a pesky little bug, and with medical help so iffy in Russia . . ."

When the Cantrells returned to the Higginbotham Building in Dallas for their second appointment, Mrs. Higginbotham had with her a gentleman about her age with white hair and ruddy skin, a lawyer named Rufus Howell.

After she introduced Howell, Mrs. Higginbotham said as she settled into her chair, "Tell me, Arthur, what is your interest in this matter?"

Egg looked a bit embarrassed. This was only the second time that he had worn a suit in five years. Yesterday was the first.

"Rip has spent every summer at my place in Missouri since his father died ten years ago. I got him interested in engineering. He's like a son to me, a son I never had."

"And you brought your brother into this?"

"That's correct. I wanted legal advice."

"I will be blunt with you, gentlemen. How much money is the saucer worth?"

Egg took a deep breath as he thought about that question. "In the short run it's worth whatever a seller could induce a buyer to pay. In the long run, I think it will be the catalyst for much of the technological progress of our species in the twenty-first century. What is it worth? It's priceless. It's the Wright Brothers' first airplane, Bell's telephone, and Edison's lightbulb, all in one object."

Mrs. Higginbotham's face glowed. "Have you seen the saucer?"

Egg nodded. "And flown in it. The experience of a lifetime, I'm telling you." He lowered his voice conspiratorially and leaned forward in his chair. "I was in the saucer when we flew over Coors Field in Denver."

Mrs. Higginbotham laughed. Even the lawyer grinned.

"How extraordinary," she said after a bit. "We are imprisoned in this place and time, and yet . . ." She fell silent.

After a discreet interval, Egg said, "I might as well tell you the rest of it, Mrs. Higginbotham, since you are in the oil business. The saucer is hydrogen-powered. It cracks water into hydrogen and oxygen and burns the hydrogen."

"I wondered about that."

"The saucer may point the way to the use of hydrogen as a regular motor fuel. It would be cleaner than gasoline and much cheaper, although motors to burn it in might be more expensive." Egg made a gesture of irritation. "All that is speculation about what might be, someday. Predicting the future without the use of a crystal ball is a risky business. Right now the saucer is just an artifact."

"Yesterday afternoon," Mrs. Higginbotham said, "I made a few telephone calls. I wanted to know some more about you gentlemen."

"A wise precaution," Olie Cantrell said.

She fluttered a hand. "You, sir, are very highly spoken of by the senior partner of the law firm we regularly use in Chicago."

It was Olie's turn to look a bit embarrassed.

Mrs. Higginbotham steamed right on. "You, Arthur, are a well-known consulting engineer. I called my chief engineer, and he not only knows of you, he knows you. He said you have worked with Wellstar on several occasions."

"That is correct," Egg told her, nodding.

"He said you have some patents?"

"Twenty-seven. Mostly in the field of manufacturing processes."

Mrs. Higginbotham looked at each of them in turn, then said, "If young Rip became the owner of the saucer, somehow achieved a legal position that allowed him to license the technology, what would be the benefit to Wellstar?"

Egg and Olie looked at each other. "We have given this a good bit of thought, Mrs. Higginbotham," Olie said. "We suggest you retain a forty-nine-percent interest in any propulsion technology derived from or based upon technology in the saucer."

Mrs. Higginbotham turned to her attorney. "Mr. Howell, please prepare a bill of sale with those provisos." She turned back toward Egg. "What is Rip's full name?"

"Stepford Sidney Cantrell."

"No wonder they call him Rip."

"Stepford was his father's name."

"And Sidney?"

"His mother was raised in Sidney, Nebraska."

"I see. Well, Mr. Howell, sell the saucer to Stepford Sidney Cantrell for the sum of one dollar cash in hand paid, with Wellstar retaining a forty-nine-percent interest in any hydrogen propulsion technology derived from or suggested by the saucer. Is that language acceptable to you gentlemen?"

"You may leave out the word 'hydrogen,' Mrs. Higginbotham," Olie said. "There is an antigravity system in the saucer that is going to make helicopters obsolete. I would think the word 'propulsion' also includes that system. I believe it would also include the nuclear reactor that is the power source for both the antigravity system and the water separator."

The lawyer and Mrs. Higginbotham stared open-mouthed.

"Sorry," said Mrs. Higginbotham, who recovered first. "Antigravity? That sounds so weird, so —"

"The modern computer would astound Edison," Olie remarked.

"It's real, believe me," Egg said. "I've seen it, touched it, flown in it. The saucer is as real as this desk." He rapped his knuckles several times on Mrs. Higginbotham's varnished mahogany.

"Go write it, Rufus," Mrs. Higginbotham said to the lawyer, who nodded and went out the door.

"I'm an old woman, gentlemen, but my, this sounds exciting! I do hope it works out for Rip, and for all of us."

"We hope so too," Egg said fervently. He

got out his wallet, removed a dollar bill, and laid it on the table.

"But what if he can't get the saucer away from Roger Hedrick?"

"That would not be an insurmountable obstacle," Egg said after a glance at Olie. "I wish I could say more at this time, but I cannot."

Mrs. Higginbotham nodded. "Since we're sharing confidences, I might as well warn you. I've known Roger Hedrick for fifteen years. He is not an honorable man."

16

Charley heard diesel engines several times during the night. The third time she went to the window to look. She saw three trucks near the horse barn, at least a dozen men. The men all seemed to be carrying weapons. As she watched, the men got into the trucks, which then drove slowly away.

She pulled a chair over to the window and sat there with the blanket from the bed wrapped around her. Her back was sore when she moved, she had a headache from the wine and cognac, and she could still taste that cigar even though she had brushed her teeth, and tongue, three times.

Of course Roger Hedrick has armed security around, probably as many men and weapons as he could muster. He would be a fool not to, and a fool he wasn't.

She wondered about Rip, wondered where he was, what he was doing, if he was getting over the loss of the saucer.

Unable to stand the silence any longer, she turned on the television. Professor Soldi appeared, talking about the saucer, how it should be in a museum for scientists to study and learn from. Well, Soldi and Hedrick were on opposite sides of a great divide.

"The saucer is a product of a great civilization," Soldi said, "and as such embodies not just the technical knowledge of the civilization, but the social organization as well. If we can learn the processes used to manufacture the systems in the saucer, we can learn many things about how the people who made it organized their lives, their society, their civilization. Just as the pyramids and hieroglyphics have taught us about ancient Egypt, the saucer will instruct us about the people who made it."

A moment later, in response to a question from the interviewer, Soldi said, "People seem to think the benefits of the saucer will be *things*. Nothing could be further from the truth. Look how the telephone has revolutionized life on this planet during the past seventy-five years. Because of the telephone, we live much differently from the contemporaries of Alexander Graham Bell."

"But can you, or anyone, predict the changes?" asked the interviewer.

"Of course not," Soldi responded. "Change is the one constant in human affairs. Change is unpredictable, unwanted, unplanned for, evolutionary, revolutionary, resisted, welcomed — and absolutely inevitable."

"Professor, several of our guests have pointed out that the change that you envision will not be change caused by man, nature, or even God. They argue that this will be change stimulated by an alien agency."

"I find that reasoning ludicrous," responded the professor. "*We* are responsible for the human condition. Life is a constant struggle to better our chances for survival. That is a law, like birth and death."

Soldi seemed to search for words. "We are trapped like flies in amber," he said, "imprisoned in our time and place. The saucer will let us see what was and what will be."

Charley Pine watched for a while longer and finally clicked the television off. That crowd Hedrick invited here could care less about the human condition.

Hedrick had not mistreated her, other than to allow a little pounding by friend Rigby. And he hadn't killed her. She had thought that he might after she flew the last flight for him, but he hadn't. Now she wondered if Hedrick was going to ask her to chauffeur home the saucer's happy new owners.

If he sent her to Beijing, Tokyo, Moscow, or Munich in the saucer, or merely let her walk out to the highway and thumb a ride into Sydney, there wasn't much she could do to hurt him. Oh, she could be a minor irritation, a flea on the elephant's ass, but that wasn't going to embarrass Mr. Roger Hedrick very much. He would probably be too busy to notice.

Of course, if she had this figured wrong, tomorrow night she was going to be very dead. Rigby would love to do her, that's a fact. The bastard would probably strangle her just so he could watch her face.

Hedrick sure seemed to be enjoying himself last night, hawking the saucer like it was a used Chevy. He was going to make a huge, heaping pile of money, then live happily ever after.

Or would he? Charley Pine mused on that question.

He would have cash or securities for the saucer, but whoever got the saucer would have the future in his hand. The saucer was a collection of seeds, many of which would probably grow and bear fruit. All manner of wondrous things would come from the saucer for whoever had it.

Ultimately the benefits from the saucer's technology would trickle down to everyone on the planet. Everyone would make money from it, have their lives improved, see new opportunities for their children.

Everyone except Roger Hedrick, that is. True, he would have money, lots of it. He was already worth forty to fifty billion dollars, and his fortune wasn't in cash. He owned things, like ships and factories, newspapers and television stations, computer companies and . . . oil companies. He owned a lot of oil, she recalled, tens of billions of dollars' worth.

Of course the cash he got for the saucer would have to be invested. Even Roger Hedrick couldn't keep all that money in his mattress; he was going to have to find someplace to put it to work.

He certainly wouldn't buy more oil. The investments in oil he already had would slowly decrease in value. Perhaps he could get out of oil before the price dropped precipitously. That must be his plan.

She gingerly put her feet up on the chair and hugged her legs. This stretched her back and gave her temporary relief. She arranged the blanket around her to keep warm.

Of course, if Hedrick were a real swine he would destroy the saucer after he was paid for it. Blow it to smithereens while it was on its way to wherever. Then he would have the purchase price, none of his existing investments around the world would be threatened by saucer technology, he would never have to defend his title in court, and no one could prove a thing. And if Charley Pine were flying the saucer, she would be neatly and tidily disposed of.

If Hedrick were a real swine . . .

She wondered if Roger Hedrick had thought that far ahead.

When the president finished lunch with the leaders of Congress, he went back to the Oval Office and turned on the television. Like half the people in America, he too was trying to keep up with the saucer story via television. In addition, he was trying to take the pulse of the voting public. He had four televisions arranged side by side so he could monitor the video on four networks at once and surf the audio channels.

Like Charley Pine in Australia, he also watched Professor Soldi. Being momentarily alone, he gave the archaeologist the finger.

The old fool didn't seem to realize how many applecarts he was threatening to upset with his visions of change, but the president certainly did. Successful politicians were those who knew which levers to pull, which buttons to push in today's world. Of course they paid lip service to change and spent their professional lives guiding it, but it was incremental change designed to benefit those people who had or would support them, usually people who were already at the top of the food chain. The president instinctively understood that the change Soldi envisioned was revolutionary, the kind that beheaded kings, executed czars, toppled republics. Soldi was the prophet of a new paradigm, and the president feared him.

He was listening to man-in-the-street interviews on CNN when his chief of staff, O'Reilly, came in.

"Roger Hedrick has four groups bidding on the saucer, Mr. President. China, Russia, and Japan arrived yesterday. A group from Europe arrived at Hedrick's station about ten hours ago. The senior negotiator is Nicholas Pieraut, a senior executive at Airbus. He telephoned the French government two hours ago and reported that he had had a saucer ride. He was very enthusiastic."

"I thought State said the Europeans wouldn't bid on the saucer?"

"That's what their governments told our ambassadors."

The president turned off the televisions

with the buttons on his desk and leaned back in his chair.

"Were they lying, or did they change their minds?"

"They were lying."

"And we can't tell them we know they were lying?"

"If we tell them . . ."

The president waved O'Reilly into silence. The National Security Agency was light-years ahead of the rest of the world in decoding encrypted electronic transmissions; it had been eavesdropping on foreign governments' conversations for years. Of course, to reveal knowledge gained in this manner would be to compromise the entire decoding operation.

"This mess keeps getting worse," the president said. He put the palms of his hands over his eyes while he thought. After a bit he removed his hands and regarded O'Reilly with a morose stare. "It will be bad if the Russians or Chinese get the thing, worse if Japan takes it home, but the Europeans would be a disaster. They have the capital and infrastructure to take immediate advantage of the technology."

O'Reilly looked as wrung out as the president. "I had lunch with the chairman of the Federal Reserve. He said that the saucer's technology could make Europe the world's dominant economy."

"Any chance the Europeans might pay too much?"

"How much is too much? If you expect the technology in the saucer to grow your gross domestic product by five percent a year for the next ten years, how much could you pay Hedrick? Ten percent of that increase? Twenty? Thirty? True, the stimulus might be less than five percent of GDP, but I'll bet it'll be more. Perhaps a lot more."

"And the Australian government?"

"They deny that the saucer is in the country."

Rip Cantrell concentrated on staying on his side of the road as he piloted the delivery van out of Bathurst at ten o'clock in the morning and headed west for Hedrick's station. He was wearing the delivery driver's shirt and cap.

He had left the man in a bar, determined to drink up the Australian equivalent of a thousand American dollars. Rip had solemnly promised to bring the van back that evening. The promise was a sop to the driver's conscience. He didn't even ask Rip why he wanted the van. The display of cash had been enough to seal the deal.

So here he was, wearing his new jacket against the morning chill, wearing a shirt that said "Fred" above the left breast pocket and a cap with the market's name above the bill, driving this old van full of food.

He hummed as he drove, trying to keep his mind off his fluttering stomach. Maybe food would help. After all, two hours had passed since breakfast. Well, why not?

He pulled over and rummaged through the load until he found a box of doughnuts. With the box open beside him and a doughnut in his mouth, he got the van back on the road and rolling westward.

So far so good, he told himself. He was going into Hedrick's home camp . . . unarmed. With no plan. To find a woman and steal a saucer.

Chance of success? Damn near zero. But what else could he do?

He didn't have a gun, wouldn't shoot anyone if he had one, didn't know if Charley was there, didn't know if the saucer was still there — though it probably was since he had seen it airborne yesterday — didn't know how many guys Hedrick had around him.

He ate another doughnut.

All too soon he came to the long straight stretch. The gate was three or four miles down there on the left. He slowed down, flexed his hands and arms, sped back up.

Well, all he could do was his best. Pray for a little luck.

He brushed the crumbs off his lap and set the cap on his head just the way he liked it, then began slowing for the turn.

Three guys in the guard shack by the gate pole, which was down. He pulled up at the shack and stopped.

One of them came out, looked him over. "Have I seen you before, mate?" he asked.

Rip just shook his head no.

"New man, eh?"

Rip nodded, then said, "Uh-huh."

"Righto. In you go." The guard pushed down on the weight on the butt end of the gate pole, and the pole rose.

Rip slipped the clutch and got the van moving. Then he took off the cap and wiped the perspiration from his forehead.

The gravel road ran straight as a bullet for about a mile before it left the flat creek bottom, then it wound over rolling terrain for another two miles. The main station complex sat on a small hill surrounded by a grove of trees. Scattered around the complex were large trucks. Around the trucks were men in uniforms, soldiers. Yes, soldiers in uniforms with weapons. Near one of the trucks he spotted a bunker with a machine gun poking out of the firing slit.

Hedrick didn't have a private army — he had the *Australian* army! Rip wondered whom you had to know and how much you had to pay to get the army to guard your house. Guard it? Heck, they had fortified it. Who did they think was going to attack?

He saw the parked airliners and the hangar, of course, and figured the saucer was in the hangar, but he couldn't just drive down there and walk in. Not past all these troops. He kept going, past the horse barn and main garage toward the main house.

The kitchen, he thought, would be around in back. He drove slowly around the house. Sure enough, there was a loading dock on the back of the building. He backed up to it and killed the engine.

He went through the door, saw a man wearing an apron and chef's hat. "Food delivery," Rip said and jerked his thumb in the direction of the truck.

"Cold storage?"

"Most of it."

"Stow it in the meat locker." Then the cook hustled off. The locker was easy enough to find. Rip opened up the van and got busy. He was done in fifteen minutes.

With the bill of lading on a clipboard, he walked through the kitchen. Only two people there, one scrubbing big pots and the other making a cake, a cake shaped like the saucer!

Rip walked on through the swinging door out into the dining area. A maid was arranging place settings. Rip continued into the main hall. He took off the cap, stuffed it into his hip pocket.

He heard voices in one of the rooms and put his ear to the door. Japanese or Chinese, he couldn't tell. He walked on.

He came to the main entrance. Looking across the porch he could see the hangar. It was several hundred feet away down a gentle grade. Three soldiers were idling by the personnel door on this side of the structure.

Tomorrow. He would come back tomorrow with the delivery driver and bring a set of civilian clothes. While the driver was off-loading the order, he could hide, and after dark, when the coast was clear, he could search for Charley. If he could just find her . . .

"What are *you* doing in this part of the house?"

He turned, found himself facing a formidable matron in a maid's uniform.

Silently he extended the clipboard and a pen.

She glanced at it. "Cook will sign that. Now scat. Back to the kitchen with you, like a good lad."

He marched, with the housekeeper right behind. As she came through the door behind him, she shouted, "Cook!"

The man with the chef's hat popped out of an alcove off the kitchen, his office apparently.

"This jackeroo was wandering about the main house. This is your tradesman, Cook."

"Right, Miss Padgett."

"Sign the bill and shove him off."

Cook signed. "See you tomorrow, laddie."

With a last glance at the cake, Rip went back to the van. He closed the rear door, started the engine, and drove slowly down the driveway, all the while looking around for any clues as to where Charley might be.

Just before he rounded the corner of the horse barn, he caught a glimpse of her, hair in a ponytail, wearing her flight jacket and flight suit, walking between two men toward the hangar.

Charley Pine!

He kept the speed down, took his time,

drove slowly by the army guys. He looked back over his shoulder one last time . . . and saw a tank parked under a tree.

The soldiers were a surprise for Charley Pine. She had seen only a few armed men prior to last night, perhaps a dozen total, and now this morning they were everywhere, at least a hundred. She too saw a tank sitting under a tree. Another was snuggled down in the midst of a pile of hay bales; all that stuck out was the turret and gun barrel.

As she neared the hangar she could see that troops were digging foxholes at the foot of the slope that led down from the house.

Three soldiers were standing in front of the hangar personnel door, all carrying assault rifles on slings over their shoulders. One of them opened the door for Charley and her escorts, a Japanese engineer and the ubiquitous Rigby. The swelling in Rigby's face had gone down somewhat, but the yellow and purple splotches were still stunning.

The engineer had his camera bag with him. He wanted more digital pictures of the engineering spaces, which he could then fax via satellite telephone to the big muckety-mucks in Japan. Hedrick detailed Charley to accompany him, escorted of course, which went without saying. Everywhere she went, there was Rigby, with his taped nose and magnificent bruised face. He didn't look directly at her even when she faced him. Perhaps Rigby sensed that looking into her eyes would be more annoyance than his constitution could stand. It was a fact she noted and filed away.

The saucer sitting in the middle of the empty hangar took her breath away again. It looked as spectacular as it did the first time she saw it, that night in the Sahara by flashlight. Smooth, sleek, dark, and ominous, with complex curves. The sight of the thing made her pause. The Japanese engineer paused too, stood momentarily taking it in, then he walked toward it.

She opened the hatch in the saucer's belly, stood aside while the engineer climbed up. She followed. Rigby could fend for himself. He entered right behind her, of course, and climbed into the pilot's seat. His logic was unassailable: Charley Pine wasn't going anywhere with him in the pilot's seat. She reached for the reactor knob and pulled it to the first detent, about an eighth of an inch. The saucer's interior lights came on.

Charley and the engineer got down on their hands and knees and crawled into the engineer bay. The light panels were quite adequate.

The engineer wanted her to help with the tape measure, to hold it against the piece of equipment being photographed while he snapped pictures.

While he was photographing the hydrogen separator and accumulator tank, the thought occurred to Charley that the best place on the ship for a bomb was probably behind the accumulator, against the bulkhead where no one could see it.

She waited until the engineer had snapped his photos and turned his back momentarily to root in his camera bag. She reached behind the accumulator. And touched something attached to the side of the tank. Something with a thin wire dangling from it.

Hell's bells! That asshole Hedrick did put a bomb in here!

She tugged at the thing. It took a serious pull to overcome the attraction of the magnets, but the bomb came loose in her hand. She lowered it to the deck, shielded it with her body from the engineer's sight.

It was wrapped in tape, plastique explosive with a hard cap, about four inches by two by two, from which a foot-long naked wire dangled. Antenna. A radio-controlled bomb.

Charley left it there. The engineer was facing this way again. She took off her flight jacket and tossed it over the bomb.

The photographs took another fifteen minutes or so. The engineer was packing the camera equipment when he inadvertently knocked his bag over. He began apologizing and making tiny bows as he picked stuff up and restowed it.

Charley took the opportunity to pick up the jacket and bomb. She slid the bomb into an inside pocket of the jacket, folded the jacket so it wouldn't show.

The engineer got all his things collected finally, and after three or four more small bows, crawled from the bay ahead of her.

Charley was right behind him. As the engineer's rump filled the entrance to the bay, she reached behind the reactor and retrieved the bomb he had just placed there. It too went into her jacket.

Ten minutes later, in a ladies' room of the main house, Charley examined her trophies. Both were radio controlled, both had magnets to hold them to metal surfaces.

She picked up the first bomb, the one

she had found behind the hydrogen accumulator tank. Who put this one there? Hedrick, the Chinese, the Russians?

Maybe Hedrick's bomb was still on the saucer.

The actual auction began after lunch in Hedrick's library on the ground floor of the house. The room was large, twenty feet by thirty, with a desk for Hedrick and smaller desks scattered about the room for the bidding groups. In the corner near where Charley Pine sat was a large, black safe, a huge thing, which bore the markings of the Brisbane, Sydney and Adelaide Railroad Company, the B, S & A.

Charley settled in to watch with her flight jacket on her lap.

At lunch Hedrick invited her to the table where he and Bernice sat. "When the auction is complete, I wish to hire you to fly the saucer to where the new owner wishes it to go. I will pay you for your time as we agreed and give you enough additional money to pay for airfare back to America. I will also ask that the new owner pay you ten thousand dollars for flying the saucer for them."

"You keep saying you'll pay me, but I haven't seen any money."

Hedrick reached into his pocket and removed a stack of hundreds. He tossed it in front of her. "There's ten thousand American there. I'll pay you the rest when we figure the airfare."

She tapped her finger on the bundle. "What if I take this, then swear out a kidnapping warrant when I get back to the States?"

Hedrick shrugged. "Do as you think best."

"Why don't you give me a check instead? That way you have proof you paid me."

"Let's not play games, Ms. Pine. Check or cash, which do you prefer?"

Charley picked up the bundle of banknotes. "Doesn't matter," she said as she slipped the bundle into a pocket.

"It is possible that the deal might be consummated tonight, but more likely tomorrow sometime. Please avoid the wine, so you can fly."

Charley nodded. Bernice smiled at her, as if to say, See, he's really very nice.

Charley managed a smile as she arranged her napkin on her lap.

"Perhaps," Hedrick said, "you would like to watch the auction?"

"That sounds interesting," Charley Pine said, trying not to sound over- or underwhelmed. After all, she didn't have anything better to do unless she wanted to go for another Land Rover ride with Bernice, and her back was too sore for that foolishness.

"Working for me didn't turn out so bad after all," Hedrick said with a smile. The bastard could really turn on the charm.

"I guess not," Charley said and smiled in reply. "I really enjoyed breaking Rigby's nose."

She did feel somewhat relieved. Perhaps neither of those bombs were Hedrick's, she thought as she sat listening to dear, earnest Bernice chatter away.

Now, sitting in the library watching Hedrick, she realized that he had paid ten thousand dollars so she would relax, not try to escape, so she would agree to fly the saucer for the successful bidders, and die with them.

Ten thousand dollars was chump change to Roger Hedrick. Bernice spent that much every half hour she shopped.

This afternoon Bernice and another secretary did the necessary paper shuffling and legwork. There were several people sitting near Hedrick whom Charley didn't know, so she asked Bernice at one point. One of the balding gentlemen was with the

Australian tax ministry. Another was from the prime minister's office.

Anyone who didn't think Roger Hedrick had connections, think again!

Each of the bidding parties had already prepared their first bids, so the first round went quickly. All four parties bid the minimum, ten billion dollars. As they were preparing their bids for the second round, Bernice wandered over to where Charley was sitting beside the safe.

Charley asked her about Siberia.

"I think Roger made some agreement with the Russians," Bernice whispered, "but I don't know what. He doesn't like it when I ask him about business matters."

"I see."

"If he doesn't want me to know anything, then why does he want me to help out with these business things?" Bernice asked. "I think he sees me as cheap secretarial help." She smiled when she said that. Actually, Charley thought, Roger wanted Bernice around so she would think he liked her. That was his hold on her.

The thought that she was overthinking this whole thing irritated Charley. Maybe Hedrick really did like Bernice. What the hell did it matter?

Then again . . . she was acutely conscious of the heft of the bombs in her coat pockets.

The Japanese and Europeans both bid twenty billion in the second round. The Chinese were next at thirteen billion, the Russians bid eleven billion, the minimum.

After the second round, each group wanted to make telephone calls, so that took some time.

The third round took even more time. This time the bids were in the mid-thirties.

After the fifth round, the high bid was fifty-eight billion and all the players were still in. They were sweating now. Ties were loosened, coats were on the backs of chairs, even Roger Hedrick was feeling a bit of the tension. He had loosened his tie and was watching each group with eyes that didn't miss a thing.

At this point Charley thought the Russians were the least likely group to buy the saucer. The Japanese exuded confidence, but Charley knew of the bomb one of the engineers had planted, so she thought they had a firm top figure that the Japanese government had refused to exceed. The only question in Charley's mind was how close to the limit they had come.

One more round, or two?

The Chinese seemed to be most in control. The senior man was as calm as if he had been playing mah-jongg for matchsticks. He was the only man in the room who was still wearing his suit jacket. If he had a limit that he could not exceed, his demeanor certainly gave no hint of it.

That thought seemed to trouble the Japanese, who kept eyeing the Chinese warily.

The Europeans were arguing among themselves. They would whisper vehemently together, then leave the room, come back and whisper some more, then leave again.

It was getting along toward five o'clock and the bids for the sixth round had yet to be filled out when Bernice came over to Charley. "Roger says this will be the last round today. Would you care to freshen up for dinner?"

"I'd like that," Charley Pine said and picked up her flight jacket from the floor beside her chair. It felt lighter with only one bomb in the pocket.

She smiled to herself as she walked for the door.

At dinner Charley Pine learned how the sixth round of bidding had turned out. All four parties were still in the game, high bid $62.6 billion by the Japanese.

Charley was wearing one of Bernice's French frocks. Ivan the Russian Romeo was too busy conferring in low tones with his colleagues to pay attention, but Pieraut found the time to give her a very pleasant smile. Ah, those Frenchmen!

That little smile warmed her.

Charley wondered if Rip Cantrell would like the way she looked, then spent the next hour feeling vaguely guilty. After all, the kid was eight years younger than she was.

Well, at least she had ten thousand bucks in her jeans. When, *if,* she got back to the States, she would call that guy at Lockheed Martin, see if that test-pilot job offer was still open. After the saucer flap maybe they wouldn't want her. If they didn't, hell, there were always the commuters. If she couldn't talk her way into the cockpit of a Beech 1900, she would tear up her pilot's license.

Thinking these thoughts, she attacked her steak.

Rip Cantrell was also eating steak. Amazingly, the delivery driver was still on his feet in the bar when Rip returned the van. He had apparently been drinking beer all day.

"Here, mate," the driver said. "Sit and I'll buy you one."

Rip insisted on buying the driver dinner after he returned the van to the market's parking lot. Now the two of them were eating kangaroo steak.

"Lucky day for me when you came along," the driver said. He had graduated from beer to whiskey.

"Are you married?"

"Oh, yeah. Little woman at home."

"Want to call her? Ask her to come down and I'll buy her dinner too."

"Here? In here? Oooh, no, mate. This is no place for her."

"Looks respectable enough."

"It's me reputation, mate. Me reputation. The mates would never let me live it down. Oh, no. The little woman stays at home. I provide for her and she takes care o' me, and that's the way it should be between men and women." He wiggled a finger solemnly. "You Americans are far too friendly with your women. That makes it hard for everyone, you see."

"You're a philosopher, Fred. I can see that."

"I like you, kid."

"How about letting me ride along with you tomorrow when you go to Hedrick's?"

"Oh, can't do that, laddie. Against company rules. No passengers, they say. Firing offense."

"It's worth five hundred American."

"How much is that in Australian?"

"About eight hundred."

"Sometimes exceptions can be made, mate."

"The high bid in the sixth and final round of the first day of bidding was sixty-two point six *billion* dollars," the aide told the sleepy president over the telephone.

"Who?"

"The Japanese."

"Anyone drop out?"

"No, sir. All four parties are still in it."

The president looked at the illuminated hands of the clock on his bedstand. 4:54 a.m. "When is the hypersonic plane going to do its photo flyby?"

"A few minutes after true sunrise in Australia, sir, about two this afternoon here."

"And the radar images?"

"Those are coming in now, sir."

"Have General De Laurio and the national security adviser come to the White House for breakfast. We'll look at the images then."

"Yes, sir."

17

Rip Cantrell was amazed when he saw what the soldiers had accomplished at Hedrick's station overnight. Foxholes and bunkers had appeared everywhere, as if a giant groundhog were in a digging frenzy. A half dozen tanks were arranged around the main station building complex.

"I haven't seen this many soldiers since I got out of the army," the delivery driver said.

"Looks like an army base, doesn't it?"

"What in the world are these people doing here?"

"Maybe Hedrick is entertaining some foreign big shot."

"Yeah. Maybe so."

The driver backed in to the kitchen loading dock. "How about helping me unload."

"Sure," Rip said. "But remember, this is a one-way trip for me. Just drive out of here innocent as all get-out and go on back to town. No one will be the wiser."

"Man, I don't like this. All these soldiers . . ."

"You want to give me my money back?"

"It's your ass, kid. Not mine."

With that the driver opened his door and stepped down. Rip got out on his side of the vehicle. Inside the kitchen the cook and head housekeeper were nowhere in sight, although two members of the kitchen staff were busy making tea.

Rip made a couple of trips into the food locker carrying bags of groceries while two waiters went back and forth to the main dining room carrying pots of tea. When the kitchen workers turned away and the waiters bustled out, Rip looked through the door glass into the dining room. About twenty people were still eating breakfast. Charley was at one of the tables with her back to the kitchen door: He would recognize that ponytail anywhere. And, of course, there was the Air Force flight suit.

He helped the driver carry one more load into the food locker, then jumped down from the loading dock and walked along the side of the house to a servants' entrance he had spotted the previous day. He tried the door. Unlocked.

He slipped inside and pulled the door shut behind him.

The hallway where he found himself was long and narrow, a passageway designed to keep the domestic staff out of the main portion of the house. No telling when he was going to meet someone, so he hurried along the passage.

On his left was a door. He opened it a few inches and looked into the kitchen, then let the door close.

Another passage ran off to the right. He took it. Fifty feet ahead was a stairway. At the foot of the stairs were two doors. He opened one: the laundry. The other was the furnace room, and it was empty. Rip slipped in and closed the door behind him.

Two windows high up in the wall allowed daylight to filter in here. He would have had a view of the yard and hangar if the windows had clear glass in them instead of the frosted kind.

Rip went across the hall into the laundry. Sure enough, he found green trousers and a shirt that could only belong to a gardener. The knees of the trousers were faded from kneeling on damp earth.

He skinned out of his clothes and pulled on the trousers. The waist was a bit large, but not too much so. The shirt was okay as long as he left the sleeves unbuttoned. He put his jacket back on, left it unzipped.

In the furnace room he found a toolbox containing a meager assortment of hand tools. These would have to do.

When Hedrick came into the dining room for breakfast, two of the bidding parties approached him. They wanted more time in the saucer. Charley Pine was sipping on a cup of coffee at the next table. She half turned in her chair to watch the discussion.

Hedrick eyed the Chinese and European team leaders without enthusiasm. "Everyone has had ample opportunity to examine the saucer. Further examination will merely delay the resumption of bidding, which by mutual consent is scheduled to resume at eleven o'clock . . ." Hedrick consulted his watch. "Twenty-seven minutes from now."

Pieraut spoke first. "My government has raised questions, Mr. Hedrick, that I must attempt to answer. I merely serve my nation."

The Chinese delegation leader echoed Pieraut. He also had no choice, he said.

Hedrick had to agree to their request and did so without further argument. He asked Charley Pine to escort the bidders, and she agreed.

On the way to the hangar she passed someone kneeling on the sidewalk working on a junction box. She and her male companions paid the workman no attention. After she passed him, however, he watched her and the four men she was with until they disappeared into the hangar. Then Rip Cantrell went back to messing with the junction box.

Rigby was standing beside the saucer when the little party entered the hangar. He stood watching as the party went through the saucer's hatch one by one, then he climbed aboard too.

Charley spent a dull hour in one of the passenger seats watching the engineers inspect, photograph, and measure. Roger Hedrick had absolutely forbidden any disassembly.

Rigby sat in the pilot's seat watching Charley Pine like a cat watches a mouse. Roger Hedrick was apparently taking no chances. Charley had been paid and promised more, but he wasn't about to take the chance that she would fly away with the saucer before he had collected a mountain of money from someone.

Is Charley going to fly the saucer? When will she come out of the hangar? Rip was toying with these questions as he inspected outdoor lighting junction boxes. He eyed the house. Maybe he should go inside. But where?

Soldiers came and went, presumably on military errands, and a backhoe lumbered by the hangar. Apparently it was being used to dig foxholes.

There were some armed civilians around too, but none of them seemed to give Rip more than a glance.

He couldn't keep opening junction boxes and dicking around inside them for too long, however, without attracting attention he didn't want. He had to go somewhere, do something, until a chance to get away with Charley came along.

But what?

"Well, as I live and breathe, if it ain't the ol' tapeworm kid himself." An American voice.

Rip looked up, straight into the face of Bill Taggart. Standing beside Taggart was the tall Aussie from the Sahara, Red Sharkey. Behind Sharkey were two other men, both carrying rifles.

Rip got to his feet, wiped his hands on his trousers. "What are you doing here, Taggart?"

"Becoming a millionaire, kid." From his shirt pocket Taggart produced a check. He fluttered it in the air. "Ol' Hedrick pays his debts, I'll say that for him. I told him about the saucer. Made myself some serious money."

Rip was infuriated. "You had no right to do that."

"All the right in the world, kid. That saucer belongs to me as much as it does to you. I figured out a way to make a dollar on the damned thing, and by God I did."

"Enough jawing," Red Sharkey said and laid a heavy hand on Rip's shoulder. Rip shrugged it off and swung at Taggart, who took the punch on his neck and went down like a stunned ox.

Sharkey and his men grabbed Rip's arms.

"I thought I'd seen the last of you when you stole the saucer in the desert, boy," Sharkey said. "Left us to the tender mercies of Qaddafi's camel jockeys, so you did. You owe me."

Red Sharkey drew back and drove a fist at Rip's chin. Rip managed to take most of the impact on his shoulder and the side of his face, but the blow staggered him.

One of the men spoke up. "You'll get us fired, Sharkey, scuffling on the lawn."

"This little bastard deserves it," Taggart snarled, rubbing his neck. He got slowly to his feet, looking sour as hell.

Red Sharkey twisted Rip's arm up behind his back. "Come along like a gentleman or I'll twist your arm right out of the shoulder socket."

Sharkey marched Rip into the house. Taggart stood on the sidewalk watching them go.

They took Rip to a small room with several chairs. "Watch him," Sharkey told the two who were with him and left them there.

Rip fell into a chair. He sat there flexing his arm, trying to work out the soreness.

In less than two minutes Sharkey was back with Hedrick in tow.

"Mr. Cantrell, it *is* you. This is quite unexpected," Hedrick said, smiling. "Welcome to Australia."

Rip didn't reply.

Hedrick's smile faded. "How did this man get here?" Hedrick asked Sharkey.

"I don't know, sir. We found him outside, playing with lawn lighting junction boxes."

"Take him down to the hangar, show him to Ms. Pine. Then lock him up somewhere. And leave someone to guard him."

Rip's legs almost failed him when he saw the saucer sitting in the middle of the hangar. So close and yet so far.

Sharkey called to Charley through the hatch. She came out, stood there looking at Rip, who was flanked by Sharkey's hired muscle.

"Mr. Hedrick said to show him to you. Now you've seen him."

Rip jammed his hands into his pockets so no one would see them tremble.

Charley looked so beautiful.

She walked over to him, reached for his cheek.

"That's enough romance," Red Sharkey said sourly. "I'm getting all choked up."

They turned Rip around and led him away.

Charley stood rooted, staring at Rip's back. Sharkey paused beside her. "Hedrick said to make it crystal clear: Any funny business and he gets it."

Charley Pine climbed back into the saucer.

The engineers announced themselves satisfied a few minutes after twelve o'clock and lowered themselves through the open hatch. Charley went through the hatch after them.

Rigby stayed in the saucer. The engineers wandered toward the main personnel door and left the building.

What is Rigby doing in there?

She stretched, did several deep knee bends, bent over and touched the toes of her steel-toed leather flight boots.

No one else in the hangar.

Where have they taken Rip?

She should fly the saucer out of here. Fly it right through the door, light the rockets and be gone.

Hedrick wouldn't hurt Rip. The man would have to let him go.

Even as she thought it, she didn't believe it.

She was standing there, forlorn, tired, and dejected, when Rigby dropped through the saucer's hatch. Bent over, he walked toward her.

He was just clearing the leading edge of the saucer and coming erect when she leaped clear of the floor and kicked with her right foot. She was aiming for Rigby's larynx and missed; her flight boot smashed into his mouth.

His head slammed back against the leading edge of the saucer, then he went to his hands and knees, blood gushing from his mouth. Rigby spit teeth, shook his head, trying to get it together.

His head came up and his eyes found her. His lips twisted. He coiled himself to rise.

She kicked him again with everything she had, with all her weight moving forward into the kick. Her foot caught Rigby square in the nose with a sickening thunk, ripping the bandage off.

The impact threw Rigby backward onto the concrete, where he hit with a splat. He lay there totally relaxed. Unconscious. Blood flowed freely from his mouth and the misshapen lump of flesh that had been his nose.

Steeling herself, Charley Pine bent down and checked under Rigby's armpits. Nothing. She half rolled him and felt the small of his back. A holster.

She pulled out the pistol, a nice little Walther .380, loaded, with a full magazine. She put it in the pocket of her flight suit and climbed into the saucer.

In the cabin she stood erect, trying to get her breathing under control, looking around, trying to think.

If those engineers hid a bomb in here, where would they put it? They must have known that the saucer might be inspected again. Or two or three times.

She started in the equipment bay.

Ten minutes later she was back in the main cabin.

One of the Chinese had looked under the floor panels.

She pried up the panels he had opened. And found a bomb with her fingertips. It was wedged as far forward as one could reach, in a cranny impossible to inspect with the naked eye. She gingerly pulled it from its hiding place and inserted it in a pocket of her flight jacket.

Did the German engineer also look in there? She couldn't remember.

She hunted for another ten minutes, looking everywhere that she had seen any of the engineers look. Nothing.

Rigby was lying on the floor of the hangar exactly as she had left him. He hadn't moved.

Perhaps he was dead.

Maybe she should check to see if he was breathing.

Naw . . .

Outside on the mat were four large jets. Two of them were Grumman Gulfstream V's, one was a Russian airliner, another was a Boeing 737. One of the Gulfstreams sported the Hedrick family coat of arms on the tail; Charley Pine walked over for a look.

The soldiers in front of the hangar made no move to follow. They were guarding the hangar, not the airliners.

Charley Pine put one of the bombs in the right main gear well of the Gulfstream wearing the Hedrick coat of arms. The Chinese bomb went in a gear well of the Boeing, which carried the insignia of the Chinese national airline.

When she walked away from the airliners, heading toward the house, the soldiers were talking among themselves, paying no attention.

Lunch was a harried affair. The members of the delegations were tense and preoccupied and said little. They ate quickly and rushed from the room to confer with their groups and make last-minute overseas telephone calls.

Charley was dawdling over a full plate, abandoned by her luncheon companions and unable to eat, when Bernice came bouncing in wearing a wide grin.

"It'll be over soon, Roger says. Somebody will get the saucer this afternoon." Bernice giggled. "Roger is *so* excited! He's going to be the richest man on earth."

"I'm happy for him," Charley Pine said.

"Oh, I am too," Bernice gushed. "He's worked so hard for this."

"Right."

"Just think, we're watching history being made! I can positively feel the electricity in the air."

She strode away, off for the library, probably, leaving Charley to her uneaten lunch.

Charley filled her coffee cup and took it across the hallway to a television room. She settled into one of the overstuffed chairs and began surfing channels.

She stopped when she glimpsed Professor Soldi's tanned mug.

". . . Of course, we have no evidence to prove my theories, but archaeologists have none to disprove them, either."

"But your thesis that Homo sapiens came to earth in the saucer would necessarily mean that the fossil record of hominid development here on earth was wrong."

Soldi shook his head. "No, sir. Not wrong. The record is fragmentary at best, and some of it may have been misinterpreted. The fact is that the earliest archaeological evidence we have for Homo sapiens — modern man — is only one hundred thousand years old. Before that we find Neanderthal man and Homo erectus."

"Could the saucer people have displaced the hominids that evolved on earth?"

"Displaced, killed, or simply survived while the natives perished. We don't know enough even to guess."

"Professor, you have admitted that your theory is based on the assumption that evolution followed a similar course elsewhere. Could you comment on that?"

"I think evolution follows similar courses when similar conditions exist," Professor Soldi explained. "All things being equal, the evolutionary pressures will also be equal. A statistician might note that while all things are rarely equal, on occasion they may be essentially so. For example, if a star similar in size to our sun had a planet of about the right size, at about the right distance, then we can expect the laws of chemistry and physics to operate to make the planet very similar to earth. People seem to forget, there are at least a hundred *billion* stars in the Milky Way, our galaxy. There are *billions* of galaxies.

"There are not one or two planets similar to earth in the universe," Soldi said with narrowed eyes. "There are hundreds. Thousands. Perhaps hundreds of thousands. Could any of those hundreds of thousands of worlds similar to ours contain creatures similar to us? I submit that it would be astounding if they didn't."

"So we are not alone in the universe?" the interviewer prompted.

"Of course not. Ask anyone who has

seen the saucer. Ask what he or she thinks."

Charley Pine reached for the remote control. After she turned the television off, a male voice behind her said, "I think the damned thing was made in Brazil."

She turned. Sharkey.

Charley Pine got up and walked down the hall to the library. The door was closed and there was an armed man sitting on a stool. He didn't say anything. Charley opened the door and went inside.

Rip Cantrell was sitting in an empty horse stall in the barn. There was no door on the stall. In front of the stall on the far side of the barn sat a guard on a stool with a rifle across his knees.

Above Rip a shaft of sunlight shown in through a small glassless window. He sat in the hay trying to think. He wasn't tied up or chained. The only thing keeping him here was the guard's implicit threat to shoot him if he tried to leave.

The guard was maybe forty, slightly above medium height, with a modest spare tire around his middle. The butt of an automatic pistol protruded from a holster under his left armpit. He kept his rifle, some kind of army assault weapon, pointed in Rip's general direction. His right hand rested on the trigger assembly.

"Hi," Rip said conversationally.

The guard didn't even blink.

Rip moved around a bit, trying to get comfortable.

He still had a screwdriver in his pocket. Sharkey had forgotten to search him. He could feel the screwdriver against his arm as it rested on his lap. About four inches long, the screwdriver had a standard bit.

Without moving, he mentally took inventory of his pockets. He still had his wallet, a key to the borrowed car, a hotel room key, American and Australian coins, some paper money, a paper clip, a ballpoint pen, and a small piece of newsprint that he had torn out of a paper a few days ago at Egg's house, a story about compulsive eaters.

Taggart . . . he had never even suspected. Well, it was his own fault for trusting him.

He wondered about Dutch Haagen. Did Dutch double-cross him too?

Well, he was good and stuck. Until that clown with a gun went to sleep or left, he was going nowhere.

Rip sighed, leaned back against the wall behind him, and tried to relax. After a bit he closed his eyes, tried to sleep.

Charley Pine . . . he touched his cheek

where she had touched him, and shivered.

Charley sat in her usual seat by the safe in the library. The tension in the room was palpable. Of all the bidders, only the Europeans looked halfway relaxed. Roger Hedrick was all business, his emotions buried behind a mask of studied calm. Still, Charley thought that she caught occasional glimpses of the man who lived in there, a man who knew that he was holding a royal flush.

Pieraut finished writing on his bid sheet, signed it with a flourish, and put it in an envelope. He handed the envelope to Bernice.

That was the last one. Bernice handed all four envelopes to Hedrick and took her seat with the Australian deputy prime minister and the tax man, who were here again today.

Hedrick opened the envelopes, arranged the bids on the desk in front of him, moved one from right to left, looked up deadpan.

"Gentlemen, we have bids for seventy-six billion, eighty-two billion, eighty-six billion, and one hundred and fifty billion."

The Chinese, Japanese, and Russians sat stunned, staring at the other bidding parties. Pieraut beamed genially.

The leader of the Chinese team stood and stuffed his papers in his briefcase. His colleagues did likewise. When they were packed, they marched from the room without a word to anyone.

The Japanese slowly picked up their papers. One by one, the members of the delegation bowed to Hedrick, bowed to the remaining bidders, then filed out.

"I must consult with my government," the senior Russian, Krasnoyarsk, said.

"Please do," Hedrick said genially. "We will reconvene here in twenty minutes."

The Russian left the room.

Pieraut lit a cigarette and savored the smoke. "If no one else chooses to bid in the next round, I presume we are the winners?"

"Under the rules," Hedrick acknowledged, "that is indeed the case."

"Where do you want the money wired? If we win the auction."

Hedrick handed a sheet of paper to Bernice, who delivered it to Pieraut. "Those are the banks," he said. "If you win the auction, wire the money. When the banks confirm that they have received the money, the saucer is yours."

"You expected to sell the saucer for such a large sum?"

"I try to avoid idle speculation. As always with rare and precious things, the price depends on how much the object is desired."

"*Oui*," said Pieraut and smoked the rest

of his cigarette in silence. He looked self-satisfied, Charley thought, as did the two German engineers and the Italian.

She decided she had had enough. She got up and walked from the room.

In the foyer, Krasnoyarsk was grunting into a telephone. The news he was hearing was written on his face.

Charley was sitting on a stool in the kitchen drinking a cup of coffee when Bernice came charging through the door. "The Russians excused themselves from the next round! The Europeans have won!"

"Roger is now the world's richest man?"

"He's so close. In just a few hours. I am *so* happy for him."

"He doesn't deserve you, Bernice. Why don't you dump him and find yourself a decent fella?"

Bernice was horrified. She whirled and marched from the kitchen without another word.

It takes all kinds to make a world, Charley decided, and poured herself another cup of java.

The head cook came over to see if she liked the coffee.

"You got any peanut butter?" Charley asked. "I could do with a sandwich."

18

"Mr. President, the Japanese delegation just informed their government via satellite telephone that the Europeans got the saucer for one hundred and fifty billion."

P. J. O'Reilly whistled softly. "That's sixty billion above the maximum amount the Japanese government was willing to pay," he said, shaking his head in disbelief.

The president took the note from the aide, then nodded, dismissing him. He stared at the note for a moment, wadded it up, and tossed it in the out-basket.

"That tears it," he said to the chairman of the Joint Chiefs, who was sitting on the Oval Office couch beside Bombing Joe De Laurio. "Let's get on with it."

The chairman, an army four-star, looked as if he had been sucking a persimmon. "I want to go on record as opposing this."

"You're on record," said the president, who hated people who wanted their objections formally noted. When events proved them correct they were insufferable; when events proved them wrong they conveniently forgot their bad advice.

"I wish we could have flown that thing to Area Fifty-one," Bombing Joe said wistfully, "but I guess it wasn't to be. I don't see that we have a choice in this matter now."

The president eyed the general without affection. Bombing Joe wasn't the man to share a lifeboat with — the pit bulls in Congress would eat him alive.

"I should have gone into the hardware business with Dad," the president muttered.

"I want to see Rip," Charley Pine said to the guard in the barn.

"What's on the tray?" the guard asked suspiciously.

Charley lifted the cover on the main dish, revealing a heaping, steaming hot plate of beef, boiled potatoes, and vegetables.

"I've got my orders," the guard said. "Any funny business, I shoot him."

Charley replaced the dish cover.

"I'll do it, too. If you think I won't, you're making a big mistake."

"You look like the type who would kill an unarmed man."

"Listen, lady . . ."

She bent down and placed the tray on the floor, then straightened. If she could just get the man off guard, just for an instant, she could take him out with a karate kick or elbow to the neck, whatever opportunity offered.

The Aussie was too suspicious. He kept his finger on the trigger of the rifle and the muzzle pointed right at her belly. Shooting him with the Walther would be suicidal.

"No closer," the guard said. "I seen Rigby after you kicked him."

She took a tentative step toward him, shifted her weight.

"Don't, Charley!"

That was Rip.

The guard had his left hand on the forearm of the rifle, the muzzle dead center in her stomach. His face was white, drawn.

"Don't try it, Charley," Rip whispered. "Thanks for the grub."

"They want me to fly the saucer out of here," she said, her eyes never leaving the guard's. The man was stupid and scared, a dangerous combination.

"Maybe Hedrick will let me go after you leave," Rip said softly.

"Maybe."

"Sorry it worked out like this."

"I'll see you back in the States, Rip."

"Yeah." His voice was husky.

She backed away from the guard, then turned and walked out of the barn.

Hedrick was in the library seated at his desk while he waited for his European banks to call. The European bidders and two Australian politicians sat around the desk smoking Cuban cigars and drinking whiskey. Pieraut looked to be in an especially good mood.

Charley stood in the doorway. Hedrick excused himself and walked over to where she was standing.

"You owe me some money," she said.

He reached in a jacket pocket and extracted a bundle of hundreds. "I believe we said three thousand for each day you were here, plus three grand to ride the Concorde home from Paris. Here's twenty."

"They want to go to Paris?"

"Yes."

Charley took about a third of the bills and pulled them out of the bundle. "I don't take tips," she said and handed back the excess bills. She put the rest in a chest pocket of her flight suit. Then she put her hands in the pockets of her jacket. She used her right hand to get a firm grip on Rigby's Walther.

Hedrick's eyebrows went up. Apparently he wasn't used to people refusing money.

"I expect you to let Rip go when the saucer arrives in Paris."

"And I expect you to fly the saucer to Paris and leave it with Pieraut and company."

"Uh-huh."

"If you ever want to see Rip alive again."

Charley Pine's eyes narrowed. She was sorely tempted to haul out the Walther and shoot this son of a bitch then and there. She took a deep breath, exhaled slowly, then said, "If Rip doesn't come home hale and hearty, all in one piece, I'll kill you someday, Roger. Sure as shootin'."

Hedrick seemed to be measuring her. "You know, I think you mean that. I think you'd try."

She pulled the Walther from her pocket and pushed it against his stomach. "This is how close you are to the next life, Roger. I could send you on your way right now. You hurt Rip, you'll be the richest dead man on this planet."

Hedrick had balls, you had to give him that. He glanced down at the pistol, then smiled genially. "We understand each other, Ms. Pine. That's rare in human affairs, but it's good. Misunderstandings can be quite messy."

She put the pistol back in her pocket and kept her hand on it.

"By the way, where is Rigby?"

"I wouldn't know. Have you lost him?"

"Never mind."

"When do I leave?"

Hedrick glanced again at his watch. "The banks in Europe don't open for another hour. The transfer will be made then."

He went back to the men sitting around his desk.

Charley removed her hands from her jacket pockets and dropped into the nearest chair.

The American nuclear-powered attack submarine rose slowly to periscope depth. For an hour the technicians had been carefully searching the sea with passive sonar. There were no ships within fifty miles of the submarine.

When the boat was stabilized at periscope depth, the skipper ordered the scope raised. All he could see was empty ocean and sky. The electronic signal detectors (ESM) on the scope remained silent. He lowered the scope back into the well.

"We have green lights on tubes one and two," the OOD reported.

"Roger."

The commanding officer looked at the digital clock ticking down on the fire-control computer. Forty-four seconds, forty-three . . .

"Commit," he said.

"Commit to fire automatically," replied the weapons officer.

Twenty-six hours ago the sub had raised its antenna above the waves and received a data dump from a computer in Washington, an encrypted signal that had been retransmitted by a satellite. Then the sub had run submerged at thirty knots for the next twenty-five hours, racing for this position. An hour ago, while the submarine was five hundred feet deep, it slowed to three knots and began the passive search. Ten minutes later the boat's com gear picked up a very-low-frequency radio signal that had traveled completely around the planet. This signal was the fire order.

Now the time had arrived.

The skipper stared at the screen of the fire-control computer. Who would have thought the president of the United States would ever order live missiles fired into Australia? The world just kept getting weirder.

The seconds counted down. The instant the clock registered zero, the skipper felt a jolt as compressed air pushed a Tomahawk cruise missile from tube one.

The missile's wings popped out and its engine ignited as it broke the surface of the sea. It roared into the air and climbed to several hundred feet above the water before it leveled off. It was already headed west, pointed almost exactly at its target. As the missile flew it acquired the signals from eight GPS satellites and updated its position.

Sixty seconds later, a second missile came out of the water and roared away after the first.

Its work done, the submarine turned back to the east and silently descended below the thermal layer.

The staccato, irregular ripping of fully automatic weapons firing bursts echoed down the long interior corridor of the horse barn. Then came the louder booms of explosions. The ripping of assault rifles, a deeper, louder belching of machine guns, and the boom of explosions mingled into a rising roar.

The guard stared at Rip, consternation written on his face.

He looked right, then left at the main doors to the barn.

Rip started to get to his feet.

"Hold it," the guard shouted, raising his rifle to his shoulder. "Don't move."

Rip sat back down.

The guard stood up, backed into the stall behind him so that he could not be seen from the doors on either end of the barn.

"Gonna wait until they come kill you?" Rip asked over the cacophony.

The guard didn't know what to do, that was obvious. He opened the window in the stall behind him and peered out carefully.

Rip gathered himself. This was his chance, if he could only get the hell out of this barn!

Several bullets struck the wood around the window that the guard was looking through. Little puffs of wood and dust exploded into the still air.

The guard rushed to the corridor. He looked both ways, then ran for the end of the barn nearest the house as the rifle fire grew louder. It sounded as if someone were shooting just outside.

Rip peered around the edge of the stall, watched as the guard scanned the area outside the barn, then ducked out the main door.

He trotted down the corridor and

peeked around the large board door that the guard had just gone through.

The guard was lying twenty feet from the door, his rifle beside him. The man lay absolutely motionless, apparently shot dead.

Rip drew back. He could hear bullets thunking into the upper walls and beams, like the patter of rain but more irregular.

Just then the booming crack of a tank gun rolled through the barn like thunder. Then another.

What in hell was going on?

The sounds of battle apparently caught Hedrick and the European delegation off guard. Pieraut loudly demanded to know who was shooting and what did it mean. Hedrick picked up the telephone and dialed it.

Within thirty seconds Krasnoyarsk and the senior Chinese bidder rushed into the room.

Pieraut went to the big window behind Hedrick's desk and looked out across the lawn. Just as he did so, something came through one of the top panes, shattering it. Pieraut ducked for cover as shards of glass rained down onto the carpet.

Hedrick shouted into the receiver. "Find them. Bring them to the library under armed guard." He banged down the telephone receiver. "Japanese commandos," he said. "At least a dozen, trying for the saucer."

"If we don't get the saucer intact, we won't pay you a cent," Pieraut said, loudly enough for Charley Pine to hear.

"Obviously," Hedrick snapped.

"We should leave now, fly it out of here while we still can."

Hedrick wiped his forehead with a handkerchief. He dabbed at his palms. A bullet hit another small pane of glass in the big window, shattering it. Hedrick didn't even flinch.

Charley Pine put on her flight jacket, walked over to the small refreshment bar, and poured herself a drink of water.

Hedrick has a heck of a problem, Charley thought. If she had needed any confirmation of Hedrick's intentions, his indecision just now certainly supplied it. He never intended for the saucer to reach Paris. However, if he destroyed it before he received the Europeans' money, he would probably never get paid. The saucer had to be intact and Pieraut alive and well when the money arrived in Hedrick's banks or he would never be able to hang on to the bucks.

And then there were the Japanese. The

commandos were either trying to steal the saucer or destroy it, and if they succeeded at either mission Hedrick wasn't going to collect money from anyone. It was a nice problem.

Charley helped herself to another glass of water. More bullets came through the main window, and the crowd around Hedrick's desk ducked below the level of the windowsill.

"Where is my army protection?" Hedrick roared at the two government ministers, who were huddled on the floor beside him.

As if in answer, a tank loosed off a round nearby. The boom took out another couple of windowpanes.

Just then Red Sharkey and two of his men marched the senior Japanese delegate, Hideo Ota, into the room at the point of a gun. Sharkey had a battery-powered radio transceiver in his hand. It was squawking gobbledygook.

Hedrick went at Ota like a tiger. "*What* is going on?" he roared.

Hideo Ota had had it with Hedrick. His face twisted in a snarl. "How would I know?" he asked in heavily accented English.

"I think your government is trying to steal the saucer or destroy it. You *knew* your government wasn't bidding in good faith."

"I don't care what you think," Ota replied and calmly crossed his arms. Hedrick slapped him. To his credit, the negotiator pretended not to feel the blow.

Apparently shocked by his own behavior, Hedrick backed away several steps and wiped his face again. He put the handkerchief in his pocket, squared his shoulders, shot his cuffs, checked his tie.

His eyes came to rest on Charley Pine. "Fly the saucer to Paris," he said.

"How is she going to get to the hangar?" Red Sharkey asked. "They're having a war out there."

The two Tomahawk missiles flew only a hundred feet above the waves. They flew into a rain shower, rode through the turbulence, and came flying out the other side unaffected.

The crew of a small fishing boat making a set saw the missiles. Before the sailors caught sight of the missiles, they heard the engines over the noise of the boat's diesel engine. One of the men pointed, and seconds later the first missile flew almost over the boat. The second one passed a hundred yards to the south about a minute later.

When the missiles had disappeared in

the haze to the west and the noise of their engines had faded, the fishermen talked about what they had seen. The captain radioed his base in Sydney — his wife — and left it to her to decide if the government should be informed about the missiles. Then the fishermen went back to work.

Rip Cantrell ran back down the central corridor of the horse barn. He looked in every stall. If he could find a vehicle, figure out a way to get to the house, where Charley was . . .

Nothing. Four very nervous horses were prancing in their stalls, nickering loudly, their eyes rolling, but there wasn't even a golf cart in the barn.

He reached the end farthest from the house and peeked through tiny cracks between the boards of the door. Two tanks were clanking down the hill, men were running for the foxholes at the base of the hill, wisps of smoke were rising from a far tree line.

Even as he watched, something struck one of the tanks. It seemed to stagger as fire and smoke erupted from the open top hatch. The tank ground to a halt. One man tried to climb from the hatch with his clothes on fire. His face was blackened. He got halfway out of the turret and collapsed face-down. Smoke rose from his clothing.

Rip went back through the barn, opening tack-storage closets and food bins. He was near panic when he saw a silver serving tray sitting on top of a barrel. On the tray were two empty wineglasses.

Rip opened the door to the main storage room. Tools, saddles, bridles, brooms, sacks of feed . . . and a door. He jerked it open. A stairway led down. Rip dashed down the stairs as the door swung shut behind him.

At the bottom of the stairs was a narrow corridor that turned right, toward the main house. The underground corridor was lit by bulbs every thirty or forty feet. Rip ran along it.

He saw a stairway ahead. The door at the top was unlocked. On the other side he found himself in another narrow passageway.

There was something familiar about this one . . .

He had been here before! He was under the main house. He kept going, went around a turn, and was looking through a glass panel in a door into the kitchen. No one in sight.

Staying low, below the tops of the counters, he slipped through the kitchen and took a look into the main dining room.

A man with a rifle was moving from window to window, looking out.

Rip looked around the kitchen. A rolling pin was handy, so he picked it up. As he turned he saw the dining room door opening, and he ducked down.

The man came along between the work islands. As he hurried by, Rip smacked him in the knee with the rolling pin.

The man went down hard, swearing. Before he could get the unwieldy rifle around in that confined space, Rip tapped him experimentally on the head with the pin. The thunk of wood against skull was sickening. The Aussie collapsed to the floor and let rip a mighty oath.

Rip gritted his teeth. He was going to have to hit the man harder, take the chance of cracking his skull. He swung the pin again, put more muscle into it.

The gunman went limp.

Rip got the rifle, checked the magazine, eased the bolt back for a look. Yep, he saw the gleam of brass.

The safety must be this lever here, and it was on.

He had done enough hunting as a teenager to be familiar with rifles, but he had never before handled a genuine assault weapon. Two spare magazines were in the unconscious man's pockets. Both were full of cartridges.

The gunman was out cold. Or dead. Rip felt his carotid artery for a pulse. Still there. He touched his skull where the rolling pin had whacked him. A large knot, big as an egg, was swelling up. The skull didn't feel pulpy.

With the rifle at the ready, Rip Cantrell slipped out of the kitchen into the dining room, then made his way deeper into the main house.

Captain Koki Owada of the Japanese Self-Defense Force threw himself against the bottom of the hangar personnel door and tried to catch his breath. Four of his men threw themselves to the ground near him.

He had had six men with him when he started; two were now dead.

Owada keyed the microphone switch on the back of his left hand and spoke into the headset he wore. "Red One is at the hangar door. We're going in now."

"Blue One, roger. The Diggers have their heads down." Blue One started the day with two dozen commandos. Koki Owada had not asked how many were still alive.

"Red Two, open the door."

Lieutenant Kawaguchi complied.

Owada dove through the door with his rifle at the ready.

No people visible.

The saucer sat in the middle of the bay facing the door.

Owada scanned the gloomy interior, ready to shoot. Not a soul in sight.

He posted two of his men outside, then he and Kawaguchi approached the saucer.

Extraordinary. It was so large, so . . .

"Red One."

Owada looked at Kawaguchi, who was pointing to a bloodstain on the concrete floor. Owada nodded, then turned back to the saucer.

The captain circled it once. The exhaust pipes were pointing toward the back wall, so apparently the thing was facing the closed hangar door.

"Red Three, it's all yours."

Red Three was a test pilot. Getting him and his colleague, Red Four, here was Owada's mission. Unfortunately, Red Four had stopped a bullet ten minutes ago and died instantly.

Everything now rested on Red Three's shoulders, Captain Ikeda. He had been on the secure satellite phone with the Japanese engineers who had inspected the saucer — and were now safely hidden in the rooms of the main house — so he knew where the main entrance hatch was. Unfortunately, he didn't know how to open it. The American test pilot had always opened and closed the hatch, and the Japanese engineers were afraid of making her suspicious by asking how it was done. After all, how difficult could it be?

While Red Three examined the hatch mechanism, Owada inspected the hangar door, a simple electric overhead door. When the time came, he had merely to push the button.

Owada permitted himself a smile. Things were going well.

Red Sharkey and Roger Hedrick huddled together in the back of the room around Sharkey's handheld radio transceiver, trying to get a handle on the military situation. Charley Pine seated herself in a huge stuffed chair well back from the window, facing the door to the hallway. Once again, she had both her hands stuffed in her jacket pockets, her right wrapped around the grip of Rigby's Walther.

Why no one had found Rigby Charley couldn't imagine. Maybe they found him and thought the Japanese commandos worked him over. Maybe Hedrick didn't gave a fig about Rigby. This possibility was the most likely, she decided. All Hedrick's lieutenants were expendable, like so many paper clips.

The pistol in her pocket gave her a fool's confidence, and she knew it. She tried to fight it back. Still, she had made up her mind: If anyone came at her in a belligerent way, she was going to start shooting.

She watched Pieraut — he was nervous now — and the Australian politicians, who were trying to telephone someone for help. The politicos were seated side by side on the floor in front of Hedrick's desk with the telephone. Finally they realized that the lines must be down. They abandoned the phone and hugged their knees.

She was facing the main doorway to the library, so she was the first to see Rip when he eased his head around the opening and looked in. He saw her too.

She glanced around the room to see who was paying attention, then stood and walked for the door. Out of the corner of her eye she saw Hedrick look up, then elbow Sharkey.

She walked through the door, saw Rip and his rifle.

"Could you shoot someone with that?" she asked.

The look on Rip's face was the answer.

Charley Pine took the rifle, flipped off the safety, then stepped back through the doorway to the library and leveled the weapon hip high at Red Sharkey, who was striding toward her with a pistol in his hand.

Sharkey was almighty quick. He leaped sideways as the rifle went off. The bullet smacked into the glass door of a cabinet near Hedrick, who dove for cover.

All of a sudden everyone in the room wanted to be flat on the floor.

Charley Pine took another shot at Sharkey. She hit him this time. Wounded, he started to rise, the pistol still in his right hand. Somehow he snapped off a shot, which missed her.

She lifted the rifle to her shoulder, aimed, and shot Red Sharkey in the chest.

"Holy damn!" she heard Rip exclaim, then he was reaching for her arm. "Let's go!"

One of Hedrick's thugs was on the floor eyeing Charley as he drew a pistol. She shot him too, then turned and followed Rip.

"We're going to have a hell of a time getting to the hangar," she called as they ran down the hall.

"Upstairs! Let's go upstairs! The room with all the windows!"

"On top of the house? What good will that do?"

Rip bounded to the stairway and charged upward. Charley had no choice but to follow.

The Tomahawk missiles crossed the Australian coast just north of Sydney harbor. They were in the terrain-matching mode at this point, flying a mere two hundred feet above the ground. The radar in the noses of the missiles scanned the flight path ahead for obstacles, then turned or climbed the missiles to avoid them. They eased over low hills, went around a radio tower, all the while continuously matching their computed position against the information they received from their GPS receivers. Course corrections were minute.

Red Three, Captain Ikeda, called Koki Owada over to the saucer. "I can't open this hatch," the test pilot said, obviously agitated. "I can't figure out how to do it."

"Is there another way in?"

"Not if we are going to fly it out of here."

"Keep trying."

Owada called on his radio for a situation update from Blue One.

"We have them pinned down. No one seems to be in a hurry to leave their foxholes or bunkers."

"And the people in the house?"

"Still there. Someone shot from one of the windows a while ago, but nothing lately. Are you in the saucer yet?"

"We're working on it."

Owada asked the test pilot, "Do you need some tools?"

"The engineers said the American woman opened this with her hand. No tools."

"Take your time," Owada said, pretending to a calm he didn't feel. To give the man time to think, he walked back to the open personnel door to check on his troops.

Owada kneeled by the door.

They were so close! Yet if they couldn't get into the saucer, they would have to destroy it. One of the troopers lying beside the hangar was carrying two optically aimed, wire-guided antitank missiles. The team had already used two: one on a fortified bunker and another on a tank. A missile warhead would punch a hole in the saucer and start a hot fire. A couple of magnesium grenades tossed into the hole should finish the job. *What a waste that would be,* Owada thought.

"Don't let them get in here," Rip shouted at Charley Pine as he topped the stairs and entered the atrium. Charley rushed over to the private elevator and pushed the call button. She listened with her ear to the door and heard a hum.

Rip ran through the large room looking for people.

There was a woman with a telephone pressed against her ear sitting behind the large desk in the center of the room.

"Who are you?" Rip demanded.

She put her hand over the mouthpiece of the telephone. "I'm Bernice Carrington-Smyth, if it's any of your business. And who, may I ask, are you?"

"Later. Who are you on the telephone with?"

"That's none of your —"

He lunged across the desk, grabbed the phone, and slammed it into the cradle.

"That was my mother I was talking to," Bernice said hotly. "Just who are you, anyway? I'll have Roger throw you off the place if you can't mind your manners."

"We're in the middle of a war and you're talking to your mother?"

"A war?" Bernice looked around wildly. The noise of small arms fire was quite plain here. "I thought those soldiers were just practicing."

Charley came trotting over. "I've disabled the elevator. Hi, Bernice."

"Charley, what is all this? I was on the satellite phone, Roger's private line, when he —"

"Maybe you ought to get under the desk, Bernice, so you don't accidently stop a bullet."

As Bernice took that advice, Charley asked Rip, "Would you mind explaining what we're doing up here when —"

"Later. Don't let anyone get in here." He pointed toward the stairs. "Oh, here are a couple spare magazines." He tossed them on the desk.

Charley got behind the desk and pointed the rifle toward the stairs. "I'm waiting for a miracle, Rip. Get busy."

Bernice spoke up. "Would you mind terribly, Charley, explaining what is going on?"

Rip ran to the corner of the room facing the hangar. He got down on his knees so only his head was visible through the window.

This had better work!

He tried to clear his mind. Closed his eyes, pressed the palms of his hands against them, took three or four deep breaths.

Okay.

He visualized the saucer, how it would look if he were sitting in the pilot's seat.

Reactor on!

He waited a moment.

Up a smidgen! Maybe a foot.

Another small wait, three or four seconds, then he commanded, *Gear up!*

Captain Ikeda, Red Three, was ready to call it a bad job. He couldn't figure out a way to open the saucer's hatch. Such a small thing, and yet it had beaten him.

He was walking toward Red One, Koki Owada, who was still crouched by the hangar door, telling him on the radio to destroy the saucer with the antitank missile, when he heard a hum behind him. Not loud, just a gentle hum.

Ikeda glanced back over his shoulder. The saucer was suspended in midair about a foot off the concrete.

Ikeda staggered, then caught himself. He

turned, faced the ship.

Now the gear was retracting.

"Red One, this is Three. There's someone in the saucer. You'd better destroy it now!"

Koki Owada turned to the soldier outside the hangar, who passed the antitank launcher through the door.

When Owada turned around, the saucer was moving!

It crossed the concrete floor, accelerated, and smacked into the closed hangar door. The building quivered from the impact.

From his perch in the atrium, Rip saw the roof of the hangar ripple. Okay! He backed the saucer up, ran it at the door again, faster. The impact made the hangar roof shimmy.

Should he raise the saucer, use it to lift the hangar roof? The saucer would be lifting against the joists that held up the roof.

First the door. Overhead doors were relatively flimsy; this one should cave in easily.

The saucer rammed the door so hard the upper hinges tore loose. Only the lifting cables were still holding it up.

Owada was right beside the lower right

corner of the overhead door. He was trying to activate the battery in the missile launcher when the saucer hit the door again and the near door edge whipped out, just flicking against the toe of his boot.

Owada lost his balance and fell.

He picked up the launcher as the saucer backed up for another ram. The door was off its hinges. It would go through this time.

Before he could get the launcher on his shoulder, the saucer shot forward, tore the door loose from the building, and went soaring upward. Owada ducked to get out of the way of the falling door panels.

When Rip saw the saucer clear the hangar on the far side, a wave of relief flooded over him. Yes, yes, yes!

He brought the saucer around in a turn, flew it up to his level, then slowed it as it neared the atrium.

The first Tomahawk missile reached its initial point and pitched upward. It climbed quickly to three thousand feet, then pitched over steeply. The radar in the nose went into its target acquisition mode.

The aim point was a ventilator shaft on top of a roof. There! Computer analysis of the radar return identified the shaft to a 99 percent certainty. The computer checked the shaft's position in relation to the missile against its predicted position based on GPS coordinates, determined that it was within parameters, and began issuing steering commands to the missile's canards and flying tail.

The missile accelerated downward.

Rip Cantrell brought the saucer gently in against the glass and framework of the atrium as a burst of rifle fire sounded behind him. He was distracted for only a second, then concentrated on the saucer before him.

Glass exploded from the windows, blew around in a cloud as the framework twisted, buckled, and collapsed from the force of the saucer pressing against it. Punctuating the sound of falling glass and twisting metal was the staccato hammering of Charley's rifle and the high-pitched eerie wail of Bernice's screaming.

Koki Owada, Red One, came around the corner of the hangar with the launcher on his shoulder. He leaned against the side of the building to steady himself, put the crosshairs of the optical sight on the saucer, which was settling down amid the twisted wreckage of the atrium.

The first Tomahawk missile plunged through the hangar roof a scant six inches from the ventilator shaft and penetrated two feet into the reinforced concrete floor of the hangar before the warhead exploded.

The force of the blast lifted the roof of the empty hangar and pushed its walls away from the building.

Koki Owada was struck by the wall just as he pulled the trigger of the missile launcher. The antitank missile roared from the launcher, shot across one hundred yards of manicured lawn, and punched a hole in the side of Hedrick's house. The missile went through three walls before the contact fuse impacted something solid enough to detonate it — the concrete elevator shaft in the center of the house.

The force of the exploding warhead bulged every door on the shaft and caused the elevator, which was at the top — atrium — level, to smash upward against the lifting machinery, ripping it from its mountings. The entire elevator and all its equipment fell down the shaft with a mighty crash.

★ ★ ★

Huddled in the library as explosions rocked the house and sifted dust down from the ceiling lights, Hedrick heard Red Sharkey's radio squawking. He picked it up and held it against his ear. Sharkey certainly didn't mind: He was lying dead five feet away.

"Hedrick here."

"Mr. Hedrick, the saucer is sitting on top of your house, and the hangar just blew up."

"On top of the house, you say?"

"Right on the bloody top. Collapsed the atrium framework, it did. Now it's sitting up there like a hen on her nest."

That bitch, Charley Pine! *She* was to blame. *$150 billion!* Down the bloody sewer. Of all the rotten luck!

Crouching, he made his way to his desk, opened the bottom drawer. The radio-control device for the bomb was still there, right where he had left it. He got out the device as the Europeans and politicians watched, set it on the desk, flipped on the battery switch.

Green light.

With the saucer at rest on its gear amid the wreckage of the atrium roof, Rip

Cantrell made his way to the hatch and opened it. "Come on, Charley. It's time to go."

She crawled over twisted beams, trying to avoid the shards of glass that threatened everywhere. She turned, called to the now-silent woman under the desk. "Bernice, this is your chance. Do you want to go with us?"

"No."

Bernice was staying with the money. Charley shrugged and crawled on.

Rip was very agitated. Any second Hedrick's goons were going to come up the staircase shooting like wild men.

"Want to tell me how you got this thing to fly up here?"

"Later. In, in, in! Let's get the hell outta here!"

The second Tomahawk couldn't locate its discrete target to guide upon, so its computer opted to impact at the GPS coordinates programmed in before launch. It hit within three feet of the place the first missile impacted.

The force of this blast was not impeded by the hangar walls, so the nearest Gulfstream V, Hedrick's, soaked up some of the warhead's shrapnel. Fuel began running from holes in the wing.

★ ★ ★

As Charley climbed into the saucer, a tremendous force slammed into her right shoulder.

Her shoulder and arm went numb, and she dropped the assault rifle she had been carrying. She tried to fall back through the hatch, but Rip was pushing hard on her bottom. Against her will, she was propelled into the saucer and sprawled on her face.

Rigby kicked her viciously in the ribs, bringing forth a grunt.

Rip crawled over her, going for Rigby.

Rigby screamed. No words, just a high-pitched, keening wail came out of the bleeding hole in the swollen, bloody mess that was his face.

He kicked at her again, this time getting Rip. On the next kick, Rip got hold of a leg and held on. Rigby went down, still screaming.

Charley rolled over, trying with her left hand to get the pistol out of the right-hand pocket of her flight jacket. She was having trouble breathing against the pain in her side.

Rigby had the strength of ten men. It was all Rip could do to hang on to his leg as he kicked and smashed Rip about the head and shoulders with his fists.

Charley finally dug the damned pistol out, tried to use her right hand on the safety. Numb. She fumbled with the safety with her left. Got it off.

Pointed the thing at Rigby and fired.

The shock of the bullet hitting Rigby was like a cattle prod on a bull. He went nuts, still screaming at the top of his lungs. He kicked so wildly that Rip lost his grip on his leg.

Completely insane, Rigby went for Charley. She shot him again and again as fast as she could pull the trigger.

He got his hands around her throat.

He was strangling her when she saw another bomb clinging to the underside of the pilot's seat. The realization of what it was sunk in despite the physical agony she was feeling. She still had the pistol in her left hand. She fired it twice more into Rigby's body before it stopped working — empty!

With blood pouring from his mouth, Rigby was starting to topple over when Rip grabbed him by the hair and jammed a screwdriver into the side of his neck.

The screaming stopped. Rigby fell over.

Charley reached up, grabbed the bomb, and jerked it loose.

"Get us airborne, Rip. We'll put Rigby through the hatch."

With her left hand she stuffed the bomb into Rigby's shirt, then helped Rip pull him toward the hatch.

"You fly," Rip shouted. "I'll crash us."

She clambered up into the pilot's seat. Using her left hand, she raised the collective. The saucer rose from the roof. Now gear up.

Still using just her left hand, she moved the stick sideways and took the saucer out over the lawn.

Rip dragged Rigby to the hatch and pushed him through.

The body fell halfway to the ground, about thirty feet, and stopped in midair.

Looking through the hatch, Rip shouted, "He's trapped in the antigravity field."

Hedrick and the Europeans were crowded around the window in the library when the saucer came into view with Rigby suspended in midair beneath it.

"That's your man, Rigby, isn't it?" one of the Europeans demanded of Hedrick. "Look at his face!"

Hedrick pushed the button on the radio control.

Behind him there was an explosion. He turned. A cloud of plaster dust filled the far end of the room. As it thinned somewhat, he could see the safe. The door was off its hinges and smoke was pouring out.

God *damn* that Charley Pine!

Pieraut looked thoughtfully at Hedrick's radio-control unit. If he and his delegation had departed in the saucer, Hedrick would have murdered the lot of them. Pieraut reached into his pocket for his own radio-control device. He flipped the switch to arm it, then pushed the firing button.

"You come fly this," Charley shouted, getting down from the pilot's seat. Having managed to close the hatch, Rip got into the seat in her stead. He put on the computer headband.

We want to light the rockets and go.

Behind him he heard a rumble of the rocket engines lighting off.

Pieraut was looking out the window at the accelerating saucer when he pushed the button on his device. Rigby's body, which was still trapped in the antigravity field, disappeared in a ball of fire.

The saucer sped away as the roar from the engines shook the library window glass, cracked it, then caused it to collapse.

Staring through the hole where the

window had been, the audience in the library watched the saucer disappear in the haze, still low in the sky.

As they stood watching, two fireballs rose from the planes on the parking mat in front of the hangar. Mr. Ito of the Japanese delegation and the gentleman from Beijing had both detonated their bombs.

Up in his bedroom, Krasnoyarsk was futilely pushing the button on his radio-control device. The battery in the device would not cause the green test light to come on. He pried open the radio controller.

The battery was Russian.

Krasnoyarsk cursed, then threw the controller against a wall, shattering it.

After the saucer had traveled a distance of about fifteen miles, Rip Cantrell laid it into a turn. He still had not touched the controls. With the headband on, he was telling the computer what he wanted the saucer to do, and it was flying the ship.

When the saucer was straight and level, pointing back at Hedrick's station, Rip let the machine accelerate through Mach 1. Charley was in one of the forward-facing seats. The G's pushed both of them back into their seats and held them imprisoned there.

The saucer was passing through Mach 6 when it went over Hedrick's mansion at two hundred feet.

The shock wave from the saucer blew out every window in the building and pushed the top story of the house down into the structure. The walls bulged, then blew out. The whole house collapsed.

The nose of the saucer rose until the ship was going straight up atop a pillar of fire.

19

It was one o'clock on a rainy, foggy summer morning when Rip Cantrell brought the saucer in over the treetops and landed in front of Egg's hangar in central Missouri.

He had reentered the atmosphere over the Southwest — which had probably made lights flash and bells ring all over the country — but he had flown the last two hours at a couple hundred knots and less than a thousand feet in altitude. A half hour ago he had run out of water, so he had slowed to the speed the antigravity unit could give him, which was about a hundred knots.

Just now Rip couldn't see anything through the canopy. He was afraid to use the landing lights, so when the computer said they had arrived, he told it to land. That was literally an act of blind faith. Still, he was wound as tight as a banjo string until he felt the landing gear touch something solid, and all motion ceased. A warm flood of relief brought tears to his eyes.

Charley was asleep on a reclining couch.

The side of her head was heavily bruised where Rigby had kicked her, and her right arm was numb, partially paralyzed. She probably had some cracked ribs too. The G's of acceleration over Australia had made her faint. He should have thought of her injuries before he told the computer to goose the throttle.

He stood in the darkness of the saucer's cabin thinking about all that had transpired in the last few days.

Ah, me! Ramming a screwdriver into that maniac's neck . . . Charley shooting him eight or nine times . . .

Was the saucer worth it?

He opened the hatch and dropped through.

The warm, moist air smelling of the earth enveloped him. Reeling, he climbed the gentle grade toward Egg's house.

His uncle would be sleeping with an open window. Rip stood outside the window and called his name.

"Is that you, Rip?"

"Yeah, Uncle. It's me. I need some help."

"I'll get dressed. Be right down."

"Come down to the hangar."

"Okay."

Together they woke Charley Pine and assisted her up the hill and into a bed. It was the same bed where Rip spent his summers growing up. Egg didn't turn on any lights. They got her into bed and Rip held onto her hand.

"No use letting the neighbors know I have visitors," Egg said. "I'll get you to a doctor in the morning," he told Charley.

"Is the press still camped out at your front gate?" Rip asked.

"Yeah, but I'll have her lie down in the front of the truck where they can't see her. The sheriff keeps them back a bit."

"Sorry to do this to you."

"Glad to help," Egg said and left the bedroom.

Still holding Charley's hand, Rip knelt by the bed.

"Thanks for everything," he whispered.

"You could have flown the saucer out of there any time," she said. "You weren't going without me, were you?"

"I sorta thought we should leave together."

She squeezed his hand.

"I'll see you in a few weeks," he whispered. "You get well."

"You could kiss me good-bye, if you wanted to."

He wanted to.

Egg was making a pot of coffee in the kitchen when Rip came downstairs. He had the lights on. Rip opened the refrigerator and stared in. For the first time in his life he wasn't hungry. He sat down at the table.

"There was a guy in the saucer when we got in. He tried to kick Charley to death, then tried to strangle her. She shot him six or eight times and I stabbed him with a screwdriver." He wiped the sweat from his face as the memory swept over him. "There's blood all over the floor of the cockpit."

"It'll wash off," Egg said calmly. "Why don't you tell me the rest of it?"

Rip had finished his third cup of coffee when he ran out of words.

"Seems to me you didn't have any choice about stabbing that guy," Egg said.

"Charley shot those men, boom, boom, boom."

"Does that bother you?"

"Maybe I should have let the bastards have the saucer, got Charley out of there somehow."

Egg snorted. "You can't go through life as a doormat, kid. You did the right thing."

"So tell me about what's been happening here."

"Rip, I don't even know where to start. The saucer is still a media event. The television only does three or four hours of coverage a day now, the soaps and talk shows are back on, but the whole country is buzzing. The media is hunting desperately for you and Charley. This is your fifteen minutes of fame."

"They can have it. I don't do interviews."

"You may ultimately have to. You own the saucer."

Rip gaped at Egg. "You mean legally?"

"Wellstar Petroleum has given you a bill of sale for the saucer in return for an interest in the propulsion technology. Tomorrow morning — no, this morning — your Uncle Olie is filing a lawsuit in federal court in Washington. We're asking the court for a temporary injunction against the federal government, a cease-and-desist order. Of course, there are no guarantees, but Olie thinks we have a good chance."

Rip whistled softly.

"I'd like to take Charley to Washington with me in a few days, whenever they schedule the hearing. She'll make a great witness."

"She needs rest."

"I understand. I'll take care of her. For the next few weeks you must keep the saucer hidden where no one can find it. And you stay out of sight."

After a moment's thought Rip said, "I'll go home. The hired men won't tell anyone I'm there. They've worked for us over twenty years, have lived in tenant houses on the place ever since Dad died. They're loyal friends."

"Hide the saucer so it can't be found."

"I've been thinking about that."

Egg stood. "Can you fly out of here before the sun comes up?"

"I just talk to the computer, and it does the flying."

"We'd better get you on your way. Every minute that ship sits here is another chance for the wrong people to find it."

"Thanks, Egg."

"I'll take care of Charley, Rip. And Olie will take care of the government. You stay hidden."

Rip hugged his uncle. "I love you, Egg."

"I love you too, Ripper. Now come on. I'll help you fill up the saucer."

"Do you have a pocket knife I can borrow?"

Egg handed him the one from his pocket.

"Some fishhooks and matches?"

"In the hangar. Take what you want."

They were standing with hands in their pockets listening to water running into the saucer's tank when Rip asked, "You said Wellstar retained an interest in the propulsion technology. Does that mean we have to keep the saucer?"

Egg hesitated before answering. "Not necessarily. Why do you ask?"

"I helped kill a man because of the saucer. He got what he deserved and I'm not sorry I did it, but I don't want to have to do it again."

"What do you suggest?"

"I want the saucer, yet I don't want to have to kill people to keep it. I don't want it that much."

"You risked your life to get it back from Hedrick."

"I risked my life to get Charley back. Okay, okay — *and the saucer.* But everyone born has to die. Dying is the easy part. Killing — that is something else."

Not a hint of the events in Australia at Hedrick's station ever reached the press. Which was, perhaps, a good thing: The press splashed the news of Olie Cantrell's lawsuit naming the president and Bombing Joe De Laurio as defendants on front pages all over the nation.

In Missouri, Egg enlisted the help of the county sheriff to sneak through the press mob besieging his gate. Charley was X-rayed at a local clinic. The doctor said she had two cracked ribs and a badly bruised shoulder. The feeling in her arm and hand had returned, but the deltoid muscle was so sore she couldn't lift her arm. The doctor prescribed ice packs to combat the swelling and a sling for a few days.

Egg and Charley didn't return to the farm. They hit the road for Washington.

Charley found that she liked Egg a lot. As Rip had promised, he was extraordinarily smart, with a wit and personality to match. After her adventures in Australia she found Egg's company pleasant and relaxing. Part of the reason, she suspected, was that Egg liked to talk about Rip. As the pickup rolled through the American countryside, he told her the family history and every anecdote about Rip that he could remember.

Rip, Rip, Rip, she couldn't hear enough about him. Just the sound of his name brought a smile to her face.

Oh, it was pleasant driving through America on a hazy late-summer day with the windows down, the corn high, farmers making hay, and road crews laying hot as-phalt. Egg and Charley talked and talked as the radio broadcast a ball game and the miles rolled by.

Two days after they left Missouri, Egg and Charley came to rest in an expensive New York City hotel with an excellent security system. "We guarantee privacy, Mr. Cantrell," the manager promised. "Heads of state pick this hotel for their New York visits for that very reason. The press wouldn't dare."

They wound up with a two-bedroom corner suite on the eighteenth floor.

"Uncle Egg, let's go dutch. I have some money. Hedrick threw some chump change at me." She extracted a wad of bills from a pocket.

Egg waved her money away. "Don't worry. I drive a pickup and live on a Missouri farm because I want to, not because I have to. Now go put some ice on your arm while I make telephone calls. We'll have some clothes brought over, you can choose several outfits. Jeans won't do where we're going. And I'll see if I can make a hair appointment for you here in the hotel."

"That would be fantastic," said Charlotte Pine. "I'd like to feel like a woman again."

That evening Charley and Egg had an invited guest.

Charley opened the door on his knock. "Professor Soldi, please come in."

The archaeologist stood there for a second looking at Charley with a furrowed brow. With her new hairdo and new clothes she felt like a new woman and looked like one.

"Ms. Pine, I despaired of ever seeing you again."

She smiled broadly and closed the door behind him.

After Charley, the professor, and Egg Cantrell had discussed the saucer situation for fifteen minutes or so, Egg said, "I invited you to meet with us, Professor, because I have been very impressed with your grasp of the importance of the saucer. I certainly haven't been glued to the television, but I've seen several of your interviews. Your theories are well thought out and provocative."

Soldi bowed his head a fraction of an inch. "Thank you."

Egg continued, "I wanted you to be the first to know that your theories about the saucer are absolutely correct in every major detail."

The archaeologist sat openmouthed, at a loss for words.

Egg got out his biggest suitcase and

opened it carefully. From it he took a bundle wrapped in bubble wrap. "This computer was in the saucer. It's the one Hedrick's men partially disassembled in the Sahara."

"Oh, yes," Soldi said.

Charley looked surprised. "I had forgotten all about it."

"Rip and I removed it from the saucer at my farm in Missouri the first afternoon you were there, before Hedrick arrived. While you were napping we experimented with the computer, learned some extraordinary things, and decided to remove it from the saucer so I could study it at length."

Charley shook her head. "I was too busy to notice that it was no longer in the saucer."

"I managed to determine the proper wattage and voltage to run the computer and put together a transformer so that we can power the computer even when it is out of the saucer." Egg removed the transformer from the suitcase, plugged a power cord into a wall socket, then plugged another cord into the computer. "I have also incorporated a surge protector to buffer voltage surges."

From the suitcase he removed the headband, the wire of which was already attached to the computer.

"This past week I devoted three days to this computer." Egg chose his words with care. "I believe there is enough information stored on this computer to keep a large research university's faculty fully employed for a century. I haven't even scratched the surface."

Soldi pursed his lips thoughtfully as he eyed the machine. He laid fingertips on it.

"As you will see, Professor, the main pathway offers you a dozen choices. Rip and I chose the first one, which turned out to be a maintenance and operations manual for the saucer."

Charley's eyebrows rose. "Rip never mentioned this computer to me."

Egg grinned. "Rip is discretion personified."

"Learned it from you, apparently," Charley shot back.

"The second pathway is the one I want you to take this evening, Professor," Egg said. "That is the path that fascinated me, that absorbed my every thought for three days. It is my hope that in a few months I will be able to devote the rest of my life to exploring that pathway."

"And the other paths?" Soldi asked.

"I haven't had the time to journey down them. For all I know they are even more compelling than the second one. Still, tonight I ask you to take the second pathway. It proved to me that your theories were correct. I wanted you to personally experience this . . . *moment*."

"I will do as you ask," Soldi promised.

Egg looked at the headband. "This headband is the way you communicate with the computer. Merely move along the pathway you choose, approach any selection that interests you."

Soldi nodded.

"I found that it helps if I make myself comfortable and relax. You will not go to sleep."

Soldi nodded again, with just a hint of impatience.

Egg adjusted the headband over the archaeologist's head.

Soldi leaned his head against the back of the couch. His eyes remained open but unfocused.

After about a half minute, Charley rose from her chair and went to stand by the window, where she could look out at the lights of Manhattan. Egg joined her.

"What is on the second pathway?" she asked.

"An encyclopedia. I suspect that it covers everything the makers of the saucer knew about the universe."

"Are the saucer people our ancestors?"

"At this point the evidence is circumstantial. In all probability . . . yes."

After she had thought about that for a moment, Charley said, "My father had a flip comment that comes to mind. He said that the world is full of idiots, an indisputable scientific fact that proves that evolution is bunk."

Egg chuckled. "It isn't bunk, but it's an extremely complex process which takes place over enormous stretches of time. The human mind just cannot fathom time in the quantities available to Mother Nature."

Charley turned to check Soldi. His eyes were closed now.

"Did the saucer people discover the Grand Unified Theory, the theory of everything?"

"Yes. They knew how all of the forces in the universe are related, which is why they could design and build the antigravity system on the saucer. It is a practical application of that knowledge."

Charley Pine turned back to the window glass and rested her forehead against it.

After two hours, Egg removed the computer headband from Soldi's head. The archaeologist blinked repeatedly and scrutinized his surroundings. He reached for the coffee table before him, caressed it with his hands, apparently reassuring himself of the solidity of the real world. Then he touched the saucer's computer, ran his fingertips across it, laid both hands upon it.

"I must think about this," he murmured finally.

As he prepared to leave, the archaeologist paused, felt the pocket of his sports coat. "Just a moment," he said. "In the excitement I almost forgot. This afternoon I received a report from my university lab on some material Rip and I found in the equipment bay of the saucer. The material was the decomposing remains of a collection of personal items, something like a wallet, if you will. I want to share one of the items with you."

He removed several envelopes from his pocket, examined them, and selected one. Out of it he took a sheet of paper, unfolded it carefully, and laid it upon the coffee table. Charley and Egg bent over to look.

On the paper was a picture of a woman. Obviously a woman, with a woman's facial features and throat. She was smiling, happy. Her race, however, was difficult to determine.

"What we are seeing," the professor said, "is a computer reconstruction of a piece of the decomposed material that I gave them. I hesitate to call the material a photograph — it was an image on some kind of paperlike substance. They are still trying to determine exactly what."

"It's a portrait of Eve," Charley Pine said.

"Something like that, I suppose," the professor said. He carefully folded the paper and returned it to the envelope.

At the door he seized Egg's hand and pumped it repeatedly. "Thank you, sir. Thank you from the bottom of my heart."

"Come back in the morning, Professor. We will talk then. Good night."

Before she went to her room, Charley Pine asked, "How will the universe end, Uncle Egg?"

"It will be reborn," Egg Cantrell told her, "again and again and again . . ."

20

When he left Missouri the sun was within an hour of rising, so Rip Cantrell flew the saucer north into Canada. He parked it on a sandbar beside a wide river that ran north to the Arctic. That afternoon he fished with Egg's tackle and managed to catch a couple of good ones. They looked somewhat like trout, but Rip doubted that they were.

He cooked them that evening over a fire built of debris he gathered along the riverbank, wood that had apparently been washed north with the melt each spring, hundreds of miles from the forests to the south, until it ended up in tangles on this sandbar.

At these latitudes at this time of year, twilight lasted until late in the evening. The stars came out one by one as a slice of moon crept over the horizon. Finally, as the fire was dying, the black velvet night was ablaze with stars flung like sand against the sky.

Which one was *the* one? From which one did the saucer makers come?

He sat by the fire hoping to see the aurora borealis until the stars began to fade with the coming of the new day, but it never appeared. At peace with the universe, Rip Cantrell crawled into the saucer and went to sleep.

After two days he decided he had been there long enough. Reconnaissance satellites had undoubtedly located the saucer; it was just a matter of time before someone came to steal it. He wanted to be gone before that someone arrived.

That night after a fish supper, he put out the fire, strapped himself into the pilot's seat, and took off heading south.

Staying low and slow, less than a thousand feet and below three hundred knots, he thought that he would be able to fly under the coverage of most radars. He experimented with hand-flying the machine. It was almost too responsive for a novice: He found himself overcontrolling. Remembering Charley's advice, which she had given him in an odd moment, he released the controls, waited while the saucer settled down, then grasped them gingerly again.

The whole gig was a rare hoot. Here he was, a farm kid from Minnesota at the helm of a real flying saucer. He laughed, at himself and the situation and the whole darn mess.

Rip got to his destination just before dawn. He hid the saucer and walked the six miles home as the sky grew light and the sun peeped over the rim of the earth.

The swing on the front porch looked inviting. He settled into it to wait for his mother to awaken and come downstairs to the kitchen.

The farm looked clean and verdant at the end of summer. He could hear cattle lowing for their breakfast, and he could smell them. He had grown up with that smell, which he rarely noticed unless he was just returning after an absence of several days.

The swing rocked back and forth, the chains squeaking on their hooks, just as they always had.

Rip was dozing when he heard his mother in the kitchen. He stood, stretched, and yawned, then went inside.

"Hi, Mom."

"Oh, *my God!* You scared me, Rip." She reached for him and gave him a mighty hug.

"Where on earth have you been, boy? When those men came, I didn't know what to say." She searched his face. Tears welled in her eyes. "I was scared, Rip. For you. And me."

"It's okay, Mom. You didn't have any choice. You had to answer their questions. I know that."

She tried to talk and couldn't. Rip held her tightly. When she seemed to have calmed down, Rip relaxed his grip. His mother grinned nervously and wiped the tears from her eyes.

"They talk about you on television every day. You're the most famous man on earth."

"It'll pass, Mom. It'll pass. Next year no one will remember my name. They'll talk about ol' what's-his-name, the saucer guy."

"How about breakfast? Ham and eggs and potatoes?"

"You fix it, I'll eat it."

She paused for a good look at his face, then got busy. "All I know is what the television said, so tell me all about it."

He seated himself at the kitchen table and began with the desert, hot and dirty and empty under a brassy sky, with a gleam of sunlight reflecting off something far away, on a distant ridge.

He finished the story as he finished his breakfast. The part about Rigby he left out. His mother was leaning back against

447

the sink sipping a cup of coffee.

"So where is the saucer now?"

"Hidden."

"You aren't going to tell me?"

"No. Those men might come back."

He saw panic in her eyes.

"I doubt if they will, Mom, but if they do, answer any question they ask."

She nodded, repeatedly. "Okay," she said. She turned back to the sink. "So where do you go from here? When this is over?"

"I don't know. I haven't even had time to think about it."

"Classes at the university started three days ago."

"Maybe I ought to sit out a semester. I could work here on the farm."

"Until this saucer flap is over, the only place you could get work would be in the state pen making license plates."

"I suppose."

"You could help out some on the farm, I guess. I'd be lying if I told you we needed you desperately. The boys get the chores done every day."

Rip nodded. "Uncle Egg is supposed to call in a couple of weeks. He wants me to stay out of sight until then. You can tell the guys I'm here if you make them promise not to tell anyone else."

"They might tell, Rip. They like to drink beer on Saturday nights and they've got girlfriends."

"If they suspect I'm here and we didn't tell them, we'll have problems. Ask them not to tell. That's all we can do."

"Okay."

"The saucer is hidden where no one can find it. I thought maybe after dark tonight I'd take some clothes and grub and walk up to the lake. I could stay in the cabin up there, fish a little, read some of those books I never seem to have time for."

"People fish that lake, Rip. It's open to the public."

"Anybody in a boat will be too far out to see who I am."

"Reporters have called here two or three dozen times this past week, pestering me something fierce. I'm surprised the phone hasn't rung this morning."

"When Uncle Egg calls in a couple of weeks, you could drive up to the lake and get me."

"If that's what you want."

"If no one finds out I'm here, this whole thing will blow over. The press will write about something else tomorrow. The politicians will want another tax, one of the president's old girlfriends will tell all, there will be another scandal du jour in Hollywood . . . *something.* The papers are full of something every day."

"Is that a prediction?"

"It's a prayer. I can't live like this for very long."

"How serious are you about this Charley woman?"

"Mom!"

"That's a fair question."

"Who said I was serious?"

"I wasn't born yesterday. You didn't go all the way to Australia to rescue a piece of machinery."

"I like her. All right? Is there anything wrong with that?"

"Well, I don't know. You never tell me anything. Exactly how old is she, anyway?"

"I don't know exactly. I didn't ask to see her driver's license."

"She sounds pretty old to me. A test pilot, retired from the Air Force —"

"She is *not* retired! She resigned."

"I never thought of you with an older woman. It's . . . upsetting, somehow . . ."

"I'm going upstairs and lie down, Mom. Okay? I didn't get any sleep last night."

"If she calls, should I wake you up?"

"Oh, Mom!"

As Rip climbed the stairs, she called after him, "Has Charley been married before?"

His room looked like he remembered it: kid stuff stuck all over, a couple of pinups, a football he had scored a winning touchdown with his senior year, a movie poster, souvenirs from baseball games in Chicago . . . It was time to throw most of this junk away.

His father's old Winchester was in the closet under the eaves. Rip got it out and worked the lever several times. He dug through the closet until he found a box of ammo for the thing. The stuff was five or six years old but it would have to do.

He loaded the rifle, made sure the hammer was down, and set it beside the bed within easy reach. Only then did he take off his shoes and lie down.

Rip got to the cabin a little after midnight. Jet lag still had him in its grip, so he got the broom and swept out the place, put his knapsack of canned goods on the shelf. Mice had eaten a few holes in the sheets and blankets. He shook them out, put them on the bed anyway.

Rip's father built the cabin two or three years before he died. Rip remembered coming here several times with his father that first summer, then his father's health began failing.

During his high school years Rip spent a few nights here with his pals, drinking beer and smoking cigarettes they weren't supposed to have and generally acting stupid.

The cabin was just a place in his life, a place without a lot of memories good or bad.

The kerosene lamp didn't really give enough light to read by. Rip sat on the porch in the darkness listening to the night sounds of frogs and insects. The mosquitoes weren't ravenous, they just nibbled now and then.

Toward dawn he found himself nodding off, so he went to bed.

The days settled into a routine. He slept when he was sleepy, ate when he was hungry, fished when he wasn't reading. The fish he caught he ate. The third day he was there rain fell for several hours.

He had been at the cabin a week when one of the hired men brought him two bags of groceries. "Your mom sent the food. Me and Otis chipped in for the six-pack."

"Thanks, Sherman. 'Preciate it."

"Me and Otis won't tell a soul you're here, Rip. Honest."

"I believe you."

"We've really been asked, that's for darn sure. Reporter outta Los Angeles offered me a hundred bucks to tell him what I know. Mainly he wanted to know about you when you were a kid. I turned him down cold, of course. I wouldn't run my mouth against my friends for any amount of money. You know me."

"Right."

"Everybody in town is dying to ask you all about that saucer, where it is, how'd you learn to fly it, all that stuff."

"Uh-huh."

"Sorta curious my own self too, you understand."

"Soon as I'm able, I'll tell you all about it."

"Me and Otis won't tell a soul, Rip. Honest."

"It's good to have friends like you guys."

"You know, I never even seen a flying saucer. Not a one. In this day and age, can you believe it?"

"They're kinda rare."

"Maybe you can give us a ride too, huh?"

"Well . . ."

"My girlfriend Arlene, she is so excited. She's really into aliens and parallel universes, reads a lot of books. Knows all about saucers.

She'd think I was the hottest thing in jeans if you gave her a ride too."

"I'll try to do that for you, Sherman. Thanks for coming up."

"Yeah, Rip. Me and Otis won't tell a soul. Honest."

Sherman and Otis would talk, and Rip knew it. In fact, he would bet a hundred to one that Arlene and all her friends knew the saucer was somewhere nearby.

As Rip watched Sherman drive away, it came to him that someone would soon come to get the saucer. He had been assuming that because the saucer was hidden, no one would know where he was.

Ha!

The question was who would arrive first, government agents or Roger Hedrick's thugs. Or some third party.

The saucer was too valuable. $150 billion, Charley said.

Having that much money would be like owning California.

He had been a fool, sitting here dumb and happy reading books and fishing, confident that Hedrick was beaten and the government was stupid.

The miracle was that they hadn't already arrived.

So what should he do? Take the saucer

and skedaddle? Leave the saucer hidden and boogie for a week or so, giving Egg and Olie time to litigate?

Or stay right here?

He took the groceries inside, opened a couple cans of chili, and put the contents in a saucepan to heat on the wood stove.

The thing to do was get the hell out of Dodge. The only place the saucer was absolutely safe was in orbit. Where it was now was second best, but better than sitting beside a Canadian river or on an ice floe in the Antarctic. He needed to eat and sleep and go to the bathroom on a regular basis.

He ate the chili and cleaned up, then packed his knapsack. After dark he would walk out.

He put the Winchester on the table in front of him, checked that the hammer was on half cock.

They might be out there this very minute, watching . . .

Watching for what?

Watching to see if he would lead them to the saucer.

Okay, he would leave the saucer where it was. What he needed to do was hide himself. Get in motion and stay that way. Sleep in a different place every night, never go to the same place twice.

He walked out on the pier, looked around the lake. Two men were fishing from a boat anchored fifty yards offshore, maybe six hundred yards east along the shoreline, but they were in the only boat in sight.

That struck him now as unusual. This time of year there were normally six or eight boats somewhere on the lake. After all, the woods around the lake held dozens of cabins.

There had been five boats out there yesterday.

Where were all the people?

A wave of disgust washed over him. He was being paranoid. Just because bighearted, bigmouthed Sherman Hockett delivered two bags of grub wasn't any reason to go to battle stations. Rip had been in the cabin seven days . . . no, eight.

Ample time if Hedrick wanted to make another grab for the gold.

Ample time for the government, too, if they were interested.

Rip pursed his lips, tried to whistle. Nothing came out. He walked off the pier and up the bank to the cabin consciously trying to look as relaxed as he had every day for the past week.

An hour before sunset.

After dark, he was out of here.

He went into the cabin and sat down in the kitchen chair facing the door. He sat with the rifle in his lap.

When the night was as dark as it was going to get, Rip Cantrell stood the rifle in a corner, put on his knapsack, and locked the door behind him. He left the kerosene lamp burning. It would run out of fuel tomorrow some time and go out of its own accord. With a little luck, he would be in Canada then.

The gravel road ran for a half mile through the woods to the highway. Rip had been walking about five minutes when he heard the sound of a car engine. He turned off the road and felt his way into the woods. The car was coming closer.

He almost fell over a fallen tree trunk, so he lay down behind it and listened.

The car crept along the road without lights. Behind it came another . . . And a third. All without headlights.

Holy . . . !

At least he was out of the cabin, and just in time. Somebody up there was looking out for the Ripper.

These people wouldn't find him in the

woods at night. When the sun came up tomorrow, perhaps, but if he played it right he would be two counties north by then.

Which crowd is this?

Didn't matter, he told himself. They wanted the saucer and they had to go through him to get it.

When the sounds of the cars had faded, he got to his feet and adjusted the knapsack on his back.

He could see a little. Not much, but the night wasn't totally dark and his eyes had adjusted to what light there was.

He began walking slowly, feeling his way through the trees and brush, toward the highway. Once on the highway he could walk toward town, which was four miles away. Tomorrow morning he could rent a car from Honest Ed White, the used-car dealer, and by midafternoon he would be in Canada.

About once a minute he paused and listened carefully. Nothing.

He fell several times and got scratched up a bit from unseen limbs. Still, he was making good progress toward the highway when he heard voices.

He stopped, stood stock-still.

Male voices, at least three, but he couldn't make out the words. The men were ahead of him. Perhaps on the road, perhaps in the woods.

If he could hear them talk, they might be able to hear him thrashing through the brush, if they hadn't already.

He sat down right where he was.

The voices were coming closer. No flashlights, though.

Rip laid face-down, as quietly as he could. Closed his eyes, covered his exposed neck and ears with his arms, kept his face in the leaves and debris of the forest floor.

". . . over this way, Tony."

"Watch that log."

"Goddamn Daniel Boone, out here hiking through the goddamn woods in the middle of the goddamn night . . ."

They were tramping along, not trying to be quiet, getting closer and closer. Rip lay absolutely motionless.

They walked right to him.

"Get up, Daniel Boone. We ain't going to sleep out in the woods tonight."

Rip rolled over. Someone shone a flashlight in his face.

He stood.

"It's him, all right. Shine your light over here so I can see this radio."

Someone put a flashlight on the man's hands. He fiddled with a small radio, lifted it to his mouth. Rip got a glimpse of goggles. Infrared or night-vision goggles. These men could see him as plain as day.

"This is Tony. We got him. He was Injuning through the woods."

Rip heard the reply over the radio's speaker. "Bring him to the cabin."

"Turn around, kid. Dinky, take that knapsack and carry it. We'll search it later. Fats, put a tie around his wrists."

Someone jerked his wrists together in front of him and pulled a plastic tie tight. The tie cut into his flesh.

"Okay, kid, start hiking. Fats, you go in front of him and he can hold on to your belt. Let Dinky carry your weapon."

Six cars sat in the parking area beside the cabin. Three of them were arranged in a semicircle with their headlights on. Rip's captors led him into the lights, turned him around, then the man they called Tony hit him.

He didn't see it coming. It was a jab out of nowhere right on the button and knocked him sprawling in the dirt. Half knocked out, he was jerked to his feet by a man on each arm. Tony was in his late thirties, maybe, with short hair and bulging biceps. He hit Rip again. This time

Rip rolled with the punch, but down he went. Hot liquid ran into his mouth when they jerked him erect.

He tried to block the next shot with his hands, but Tony was cat-quick. Rip took it in the left eye.

He was trying to anticipate where the next punch might be coming from when someone said, "That's enough for now."

A man stepped into the light, reached for his face, and turned it so that he could see the bloody nose.

"You cost me a great deal of money, Mr. Cantrell, and a great deal of aggravation."

Roger Hedrick!

Rip said nothing. His mouth had blood in it, so he spit the coppery-tasting stuff out on the ground.

"Where is it?"

Instinctively Rip knew that as soon as he started to talk, Hedrick had the upper hand.

"We have all evening, Mr. Cantrell. All evening to cause you pain. Believe me, these men can administer more pain than you can stand."

Rip tried to wipe the blood from his nose on his arm. He almost missed Hedrick's nod to Tony, who was sinfully quick. Rip just had time to let his head go with the punch.

They left him lying on the ground. Hedrick stood just beyond reach of his feet.

"No one is going to ride to your rescue," Hedrick said. "I have almost thirty men surrounding this whole area. We've sealed it off. You couldn't get away even if we cut your hands loose and gave you an hour's head start."

He stood there measuring Rip, sizing him up. "Break his leg," he said to Tony.

"How'd you know I was here?" Rip asked. His voice was hoarse, a croak.

Hedrick's hand stayed Tony. "I had your mother's house bugged and her telephone tapped forty-eight hours after I knew who had taken the saucer from the desert. We waited for you to call, futilely of course. Then, finally, you showed up on her doorstep. You can't get away, Cantrell. The world is too small. I can raise an army in an hour anywhere on this planet."

Rip heard one of the onlookers say, "Is it raining? Is that rain I hear?"

Hedrick glanced around at the speaker.

Rip spoke to Hedrick: "You get the saucer, how you gonna get it out of here?"

"I want you to meet Herr Zwerneman," Hedrick said, "Europe's finest test pilot." Zwerneman stepped into the headlights.

"If you can fly the saucer, Cantrell, he can. He can fly anything with wings or rotor blades."

"Some people will do anything for money, I guess," Rip said, because he had to say something.

"That is oh so true, Cantrell. Oh so true. I am one of them. I will do whatever it takes to get that saucer. I will buy it from you here and now, torture you, have your mother raped, whatever."

"Leave my mother out of this."

"Whatever it takes."

His face hurt like hell.

"You said you'd buy it. How much?"

"One million dollars."

"That's rich. You're going to sell it for a hundred and fifty *billion!*"

"There will be a markup, of course. I intend to make a profit as the middleman. One million dollars to you, that's your profit. Take it, or I will take one hundred and fifty billion dollars out of your hide."

"My hide isn't worth that much."

"Taggart!" Hedrick called the name like he was summoning a butler. Bill Taggart stepped into the headlights where Rip could see him.

"Tell him how much I paid you, Taggart."

"He paid me a million, Rip. Cash. Paid me another hundred thousand to come with him tonight. Give him the saucer and you and I can both retire, never work another day in our lives."

Rip looked at Hedrick, looked at Taggart, spit blood down the front of his shirt.

"You're a dirtbag, Taggart."

"Be that as it may, a million dollars is a million dollars. And when you're dead, you're dead."

"If I'm dead, Roger Hedrick will never get the saucer."

"Enough of this," Hedrick snapped. "We've wasted enough time. You know I can't kill you. What I can do is kill your mother. If you don't answer my questions I'm going to send some men to get her now. Let's start with an easy one: Who flew the saucer out of my hangar in Australia?"

"What?"

Rip had taken several brutal punches, so at first he didn't understand.

"Who flew it from my hangar to the atrium to pick up you and Pine?"

"You really don't know?"

Hedrick took a deep breath. "I am fast losing my patience with you, kid. For the last time, where is the saucer?"

Rip put his head down, wiped his bloody nose on his shoulder. He didn't see Tony's punch coming. It exploded against his cheekbone.

He wound up on his face with dirt in his mouth. He rolled over, tried to focus on Hedrick.

Hedrick was talking to Taggart and Zwerneman, who were one or two feet closer to the lake. They were standing facing Hedrick, then they were rising into the air. Bits of leaves and twigs and dirt rose with them.

Taggart screamed. Zwerneman shouted something in German, a curse probably.

Hedrick stepped back quickly, looked up at the rising men and the black shape above them, darker than the night.

"Oh, Jesus," someone said and pointed with his flashlight. The flashlights and the glare of the automobile headlights reflected from the glistening wet belly of the saucer, suspended in the air above the rising men.

Taggart and Zwerneman rose halfway to the saucer, screaming, then were crushed.

"Oh, my God!" Hedrick shouted. He bent over Rip and screamed in his face, "What happened?"

"The earth and the saucer repel each

other. The saucer crushed them."

Rip got his legs under him, got to his knees. The flattened bodies were suspended between the saucer and the ground, about twenty feet in the air, trapped in the repulsion zone of the antigravity field. Blood from the corpses was making the repulsion zone visible. It was almost as if the bodies were trapped on a glass laboratory slide.

"Where was it?"

"In the lake. You want to be next?"

Roger Hedrick grabbed him by one arm, jerked him. "It'll have to be you *and* me, kid."

The saucer moved toward them. The men nearby scattered like quail.

Rip kept the ship creeping closer and closer. Leaves, debris, and gravel rose skyward as it moved. As he felt himself getting light on his feet, he turned and dove with his hands outstretched, reaching for the bumper of the nearest car. He got his hands around it just as he felt his feet leave the ground. He was hanging upside down from the automobile's bumper, being pulled upward toward the saucer just as Taggart and the German test pilot had been.

Hedrick was hanging on to his waist.

"Who's in that thing?" Hedrick shouted.

"Tell them to stop! They're going to kill us too!"

Hedrick was off the ground, his feet pointing toward the saucer, his arms around Rip's waist.

"Make them fly it away, kid, or I'll take you with me."

Rip was supporting his weight and Hedrick's, dangling from the bumper, hanging on to it for dear life. The edges of the bumper and the plastic tie that bound his wrist cut painfully into his flesh.

He felt Hedrick's grip slip.

Rip's fingers were supporting the weight of both men. The *pain* . . .

"There's nobody in the saucer, is there?" Hedrick hissed. "It obeys *you!*"

Incredibly, in a fantastic exhibition of physical strength, Hedrick held on to Rip's waist with his left arm and lifted his right hand to Rip's shoulder. Then the left. He wrapped his legs around Rip's, then managed to get his hands around Rip's neck.

With his face inches from Rip's, Hedrick began strangling him. He was past the edge of reasoning.

"You'll kill us both," Rip managed as Hedrick's hands closed like a vise around his windpipe.

"It's *mine!*" Hedrick grunted. "Mine!"

And he squeezed on Rip's neck with all his strength.

Rip used his knees. Kneed Hedrick in the stomach, in the groin, bucked and pummeled him with his knees as he fought to breathe.

Roger Hedrick screamed as he lost his grip.

Hedrick dug in his fingernails, raking away strips of Rip's skin and shredding his shirt as he fell upward toward the waiting saucer, still screaming . . .

Rip backed the saucer away before he too fell upward. As the saucer's antigravity field released him, he lost his grip on the car bumper and fell to earth with a thump.

One of the flattened bodies fell nearby in a shower of blood.

Two were still up there, crushed in the transition zone between earth and saucer. One of them was Hedrick.

Tony came over toward where Rip lay, but he kept his eyes on the now stationary saucer. He was ready to run.

"You win, kid," Tony said. He raised his voice, "Let's get outta here."

"Are you nuts?" one of the onlookers demanded. "That saucer is worth billions!"

"Don't be a fool!" Tony said bitterly. "The moneyman is dead. Do you want to join him up there, squashed like a bug? And who would pay *you* ten cents for the saucer, *if* you could manage to get your hands on it and fly it out of here?"

Rip moved the saucer toward the nearest automobile. The front end of the car rose about three feet in the air. He stopped the saucer, left the car hanging as men dove into the remaining cars and backed up hurriedly. Finally he moved the saucer a few feet, enough to release the front of the suspended car from the saucer's grasp.

Some of the remaining men made a dash for the cars. The few still standing were restless, shining their flashlights over the saucer's belly.

"I'm leaving," Tony announced. "Anybody who wants to take the saucer from the kid can shake hands in hell with Roger Hedrick." He got behind the wheel of the car nearest Rip and started the engine.

Rip left the saucer where it was and walked for the cabin.

Behind him he could hear car doors slamming, engines roaring into life, gravel being thrown as wheels spun.

There was a paring knife in the tableware drawer. Rip managed to cut himself a little. Eventually the plastic tie around his swollen wrists gave way.

He sat on the floor in the lamplight, massaging his wrists, wiping blood from his face with his shirttail, listening to the frogs and crickets.

21

The headline screamed, CANTRELL OWNS SAUCER, JUDGE RULES. The president frowned at the headline and scanned the story.

"Yesterday in Washington a federal district judge granted Olie Cantrell's motion on behalf of his nephew, Rip, for summary judgment after an expedited hearing. 'The government has no case,' the judge said. 'The government has no colorable claim to title to the saucer.' "

"No colorable claim," the president muttered to the people gathered around his desk. He cast a withering glance at the attorney general, who reddened slightly.

Another headline on the front page caught his eye, down near the bottom on the left side: BILLIONAIRE MISSING. The story began: "Australian billionaire industrialist Roger Hedrick, the world's second richest man, was reported missing yesterday by his companion, Ms. Bernice Carrington-Smyth. A crew of a chartered jet dropped Mr. Hedrick at the Minneapolis–St. Paul, Minnesota, airport nine days ago. The industrialist was seen leaving the airport in a limousine and has not been seen since. Ms. Carrington-Smyth suspects foul play . . ."

The president tossed the newspaper on his desk. "What do you people have to say for yourselves?"

"There's more, Mr. President," O'Reilly, the chief of staff, said.

"More?"

"This morning on the *Today* show Olie Cantrell announced that his nephew was donating the saucer to the National Air and Space Museum. There are a few conditions: The nuclear reactor must be removed from the saucer, it must never fly again, and it must be put on permanent public display."

"A political masterstroke," the president murmured. "Thank God Olie Cantrell isn't in politics."

"The director of the museum agreed to all three conditions, of course."

Bombing Joe De Laurio's face turned purple. "They can't accept it! That saucer should be confiscated for national security reasons. I'm tired of pussyfooting around with these people. Too much is at stake here."

"Pussyfooting?" the president purred.

472

He looked at the director of the FBI, who was sitting beside De Laurio. "Go over it again, please, one more time, so all these people have it straight. Including the general."

The director of the FBI took a deep breath, glanced at De Laurio, who had set his jaw, then began: "At your order we bugged Rip Cantrell's mother's house. When Rip came home sixteen days ago, we put a team around the lake cabin in which he was staying. As you know, our orders were merely to observe and report to you while the Justice Department litigated title to the saucer."

The FBI director looked around. "On the night of September ninth, Roger Hedrick and several dozen Mafiosi from Chicago arrived at the lake cabin in Minnesota. Rip Cantrell was tied up and given a physical beating. Hedrick and two of the others were crushed by the saucer, which was probably under Cantrell's control. When the saucer is in the museum, perhaps we can examine it and determine how he controlled the thing, if he did.

"In any event, after Hedrick's death the surviving mobsters departed the scene. We believe Mr. Cantrell wrapped the bodies in bedding from the cabin, loaded them in the saucer, and flew away. NORAD lost the saucer off the California coast. The following night Cantrell returned to Minnesota, once again submerged the saucer in the lake, and resumed reading and fishing."

The president scratched his head, then smoothed his coiffured hair. "When we discussed this before, you said that you believed Hedrick's death was self-defense, did you not?"

"Yes, sir," said the director. "I did."

"And after consultation with you and the attorney general, I decided not to have Mr. Cantrell arrested."

"We should have taken that saucer," the general rumbled. "It's a national security treasure."

The president's patience was fraying. "If I had authorized seizing the saucer while the courts were litigating the title, I would have opened myself up for impeachment."

"We can appeal the judge's ruling," De Laurio said.

"We could," the chief of staff replied, "but we won't. Olie Cantrell torpedoed that option with his announcement that Rip was donating the saucer to the people of the United States for display at the Air and Space Museum. We were litigating title on behalf of the American people — now he is donating the saucer to them. An appeal is politically impossible."

The president leaned forward in his chair and wagged his finger at the Air Force chief of staff. "It's over, General. The saucer crisis has been a mess from day one: I got bad advice and was stupid enough to take some of it. The crisis is *over*. I am not going to risk my tenure in this office or my place in American history over a flying saucer."

"We should destroy the saucer now," De Laurio insisted.

"We were lucky the Australians decided not to raise a stink about those two Tomahawk missiles."

"They are corrupt." Bombing Joe's upper lip rose into a sneer. "Hedrick owned them."

"Hedrick owned half of Sydney," the president explained. "Politicians can't ignore such men. That's the reality of the world we live in."

"Politics!" Bombing Joe said contemptuously.

The president appraised the general thoughtfully. "I still don't understand, Joe, why you argued so vehemently that the saucer should be destroyed. The benefits the saucer can confer on all mankind are beyond calculation."

The general leaned forward and automatically lowered his voice to a whisper. "Mr. President, we already have a saucer. It's in a hangar in Area Fifty-one. The technology was the basis for the hypersonic spy plane. We don't need another one."

The president gaped.

The deepening silence was broken only when the president asked, "Why wasn't I told about this?"

"That's classified," Bombing Joe said, his face beet red.

"Don't give me that, General," the president snarled.

"My predecessors decided years ago to keep the saucer's existence secret," Bombing Joe explained. "Really secret. Politicians get voted in and out, they talk in bedrooms, whisper in congressional hallways . . ."

"*Where* did the Air Force get a *saucer?*"

Bombing Joe took several deep breaths before he answered. The president could see that he didn't want to say anything. "New Mexico, forty years ago," Bombing Joe said after a bit, then shrugged.

The president sat erect in his chair, played with the items on his desk. Finally he asked, "Aren't you due to retire in about eighteen months, Joe?"

"Yes, sir."

"Put in your retirement papers today. Effective tomorrow."

Bombing Joe swallowed hard. He squared his shoulders. "Yes, sir," he said, and stalked from the room.

The president picked up the morning newspaper, glanced at the headlines one more time, then tossed it in the wastepaper basket beside his desk.

"What time is Rip delivering the saucer?" he asked P. J. O'Reilly.

"Two this afternoon, sir."

"Clear the calendar. I'm going to the museum to watch the thing fly in."

There were at least a hundred thousand people on the Mall outside the Air and Space Museum when the saucer came into view. Apparently every government worker within five miles of the museum had taken the afternoon off. A gaggle of congressmen and senators hoping to get on the evening news surrounded the president, who was surreptitiously scoping the crowd for pretty girls.

The museum staff had opened the front of the main display bay, an emergency operation that had taken all night and most of the morning. The last of the workmen finished cleaning up just minutes before the saucer became visible as a black dot in the western sky. At Olie's insistence, a clear area a hundred feet wide and a hundred yards long was roped off leading to the open bay.

"There," someone said, pointing. Hundreds of other fingers probed the air, thousands of eyes scanning, then as one the whole crowd saw the dark circular shape and fell silent.

Rip dropped over the Lincoln Memorial, still decelerating. He was flying hands-off, letting the computer do the work. Now he knew: Flying the saucer over a crowd was extremely dangerous. If the saucer got below fifty feet and needed the antigravity rings after aerodynamic lift was lost, the earth would literally push anything loose toward the saucer. When the saucer was above fifty feet, objects on the ground didn't seem to be affected.

To think that he and Charley had blithely flown this thing into the baseball stadium in Denver! It was a miracle that someone, or a group of someones, hadn't been sucked out of his seat to his death.

He could see the spot where he wanted

to go, the clear area in front of the Air and Space; he kept his gaze on that area except for an occasional glance at the computer graphics. The vector crosshairs were in exactly the right place.

Past the Washington Monument at about three hundred feet, still making a hundred knots but decelerating . . . He was on the antigravity system as he slowed through fifty knots at about two hundred feet, still above the treetops.

Then the saucer was settling onto the patio area in front of the museum, just to one side of a silver-and-gold monument.

As the saucer neared the pavement, dirt and trash began to fly.

Hovering just above the patio, Rip looked at the spot inside the museum where he wanted the saucer to come to rest, in the clear area under the Wright Flyer. The saucer moved toward it, closer and closer, through the open side of the building . . .

Gear down!

He could feel the thumps as the landing struts locked down.

Then the saucer touched down . . . swayed once . . . and gently came to rest.

For the first time he really saw all the faces looking at him. A sea of faces, thousands packed into every square foot inside the building. Suspended from the ceiling near the Wright Flyer were Lindbergh's *Spirit of St. Louis,* Chuck Yeager's Bell X-1, and an X-15.

Rip killed the reactor, took off the computer headband, and unstrapped from the pilot's seat.

On the floor of the compartment he paused, took a last good look around.

"You've come to the right place, ol' girl," he said and bent to open the hatch.

The first people Rip saw as he came out from under the saucer were Uncle Egg and Charley Pine. He hugged Charley and shook hands with Egg, both at the same time.

"Hey, Charley."

"Hey, Rip."

"Right now you are on every television set on this planet," Egg said above the buzz of the crowd.

"If everyone is watching, we might as well give them a show," he said to Charley and kissed her. When they came up for air, Charley asked, "What happened to your eye? And your neck?" The marks from Hedrick's fingernails were raw scabs.

"Had an accident. Tell you about it later."

"I'd like you to meet the director of the

museum," Egg said and put a hand on Rip's arm. Rip shook a hand.

Egg whispered into Rip's ear, "We need to go upstairs to sign some papers."

The director led the way up the stairs to the second level of the building while flashes popped and television cameras pointed. When they entered the administrative office area they were alone.

Once they reached the director's office, he shook Rip's hand again. "It's a pleasure, Mr. Cantrell, a real pleasure. We are so thrilled you are presenting the saucer to the museum."

Rip just nodded.

"Here are the papers transferring title. Perhaps you'd like to read them?"

"Who wrote these?" Rip asked Egg.

"Olie did," his uncle told him.

Rip borrowed a pen from the director and signed three copies. He handed his copy to Egg. "I left the hatch open."

"Ms. Pine has been very helpful. She has spent the morning telling us all she could about the machine, including the operation of the hatch."

Rip nodded. "I must caution you that anyone under the saucer will be killed when the ship is lifted off the ground."

"Under the terms of your gift, we cannot

fly the saucer. And I assure you, we will have the reactor removed as soon as possible."

The director wanted him to meet some of the staff. Rip shook more hands, smiled, didn't even try to remember names.

"Perhaps you would like to say a few words to the public, answer some questions from the press?"

"No, thank you," said Rip Cantrell.

"The president is here. He has asked to meet you."

Rip tried to decline graciously. "I voted for the other guy. Maybe some other time, huh, when I'm older."

With that he led Charley and Egg out of the administrative suite by a side door, picked his way through the crowd. They wound up on the balcony, looked at the saucer on the main floor below surrounded by people.

Anonymous bits of humanity, they were pushed and shoved until they found themselves against the balcony rail. Egg gestured at the *Spirit of St. Louis.* "You made the right decision, Rip. *This* is where the saucer belongs." He put his elbows on the rail, intent on the scene below.

Rip and Charley found themselves being pressed together by the warm, restless crowd. "You can kiss me again, if you want," Charley whispered.

On the main floor below, the president and senior congressional leaders were examining the saucer, touching it, running their hands over the landing gear and rocket nozzles as the museum security staff and Secret Service held back the crowd.

A half hour later, out on the street, Rip asked, "Is there a decent restaurant not too far?"

As they walked, Egg asked, "Why did you decide to donate the saucer to the museum?"

Rip told them about the night at the lake, about Hedrick and Taggart and the German test pilot. Charley Pine gripped his hand even tighter.

"So what did you do with the bodies?"

"I recycled them. Mauna Loa in Hawaii is erupting."

The weight of the saucer was gone from his shoulders, the sun felt good, Charley's hand felt terrific . . . It was time to shift gears, to come back to earth.

"What's with the briefcase, Uncle?"

"Patents. Remember the computer you and I took out of the saucer?"

"Yeah."

"I figured out how to wire a laser printer

to it. This morning Charley and I filed twenty-six patents on saucer technology."

"Twenty-six?"

"Wellstar sent us a couple of engineers to help with the applications. You remember Dutch Haagen? He works for us now."

Rip shook his head in amazement.

Egg continued, "We figure if we can do maybe three patent applications a week for the next ten weeks or so, we'll pretty well have the critical stuff covered. I put all three of our names on the patent applications, signed for you as your attorney in fact."

"Okay, but . . ."

"You may recall that we gave Wellstar an interest in the propulsion technology in return for a bill of sale. I thought we might license the propulsion stuff, make enough money to keep me in a nursing home and you and Charley in tall cotton. With your consent, I thought we might put the rest of the patents in the public domain, make them available to whoever wants to use them, anywhere in the world."

Rip grinned broadly. "Sounds great to me. Charley, what do you say?"

"The saucer used to belong to everyone, didn't it? Now it will again. I like that."

Rip and Charley had walked a couple of blocks hand in hand when Charley remarked, "Do you realize that we don't have anything to fly?"